ALL THE WINNING NUMBERS

RACHEL MARIE SERIES
BOOK THREE

DAVID B. SMITH

Copyright 2018
Waldo Publishing
San Bernardino, California

ISBN: 9781980214618

This is a work of fiction. Except for well-established Bangkok landmarks, names, characters, businesses, places, events and incidents are either the products of the author's imagination or used in a fictitious manner. Any resemblance to actual persons, living or dead, or actual events is purely coincidental.
Cover art by Roy Ice.

CHOICES

Here in Perelandra the temptation would be stopped by Ransom, or it would not be stopped at all. The Voice–for it was almost with a Voice that he was now contending–seemed to create around this alternative an infinite vacancy. This chapter, this page, this very sentence, in the cosmic story was utterly and eternally itself; no other passage that had occurred or ever would occur could be substituted for it.

He was no longer making efforts to resist the conviction of what he must do. He had exhausted all his efforts. The answer was plain beyond all subterfuge. The Voice out of the night spoke it to him in such unanswerable fashion that, though there was no noise, he almost felt it must wake the woman who slept close by. He was faced with the impossible. This he must do: this he could not do. In vain he reminded himself of the things that unbelieving boys might at this moment be doing on Earth for a lesser cause.

Then some cross-wind of the mind changed his

mood. Perhaps he would fight and win, perhaps not even be badly mauled. But no faintest hint of a guarantee in that direction came to him from the darkness. The future was black as the night itself.

"It is not for nothing that you are named Ransom," said the Voice.

Perelandra, by C. S. Lewis, 1944

ONE

"Three . . ." *Trickle trickle trickle.* "Four . . ."

The high school girls whooped with good-natured derision as the orange golf ball slowly rolled back toward the tee in ignominious retreat.

"Come on, Pastor Sue. Can't you hit that little ramp?" Evie reached out with her putter and gave the narrow strip of metal an encouraging tap. "Just pop that baby right up here, Rev. Put some muscle into it. Like Samson."

Sue sighed theatrically. "I've already hit this idiot ball four times. Just give me my default six and let's move on to hole number fourteen. Don't be mean."

"No way." Rebecca, a stunning Hispanic girl wearing an abbreviated pink tank top, wagged a finger at the church administrator. "That's a copout, man. We're just gonna stand here until you put the ball right up the middle and into the hole. Now come on, Pastor Sue. I think you're not concentrating."

It was a funky Tuesday night outing at Golf City.

The girls were a robust collection of high school seniors and a few seasoned veterans of Glendale Community College's blistering summer session. Sue peered back to the hole just behind them, where Naree's foursome was huddled around the obligatory windmill, taking comic stabs at their balls and laughing as shots bounced clumsily off the wooded blades.

"Are you guys trying your hardest?" she called out.

The Korean girl grinned. "We saw how many sixes you're getting, Pastor Sue, and thought we should flub a few shots too, just to make you feel better."

"Don't you worry about my feelings none," the graying pastor retorted. "Tell everybody to play their hardest. Low score gets a free milk shake when we're done."

Girl Power Ministries was one sliver of Pastor Sue Baines' growing portfolio of assignments at New Hope Church, and she scoured the Internet to put together an eclectic lineup of summer activities for the mass of feminine energy. Once a week they hit the beaches or descended on Dodger Stadium for one of its 5:00 p.m. Sunday contests. Most of the girls seemed to have entertainment money, but Pastor Sue doled out her own spare dollars in cases of real need.

The foursome holed out and Dominique pulled the tattered scorecard out of her hip pocket. "What'd you guys all get?" She peered at Sue. "Six for you, huh? Ooh, look at that. Six–six–six. Satan must be kicking your ball out of bounds, I bet."

The group guffawed at the apocalyptic reference, and Sue impulsively pointed her putter at the upcoming water hazard. "Here's what's happening. If I get a hole in one right now, *you*, young lady, are going to sing a solo at church next weekend."

"No way!" Dominique dropped her putter and made a show of being horrified. "New Hope is doomed if I sing."

"Huh uh." Lupe set her ball down on the rubber mat and took a healthy swat. "You're really good, Dominique. I say go for it."

The taller student looked from one to the other. "I don't make no one-way bets," she sniffed. "If Pastor Sue gets a hole in one, I sing. And if she doesn't get a hole in one, then what?"

"Name your price." Sue grinned, getting into the wild west gaming spirit.

"I get into Disneyland free when we go Fourth of July."

"No chance. That's an $100 wager. Pastor Mike'll fire me."

The dark-haired girl's eyes danced wickedly. "Hang on, hang on." She waved her putter around triumphantly. "Okay, here it is. If you miss, then *you* sing next weekend. Plus I get a milkshake too, even if I don't have low score tonight."

The girls from hole #14 backtracked, eager to join the action. "What's up?"

Dominique bounced up and down on the balls of her feet. "If Pastor Sue gets a hole in one, I gotta sing a song at church next weekend. And if she messes up, then she sings."

"Plus the milkshake," Lupe reminded.

The girls chattered animatedly like sports enthusiasts lined up along the rail of a dog track. Sue, grinning, eyed the upcoming hole. It was a straight-up shot, a narrow lane between two half-empty water puddles, one on each side. Lupe's initial shot had eased through to the rectangle containing the hole, and was perched a couple feet off to the left.

"Come on, you guys." Esther gestured to the trailing quartet of girls. "Pastor Sue's going for it. A hole in one, and Dominique's got to sing in church."

"That'll bust the TV cameras," Evelyn put in as the golfing action ground to a halt for the big moment.

"Okay, ladies," Sue announced. "Stand back now. You're using up my oxygen; know what I mean?" It was a vague reference to an old *Cuckoo's Nest* cinema moment, and the teens shrugged, not getting it. Sue peered at the hole and lined up her shot, already knowing it was going in.

She stroked the ball smartly, lapsing into a pleasant reverie as she did so. All her life, jackpot moments of good fortune had simply fallen into her lap. She'd never been particularly athletic, but once in a high school JV basketball game, she had heaved up six straight shots from long range. They were the kind of desperate bricks that often missed the entire backboard, but for Sue Baines, #21, all six sailed right into the basket, barely rippling the net. Once she and her parents had stopped by some real estate office to look over a condo her dad wanted. "Come on, Susie Q," he teased, spotting a contest entry form. "You fill it out for us. Maybe we'll win the big prize." Less than two hours later, the agent had called, bubbling with the news. Didn't she know that third grader Susie Baines had a hundred silver dollars waiting for her, just piled up on the guy's desk? Grumbling, Dad had allowed her to keep the entire stack of coins.

It had been the same in adult life. Mutual funds

soared when she bought in. Her Glendale house had doubled in price within eighteen months of her signing escrow papers, holding steady even during California's long slide into real estate panic three years ago. She was forever winning raffles, scoring on baby shower pools, getting her ticket number drawn when bidding on a Christmas basket. Just once, Pastor Mike teasingly said it might be forgiven if she put a single coin in a slot machine when the pastoral team attended a gospel-and-blues concert at Morongo; she waddled home with fifty bucks of quarters jingling in the pockets of her blazer.

She had wondered during the uncanny winning streak if the twinkling moments of luck were God's way of compensating her for the otherwise barren parking lot that had been her adult life. Her peers in college had tumbled easily into relationships; impressive guys had come and gone . . . and continued arriving in steady numbers. But not for her. One by one, serendipitous pairings mounted up on all sides. The weddings and baby showers peeled away her intimate circle of friends as she quietly went out each December to put up her own Christmas lights and hang a stocking for Pickles.

But hey, at least I keep winning those door prizes . . .

Her golf ball rolled confidently between the two water hazards, bouncing just slightly over the uneven stitching in the green felt and onto the rectangle of hope. The girls squealed in anticipation. As if on a mission of destiny, the orange sphere charged the cup, hitting it dead center. For the slightest moment, it clanged against the iron pin, threatening to spin back out, but the hoots of the female army drove it to cover.

"All right, girl!" Lupe swung her hips back and

forth in a giddy moment of mocking celebration, jabbing a finger in Dominique's face. "Showtime! Showtime! Man, I'm gonna have all my relatives there on the front row this weekend. Maybe call Univision to send over a camera crew. Girl, you are in deep trouble." She came over and embraced the chaperone. "Pastor Sue, you are so awesome! How'd you know that ball was going in?"

Sue, still flush from the expected miracle, gestured casually to indicate that it was nothing. "Hey, I set her up with those three sixes, and then reeled her in." She turned to face Dominique. "So I guess I better call up Pastor Frank and let him know who's got special music."

"No way." Panic-stricken, the girl fell to her knees in a comic desperate gesture. "Pastor Sue, don't make me. You were just kidding, right?"

"I don't know. A woman of honor makes a promise, she ought to keep it."

"Yeah, but . . ." Dominique reached out for her mentor's hand. "Make it something else. I'll come babysit your cat or something. Huh?" Pastor Sue's devotionals often mentioned the persnickety feline, and the girls whooped.

"That might work," Sue allowed. "Tell you what. If you beat me for the whole eighteen holes, I might let you trade in for something less high-profile than singing on TV."

It was a lively postgame celebration as Sue relented and treated the entire entourage to malts out of her own purse. Along with Pastor Mike and the growing ministry team at New Hope Church, she accepted a modest salary for her efforts. But her successful years as an executive in high-flying finance, plus her astute investing, gave her the pleasurable liberty to occasionally treat both her friends and youthful ministry charges.

"This is great, Pastor Sue." Naree nursed her chocolate shake, perusing a text message before rejoining the conversation.

"Okay, ladies," Sue began as the party started to wind down. "First of all, I want you to take notice that I'm doing like Jesus commanded and forgiving Dominique. She doesn't have to sing a solo after all, even though, man, I put that ball right in the bucket."

"You did, Pastor Sue," the teen conceded. "That was amazing."

"Well, that's okay." Sue glanced around to make sure all the girls were tuned in. "Now, this Friday we're going over to Rainbow Medical Center right at seven. I need somebody here to do, like, a seven-minute devotional. You guys know what old folks like: something sweet, maybe about one of Jesus' parables." She returned to Dominique. "How about it? Can you maybe cover that for us? Since we let you off the hook going on *American Idol*?"

The girl knew she was beaten. "Sure. I'll be there."

"Terrific. And of course, we all sing. I'll have a guitar there. Lupe, you too, huh?" A nod.

"Now, next weekend, Pastor Mike is really counting on this whole group," Sue went on. "'Blood for Life' is coming out to the church right after services, setting up cots in the gym, and we're hoping that lots and lots of people stick around and donate a pint."

"Barf! No way." Jennie, a gangly Chinese teen still in high school, shook her head. "I'm not going near that place."

"Well, you're not seventeen anyway. But I think the rest of you are good to go. Right?" She looked from one to the other.

"Long as you go first, Pastor Sue." Esther folded her arms across her chest and gave the supervising pastor an insolent look.

It was an awkward moment. "Well, I'm supposed to be organizing everything," she said, sensing how lame it sounded. "You know, getting everyone through line for needle sticks and BP and all that. Plus . . ." Her mind raced, trying to seize on an excuse. "I'm kind of an old lady. Who's going to want fifty-five-year-old blood that can barely make it around the track?"

The girls were having none of it. "We give, you give, Pastor Sue. You can run the show and still plop down on a gurney for ten minutes while we take over passing out the wheat thins."

Inwardly she cursed herself for not gaming out the blood drive pitch with better forethought. "We'll see." A fit of honesty forced her to admit, "Frankly, I've always been a chicken. I know that's lame. But ever since I was six, needles have always freaked me out."

Dominique, finishing off her strawberry malt, draped a teasing arm around the pastor. "You gonna let a little needle poke cancel out Philippians 4:13?"

"I hate you."

IT WAS A SPLENDID summer night and the California moon drenched the hills rising in ghostly silence above Glendale. Sue threaded her way through the evening traffic below, reflecting on the banter and the cheerful camaraderie of playing miniature golf with eleven hormone-supercharged girls.

She ducked in a trio of quick hands-free calls, reminding old church friends that Pastor Mike was seeking sponsors for the Haiti mission trip in August. But the surface streets leading away from the Pasadena Freeway were a confused snarl, and she lapsed into an internal reverie.

It was odd how a brilliant career woman could fashion a lifestyle so filled with people and buzzing emotions and yet be achingly alone. Her days and evenings spilled over with high-powered committees, banter with kids, repartee and worship with young married couples in New Hope's kindergarten department, where she directed traffic one weekend a month. Just minutes ago, in the Golf City parking lot, it had been a pleasing round of hugs and compliments. "You're so awesome, Pastor Sue" was a familiar refrain; one by one the girls had offered quick embraces mingled with teen perspiration and Target perfume. Every October the entire church staff hijacked her away to Acapulco, her favorite Tex-Mex restaurant, and endlessly roasted her with virgin strawberry daiquiris and inside jokes.

But the mad merry-go-round of embraces and Bible studies, of visiting nurseries and ICU patients always ended up the same way: wheeling this lonely Lexus SUV into her spacious two-car garage and being mocked by the empty space next to it. Her house was a veritable estate, with a well-manicured lawn and sumptuous pool overlooking old Pasadena. Subtle evening lights created dancing shadows in the sculpted shrubs along the cast-iron fence, and she could relax on the deck with a tall glass of lemonade and make phone calls for Jesus. *But dear God, what an isolated tower . . .*

Mail was nothing but bills and political ads and she tossed the pile on the kitchen counter. Peering at her watch, she committed herself to ten more minutes of phone calls before the self-imposed courtesy deadline of nine p.m. It had been six years since Pastor Mike Russell and New Hope's board of trustees had encountered such a business-savvy player who could keep multiple plates aloft and spinning, tracking ten projects at a time. She had been the first of her friends to master social networking and Blackberry technology, dashing off project white papers and grant proposals on a laptop while carpooling with an associate to a training seminar. Ever since being recruited to accept a cut in pay and a cubicle at the church, she had been the cheerful pot of superglue holding the bustling Christian center in one dynamic piece.

"Mr. Wiggins? Sue Baines here. I hope it's not too late. How's Consuela?" She juggled a can of soda in her spare hand and edged outside to the poolside chairs.

Nearby streetlights from the level just above hers beamed cheerful shadows into her backyard, and the dancing ripples on her pool cast a blue-green reflection in the sliding glass doors, framing her own outline. There was a renewed nudge of sad frustration as the doughy shape in front of her was a reminder of her futile girlish dreams.

She clicked from one phone call to the next, forcing a faux cheerfulness into her voice, but the image remained indelibly stamped on her soul. Ever since childhood, all the mirrors in the Baines household had carried a consistent and inescapable message: *Girl, you are as plain as they come.* Growing up, her shape had never changed: not as a scrambling kid, not as a preteen, not when puberty arrived at long last, delivering virtually nothing to her doorstep, not as an adult. Her body was a good-hearted but uninteresting *lump*. Hers was a chunky, nonthreatening presence, not offensive and also not noticeable. Men slipped past her at Trader Joe's or on the glittering mezzanine of Staples Center before Laker games and simply didn't see her.

Sue's face was warm: nice cheeks and warm brown eyes. A kindly smile forged in Christian maturity. But her hair, now mostly gray, had defied all efforts to be shaped into any kind of good design. As a child, perms invariably turned out poorly and went limp in a hurry. Her eyesight had gone blurry in high school but contact lenses made her squint and get headaches. So the necessary glasses were one more digit in this physical sum that always seemed to add up to a romantic zero.

During her corporate days, and even more now that she was working for the Lord, Sue compensated by being diligently friendly. Even plain people could make their positive mark in the world, and she was determined to honor and grow God's kingdom by loving everyone, by serving with selfless charm and good will. She dispensed hugs and compliments right and left; she tracked birthdays and forced herself to smile as friends and newbies at the church invited her to celebrate weddings and baby showers. And then, as the lonely Lexus took its place in the spotless garage next to the empty stall, she would dissolve into sobs and ask Jesus to forgive her.

The phone curfew slid into view, and she set her cell down, nursing her soda and trying to force her thoughts to a better place. *Nobody gets everything they want. God chose your list of blessings, and you could do a lot worse.* All this was true, she mused. And yet the stark reality was that she, Sue Baines, would willingly trade in most of God's pre-assigned blessings in exchange for just one man who would choose to love her.

It took a moment of easy math to figure out that one of her treasured friends was living well beyond the curfew of American darkness at this very moment and she picked up her cell phone again. Scrolling down until she spotted her name and the country code of 66 just below it, she hit the green button. It took two rings before Rachel Marie answered. "Hello?"

"Hey, Thai lady. Sue Baines here."

There was a gasp of pleasure, and Sue savored the long-distance strands of friendship. "Pastor Sue! What a nice surprise!"

"I figured with it being summer time, you might be at home. Straight-up noon, isn't it?"

"Huh uh. Not quite eleven. It's fifteen later in the winter, but only fourteen now."

"Oops, I flubbed it."

"No problem. Anyway, Khemkaeng said we might go out to dinner this evening. With John and Marilyn. But I'm just puttering around the house, trying to catch my breath after school letting out and all."

"Everything going okay?"

"Oh sure. We're good."

"How about . . . with that kid? What was her name again?"

"Pranom. Yeah. Well, I told you Samantha and Tommy got things all firmed up. They're getting married next Christmas and then the adoption can go forward."

"Quite a story," Sue responded.

"No kidding."

"Did Pranom come through all the . . . well, you

know?" Her voice trailed off. It had been a wrenching tale, with the young seventh-grader hijacked into a life of go-go bars and prostitution. Rachel Marie's lengthy emails back to New Hope had outlined a thrilling rescue saga.

"You know, I honestly think it's a miracle. I got an email from Sam last weekend, and as near as she can see it, that kid is just amazing. She took her a couple of times to a Christian therapist there in Oregon, but–praise Jesus–no lasting effects. She and Paloma get along great, calls Samantha 'mom' already. Addicted to Nickelodeon, wants to go to Del Taco twice a day, Sam says."

Sue laughed despite the wistful maternal longing in her own heart. "It just is so terrific how this whole Thailand mission thing has worked out. You chug out there and meet the man of your dreams first day you get there. Your cousin follows you to Bangkok the next year, and finds Mr. Wonderful out there playing the piano in church. What is it with that place?"

Rachel Marie's laughter was contagious. "I know." The international call crackled for a moment before her voice came back on strong. "Maybe you better come out here for a peek too, Pastor Sue. Third time's the charm, they say."

The unintended bit of nonsense struck her right in the heart, and Sue felt moisture spring into her eyes. Resolving not to let on, she managed a feeble crack. "Well, goodness knows I'm sure not sailing on the Love Boat here in Glendale. What was that boat outing you Bangkok folks always talk about? With that temple by the river?"

"The klong trip." Rachel Marie was innocently

unaware, and Sue could hear her chewing on something crunchy in the background. "If you think you'd like teaching third grade, I'll bet John could fit you in starting this August."

TWO

The piano was a tinny upright, with a third of the white keys missing their ivory. But the seniors seated all around sang with reedy gusto as Sue pounded out clumsy chords. "How about 'Let Me Call You Sweetheart'?" She winked at old Mrs. Diggs, an Alzheimer's patient who was a regular each Thursday afternoon.

A white-haired man in hospital pants and a ratty tank top undershirt clumped unsteadily toward the knot of retirees. He leaned against his walker and joined in, adding some surprising baritone strength. *Keep that love light glowing in your eyes so blue. Let me call you sweetheart; I'm in love with you.*

"Well, well." Sue swiveled on the bench and welcomed the newcomer. "Mr. Jankowski. That's a nice voice you add to our little choir."

Nonplussed, he shook his head, the white tufts of unruly hair trembling in the humid warmth of the day room. He muttered something about "my Eleanor," his unblinking eyes sliding from one patient to the next.

"Well, we've probably tormented the other guests enough. But if we don't sing 'Amazing Grace,' I think the kitchen staff will confiscate that delicious jell-o I know you nice people have been craving all day."

"It sucks!" A lady well into her nineties, thin wisps of pure white hair pulled over a freckled scalp, pounded her cane against the linoleum, and the group chuckled.

"Now, now." Sue hit the opening chord and then turned to face the aggrieved woman. "Don't be like that, Annabelle. This place is famous for its strawberry jell-o. I drove fourteen miles over here from Glendale just to get my share."

"You can have mine too then."

A trio of African-American men, all in Bermuda shorts and with knee-high black socks, draped themselves on a couch against the opposite wall, listening passively as the piano thumped out the familiar gospel tune. Sue could hear one of them timidly joining in on the third verse: *Through many dangers, toils, and snares, I have already come. 'Tis grace hath brought me safe thus far, And grace will lead me home.*

Rather than undergo the laborious trek down to the library where the group usually convened for the devotional, Sue simply pulled a Bible out of her purse and pivoted around on the piano bench. "Let's just stay right here," she suggested, drawing the group of elderly saints closer. "'Cause what I have today is pretty short."

Mr. Jankowski appeared frozen over his walker, limbs set in concrete as he held himself in a state of static tranquility. Sue flipped to the back of the Bible and carefully read from the next-to-last page. "I know you folks all remember these great promises of God.

Listen to this from John the Revelator: *Now the dwelling of God is with men, and he will live with them. They will be his people, and God himself will be with them and be their God. He will wipe every tear from their eyes. There will be no more death or mourning or crying or pain, for the old order of things has passed away."*

"From *Titanic*," one of the women declared emphatically. "That there's *Titanic*."

"Huh?" Sue peered at the overweight patient from somewhere in the Deep South, hiding behind massive sunglasses.

"They just showed it last Sunday night. In the rec center, you know."

"*Titanic*?"

"That's right. And right at the end, the preacher man–you know, the priest–was hanging onto that rail 'cause the ship was all tippy-upside-down, people hangin' on with him, like forty-five degrees and all. And he was saying all that same thing you just did. God being with us and wiping the tears and no more death."

"Oh, yes." Sue nodded, remembering. "And of course, they all knew that the end was near for them."

"Yes'm. Except that, look, if you've got the Lord, then it's all right, see. The ship goes down, okay. But if you surrender it all to Jesus and all that, well, then, the Lord's got your mansion ready and waiting."

Sue reached out and took her hand, giving an affectionate squeeze. "That is just so true. It really is. I didn't think of that, but when we have Christ in our lives, then we don't have to fear anything. We could be facing problems, or illness, or even death. But the Word of God promises us eternal life. A million tomorrows."

"World without end," the Mississippi visitor stated.

"Amen to that." Sue looked from one to the next. "And I don't have to tell you what that means." She pointed to her own unruly curls. "No more gray hair. No more glasses. No more cancer treatments. No more cemeteries. No more funeral homes."

"And no more red jell-o!" The old biddy was still on a diatribe about the diet. "It sucks!"

The group guffawed. "Well, you know what?" Sue couldn't hide her mirth. "If you don't want any more red jell-o, Annabelle, I can guarantee you that the chef in heaven will rustle you up something else. You can have caviar and maple bar donuts every single day of the year if you want. And double on Christmas morning."

"Pancakes!" The aged warrior looked defiantly from one to the other. "Pancakes for dinner. Now that's heaven. But no more of that rock-hard red jell-o."

Jenjira, one of the long-term kitchen workers, slipped over to the group just as Sue was wrapping up. "You wish to stay for dinner, ma'am?"

She shook her head. "Not this time."

"Okay. But I bring you cake." The Thai employee held out a small green plate with a square of chocolate cake topped with a stiff swirl of Cool Whip.

"Wonderful!" Remembering, Sue proudly added: "*Kop kuhn kah.*"

She was rewarded with a bright smile and widened eyes. "How do you speak Thai?"

"Oh, don't get excited; that's the only phrase I know." She took a bite and managed with her mouth full: "One of my church friends went to Bangkok two years ago to work. So when we talk on the phone, sometimes I learn a word or two."

"You speak Thai very good." The Asian aide

loitered until Sue finished with the delicacy and accepted the plate back.

"Thanks again."

"Sure." Beaming, the woman added: "We always say *mai bhen rai.* Means 'you are welcome.'"

"I think I remember that one too."

Sue bent over, dutifully fussing over each patient, accepting their feeble hugs and murmuring words of encouragement. "You hang in there, Ethan. And when that pretty granddaughter visits tomorrow, tell her Pastor Sue really likes her painting."

It always tore at her heart when visiting the center. More than a third of the clients were struggling with dementia and other bleak challenges. One man, rail-thin and alone, invariable sat in the hallway in a threadbare rocking chair, pushing himself angrily back and forth. Every minute or so, he would call out in a hoarse protest: "I want to go home. . . . I want to go *home!*"

"Sweetie, you *are* home, I fear," Sue muttered to herself as she passed by, her own heart aching over the unsolvable mysteries of a sin-scarred world.

THE NEW LIFE WORSHIP CENTER was pleasantly filled the following weekend, as the praise team led the congregation in an extended set and Pastor Mike shared from First Thessalonians. Pastor Sue was everywhere, Bluetooth stapled to her ear, checking in with the PA operators, poking her head into the control room to make sure Cammie had the camera crew under control.

"You have your own wireless already on?" the technician asked.

"Uh huh."

"Okay. Just stay on Camera One the whole time.

How long you need?"

She hesitated. "Three minutes tops."

New Hope Church had a thriving Internet feed, and the TV people managed to record a professional program without intruding on the worship experience. Right after Mike's closing prayer, Sue bounded onto the stage and gave the large congregation a reminder about the blood drive.

"They brought a whole team with them," she said, trying to encourage a large turnout. "So they can process you guys really fast. For all of you who are regular donors, if you remembered your ID cards, they can zip you through in about three minutes is all. Course, they got to check temperature, blood pressure, and a needle stick." She held up her index finger and pretended to grimace. Everyone laughed. "Now, don't any of you lie when you do the touch-screen medical history thing. If you got a Jesus tattoo in the last week, say so." More laughter.

Fumbling in her handbag, Sue held aloft a still shrink-wrapped Kindle. "Plus look at this, ladies and gents. Stick around in the juice bar area after donating. Pastor Mike says we're going to have a drawing, and one lucky blood donor is going to walk home with a brand new e-book reader. Wouldn't you like that?"

There was a smattering of applause, and she quickly added: "Plus I think all of his books have already been downloaded. That's got to save you, what? Maybe three bucks?" She grinned and pointed to the exits on the right-hand side. "I expect all my miniature golf buddies from Girl Power Ministries to be first in line."

"Right after you!" one called out, and there was another buzz of amusement as people began streaming toward the exits.

The athletic center smelled slightly of rubbing alcohol as medical trainees queried parishioners about overseas travel and conjugal visits with hardened criminals. Dominique and Lupe, toward the front of the line, gave smirking answers to the behavior-related HIV questions, and Sue pretended to scowl at them. "You girls behave now. I'm afraid they'll take your pint and just heave it out the window by the side of the road."

"Doesn't matter to me," Dominique quipped, tossing her dark curls. "Long as I win me that Kindle, hey, they can take five gallons."

The Foster twins had arrived with a well-stocked canteen, and members loitered over mini-bottles of grape juice and fig Newtons, their arms proudly adorned with bright red bandages. Pastor Mike, protesting loudly, finally sank down in one of the cots and offered both veins for inspection. "If you stick me, then you've got to suck a quart or so out of Sue over there as well," he complained, his eyes twinkling.

"Hey!" Naree, nursing her apple juice, wandered over to where Sue was tidying up. "You got to give too, Pastor Sue. That was the deal."

"Come on." She shook her head, keeping her pleading low. "Really. I'm just no good at this stuff."

Rebekah heard the confrontation and bounded over, her own bright yellow bandage flashing authority. "Come on, now, Pastor Sue," she dared. "All ten of us just got sucked dry. Everyone 'cept Jennie because her birthday's in January. But you got to do it."

The rest of the girls gathered around, bouncing up and down in their amusement. "*Pastor Sue! Pastor Sue! We want blood from Pastor Sue! Pastor Sue Pastor Sue*

. . .”

She glared at them, trying to still her own racing pulse. She honestly was scared of needles, and almost blanched at the idea of feeling that hostile tourniquet tightening around her arm, the sinister rubbing of alcohol, the stabbing moment of truth . . .

"What will it take for you guys to give me a pass?"

"Nothing!" Dominique grabbed her hand and began dragging her toward the sign-in desk. "Well, you get each of us a new Prius, then maybe."

Maybe I'll flunk the BP test. Reluctantly she eased into a chair and rolled her eyes.

"Are you our last person?" The screener, a chunky Asian kid with tattoos over both eyelids, took her wrist as he eyed his watch.

"I'll give you fifty bucks if you say my heart's stopped," she muttered conspiratorially.

He grinned, appreciating what he took to be humor. "Nope. Seventy-two." He applied the blood pressure cuff and scanned the digits. "'Pastor Sue,' right? Everything's looking good."

"Thanks for nothing."

A blond novice who looked to be no more than seventeen accepted her donor sheet. "Could you state your name and birthday for me, please?"

Sue complied, feeling the noose tighten around her neck.

"Okay." The girl scanned the document. "Oops. I guess Alan forgot to ask you this. 'Are you willing to be screened as a possible marrow donor?'"

"Huh?"

The nursing aide shrugged, eager to get on with the procedure. "They just add one more blood vial to the test sample. It gets sent off someplace, and if you ever match somebody who needs it, they can figure out where to find you."

"I never heard of it."

"Me neither. I never heard of anyone matching or anything. But you never know." She cocked her head, waiting. "Can I put down yes?"

Just get me out of here, kid. She nodded unhappily. "Sure. Whatever."

"Good deal. Three squeezes, please." The child affixed the cuff to her upper arm and examined the vein. "Not much to go on there." She patted the area and waited, humming a vague pop hit to herself. "That's better." She popped open an antiseptic vial and began swabbing.

"Have you done this for very long?" Sue tried to force herself back into the familiar role of a pastor: making conversation, drawing people out, seeking a connection, steering topics toward the glories of the kingdom.

"Huh uh. Just started last week." She could see the blonde pulling out the plastic bag, affixing it to the metal stand just beneath the cot, safely below eye level. The needle was a sinister, chilling spike, spelling pain and the slow ooze of her precious life fluid. *I hate this job. I hate it I hate it I hate it . . .*

"'Bout ready?" The nurse hit the nozzle, lessening the tension of the blood pressure cuff. "Little stick now."

There was a tight jab and Sue winced. The hurt simply *sat* on her arm, spreading in a painful oval.

"Come on come on . . ."

There was a nasty moment as the employee jiggled the spike, inspecting the plastic tube. "We're not getting anything." She pulled back on the needle, trying to probe for the elusive vein.

That really hurts! Sue wanted to speak, but could feel her entire face going clammy. Out of the corner of her eye, she could see Pastor Mike approaching, serious concern in his eyes. "Nurse, is she all right?"

The sting in her right arm was a wave now, a crash of throbbing terror. "It's not working . . ."

Her own voice was feeble, and she heard one of the other aides hollering toward the gym exit: "Get Mona back in here!"

There was a sick flutter as her pulse vainly protested, and then the lights went dark.

IT WAS A WOOZY recovery, but at last she staggered–sans the requisite pint–over to the food table where the Girl Power bunch was waiting with open arms. "Pastor Sue, we're so sorry!" Lupe moaned, enfolding her in a gingerly hug. "We didn't know you were going to faint!"

Sue's face was still damp from the cool washcloth the blood bank team had used to revive her. "Well, that was exciting."

"Here." Pastor Mike eased over and put a bottle of chilled grape juice in her hand. "Sure sorry, Sue. Yikes."

"It's okay." Baffled, she shook her head. "What was all that, anyway?"

Mona came up from the other side and put a sympathetic hand on her shoulder. "Happens every now and then," she explained.

"What?"

The girls stepped back so the supervising nurse could sit next to her still-fragile patient. "You had what we call a vasovagal episode."

"Huh?"

The younger woman was all business. "It's just a syndrome, like a panic attack. Something called the vagal nerve senses that you're, you know, kind of nervous."

"As in about to wee-wee in her pants." Dominique interrupted, and the girls gave a tentative laugh.

"Yeah. Anyway, the vagal nerve seems to send out some kind of signal, and it triggers lightheadedness."

"That wasn't lightheadedness," Sue protested. "I was clean out."

"I know." Mona nodded sympathetically. "When people pass out like that, they usually keel over, blood rushes to their head, and that reverses it. We call it a 'vasovagal syncope.'"

"How long was I out?"

"I missed the first part of it. But maybe half a minute."

"Yow."

Mike leaned over and patted her good arm. "Well, you're a saint, Sue," he grinned. "Next time we have one of these, we'll let you just stand by the cots with your guitar and play 'Jesus Loves Me' for everyone."

"Deal."

Most of the donors were still milling around, nibbling on bonus cookies and offering high fives to first-timers. Mike glanced around. "I think we got all your stubs in this offering plate. Ready for a lotto drawing? Who wants to go home with a brand new Kindle from Amazon?"

"Me! Me!" Sue's golf friends, their sympathies forgotten, were first in line, clamoring for the door prize.

"We need an impartial bystander." Mike's eyes fell

on the young blonde who had botched Sue's crucial medical moment. "How about you, young lady?" He motioned her forward. "Just reach in here and make one Christian really, really happy."

Sue tried to choke back the twinge of resentment she could tell was flushing her cheeks. *She didn't do it on purpose; you just have lousy veins. And are definitely California's biggest ever chicken.*

The blonde gave a delicate squeal, the kind of juvenile affectation that belonged on a Saturday morning cartoon show, Sue thought grumpily. Reaching in, the kid made a big show of swirling the papers around. Finally seizing one, she held it aloft. "The winner for best supporting actor is . . ."

"Just read it!" Rebekah put both hands on her hips and pretended to glare at the visitor.

"It says . . . Susan Baines."

The gym rocked with laughter. "Pastor Sue! Pastor Sue! Pastor Sue!" The jovial chant went up from all sides.

Sue shook her head in disbelief. "No way. I know you guys pity me and all, but this is ridiculous." She was in no mood to proclaim faith in her continuing streak.

Mike took the slip of paper from the medical trainee and inspected it for himself. "I wouldn't believe it either," he admitted, pretending to be ashamed. "I mean, we all know that Pastor Sue set up this whole vampire show here. It was all her idea, folks. Including the big prize. She begged me to make it a Kindle. And now she wins it for herself?" He snickered. "That's like Dick Cheney heading the VP search committee for President Bush and then just picking himself." He thrust the medical form and the digital prize into Sue's reluctant hands. "There you go, Sister Sue." He grinned at the crowd, now beginning to trickle toward the parking lot. "The lady never loses, folks. I keep saying . . ."

THREE

There was a tap on her office door, and Sue looked up. "How are things, Hannah?"

The church secretary, a slight young lady barely out of community college, was juggling a beverage holder that still held two Jamba Juice treats. "Dr. Low came by again."

"That guy's such a saint." Sue reached out eagerly. "What'd you leave me?"

"Let's see. Strawberry . . . and . . . strawberry."

"Ah. In that case, let's see. Gimme a strawberry."

The ladies both laughed. "Don't forget five o'clock."

"Got it." Sue sagged as she looked at her crowded computer screen, where she had two Excel sheets sharing space with a possible fall schedule for her Girl Power Ministries group. Plus the Tuesday meeting agenda. "Tell the boss man I'll be there."

Hannah hesitated. "You feel okay? After that blood thing."

Sue didn't have to feign embarrassment. "I suppose I'll hear about it from now until Christmas at least. 'Pastor Sue collapses in a dead heap from a needle stick.' I'm just glad you guys didn't post photos of me on the church site."

"Hey, those big needles can freak you out," the secretary soothed. "I never give blood; no way."

"Well, I had to be a good example." She took a satisfying pull on the icy drink and savored the mix of juices. It took just a few minutes to reconcile the numbers for the Haiti project, and she quickly checked emails before shutting down. It was rare to have an evening free, and she was anticipating a few laps in the pool and then back-to-back-to-back episodes of her favorite cop show on TNT.

Pastor Mike was slogging through a Christian book catalog in the conference room and looked up as she entered. "Hey, Susie dear. Are you all well?"

"All well and packing bestsellers into that Kindle," she retorted. "I still feel like you guys stacked the deck out of pity."

He snickered. "I know it looked that way, but, hey, Pastor Sue's nickname is Lady Luck."

Lucky at cards, unlucky at love. She pushed the self-pitying thought away and shoved an agenda sheet toward him.

He scanned it with a grin. "Sweet! We might get out of here in less than an hour. Looks like the church picnic is the main thing you've got for us. Oh, I forgot to text you, but we're going to get the BCS guys on the phone for maybe ten minutes."

"Okay."

He set down the magazine and looked right at her.

"I was thinking about the . . . you know, the blood thing. Sure sorry about that, Sue."

"Don't worry about it."

"I know." He stifled a yawn and peeked at the wall clock. "But I just had a thought going home that night. It's just that . . . well, you know, we don't have to say yes to every single thing that people push in our faces. You didn't want to donate a pint of blood; you shouldn't have to."

"I know, but . . ." Blushing, she explained about the golf match.

He chuckled. "I guess that's what you get for gambling on the golf course then. But I still say: you're entitled to say to someone, even to those girls: 'I serve Jesus by doing x and y and z. But for some reason q is just not my thing. I don't like it; it creeps me out, and while you girls are donating blood, I'll be sweeping up the Band-Aids. Or whatever."

She digested this. "You're right. But the plain fact is that some ministry things are just no fun. For anyone. It still has to get done, though."

"I suppose." Mike was wearing a short sleeve shirt, and without meaning to, inspected the tiny bruise on the inside of his own arm. "The nurse always says not to do any heavy chores for about a day, so I used that as an excuse not to mow the lawn." They both laughed.

Ivan, the youth pastor, eased into the room holding his newborn son. "Sorry, you guys. Maria had a thing with her doctor and we couldn't change it."

"No sweat. As long as he votes my way on everything." The senior pastor pulled himself out of the chair and went over to the baby. "How's my little man Noah?"

"He's good."

"Sleeping through the night?"

"Are you kidding? Wakes me up every twenty minutes, wants to know the Angel score."

The other two staffers came bustling down the hall and found seats. "My bad," Jose apologized. "The guy to replace the AC condenser took longer than he said he would."

Sue distributed agendas to the group and opened with prayer. As administrative pastor, it was her job to oversee the general health and operation of the place, and Mike deferred to her in the day-to-day running of New Hope Church. With a minimum of fuss, she outlined plans for the Fourth of July picnic and the staff retreat to Forest Home Christian Camp in mid-August. "Trivia time: you guys know that's where Billy Graham had his big one-on-one with the Holy Spirit. Way back a million years ago. Made up his mind to serve the Lord without questions, without doubts, without ever looking back."

"And the rest is history." Mike added the tag line respectfully and the group nodded. He glanced at his wristwatch. "Sue, can we get John on the phone and see what all our friends in Bangkok want?"

The conference room was set up with a Skype video system, and she punched in the overseas codes, consulting her own phone directory for the number. The line squawked for a moment before the high school principal from Bangkok filled the color monitor. "Hey, everybody! *Sawatdee!*"

"Is Khemkaeng there with you?" Mike called out. There was a subconscious tendency to bellow when making international calls, and Sue nudged him. "Don't shout, Pastor Mike. He'll be able to hear you even without the Internet."

"Sorry." Mike grinned, then peered into the camera. "'Scuse me, John. My disloyal staff here is giving me grief. I was asking: did Khemkaeng come in this morning?" Sue had to remind herself that with a fourteen-hour time difference, it wasn't quite eight o'clock Wednesday morning in Thailand.

"Huh uh." John shook his head. "I sent him over to the government liaison office for this year's updates. They keep changing the rules, and he's the only person who knows the ins and outs of their system."

It was hard not to smile as the two men bantered. John and Mike were virtual twins: both large, cheerful men, passionate about the gospel of Jesus. Neither could resist the temptation to tease. Sue had only met the missionary a couple of times; John's yearly trips to the States were jammed with appointments, and he had family in Texas. But New Hope Church had been a charter player in the founding of the huge mission school, and Mike was a member-in-absentia of the board. At least once a month the two leaders conferred via Skype, and she knew Mike routinely traded phone ideas with his counterpart in Bangkok.

"Anything pressing this time?" Mike called out, his voice still booming. Sue and Hannah traded amused glances. "I saw the graduation video clips you sent over. Very nice. And wow, your enrollment is exploding, Sir Garvey. Well done."

"We had an excellent year," the older man nodded. "Good teachers. Your Rachel Marie truly came into her own; one of our best. And her cousin Samantha was an absolute gem. We're going to miss her, but the new math guy seems all right."

"Tell me about this new sponsoring church then."

Sue had received an email earlier in the day but hadn't found the time to open it up yet. She blushed, but leaned forward, eager to absorb any critical factoids.

"Well, you guys know that we've been linked with UCC from the get-go."

"United Christian Church, downtown Bangkok," Sue whispered to the others.

"They put in an annual subsidy of something like 140,000 baht–just about four grand. The tradeoff is that members of the church then get a tuition discount of fifteen percent."

"Which, last time you ran the numbers, was essentially a wash," Mike recalled.

"Right. But then two of their people sit on our board and it just encourages all of us to work together over here. Common cause and all. Anyway, now we have this second church wanting to buy in. Nice folks, growing congregation, over by Mission Hospital. We already have about twenty of their kids coming here, and they want to set up the same program."

"Exact same numbers all the way around?"

"Right. A hundred forty thousand baht traded for a fifteen percent break. Khemkaeng visited with the pastor and he's just golden. Nice guy. Sawat, I think his name is. Not as good with English, but trying to learn. And of course, with all the kids picking up English here at school, it's a nice partnership."

"What do you need from us?"

"Just approval to go ahead. The charter makes allowance for new sister churches to join on any reasonable basis, so it's just a case of voting it. We don't meet again till July, but I think it's just a formality."

Mike glanced around the room. "What do you guys think?"

Everyone nodded, looking at Sue. "Sure," she agreed. "Even if the discount was to slightly outgrow the subsidy, if it encourages families to be an active part of a Christian church in that Buddhist culture, man, that's huge. We're way ahead."

Mike was about to speak again when there was a sudden flicker on the TV monitor. "John? Hey . . . did you run out on us?" The screen was empty, showing just the bare table and two unoccupied chairs.

The five New Hope team members waited for a moment, expecting the jovial principal to pop back into the picture. But there was nothing. "Yo! Mr. Garvey!" Mike glanced around at his team, then back to the video feed. "Everything okay over there?"

All at once Sue saw the bulky form of the Bangkok administrator. His face was pale and drenched with perspiration as he struggled to pull himself back into the picture. "Mike . . . man . . . I can't breathe. My chest . . ." He leaned heavily against the formica table top. "You better . . . call somebody." He pitched heavily forward, jarring the equipment loose, and the video feed vanished.

It was pandemonium in the Glendale conference room as the panicked members looked at each other. "What do we do?" Mike was on his feet, breathing hard. "Sue, do you have any numbers?"

She thumbed through her phone index. "I have Khemkaeng's house number."

"Call it! Maybe we'll get Rachel Marie at home."

A prayer in her throat, she hit the number and waited. *Please, Lord.*

"Hello?"

Trying not to cry, she blurted out: "Rachel Marie, it's me. Sue."

"Hey! How are . . ."

"Hang on! We were on the phone with John. Over at the office. But we think he just . . . collapsed. Maybe his heart. This was, like, half a minute ago."

"Oh, dear God." There was an awful stillness for a moment before the young teacher came back on. "You guys, what do I do?"

"Can you get Khemkaeng on the line? But . . . I guess, first, an ambulance?"

"I'm on it." Sue could tell that Rachel Marie was crying, and she felt tears in her own eyes. "I'll call you right back. Oh no . . ." The line went dead.

The five Californians sat in numb helplessness, not knowing what they could do. "Come over here." Mike, his voice gentle, motioned to the others. "Let's just say a prayer for our brother. While we wait."

Sue felt moisture on her cheeks as the senior pastor reached out and clasped her hand. "Mighty Savior, we need you in an urgent way," he managed, fighting his own emotions. "John is in trouble, and we know you're present with him in that office right now. Please help Rachel Marie to make contact with the right people. Be with whoever is on their way. Father, send your angels to that school right now and make all this right. Please, Jesus   . . ."

For a moment he couldn't go on, and it was with relief that Sue felt her own cell phone ringing. "Rachel Marie?"

"Yeah. It's me." The fierce buzz of city traffic was bleeding into the call.

"Is help on the way?"

"Yeah. I called 191, which is what they use here. Took a minute to find someone who spoke English, but an ambulance is on its way to the school. I'm in a cab and we're going too. Fortunately, traffic's okay."

"Did you get Khemkaeng?"

"Just his voice mail. But I left a message, so hopefully he'll get there ASAP."

Mike put his voice up close to Sue's. "This is Mike. Just wanted you to know we're praying here, and we won't leave until we hear back from you. Call us as soon as you know something, okay?"

For a moment there was no reply. *She's crying.* Sue felt her own insides heave with the anguish of the moment. John Garvey wasn't just an effective and dynamic missionary; she knew he was one of the kindest Christian men anywhere. How was all this going to end? Would God permit this bigger-than-life force for Christian victory to meet his destiny all alone in such a lonely outpost on the other side of the world?

SHE SWAM A FEW aimless laps, quailing at the obscene luxury, the safe comfort of her life. Nine thousand five hundred miles away, her friend was in the ICU of a Christian hospital, tubes and needles and EKG machinery humming in an attempt to hold back the forces of evil. But there was really nothing a California friend could do but wait and pray.

Sue pulled on a pair of baggy sweat pants and T-shirt and slowly trudged down the hilly street for her evening walk, heading into the gathering sunset. Without warning, another lump came into her throat, and she dabbed at her eyes. The ambulance had gotten to BCS in good time, and the medical prognosis, while guarded, seemed to indicate some hope. But the ways of destiny, of God's flickering providences, were a formidable wrestling match for a Christian.

One had to read the fine print; that was for sure. If you had talents, God seemed to always call them into service. The servant who had five was expected to use all five. And if the terms of the contract were written in Thai, or hinted at poverty, or spelled out a celibate journey, or a harrowing ambulance ride–well, that was what God asked for. The reward was heaven, of course, but the attendant bumps and bruises were oh so hard to fathom.

She had worked for the Lord long enough now to have discovered that ministry, taken as a whole, was a fabric of joy. It was good to be a blessing to others, to be a part of changing lives, and there was a lot of pure *fun* in this life of service. There was nothing like the hugs of a grateful teen, the thank you notes of a new convert, Universal Studios with the kids, the many Christmas trinkets and gifts from church friends. As administrative pastor, she was only able to schedule a couple of Bible studies a week. But on the rare moments when she went into the baptismal font with a new friend and felt the radiant wetness of that celebratory hug–well, that was a pinnacle blessing.

Yet, without explaining himself, or providing any context, God sometimes seemed to slam a door in your face and say nothing. Dead silence. Figure it out. *You have reached a number that is no longer in service.* She glanced up as she did a weary U-turn and trudged back toward home, passing an empty house that had been for sale since February. A green foreclosure sign from the bank marked an abandoning of hope.

Sue breathed another prayer, envisioning Marilyn Garvey in a Bangkok hospital room, waiting, praying, watching in a solitary vigil the slow creep of a wall clock marking the long moments of cardiac battle.

"ARE WE SKIPPING the game?"

Mike peered at her queerly. "What's the matter with you? No, we are *not* skipping the game." He reached into his back pocket and pulled out a tattered Angel hat, slapping it defiantly on and thrusting both hands in his pockets. "Cindy packed a whole cooler full of egg salad sandwiches and you'll hurt her feelings if you don't come with us."

Sue managed a smile. Twice a year, she enjoyed tagging along with the senior pastor and his wife to a baseball game in Anaheim. A fairly new convert who worked in the L.A. music business enjoyed an oddity: a strip of *three* season pass tickets to the Halos, fourth row in, first base. New Hope folks often got the freebies, sometimes on short notice, and this was one of those nights.

"I just meant . . . you know."

It had been five days since the stunning bad news from Asia. But John was recuperating well, managing weak bits of humor with the nurses, and the crisis seemed to be under control.

"Yeah." Mike brightened. "But, hey, John's a big Angel fan. Best thing for his heart is if we tell him we beat the Yankees."

"He'd probably die from the shock." It was an acceptable bit of gallows humor, and the older man laughed as he pointed out to the parking lot. "I'm driving. You and Cindy can gossip about Brad Pitt movies or whatever."

It was a beautiful night under the California stars–a sellout, of course, with New York thundering into Southern California toting their scary bats. But the Halo batters carved out a tenuous two-run lead and handcuffed the Bronx visitors, much to the delight of the rally monkey. Sue munched on the delicious sandwiches, thankful that the Russells weren't the kind of married couple who made an accompanying friend feel like an awkward third-wheel.

"Get enough to eat?" Mike peered behind him at the retreating back of a vendor. "We could split a malt three ways."

"I've got it." Sue fished in her purse and generously signaled for three of the frozen treats. They took dainty bites, enjoying the banter and clean night air as the visiting hitters surrendered meekly in the ninth.

"Can't believe we beat 'em!" Mike fished under the seat for his ragged jacket and collected the trash. "Pastor Sue, your lucky DNA must have spilled into the dugout."

"Yeah." She accepted his chivalrous help in putting on her coat. "Thanks, you guys. This was terrific."

"Sure."

The parking lot was gridlock, and the trio loitered for a few minutes, waiting to let some of the traffic ease onto the 57 Freeway. "Hey, we ought to see if Marilyn is up," the pastor mused. "She'd love to hear about Angels winning with the three of us being here and all." He peered at his watch. "Ten thirty-five plus fourteen hours is what?"

"A little past noon," Cindy said.

"Shall I try it?" He scrolled down and tried to dial. "I guess we can afford eight cents a minute. Considering that popcorn is seven bucks in this place." He waited, listening. "Hello? Marilyn? That you?" A pause. "I got Cindy and Susie here and we just cheered the Angels to victory. Yeah, over New York. Thought John would like to hear about that."

He covered the receiver. "She's with him right now," he whispered. "Out of ICU, so that's good." He punched a button. "We got you on speaker phone. John, can you hear us?"

There was a crackle, and Sue felt a tear spring into her eyes as the principal's faint voice came on. "Hey, Mike. Cindy. What are you folks doing out so late? Old folks like you should be in bed . . . like I am."

Mike laughed. "Speaking of beds, Marilyn says you're in a new one. Excellent! We don't like for our good friends to loiter around in Intensive Care, burning up the Lord's money. That's too many baht, my friend."

The laugh on the other end was weak. "Well, I'm not ready to run the bases just yet, but the doctor says I might live. Course, he said it in Thai; maybe I misunderstood him."

"Listen, pal," Mike boomed. "I've worn out the knees in three pairs of pants praying for you. All of us, John. I mean it. So praise God you're doing all right."

"Yes, we're very thankful."

"Marilyn, are you hanging in there?" Cindy leaned closer to the phone. "We just love you guys so much."

"We're good. And you folks . . . your prayers . . . just . . . we can't tell you how much that meant to us. No kidding."

Mike swallowed hard. "Well, again, we absolutely

love you both. But the Lord had you in his hand all the way, brother."

"That's right."

"Khemkaeng's managing all right?"

The digital traffic threatened to bury the signal, but a moment later John's voice returned. "Sorry, what was that?"

"I was just asking: how's Khemkaeng holding up? I mean, I assume all your folders have pretty much landed on his desk." He shot a wink over at Sue.

"Well, you know what?" A bit of raspy pain crept into John's voice, and Sue winced. "I've got a big, big favor to ask. And maybe it's good that all three of you are on the line."

"Listen," Mike said, trying to sound carefree. "You say what you want, Johnny, and I'll make it happen. Up to half my kingdom, sir."

John managed a feeble chuckle. "Well, I'm mending all right, but crawling back at about a third of a percentage point a day. I'm in here for at least four more weeks, and then living a really quiet life for a while past that."

"Okay." Mike digested this. "Bottom line is what? Are you guys coming home? Staying put? What?"

"Oh, we think staying right here is best," he managed. "Doctor's orders and all. But it would sure save Bangkok Christian School if you could loan us a certain whiz kid named Baines for the next few months."

FOUR

It was a splendid Sunday night with the incoming ocean waves an orderly pattern of distant white flecks barely visible from the elevated patio. Sue accepted a paper plate from her mother and peered at it. "What did you guys get?"

"It's Greek. Dennis discovered them a couple of months ago at a convention, and we get it sometimes now when company pops by."

She nibbled on the *orektika*–dainty European appetizers–as the twins scrambled around the well-appointed backyard. "Katrina! You run right over here and give your Auntie Sue a kiss."

The four-year-old lurched over, snickering, pressing her jam-stained cheek close to Sue's face. "Do you want Charlie to kiss you too?"

"What do you think? Certainly so. Course, he's a boy. Is he still willing to kiss an old lady like me?"

"You're not as old as Grandma."

"That's very true."

It had been Pastor Mike who initiated the Baines family council. The startling mission request from Thailand had sent New Hope Church into emotional convulsions. Pastor Sue carried a substantial portfolio for the growing California congregation; she chaired commit-tee meetings, balanced budgets, recruited volunteers for her own panoply of initiatives. "I can't imagine how we'd do without you for even a week," the senior pastor had lamented. "But it sure looks like the Lord needs for you to take this on, Sue." He and Cindy had offered to carpool with her down to the beach community for an evening of prayer and soul-searching.

Sue's father, a successful physician for many years, had retired years ago to an exclusive San Diego villa less than a mile from the beach. Sue had one sister, Natalie, married to an accountant. Their two sons both lived in the area as well, and Sue spent a small fortune on Christmas gifts for the twins and now Rod's infant daughter, Belle.

A feeling of foreboding crept over her as she worked her way through the delicious ethnic fare and then accepted a slice of pie. She'd always been close to her family; Mom and Dad generously arranged for weeklong cruises with the three of them sharing an oversized cabin. Natalie often scheduled impromptu drives up to Los Angeles, where the two sisters snuck away to day games at Dodger Stadium whenever the Padres were visiting. They would trade baseball insults and guzzle overpriced sodas, with Sue conducting New Hope business on her iPhone between innings. Thanksgiving and Christmas were ironclad commitments; Dad's taco barbecues on the Fourth of

July were gala highlights each summer.

Beyond the warm family strands of affection, there was an indefinable *bond* to the California lifestyle. Her Lexus was a well-appointed haven of comfortable luxury on the Golden State's broad freeways. Sue loved the beach, the Hollywood sign, her flat-screen TV over the mantelpiece, with six HBO channels. Summers were long and lazy, but she treasured the shrinking days of late fall when the sunsets grew in exponential glory, followed by three months of snow-capped splendor overlooking Santa Anita Racetrack.

I don't want to go to Bangkok! No way.

Dad tooled around the patio now, collecting dessert plates and stuffing them into a green trash bag. "All done, Pastor Mike?"

"Yeah." The visitor smiled his thanks. "Tell the cook that was some terrific berry pie."

"She does all right, doesn't she?" Her father motioned to the children. "You hustle inside, now. I rented a movie I think you'll really like."

"How come we can't stay out here?"

The elderly man swooped up his great-grandson. "Because, Mr. Charles, we're going to be doing some big-people talk out here. Way way way way way boring. So you'll have more fun watching TV. Don't you think?"

He convened the group around the fire pit. "Well, you know what we're here to talk about. Sue's been invited to head over to Bangkok and help out for a while. And she needs our advice." He swiveled around to face New Hope's senior pastor. "First off, Mike, tell us the latest."

A nod. "Well, John's doing well in rehab. They

upgraded him to stable, and he's mending all right. But for sure, he's got to take it easy for the rest of this year. Doctor's orders."

Natalie, still finishing up her own dessert, raised a hand to interrupt. "What all does he do? I mean, so he's the principal. Day to day, did he give you an idea of what that entails? Why do they think Sue's the one they need?" She glanced over at her younger sister. "No offense, sis. I mean, we all know you can work circles around just about anybody. But how does what they need match up with you?"

"It's pretty standard," she said. "Lots of personnel stuff, juggling fifty-three teachers–with probably a thirty-percent turnover every year. Supply requisitions, parent-teacher conferences. Agendas for faculty meetings. They run a huge meal program, so that's complicated. The principal has to organize a lot of the spiritual awareness programs for three groups: K-3, 4-6, and then what they call *Matthayom*, which is the higher six grades. Plus a lot of social activities: banquets, choir concerts, field trips. A lot of times, it's simply having a presence at events, letting parents and community people know that you're integrated with the whole program."

Her mother, who had spent a long, cheerful career in the classroom herself, drew her sweater tighter. "Sounds like you've done your homework already. But how hard would it be for you to get up to speed, dear?" She gave Sue a friendly but probing look. "You'd be facing two big challenges: it's a new field for you, plus over in Thailand. So you'd be scrambling on both fronts."

"It's a big hill to climb," she conceded. "I mean, at New Hope it's just stuff coming at you all day every day. If you're not careful, you can spend your whole life putting out fires. You know, 'letting the urgent crowd out the important.' Reacting instead of acting. And then you never get around to really strategizing."

"The good news," Mike said, "is that Sue's basically twice as fast as anybody else there is. I'm telling you: she handles paper flow and organizing and delegating as good as anybody on the planet."

Her dad nodded, pleased. "How do you feel, sweetie, just about the challenge of uprooting your life? Thailand's clear around on the other side of the globe. You'd have to rent out your place, wouldn't you? Even if you're away for six months, you can't keep up with your mortgage." He cocked an eye at the senior pastor. "Or, with this being short-term, would the church just keep her on payroll like always?" His face reddened. "Sorry, Pastor Mike. I mean, we're all friends here. I was just thinking out loud."

"This is all new to me too," Mike confessed. "My first impulse is that, Sue, you'd be over there at least till Christmas and maybe even more. From that point of view, you'd probably need to go on their payroll. Which would be substantially less, but it all comes out in the wash with their standard of living being dramatically discounted. And then here, we'd scramble and make do with a couple people trying to cover as much as possible of your kingdom." He forced a reluctant smile.

She nodded, digesting the flow of options.

"So that would mean–I assume–trying to lease your place out."

Dad, not wanting to overplay his influence, but still concerned, gave a dismissive wave. "Well, things like that can always be resolved," he said easily. "Sue's a genius at that stuff. The bigger question is the work itself. Is Sue the person for the job? How does the church here manage in the interim? Etc."

"Hold on a sec." Natalie, still working through a big piece of pie, handed the plate to her husband, who set it down on a nearby tray. "I don't know lots about this, but you've got John What's-His-Name, and then their vice principal. That Thai man, right? Who married your friend from New Hope."

"Uh huh." Mike rolled out the Asian name with precise care. "Khemkaeng. Awesome man, new Christian now."

"Wouldn't the normal thing be for him to step up and take the top spot? Be acting principal while John's rehabbing?"

It was a new thought, and Sue flushed. The last thing she wanted to do was walk into a delicate turf war and accidentally offend local sensibilities.

"Good point," Dad agreed. "What do you think, Pastor Mike? Here's a school with a thousand Thai kids. One of their own is the number two man. Then when something like this comes along, they pass him over and bring in Sue instead. Could be, you know, a real lead balloon."

The senior pastor was unfazed. Fishing in his khakis, he pulled out a flash drive. "Got a video file from Khemkaeng just last night. Can we take a peek? I think it'll answer your questions."

Carrying their leftover plates into the house's expansive family room, Sue's father switched on the computer and scrolled down. "Is this it? 'BCS Khemkaeng'?"

"Yeah."

"Let's take a look."

Moments later, Sue and her family saw the clear image of the nice-looking Thai man peering right into the camera. "Hello, Pastor Sue," he said. "We are so thankful for the prayers you and your church team have given for John. He is doing well and we believe he will recover one hundred percent."

What followed was a five-minute amateur tour of the Bangkok campus. "Here is where you would work, if God makes it possible," he explained. There were unedited clips of the immaculate grounds, administration building, gymnasium and dining hall, some of the classrooms, Tommy Daggett's choir rehearsal studio. At the con-clusion, Khemkaeng reappeared on the screen, now in a wide shot to show a comfortable and modern office. "Right here is where you would work, and we are all praying that you can come help us, Pastor Sue."

He then leaned closer to the camera, smiling and fully at ease. "I have thought of one additional thing I wish you to know. My role at BCS is to have a good connection with students and also with government offices. I am Thai, and know the regulations and ways of developing friendship with important leaders who can give us help. This is a gift God has so kindly blessed me to have in service to his work. But John had a strong way of serving teachers, of crafting agenda plans. This is not so much what I wish to do." Another smile. "So, please, Pastor Sue, know that just as I felt it a great honor to serve John Garvey, I pray that God can give me the blessing of serving with you as well. My wife Rachel Marie feels exactly as I do. If you come, this will be a strong arrangement for Bangkok Christian School."

He was about to sign off, but then quickly added

one more thought. "The students at BCS all love Mr. Garvey very much, and pray for his return. I feel they are very kind to me as well, and I am happy for the blessing of working in a place where we have so many fine friendships. But it is also true that families come to Bangkok Christian School partly because it has American leadership. These parents wish for children to master the English language. Each time they meet Mr. Garvey at a graduation or a concert, it reminds them that English and also western philosophies . . . these are the top priorities. So it is best if our leadership team remains in this way, with a person like you having this position." He smiled easily, and then gave a tiny wave of his hand to whoever was operating the camera. The screen went dark.

"There's another file there too," Mike said. "Can you see it there?"

Sue's dad hunted briefly. "Got it." He double-clicked, and another short clip ran, showing the previous year's graduation ceremony. Sue watched as a long row of beautiful Thai teens, many waving at the camera, marched into the auditorium, eager to receive diplomas. She caught just a glimpse of Rachel Marie posing with her cousin Samantha and a flock of beautiful *Matthayom* Six female graduates, a bearded Tommy Daggett poking his head comically into the video shot.

"So there's that," Mike concluded as the short piece came to an abrupt halt and the screensaver kicked on. "Nice place, great kids. But man, it's a big challenge."

His words from the other day rang in Sue's ears. *You don't have to do every single thing someone asks you to do.* She was a key figure at New Hope; this was her world, her life. Her home in the Glendale hills was an elegant, comforting castle. And the church was a near-perfect fit for her abundant portfolio of talents. While she was certain she could wing it in Bangkok and help keep the huge Christian school from foundering in John's absence, success over there was by no means assured. For sure, it would be a wrenching departure from the California dream.

The family discussed a bit longer, but it was clear that–now with the variables clearly defined–it was simply a matter of Sue praying and weighing her priorities. "We can make it work on this end," Mike assured her, "but this is absolutely your call. You're needed in both places; you can make a mighty difference for Jesus there or here. If you don't go to Bangkok, they'll find someone else." His voice softened, and a note of true Christian affection crept in as he reached out and took her hand. "Ask God to bless a coin and then flip it." He smiled. "Your call, Sue."

FIVE

Even at twenty minutes past midnight, the airport was a humming beehive of airport shuttle buses and blue vans bringing travelers to their rendezvous with new beginnings. Sue accepted hugs from Mike and Cindy, then teared up as a whole row of her Girl Power friends surrounded her for a group hug.

"You guys are too much." She tried to scold them, but her voice broke and she dabbed at her eyes. "Here you've all got work in the morning and all."

"But we love you, Pastor Sue," Naree said, giving her pastor a second lingering hug. "It's so awesome you're doing this. I promise we'll keep the faith and be good girls. You know? But we're going to miss you tons."

The Christian group gathered around for a short prayer and she savored Mike's fatherly arm around her shoulders. "Take this beautiful woman's many talents, Jesus," he prayed, "and multiply them like the loaves and fishes. Make her a huge blessing to the kids in

Bangkok. And give her the rich reward of seeing your kingdom grow and prosper."

She had to remind herself, here on the curb of Tom Bradley International Terminal–this platform of tumult and hope which launched a thousand adventures a day–that life's main joy came in bringing glory to Jesus' kingdom. Life would be harder in Bangkok; no doubt about that. There would be barriers and bad moments. Heat and hard recipes. Certainly times of frustration and letdown. But despite the silent screams of the inner voice saying *No!*, she felt something spiritual tugging her toward the principal's chair in this teeming new kingdom. Sue gave the New Hope team a last wave before disappearing inside the terminal and looking for her airline.

There were long lines in front of each ticket counter, but it was a subdued and reflective crowd as bleary-eyed travelers nudged suitcases forward and fumbled in their bags for itineraries and misplaced e-tickets. The employee who accepted her passport was a slight, precisely beautiful young woman with an expensive silk blouse, her jet-black hair carefully braided. "Bangkok is final destination?"

"Uh huh."

"And two bags?"

"Yes." She accepted the ticket folder with the pair of claim stubs, relieved to be free of the bulky cases.

"Plane will board at one thirty a.m. Okay? Gate Nine."

Sue nodded. There was plenty of time, and she felt a strange reluctance to head directly for the screening lines, now shortened in the early morning hours. It was a foggy August night in Los Angeles, with the big glass windows slightly misted over. Taillights of taxis and limousines on the curve leading to Terminal Four created a slow-moving red snake sliding away from her vision.

Her tote bag and purse draped over her shoulder, she spent a few minutes aimlessly wandering through the gift shops, eyeing a row of designer purses by Fendi and Marc Jacobs, then turned away. Just outside the store, a girl barely fifteen was locked in an embrace with her boyfriend, face buried in his neck. The pair seemed so innocent, untouched by the hurts of life, but the way he was kissing her was anything but juvenile.

Sue flushed, and moved away from the tingling encounter, her own memories stirring in this nocturnal launching pad.

Tenth grade. John Muir High School, downtown Pasadena.

She was a nondescript sophomore, braces and zits, determinedly fumbling her way through geometry and world history classes. Walking the seven blocks home with Karen, retrieving the key from under the mat, plopping down on the bed with her best friend and putting a Beatles LP on. *Oh please, say to me, you'll let me be your man.* Giggling and gossiping about boys even though neither had ever had a date.

And then one day in band, there he was. Arnaud wore a beatnik turtleneck and answered Mr. Nelson's questions in a stiff European accent but he was assigned to play clarinet *right next to her!* "Sorry, what measure we are on?" he murmured, and she pointed, feeling a tiny thrill at having even this slight connection with such a cute boy.

"Where'd you come here from?" she managed to

ask between songs, trying not to blush.

"We always live in Lyon." His dark eyes danced. "You know of it?"

"Huh uh." Impossibly, her cheeks turned an even deeper red. "Sorry."

"No, of course you would not know. About five hundred kilometers from Paris." He laughed. "You know of Paris, surely?"

Even as a sophomore, she had enough poise to eke out a teasing answer. "Hey, we're not total dummies. I've heard of Paris. Have *you* ever heard of San Francisco?"

She walked home on a cloud after finding out that Arnaud–"The *d* is silent, you know"–had been assigned to the same English class as hers. And that his dad's diplomatic mission to the United States would likely last clear until spring break. "You are certain you can help me with homework from Mrs. O'Fill?"

"Sure." She lay in bed for hours, thinking what a delirious heaven it would be to help him with his English, with his spelling, with his hands, his lips, his gorgeous head of hair, with his . . . anything.

And for six glorious weeks, this magical feeling–giddy, uncontrollable–actually coalesced into something *real*. At first, it was teasing in band. Had she imagined it, or did he sometimes scoot his chair just a bit closer to hers? Then looking up in the cafeteria, and seeing him clear across the vast hall, scanning the adolescent sea of faces, clicking from Amanda to Colette to Wendy . . . to *her*. He was actually looking for her, little Sue Baines, with the spunky sense of humor, imperfect but eager smile, and nonexistent cleavage.

Finally it had happened. "This weekend I think I am

going to the cinema," he managed one Thursday as they headed for the bike racks. "Why don't you come?"

Is this a date? Huh? Oh my God! Yes! Yes! Yes! She'd been tempted to fling herself upon him and give this adorable French boy the kind of kiss he was no doubt used to, but managed to hide her galloping pulse. "Sure. That'd be cool."

Three sleepless nights later, Dad had driven her down to the theater, himself pleased and proud, and dropped her off with a nonchalant wave. She sat next to Arnaud, barely seeing the romantic interplay on the screen, so enthralled was she to be on a date with a boy. Right at the end, after innumerable false starts, her hand ended up wondrously enfolded in his own. *Jesus, I could just die right now and it'd be all right.*

There had been two more such dates–both handholdingly glorious–and numerous shared bags of McDonald's fries. She told Karen everything, of course, and her best friend unselfishly helped her fantasize about a possible life in a French chalet, summers at Monte Carlo, skiing in the Alps. Filling their incredibly romance-drenched mansion with *les enfants.* Of course, she'd fly home on a jumbo jet for Christmases with Mom and Dad.

And then, just as she could almost look in the mirror and smirk: "Yeah, we're going steady" . . . it was abruptly over. Didn't she know, Père's diplomatic mission to California had been cut short, and Arnaud was flying home to Paris. Tomorrow night. Three days before Christmas.

Sue paused now in the terminal, remembering the numb pain of those long ago thirty-six hours. She had stayed alone in her bedroom for hours, unable to eat or think. *Oh, baby. Sweetie. My love.* Over and over she murmured the teen endearments she'd never once had the courage to say to her beautiful Arnaud.

It had been a delicate matter, but Natalie finally prevailed on Mom and Dad to let the two girls drive out to Los Angeles International Airport, so she could see him off. "Honey, it's Christmas; the freeways are all jammed. What if you can't even find what gate he's at?" Mom had tried to be reasonable, but a pointed look from her big sister softened the painful moment. Natalie, new California driver's license in her purse, listened sympathetically to Sue's tale of anguish as they crept down the 405 freeway.

"You go in and find him, kid. I'll just park right in there."

"Okay."

It took several minutes, but her heart seized up as she spotted Arnaud with his parents, already waiting at the departure gate. "We board in twenty minutes," the father said, his face a disinterested mask as the young couple awkwardly slipped down the corridor.

Now, more than four decades later, Sue could still remember each moment of that romantic walk, anguish dogging every footstep, down to the end of the terminal and back. Planes slowly edged away from gates, small tow trucks tugging on people's hearts as men in yellow raincoats waved flashing semaphore signals in the misty night air. Arnaud, oddly clumsy in the stilted social situation, reached out and took her hand as the young lovers looked out at the nocturnal gloom.

"You can never know. Perhaps we shall see one another again. *Oui?*"

"Uh huh."

The walk back toward the gate was a tangle of emotions, a San Quentin death watch mingled with: *Please, Jesus, I hope he kisses me! Just once . . .*

Arnaud's parents were already standing in line, holding their carry-ons. They spotted their son, and the mother held out his expensive designer bag, barking something snippy at him in French.

"Okay, then." His beautiful dark eyes seemed to barely comprehend her level of female agony, but he turned his back to his parents and took both of Sue's hands in his own. She would never know, replaying the moment a thousand times after, if he truly meant it or was simply playing the exotic French role assigned to him, but he murmured in her ear: *"Mon cheri."* A soft look in his eyes, he leaned forward and gave her a sweet kiss. Then with a grin, one more.

And he was gone.

Sue checked her cell phone now for any last-minute messages from New Hope or relatives. But it was 1:15 a.m., and she was on her own.

A bit weary from her journey through time, she plodded toward the X-ray machines and the phalanx of security guards. Arnaud's kiss had taken place perhaps within two hundred yards of this very spot, nearly half a century earlier. She could still recreate, in exact and unforgettable glory, the tender physicality of that nice moment.

But that had been it. There had been no more dates after that pinnacle of sweet anguish. No more kisses or touches. There had never been a man who said to her: "I love you, babe." The rest of high school and college had marched its way into and out of her life, and upon graduation she had gone to work and made her living, signing all her own checks.

There was a last-chance watering hole before the escalators and rope lines, and Sue paused, self-conscious about her comfortable but rumpled jeans and sweatshirt. A flat-screen television in the corner was playing a clip from a vintage rock concert at the Coliseum, and her flesh prickled. "Lazy Day" by the Moody Blues. It was the same song she and Natalie had heard on the car radio driving home on Century Boulevard after the bittersweet Christmas kiss so many Decembers ago.

The haunting vocals of the chorus sank in deep, truly hurting her. The delicate machinery of her heart had been forced to run for forty years on just those few drops of romantic fuel, and the memories stung at her now as she turned away from the bar and stepped onto the escalator.

THE CITY OF ANGELS was a distant, tarnished jewel as she rode in the back seat of Khemkaeng's Nissan through Bangkok traffic. "Your flight was all right?"

She nodded, exhausted but strangely alert. "It actually went by kind of fast. I did some organizing for the first part, but did sleep a bit just before we got to Manila."

Rachel Marie took her eyes off the highway flow of cars and multicolored taxis. "It's sure great to have you here, Pastor Sue. You kind of pushed me out the door to come out here, and now I guess I've gotten even."

The older woman tried to stay cheerful despite the pile of time zones pressing down on her. "Well, I'll probably come crying on your shoulder a thousand times before we get through this adventure."

Rachel   Marie   laughed,   leaning   against

Khemkaeng's shoulder for a moment. "Well, you're going to be awesome. John actually left things in fairly good shape, school doesn't start for another week, and I promise you'll like the staff. Except for losing Samantha, a lot of the other teachers are staying, and it's an amazing bunch."

Khemkaeng peered at her in the rear view mirror. "Did you make a decision about where to stay?"

"Oh, definitely that house just over from where you guys are. I already booked it through December. Sent an electronic deposit last week."

"Perfect!" Rachel Marie seemed pleased. "We got to be neighbors with Sam last semester, and it was just great having friends close by. And these houses are an incredible bargain."

"Well, I toyed with a pretty nice condo clear out on the other side of the city, looking out over the river. Thirty-two floors up. Figuring since it's only for a few months, I might as well treat myself. But I did some Google searching, and the commute over to the school would have been a horror show. At least thirty minutes each way. So I dumped that idea quick."

Khemkaeng laughed. "This place is much better. Plus you are welcome to ride over to BCS with Rachel Marie and me whenever you wish."

The car was surrounded by the exotic ambience of Thai living, with packed buses rumbling by on both sides, and the ever-present *tuk tuks* ducking in and out of every possible opening in the slow-moving traffic. "I spent a little while researching cars too," Sue added, leaning into the gap between the front seats. "Leasing one, I mean. But it's so expensive, and I figured with the traffic and all, I'll do just as well to take taxis and buses."

"Yeah." Rachel Marie fished in her purse and handed Khemkaeng a bill for the toll. "Khemkaeng's had this old car for a long time, but just about everyone who comes out here decides that it's easier to use public transportation." She twisted around in her seat so she and Sue could chat more easily. "How'd it go with your house in Glendale and all that?"

"Well, not to brag, but I'm actually kind of good at stuff like that," Sue laughed. "I had to get a renter for the house, of course, but there was a family that had been itching to get into that neighborhood, and they snatched it right up. I think when the kids saw the pool, that was all it took. I got lucky with the car lease too. It only had two more months left on it, and when I went back to the Lexus dealership, they agreed to take it off my hands without penalty."

"Sweet." Rachel Marie grinned. "Pastor Sue, you're too much."

"You said you wanted to stop at a money-changing booth?" Khemkaeng pointed. "There is one right here. We can wait for you."

It took just a couple minutes for her to run into the small office, trade in four crisp $100 bills and accept a pile of foreign-looking *baht.* "How'd you know to bring hundreds? Instead of twenties?" Rachel Marie asked. "That's how you get the best exchange rate, and I meant to send you an email about that, but forgot."

"I'm the queen of the Internet."

They wheeled into the housing development, now settling into the humid shadows of a late August afternoon. "I did like you suggested and picked up the key from the landlord," Khemkaeng said. "That is us right here." He pointed. "And you will be staying just to the right down this street, and two doors down."

"Perfect." Sue was exhausted, but after the grueling flight, the American-style architecture looked inviting. "Thanks so much, you guys. This is really nice of you."

"Sure." Khemkaeng pulled her suitcases free and unlocked the front door of the two-story house. "We are having a meeting tomorrow at nine; is that okay? Most of the teachers are in town already, and even though we don't expect them to check in until the following Monday, everyone wanted to meet you. Plus, if you like, we can then have some lunch together and perhaps go by the hospital and visit with John and Marilyn."

"Excellent." She managed a grateful smile. "I was hoping to get to meet the staff already, so thanks for setting that up."

THREE HEAPING PANS of fried rice greeted the teaching staff the following morning as Sue, in between bites, made the rounds of the teachers. "Hang on–I can get this," she twinkled, her mouth half-filled with the delicious Thai recipe as she mentally groped for a name. "'Lee Eckersley–chemistry.' Right?"

"Pastor Sue, you're uncanny," Rachel Marie marveled. "How come you already know everybody's name?"

She smiled, enjoying herself despite the gnawing fatigue grinding at her bones. "Soon as I knew I was coming, I went to the school web site, collected all your pictures into a separate file, loaded them into my iPhone and started memorizing."

"Wow."

Khemkaeng, cheerfully at ease in his familiar role

as sidekick, led her toward another knot of female teachers. "All three of these ladies teach first grade for us. Sometimes we call it 'Form One'; many of the parents are more used to saying *Prathom* One."

"Got it. And *Matthayom* is the upper six grades, correct?"

"Very good." He introduced the trio. "Here is Terri Adams, whose husband is in business here in Bangkok. Then Ellen Arroyo, from the Philippines, who is now in her third year at BCS, the same as Rachel Marie. And here is a new talented lady, Gloria Garavita, who has arrived here just two days ago from Costa Rica." A laugh. "So Rachel Marie and I have become quite familiar with the highway out to Suvarnabhumi Airport."

"Excellent." Still holding her plate of rice, Sue jockeyed comically between handshakes and the traditional *wai*, and the three teachers laughed, warming to her immediately.

Khemkaeng noticed that her breakfast plate was now empty. "Would you like some more?"

"No, I'm good."

He accepted the plate from her and handed it to a passing kitchen assistant. "*Kop kuhn kah*," Sue said, and was rewarded with a smile.

"Now come over here, because I do want you to meet this good friend of BCS." Seated in a corner and just tucking away a cell phone was a tall, almost burly man with a nearly bald head; closely cropped white hair and a substantial mustache filled out his ruddy face. "This is Dr. Miles Carington. He's a physician over at Mission Hospital, but often comes by the school to assist with health presentations. He teaches so well that I have told him many times: God actually called him to be a teacher, but somehow he misunderstood."

"It was probably an accent thing, eh?" The big man flashed a smile and offered a meaty handshake which dwarfed hers. "It's very good to meet you, Miss Baines."

"Oh, please, just call me Sue," she remonstrated for the fiftieth time that morning.

"Excellent. Sue it is." He seemed pleased. "Then, of course, I must be Miles."

The mention of Mission Hospital triggered something in her mind, and she blurted out: "Can you give me an update on Mr. Garvey?"

The doctor nodded, brightening. "I popped round to see him yesterday, and he's looking much better. A week ago, Dr. Wilamart–that's his regular doctor–was rather worried because he was battling a bit of infection. But this week it's all cleared up, and we're glad to say that his recovery is right on schedule."

She felt a sense of relief. Despite her confidence about filling in at the school, it would be a comfort to know that BCS's real principal was at least available to give advice. "Tell me real quick what kinds of talks you give to our kids. And by the way, we'll take all we can get from you, doctor."

"Miles," he corrected.

"Sorry."

He shrugged. "Well, a lot of just fun stuff–you know, preventive health. What's a good diet. What kind of exer-cise keeps your heart strong. In the *Matthayom* class-rooms, they begin to care about their weight, specially the girls, so I give them tips on how to maintain an ideal level without letting it become an obsession. Then, of course, if teachers are presenting something about the pulmonary system, or various organs and their function, I like to help there too. I got lots of stories and all, and the kids enjoy hearing about our gory exploits in the OR."

"Huh." Enjoying the chat, she hesitated: "I hope you don't mind if I ask: what's your connection with the school?" Turning on the charm, she added: "I mean, how'd we get so lucky?"

The big man draped an arm around Khemkaeng before responding. "I just love kids is all. I've been over at the hospital for about five years, and of course, we have folks there on your board. So I began helping out here and there–just a bit, you know–and a little soon grew to be a lot." He gestured toward the now-empty plate of rice. "I think the ladies here feel sorry for me, and they enjoy feeding Dr. C."

Pointing at his watch, Khemkaeng interrupted politely. "We should probably start." He called the teaching staff together and formally introduced the newcomer. "At New Hope Church, the people call her 'Pastor Sue.'" He turned and gave a small bow. "Do you wish for the same here?"

It was something she hadn't considered, but quickly shook her head. "Well, for all you guys, just 'Sue' is fine. I imagine when we find ourselves in formal situations, using last names before the students and all, Miss Baines will be all right."

"Excellent." The teaching staff all nodded.

Trying to be at ease, she chatted briefly, telling a bit about her own background at the church. "I want all of you teachers to know that I'm here to serve you, not the other way around. I'm an organizer and I'm a listening post. If you have issues, those are my issues too. Back in California, it was always my job to not just come up with better ways of doing things, but to help pave the way for your expertise to flower. Whatever you men and ladies need, I'm here to knock down walls and help make it happen. Is that all right?"

She was gratified to see them nodding eagerly, ready for a positive school year. "Now," she went on, "we'll have more agenda stuff next week of course, but I had a long airplane ride and some time to think about this coming school year. Let me at least put these three ideas in front of you before the weekend."

She had already handed Yothin a computer flash drive; now she nodded in his direction. He came up to her with a remote device, and a PowerPoint slide appeared on the screen. "First off, what would you teachers think about having a supply requisition form more like this? Easy to use–and you just check the boxes right along the left. Like so. If you do it with a hard copy, then just sign it right *there.*" She pointed with the laser device. "But we'd have it online too, and you could just tick off the boxes that indicate what you need, and hit 'send.'" She had already consulted on the idea with Khemkaeng, who concurred that it was an improvement.

Sue proposed two scheduling modifications, both of them affecting just the *Matthayom* level, and the high school faculty members nodded eagerly. "I'll vote yes twice on that if you allow me," Mr. Cey hollered out and his peers grinned.

"Now, I know that we have inservice work all this next week," Sue said. "Try to get here by nine if you can, and we'll be sure to have a good lunch planned each day. Plus"–she glanced over at Khemkaeng again–"Mr. Chaisurivirat and I both agree that if everyone hustles and we can get through all our prep by Thursday afternoon, we might come up with a Friday something rather splendid for all of you." Her face crinkled up in a smile. "What's that expression, Rachel Marie? *Bhai tio*?" It was the Thai equivalent of "go on a fun outing," and the group guffawed, not minding her stiff pronunciation.

"All right, then." She set down the remote control and scanned the row of cheerful Christian faces. "I'd like to spend about an hour just poking around the campus and getting my geography straight. Then go out for a bite to eat, and if any of you want to stick around, Khemkaeng and I will find enough baht in the budget to pay for your lunch. How's that?" She looked over at the doctor, who stood in the corner watching the interaction, a cheerful grin on his face. "Miles, if your schedule lets you wait for us, you could have some lunch with us too, and then I think some of us want to carpool over to your hospital to say hello to John."

He beamed, nodding his approval.

"All right, then. Let's have a prayer together, everybody."

SIX

C ome on, boss lady. Ducks are on the pond–hit 'em in."

Sue waved a menacing bat and put a fake snarl on her face. "Be good to the newcomer."

The BCS staff had poured itself into a diligent four days of pre-term prep, hauling boxes of books into their newly assigned classrooms, making sure lesson plans were all ready for opening day, and scouring the school web site for updates. True to their word, Sue and Khemkaeng had rented an expansive athletic field from a Catholic school thirty kilometers east of Bangkok, and an impromptu but ferocious softball game was underway.

Lee, on the mound for the *Matthayom* teachers, lobbed a pitch toward her, and Sue drove a blistering line drive right past his ear. "Ha!" She trotted down to first base as two more runs went on the board for the home team.

"Just like when you were a kid!" Tommy hollered

from the on-deck circle, remembering a good-natured tale of baseball heartbreak from Lee's childhood as a missionary kid in Bangkok.

"Shush." Grinning, the chemistry professor zipped a quick fastball over the plate; the choir director lunged at it and sent an easy line drive right into the pitcher's glove. Laughing uproariously, Lee trotted over to first base and tagged Sue out for the double play. "Thank you, Lord. Revenge is just so sweet!"

The kitchen staff had prepared a feast of *kai paloh*– eggs stewed in a spicy soy sauce– buttery rolls, and platters of candy donated by Khemkaeng's family corporation. "We'd better play another game after lunch to work off these delicious calories," Sue sighed contentedly. "Tell me again how you say 'watermelon' in Thai?"

"*Dhaeng mo.*" Rungsit, the school's computer whiz, passed the fruit plate over to the new principal. "Please have more."

The two principals had surprised the staff with a bonus gift of brand new polo shirts–cotton white with burgundy edges on the short-sleeved cuffs and sporting the BCS logo. It was a day of sticky heat, though, and faculty members crowded close to one another, making sure they stayed in the leafy shade cooling the four picnic tables.

"Did our ice cream treats arrive yet?" Khemkaeng hiked over, still holding a plate of the main entrée. He scanned the front entrance to the secluded campus. "Good, here they come." The green BCS van wheeled into the complex, and a driver climbed out lugging two heavy bags. The teachers dug in eagerly, picking through the assortment of popsicles and fudge-drenched treats.

"Now before we head back into town," Sue called out, "I want you guys to line up for a couple pictures. We want it for the school newsletter, and also to put up on the web site." She turned to Rungsit. "Can you take care of it today?"

He nodded.

"Plus I know John would like to see it," Marilyn called out. Rachel Marie, sitting next to her and nibbling on an oversized cookie, draped a comradely arm around her friend.

"We'll for sure email it over to him," Sue promised.

Amid good-natured cajoling and the typical hijinks and mugging for the camera, Rungsit snapped a whole row of digital shots and quickly scanned through them. "Yes, we have several that are okay. Even with Mr. Daggett making faces." Everyone laughed.

Sue heard a soft *ding* and pulled her phone free. The screen announced an incoming email from Miles Carington, the doctor from Mission Hospital. Intrigued, she scrolled down to read it.

Greetings, Miss B, the note read. *Just a suggest that perhaps you may wish to pop by Redeemer Christian Church this weekend, since they've now voted to be partners with the school. RCC's where I attend; Rev Sawat allows you could take five minutes to promote BCS. Khemkaeng will do the same, I expect, at United Chris-tian. If interested, I could pick you up. 9:45. Catch ya. Miles.*

She read the message twice, pleased to sense another ally in her mission assignment. All during lunch last Friday, the bulky physician had entertained with cheerful anecdotes from his often grungy work at the hospital, and his buoyant attitude was infectious. She slipped over to Khemkaeng to discuss the offer.

"I think that would be excellent," he nodded. "Rachel Marie and I definitely must be at UCC; Pastor Munir has given us time to make a video presentation, and Tommy is in charge of praise music. But if you could help Dr. C in representing us to this new church, it is a good idea."

She spent a long afternoon back at BCS, working her way through files in John's office and familiarizing herself with the schedule. Part of her role beginning Monday, she realized, was to simply be a presence on campus, being visible and supportive to each of her teachers. Before hailing a taxi for the short ride back home, she flew through short personal emails to each of the teachers on her roster, letting them know how grateful she was to have them on board. Adding a unique touch to each note was a skill she'd honed even before joining Pastor Mike at New Hope Church. Instead of sterile, one-size-fits-all corporate memos, someone quick on a laptop keyboard could easily personalize messages and begin to seal a bond of loyalty.

SHE DAWDLED OVER a bowl of corn flakes, one of the few western-type breakfast cereals for sale in Bangkok supermarkets. In just one short week, she'd become fairly adept at finding her way to a grocery store about a kilometer away, using a few memorized words to steer cab drivers back home. Each day Sue endeavored to tuck three or four new Thai words into her growing vocabulary arsenal, and she grinned now as she splashed a bit more *nome* onto the last of her cereal.

Miles arrived punctually and she greeted him at the door. "Good morning."

"G'day, Miss Baines." He was wearing a white suit, no tie, and she noticed again what a barrel-chested man the doctor was. *He almost looks like that Mr. Clean character on TV*, she thought to herself as she checked the lock on the front door, masking a smile. "That your car?"

"Yeh. Such as it is." He opened the left-hand door for her and waited until she climbed in. "Picked it up about a year after I first arrived here. Pretty good little Honda."

She eyed the dashboard. "I guess I didn't think about it, but this goes in kilometers, not miles, right?"

Even his laugh was ruddy. "Yes, ma'am." He pointed toward the odometer. "So it runs up to around 220. If it was miles per hour, we'd be mashed into pancakes real quick-like if we bumped into anything."

Weekend traffic was slightly less frantic, and he hummed a recent praise song as they threaded their way toward the Chao Phraya River. "Hospital's right there," he pointed. "Remember?"

"Uh huh." Sue was diligently grabbing peeks in every direction, trying to pick up bits of the Bangkok geography. "And the church is . . ."

"'Bout two more clicks."

"Okay, you got me. That's slang for . . ."

"Kilometers." He grinned again. "Sorry, love."

Redeemer Christian Church was substantially smaller than UCC, where she had worshiped with Khemkaeng and Rachel Marie the previous weekend. But there were close to a hundred worshipers filing into the sanctuary; she slipped out of her shoes and followed Miles to the front. He whispered an introduction, and she offered the traditional *wai* to the cheerful pastor. "Very nice you are visiting," he said, his face wreathed in smiles.

"Thank you." The service was translated, and people sang with gusto in both Thai and English. She glanced around during the hymns, trying to spot any potential student recruits for the school.

"Now we have special blessing," Pastor Sawat said, motioning her toward the platform. "We were very sad to hear of medical heart problem for *Adjan* Garvey. But he is in hospital still and all is well. So we thank God for kind blessings. Now, though, is his helper. *Ma'am* Sue Baines. She is coming to us from California, and now as our church and Bangkok Christian School have new partnership in work for God, she will give invitation that our young people can be to attend BCS. Thank you, Mrs. Baines."

She flushed, tempted to correct the erroneous greeting, but thought better of it. "*Sawatdee kah*," she said brightly, and the congregation hummed appreciatively. "It is very good to worship with you, and I too am so thankful that my friend John Garvey is getting well." She paused while the diminutive Thai provided a translation.

"It's very exciting to me that such an excellent school is right here in Bangkok, and we want to make sure every single young person here at Redeemer Christian Church is able to attend." On the front row, she could see Miles emphatically nodding his head.

"Let me tell you all of the big advantages of coming to school at BCS," she added cheerfully. "All my life I have believed that young people deserve advantages! Pluses, not minuses." The pastor fumbled to find words, and she chided herself for the esoteric reference. "First of all, an excellent education with wonderful teachers. Five stars," she added on an impulse, and the believers nodded to indicate that they comprehended the metaphor. "Plus some very special visiting teachers, like Dr. Carington, who is very welcome all the time!" He grinned, enjoying the moment.

"We have a beautiful campus and lots of extra activities: trips, a musical choir, a very modern computer web site. And you know that our curriculum is provided in English, which–as our world gets more interconnected all the time . . ." She sucked in her breath, but the pastor confidently provided Thai words to convey the concept. "And the best thing is that Jesus is a very real part of Bangkok Christian School. We pray. We sing Christian songs. We support this church. Our teachers have given their lives to Jesus and they love him and lift up the beauty of his character." There were scattered *amens* even before Pastor Sawat provided a Thai translation to her appeal.

"Now," she said with a broad smile, "I admit I am just a visiting helper. Mr. Garvey is still the *hua nah*." Everyone laughed as she deliberately butchered the colloquial expression for "head honcho." "But I do have his permission to tell you this: if there are young people here, either *Prathom* or *Matthayom*, and tuition is a problem for your family, I have very good news for you. We can solve your problem! I promise you this. Parents, I believe that God wants for your boys and your girls to be in this wonderful place of advantages. If you don't have enough baht for this great advantage, come right to my office and say: 'Miss Baines, you promised to help me. Here I am!'" More laughter. "And God will help me to keep this promise." She paused for effect, then added:

"*Kop kuhn kah.*"

Miles gave a masculine fist pump as she returned to sit next to him. "Aces! I wish I'd recorded that, Miss Baines."

There was a hubbub of *wais* and multilingual conversation as the church let out a few minutes past twelve o'clock. Miles frowned as he scanned through the bulletin he had tucked into his shirt pocket. "Sorry, Sue," he admitted. "Somehow I got it in my head there was a potluck lunch here today. But it's next weekend."

"That's all right."

"No, no," he remonstrated. "I'll find us something." He scratched his bald pate, thinking. "I guess, seeing as we've got the car and I don't have to make rounds till four, sky's the limit." He bowed low in a grand gesture. "After a week in Asia, is your tum craving anything in particular?"

She laughed, pleased at the prospect. "Well, the lunches at BCS have been, shall we say, extremely *Thai* all week long. I'd kill for a good old-fashioned American buffet."

"Excellent." He flashed his big smile. "There's a Sizzler back downtown in the Central World Plaza mall. Or, if you want some real ambience, let me take you to the Sheraton. Their Garden Pool Restaurant has quite a lineup, if I remember. And it's lovely by the pool, with shade trees and such. Are you game?"

Sue pretended to swoon. "Well, that sounds like heaven. If you're willing. And we can go fifty-fifty," she quickly added.

"Nonsense." Miles pretended to be indignant. "It was my mistake here, getting the dates wrong and all."

Chatting animatedly, he motored down the street,

then grunted to himself. "Oops, wrong way. Guess we'd best chuck a Uey." He wheeled the car around in a tight one-eighty and eased onto the elevated tollway ringing the city. "This should save us a spot of time," he grinned, threading his way through the flow of buses and taxis and pointing to various local landmarks.

"I still haven't gotten used to being on the wrong side of the road," Sue confessed as a tour bus eased past them on the far side.

"Takes a bit of adjusting for sure." He laughed. "Not for a down-under gent like me, though."

There was a drifting layer of cloud cover at the five-star hotel, and after going through the buffet line, Miles led Sue over to a secluded table surrounded by lush bushes and a corner of the elegant swimming pool. "This all right?"

"Sure."

There was a moment of hesitation before he picked up the slack. "Shall we say grace?"

"Okay."

"Lord Jesus," he began. "Thanks for the rest and the spiritual comfort you give to us on this your special day. We thank you as well for the Christian churches here in this beautiful city. Please bless and strengthen each one, and add to our contributions, feeble as they are. I pray that you'll bless my dear sister Sue and all her fellow teachers as they fire up this great adventure of a new school year. Be with her family, dear Lord, wherever they call home. And also now we ask your blessing on this feast; we thank you for it. In your mighty name, Amen."

She felt a flush of satisfaction, realizing that here was a kindred spirit who was fully committed to the same kingdom ideals as her own. "That was nice, Miles," she said, digging into the extravagant salad and dinner pastries.

He was a big man with hearty appetites, she noticed, as he trooped back to the buffet line for one item after another. "Try a bite of this," he offered, holding out his fork. "The Thais call this *nua paht gratiem prik thai.* Bits of beef fried in garlic and pepper." A belly laugh. "But hey, keep your water glass close by, my lady."

The concoction did sting, almost bringing tears to her eyes, and she quickly took a comically large gulp of her drink, giggling as she did so. "I guess you did warn me."

"They've got some mango ice cream sundaes that will put me back in your good graces," he announced. "Stay here and check your emails and I'll bring us back some treats." He returned moments later, a big smile on his face, toting two massive bowls of the frozen tropical dessert. "There you be, Miss Baines. To a long and prosperous life in the City of Angels."

He dropped her off at 3:45, glancing at his wristwatch. "Are you going to be late?" She fretted that the leisurely lunch had compromised his schedule.

"No worries," he said easily, lingering at her front door for just a moment. "I can make it back to the hospital in twenty, and the nurses all like me. I imagine they'll be in a forgiving mood." He tossed her a casual wave. "I should be by the school again Thursday. Lee has a thing he needs me for. Hope to see you then, Sue." He gave a tiny honk and tossed a manly *cheers* out the window as he squealed around the corner.

SEVEN

It was a new and exhilarating experience to lead others in such a *beginning* as the first day of a school term, she thought to herself. New Hope Church was a flowing stream of duties and ministry moments, but nothing ever started or concluded. One was simply always in the mad dash of the whitewater ride, the waves and rocks and eddies of unexpected currents, the occasional moments of calm. But here in Bangkok, this intense new world, August 21 was Chapter One of a great mystery novel now beckoning to her.

She dressed for the first day of work, examining her two-piece pastel suit in the mirror, sighing as the humidity already flattened her gray locks and coated her lumpy frame with a whisper of sweat. Too nervous for a real breakfast, she hastily downed a banana, peering out the picture window for Khemkaeng's tan Nissan to roll up.

"Here we go again," Rachel Marie chirped as Sue climbed into the back seat next to Pranom. "Are you ready, Miss Baines?"

"As ready as I'll ever be." She forced a smile and greeted the eighth-grader. "Hello, Pranom. We're so glad we still have you here for one more semester."

"Thank you." The girl was adorably beautiful in her maroon-and-white uniform, her jet-black hair carefully decorated with regulation ribbons.

"Who's your teacher this year?"

"I have Mr. Sinaga."

"Ah. They say he's good."

Pranom flashed a grin. "Plus I have my dad for choir."

The goateed musician, struggling to fit his bulky frame into a third of the back seat, leaned over and kissed the girl on the head. "And you behave yourself, daughter. No sour notes."

Rachel Marie gave her brunette curls a flip. "Course, when all your friends are around, don't forget to still call him 'Mr. Daggett.'"

"Yes, okay."

The campus gym was a cheerful maelstrom of human activity as small children and teens formed shifting clumps of teasing conversations. Sue, who had rehearsed this moment over and over all weekend, set her briefcase down next to the PA table and accepted the wireless mike. "Is this on?"

The girl showed her the switch. "You can press here when ready to speak. Red light means okay."

"Got it. Thanks."

Striding with Khemkaeng to the center of the court, she faced the student body and nodded to the PA operator, who pressed a button. A buzzer sounded, and kids immediately began to form themselves into lines behind their homeroom teachers.

"Thank you, BCS students!" she said brightly. "My name is Sue Baines, and I'm very happy to be here in Bangkok to help serve our school along with Mr. Chaisurivirat." The night before, over a home-cooked meal of rice and curry, she had drilled the tricky last name with Khemkaeng until her intonation had the natural Thai sound, with a falling tone on the fourth syllable. "You read in the school newsletter that Mr. Garvey got very sick this summer. But we thank Jesus that he is getting well; in fact, I hear he may be able to go home from the hospital this coming week. I know many of you have prayed for Mr. Garvey, and I appreciate that so much."

It felt almost military to be addressing such perfectly straight rows of juvenile humanity, ranging from near-toddlers to the very mature eighteen-year-olds lined up in the *Matthayom* section. "Just so you know a bit about who I am, I have always lived in California. I worked as a bank officer and in financial management for many years, and recently was blessed by God to serve him at a very good church called New Hope." With a flash of inspiration, she added: "Many of you remember Pastor Mike, who has come to Thailand to share with you. He was our leader at the church, and he and our own Mr. Garvey are wonderful friends. Anyway," she concluded, "I know it's time for our national anthem, and then Mr. Chaisurivirat will tell you some important things about this new school year."

Two students stepped forward and grandly raised the colors as the anthem boomed through the large speakers in all four corners. It was stirring to hear the Thai students singing with such gusto and national allegiance, and Sue found herself almost saluting, swept up in the nice fervor of the moment.

Khemkaeng ran through some of the trivial bits of information that were helpful on a first day, reminding students that meal tickets could be purchased on a monthly or weekly basis, and to please take care not to lose the stubs. "And remember, we have told all teachers that the twenty-baht rule for Thai language violations is . . . very firm." He grinned at his own failure to find a good metaphor. "I know when you are playing with friends or doing games, it is so easy to forget. But the best way to become proficient is to do all your speaking in English. All day!" He gave them his warmest smile. "I married a beautiful teacher, Missie Stone, who did not speak Thai! So I quickly found that speaking English all through the day, and then even at home soon helped me to improve." He glanced at his watch. "Has a student been selected for our prayer?"

To Sue's surprise, Pranom stepped forward and accepted the microphone from Khemkaeng. With poise beyond her years, she faced the crowd. "Okay. Let us pray." The vast ocean of kids bowed their heads. "Dear God, it is a fine blessing to come to school again at BCS.

We give thanks that you look after all students in our holiday time. Bless all teachers, please, and give us understanding of love of God. And also that we will come to love Jesus in our hearts." There was a pause, and then she added: "Please protect our families and also my mom and sister in U.S. Amen."

Sue glanced over at Rachel Marie, who was looking in wonder at her niece and dabbing at her eyes. A burst of contemporary Christian music blared through the speaker system and a river of maroon flowed toward the staircases leading to the maze of second-story classrooms.

Now what? This new and intimidating Everest loomed before her, but Sue was wired for these very kinds of challenges. Her pulse thumping excitedly, she went to her office, greeting each of the support staff by name, flipped on the computer, and dove into a thicket of opportunities.

She knew the high school schedule had a break promptly at ten, so made a point of making the rounds just as students were traipsing from one classroom to the next. "Everything good?" she asked teachers, poking her head in the door. "Hey, men and ladies. How's the first day?" Tong Inn, the fresh-faced calculus teacher who had stepped in to replace Samantha Kidd, gave her a big smile and nod to indicate that he had survived his initiation.

She deliberately hopscotched from one table to the next during lunch, cementing her connection with all of the middle school instructors. "No, I don't need to write it down," she protested, as Rachel Marie mentioned a screen that wouldn't pull all the way down. "I'll have Sakda look at it later today." She always waited until stepping away before texting a cryptic reminder note to herself, using the efficient Baines shorthand she'd perfected through the years.

Tommy was still conducting choir tryouts as the closing bell rang, and she offered a *wai* to as many departing juniors and seniors as she could. "I hope you had an excellent first day!" she said over and over. "Thank you for being part of BCS." Grinning as she picked up a copy of the choral music, she scanned the lyrics. "Let me know if you need a third-rate guitar player to help out on the chorus, 'cause I really like this song."

His eyes widened. "Are you serious?"

"No way," she laughed. "Back at New Hope, I could handle 'Kumbaya' and about three other songs as long as they were in either the key of C or the key of C. Otherwise, I sit in the back and make a joyful noise."

He grinned. "How was your first day?"

"Wonderful," she told him, meaning it. "This place is amazing."

"Tell me about it."

She pretended to cloud over. "For sure you and that pretty young lady have to leave us in the lurch at Christmastime?"

The chubby musician sighed heavily. "Man, for five baht I'd settle here forever. No kidding. This place is awesome for ministry." He gave a helpless gesture. "But my lady love is in Portland, you know. And Miss Paloma has to stay there for political reasons."

"I know. But in the meantime, thanks for all you do. I know you're a huge influence here." She forced a cheerful look. "Unfortunately, high on my list of impossible things is to start scouting around for a

Tommy Daggett clone." She headed resolutely for the main parking lot, determined to greet as many parents as she could.

The days of the first week fell into place like an all-strikes row of bowling frames. Without the temptation of evening television, she kept clicking out brainstorming ideas on her laptop until around nine each night, sometimes taking a comfortable hike around the neighborhood with the muted sounds of crickets adding to the exotic Thai ambience. Once she waved to Rachel Marie through her neighbor's picture window, returning to her own living room for an abbreviated dose of American TV via the DVD sets she'd tucked into a suitcase.

It had always been a workaholic temptation to spend every free moment in productive labor, and she had to reach deep inside for the self-discipline to do a bit of quiet Bible study each morning. She set the alarm for six each day, and after another brisk walk in the early cool outdoors made time for prayer and pieces of wisdom from the book of Psalms. Pastor Mike always posted a weekly devotional on the New Hope Church web site, and she now made a point of calling up a treasured dose of California inspiration.

For some reason it had stuck in the back of her mind that Miles would be back on campus Thursday afternoon. Curious, she found an excuse to amble by the chemistry lab, and stood in the back enjoying the doctor's colorful banter with the *Matthayom* Five students. He had prepared a clever talk, replete with bits of humor, about how various chemistry compounds should never be prescribed together. "Now, see, this stuff"–he hoisted an innocuous bottle of some powder–

"might grow some hair on the top of my head. And I would love that." The students tittered. "The problem is, Mr. Eckersley says I would end up looking like his wife in about five other ways too." Even Sue joined in the general merriment.

"You sure add a lot here, Miles," she enthused as he waved goodbye to the students and donned his doctor coat. "That was terrific."

"It's nothing," he said breezily. "Keeps me young, eh?"

They walked down the hall together, and he held the door open as they went outside. "Are you getting used to the Bangkok heat yet?"

"Not much." It was a muggy afternoon, with the Thai flag hanging limply from the pole in center court.

The brawny Australian peeked at a text message and shoved the pager into the pocket of his lab coat. "Thursday nights the pool at our place stays open till eleven. I asked Khemkaeng if he and Rachel Marie might like a bit of a swim. Why don't you join us? Seeing as how you're all in a carpool and everything."

It was a nice offer, and Sue felt a delicious tingle. "Boy, right now that sounds about perfect. What time are they coming over?"

"Kind of on the late side," he confessed. "'Cause I've got rounds and possibly a small surgery thing. Just routine, though. I told them about eight-thirty."

"You're on." She waved goodbye and headed toward her office.

SUE HAD LONG AGO insulated herself from the unavoidable facts regarding her appearance in a bathing suit. Her body was a saggy pillar, and being around a pool simply added to the dumpy impression she was sure she made on fellow bathers. But she did feel a wince as Rachel Marie and Pranom emerged from the ladies' restroom. Both of them were slender beauties, and Khemkaeng lit up whenever his wife paddled by.

"This water's perfect, Dr. C," Sue grinned, forcing away her unstated envy. Miles was no Greek god himself; his barrel chest, lightly coated with a manly furriness, had a good thirty extra pounds running around the equator. He floated cheerfully on his back, his scalp gleaming in the pleasant moonlight, grinning foolishly as Pranom exe-cuted a splashing cannonball aimed right at him. "Hey, you . . ."

The pool was an unadorned rectangle on the grounds of a high-rise condominium complex a few blocks east of the Chao Phraya River. "I almost leased a place just down the street from here," she told Miles as they visited amiably in the deep end, enjoying the sparkling cool liquid.

"Yeh?" He glanced at a waterproof watch adorning his left wrist. "I wish you had, then. I could use a home-cooked supper now and then." A hearty laugh.

He clambered out and went over to a small snack bar adjacent to the well-lit pool. Moments later he returned with an icy bottle of pop. "Here you go, principal lady."

She accepted the offering with a smile. "None for you?"

"Nah."

The drink was fruity and tart. "Come on, you have some too." They traded tastes until the bottle was drained, and he carefully set it close to the shallow end of the pool. "Don't let me forget that."

The evening crowd thinned out until just the BCS members were left. Rachel Marie, her damp hair plastered down her back, came up behind Pranom and gave her a teasing dunk. "Hey, sweetcakes. Isn't it your bedtime?"

The Thai girl sputtered back to the surface. "Tommy–my daddy says I can stay until ten. Because Friday is always easy day at school."

"Pretty nice. First week go all right?"

"Yes, I like it so much."

"Even algebra?"

Pranom nodded confidently.

"Sweetie, you're going to knock them dead when you go back to Portland."

Sue watched, bemused, as Tommy and Khemkaeng stood with Miles in the shallow end, bantering about this and that. BCS's resident musician was a jovial soul, and his jokes brought a barking laugh from Miles, who some-times bounced up and down in his masculine enthusiasm. "Good on ya!" he chortled over and over. "Good on ya!" He was a very physically expressive specimen, she noticed, often draping an arm around his pals when emphasizing a point or trying to dominate a good-natured debate.

There was a big clock on the side of the condominium, perched just over the outdoor shower spigots. As the time slowly crept toward ten, Miles eased back into the water and took a last swim in her direction. "It was lovely having you come over, Sue."

"Well, thank *you*." She felt a spot of color reach her cheeks. "I know you're so busy, and then for you to give up your evening for all of us . . ."

"Hey, you're welcome here anytime."

Sue was about to dry off when she noticed that a teenage boy had parked himself right on the lounge chair where she had draped her towel. He was engrossed in a handheld video game, muttering to himself as the device spat out digital warning sounds.

She gulped, hoping he would move, but the youth seemed impervious to his surroundings. After a moment of hesitation, she walked over. "Er, excuse me."

Nothing.

A gust of Bangkok breeze ruffled her locks, and she carefully cleared her throat. "Sorry," she managed. "I don't want to interrupt your game. But you're kind of on my towel."

The boy had a European look about him, but with very dark skin. His hair drooped in loose curls around his eyes, and he popped the controls with his thumbs, cursing softly under his breath.

You're a school principal now. Better get used to this kind of thing. She was irritated by the boy's callous insulation from the world around him. "Excuse me," she said again, this time a bit louder.

The teen popped the game device against his thigh and lifted his eyes to hers. "Rack off," he snapped, adding a familiar epithet.

She flushed. "Look, I don't want to get in your way. Just pop up for two seconds and I'll leave you alone."

The boy had already returned his gaze to the animated contest on the screen. "I said shut it, missie."

Nonplussed and offended, Sue stood rooted to the spot. It seemed incongruous that in this Asian kingdom where gentility and civil discourse were highly prized commodities, this uncouth boy should be challenging her. She was about to speak again when there was a retort from the pool. "Gino! Move your butt off there. Can't you see the lady wants her towel? She's my guest, eh? So belt up!"

Stunned, Sue gulped as the teen, a seething volcano, flounced over a couple of inches, his eyes still glued to his game. Scarlet-faced, she carefully tugged the towel free. "Thank you," she managed evenly, walking away and deliberately going to the far side of the pool to towel off.

Rachel Marie came over, trying to mask a sympathetic smile. "Yikes. What was all that?"

Miles, a blotchy crimson with embarrassment, came up to both of them, dabbing at his balding dome. "I'm sorry as can be, Sue. Please forgive me. There was no call."

"That's all right. I guess." Her voice was still unsteady from the X-rated encounter. "Thanks for helping out." She glanced over at the petulant youth, shaking her head in wonder.

The tall man hesitated, his composure fractured. He looked down at his feet before raising his gaze up to meet her own. "You don't understand," he whispered, his voice tinged with clumsy shame. "That there's my son."

EIGHT

She lay awake in bed for a long while, replaying the unpleasant encounter by the pool. It had been an upsetting end to an otherwise satisfying evening, and she found herself terse, almost snappish, in the car as Khemkaeng chauffeured the group home. "Sorry, you guys," she blurted out when they dropped her off. "That was just too weird."

"Shake it off," Tommy called out from the back seat, and she forced a smile, waving goodbye before digging out her house key.

Bumping into insolent kids was part of life; she knew that. Already in this first week of school, one teacher had sent a disobedient eighth grader to her office, and it had taken nearly half an hour to unravel the boy's grumbling diatribe. But when Miles' confession tumbled out, that the prickly teenager was his own flesh and blood, it left her feeling oddly unnerved and disappointed.

Unable to sleep, she flipped on a small lamp next to

her bed and simply brooded. From the first, she had considered Miles an interesting and pleasant friend. He was great in the classroom, a natural communicator. Their trip together to visit RCC the previous weekend had gone well; he was charming company and a strong, supportive ally of the school.

Why didn't he ever mention having a kid? Somehow she resented being blindsided by the revelation of his obviously dysfunctional family life. Was this guy married? The boy–*what was his name again? Gino?*–had an unusual ethnicity, and her mind spun out the various possibilities.

The clock on her nightstand said it was creeping up to midnight, and she resolutely turned the light out again. But as she drifted off, Sue admitted to herself that part of her unstated frustration had to do with Miles himself. He had seemed so nice, and being responsible for this bratty kid was obviously a chink in the man's armor. Plus–she hated to admit it to herself–the delightful lunch by the pool had made her wonder if maybe, just maybe . . .

Well, that was dumb. Go to sleep, Sue.

Friday afternoons at Bangkok Christian School were a quiet time for catching up; the campus emptied out shortly after noon, and her carpool entourage had already departed for home. She remained at her desk, BCS's solitary sentinel, still thinking about the mess with her friend. It wasn't like her to allow issues to fester. Pastor Mike had always emphasized the importance of Christians being gracious but direct in resolving disagree-ments. The biblical rules for reconciliation between believers were part of the Matthew 18 Magna Carta at the thriving church.

Breathing a prayer, she logged onto the Internet and tapped out a message. *Hi, Miles. So sorry for the mess last evening. I know it was disquieting for you too, but I've had kids snap at me a zillion times and I'm still here. LOL. If you want to talk, I'm always around. Still friends, right? You're a huge plus to this place, and we all appreciate it. Have a blessed weekend. S.B.*

It was less than a minute before her cell phone rang. Her heart skipped a beat when she saw his name on her screen. "That was quick." She tried to keep her voice light.

"Hey, Miss Baines." He seemed subdued. "Good to get your email. You're positive you don't hate me?"

"Don't be ridiculous." She felt an involuntary flush. "It was a great evening. I was just sorry for that little thing at the end."

"Yeah." A pause. "I just feel like . . . well, I mean, I should have mentioned Gino before. Don't know why I didn't get round to it."

"Well, plenty of time for that later."

"Sure."

He seemed discombobulated, ill at ease, and she tried to ease the tension. "So how old is your boy?"

"Sixteen."

"Huh." Sue forced an awkward laugh. "Why isn't he enrolled here? We could use the tuition dollars, Dr. C."

"After last night, I wouldn't think you'd ask that question." He said it evenly, but she flushed.

"Sorry."

There was a pause, and then he spoke in a rush. "Look, Sue. I feel awful about all this. And I mean, it sure feels like it put a big wall of China up between our being friends and all."

"No, course not," she said quickly, not sure if she meant it.

The big man's voice was unsteady. "I just . . . I'd really like to come by if you'd permit. Clear the air and all."

She felt torn, weighing his entreaty. Erasing barriers was part and parcel of her Christian ethic, but she still felt so stung by the brutish moments at the pool. "Of course," she assured him, her cheeks reddening.

"He's off with friends tonight anyway. How about a bit of supper when you get off work, and I'll spill the beans."

"Sure." She felt conflicted, but knew it was the right thing. "Want to meet somewhere?"

"No, I'll come by since I've got the car. How's five?"

"Very good. I'll get some work done."

He hesitated. "Thanks, Sue. This means the world to me."

"No problem."

She clicked out a careful email to Khemkaeng and Rachel Marie, brooding as she did so. *Dinner with Miles this evening. Probably to fix the #%@&! from the pool. Say a prayer. I don't want anything to mess up all he does for BCS. Sue.*

The campus was eerily still at five when he pulled up. Miles had shed his ever-present doctor's coat and was clad just in a pair of jeans and a black polo shirt, his bulging biceps straining the fabric. "You got through the first week okay, eh?"

"Yeah." Her heart was skipping beats, but she reminded herself that she was the mature, capable principal of a school with present enrollment of 1,368. And that this well-meaning gentleman was a fellow servant and team member in the army of Christ. "No bruises yet."

He wheeled out of the lot and nosed into traffic. "There's a good pizza place over at the Narai. Your friends all go there on occasion, I know. Any objections?"

"Sounds good." Her briefcase was in the way, and she awkwardly fumbled with easing it onto the backseat behind her. "Oops. Should have put it there when I got in."

They paused at a light, and he suddenly blurted out: "I just . . . I'm so sorry about last night. Gino was unforgivably rude, and all I can do now is apologize."

Sue swallowed hard. "Shouldn't that come from him?" It came out sounding prickly, but she looked directly at him, unwilling to back down.

He nodded abjectly. "Of course. Not that I'm going to get that to happen. But . . ."

She smiled. "Let's get some supper first. I tend to bite people's heads off when I'm hungry." Miles managed a short laugh and lapsed into silence.

The pizzeria outside the luxury hotel was cozy, and the tension between them started to thaw as Miles bowed his head and offered a nice prayer. "That helps," she murmured.

He looked quizzical. "What do you mean?"

Sue thought about it. "Just that . . . well, look. We're Christians. We both care about reaching this city for the Lord. And serving all these great kids at the school. We believe in grace and forgiveness and new beginnings. Sure, last night was a mess, but Jesus has an answer for it. In the meantime, I value your talents and . . ." She hesitated, then went on, her words in a jumbled rush. "I like our friendship too. I think we get along and have values in common. Going to church with you last week, and the nice lunch and all . . . I want to make sure we don't needlessly lose a good connection over something like this."

The pizza arrived and they both dug in, savoring the hot melted cheese and the elegant atmosphere of the business district. "How's a bit more soda?" he offered.

"No free refills here?"

He shook his head. "I keep telling restaurants that's the way of the world now, but they always want to sell you a second bottle for forty baht more." He motioned to a passing waiter, and she smiled gratefully.

She finished her third slice and wiped her hands clean. "All right, Doc," she said, resolving to hear him out. "From somewhere or another, you have a family life that's obviously rather interesting. Why don't you put your cards on the table?"

He nodded. "Fair enough." They were in a secluded corner of the restaurant, and the intimacy afforded him a private place to share. "I got out of med school a ways back, down home in Brisbane. Pretty tough program at UQ, but I did all right for myself."

"Hold everything." Managing a grin, she held up both hands. "Don't show off. What's 'UQ'?"

"Sorry. University of Queensland. Pretty good outfit, and I slogged through it, residency, everything."

"Okay."

He pulled another slice of pizza free and took a bite, eyeing her as he did so. "Have some more?"

"In a while."

"Right. Anyways, that's when things went south. There was a lab tech there, pretty lady, that had come in from England. A cross between Caribbean and a trace of Sicily. Cooked up a storm, spunky, I dug her accent, etc."

"And . . ."

The man sagged. "Well, you know, one thing led to another and we fell in with one another. A bit more of that and she moved in with me. I was raised better, and my dad was mad as a cut snake when he got wind. I always figured that what they didn't know wouldn't hurt them, seeing as they were clear down in Sydney, a long day's drive and all. But they showed up once, no warning, and that was it. My mum and dad told me off, said they were hurt, I said oh well."

Sue digested this, warming to the plain humanness of the saga.

"Anyway, so not long after, Elena tells me she's pregnant and what should we do? And so we face up to the music, and got married next month. That helped with my folks and it was all dandy again."

"I assume that was Gino?"

"Yeh." He chewed thoughtfully on the pizza, appreciating the low-key conversation. "So there we were. Mum and Daddy and kid makes three. I had a decent practice, Elena went to working just halves, and Gino was adorable until the first time he spit up on me. But I changed my share of nappies and sang to him at bedtime and such."

She gave a tentative laugh, trying to picture this hulking man fumbling with a poopy diaper. "Keep going."

"All right. Truth be told, I wasn't much into God

and all that, even though I'd been raised Christian. My folks were devout as Catholic candles, but not me so much. Anyway, time went on and we were having difficulties. Marriage wasn't doing so good, Gino was five handfuls, and something in me kind of went: 'Doc, you better get with Jesus or it's over.' So I began reading the Bible, trying to go to church, and Elena just wouldn't have any of it."

"How come?"

"It just wasn't her thing. She was a free spirit, liked her wine, partying a bit, hitting the clubs. So I'd be home with Gino, trying to hold things together with a clothespin, and she was soused half the time."

Sue felt a pang of sympathy, envisioning the slow unraveling of this fragile cocoon. "Then . . ."

"Okay. So Gino's around, pulling low marks, year three in primary school. Teacher's calling me once a week and it's a fair mess with his mum out and about most of the time. And Elena comes home one night and says to me, 'It's done, Milesy. I've found me another mate.' Some guy she hooked up with over at the lab, working same shift as her." He looked down at his hands. "Can't say I blame her, but I didn't smell the rat till it was over and done."

"I'm so sorry," Sue murmured, meaning it.

"Yeah. Well, I had it coming for sure." A crooked smile. "So she moves out and then we've got this thing about, 'What happens to Gino?' Turns out, this bloke, Conrad, can't stand kids, didn't want his or anyone else's around. No way, not now, not ever. Just beer and blackjack was his thing, you know? So Elena comes back and says, 'Look, just take all we got plus him, and let me out of here.' So I say, 'All right.'"

"Huh." Despite her own angst, Sue's face softened. She reached over and gave his hand a sympathetic squeeze. "There must be a chapter two because here you are having a pizza with me four thousand miles away."

He brightened. "Yeh. Well, we put in four more years there in Brisbane. I had to hire nannies now and again because I had this shift and then that one at the hospital. I tried to stay off nights, and had enough seniority to have a fairly steady schedule. But Gino was so unhappy."

"How come?"

"Well, he missed his mum. Blamed me totally for the fact that the marriage was bodgy."

"Huh? Sorry–translate, please."

"Oh. You know, went bad."

"Ah."

"So he got to around Grade Six, and I began looking around. Figured a fresh location might be all right for both of us. Now that I was Christian again, when I heard about the hospital here in the city, I thought I might look it over. Gino liked the looks of it, and said all right." He tried to force a smile. "First cheery thing he'd said in about those four years, eh?"

Sue finished her meal and dabbed at her mouth with the paper napkin. "So the two of you have been here ever since?"

Miles nodded. "And I know I've made a mess of things. I wish I could say, well, it's just a phase, a bad month or so. But it's been blue pretty much the whole way. Kid doesn't do what I tell him unless I threaten to crack him one. Mouths off at folks, and of course, when it's someone I care about, like at the pool, it hurts me bad."

She felt a twinge of sympathy, realizing how the fracas from the night before had wounded this gentle giant. "Wow. I'm so sorry, Miles."

He nodded forlornly. "Anyway, so I do the best I can, which isn't much. The job pays all right; we've got the flat by the river and enough to get by. I have him going at International School Bangkok, which, the fees are about twice the price tag of our place at BCS, but it's top drawer, and he's reasonably content there. Grades a bit better than before." He hesitated. "But at home . . ."

"Does he pop off at just anyone?" She asked the question directly.

"Sometimes yes, sometimes no. We'll go a month or so where he's actually decent. Not cheery, but he'll eat his papaya and lay off the F-bombs. But then, all at once, he'll swear a blue streak at a friend of mine, I take away his toys, he curses me to my face, and when a fortnight's gone by, then we pretend, hey, it never happened."

"Huh."

Miles picked up a menu and scanned it. "Would a dish of spumoni ice cream help patch up our friendship?"

She laughed, feeling a return to semi-normalcy. "There's nothing to patch. But if you're offering, sure."

"Aces." He motioned for the waiter and pointed to the delicacy. "*Au song.*" He held up two fingers for confirmation. The Thai youth nodded and scurried away.

It was nearly dark outside and the evening stars, muted because of the radiant city lights all around, began to twinkle through the skyscrapers. A few blocks away, Bangkok's efficient sky trains glided in and then away, moving their human cargo through the restless metropolis. Sue took careful bites of the gourmet treat, feeling better. Miles' family life was a dubious adventure, but he was trying his best to patch up a bad situation and live with integrity. "Are you coming out our way next week?"

"Nothing's on my slate. But sometimes if I'm free I simply show up and mingle with the kiddies at their chapel. Sing along with the songs, you know."

"That's so awesome," she told him. "Please do keep coming. And about last night, just let it go. As far as I'm concerned."

Overcome, the big man reached out and took her small hand in his own. "That means the world, nice lady."

THERE WAS A THUNDEROUS downpour outside, typical for early October, and Sue popped an umbrella as she made her way over to the crowded cafeteria. It had been a difficult morning trading emails with a pastor in New Zealand who had promised to come to Bangkok for the school's annual Week of Spiritual Emphasis. "But he came down with a destructive case of dysentery," she told Rachel Marie as the pair loaded up plates with a Thai version of spaghetti. The cafeteria matron had picked up a cache of mangos, and the California ladies savored each scrumptious bite of the heavenly fruit.

"So what's Plan B?"

Sue bit off half a piece and chewed before answering. "There's this guy Marilyn recommended from three years ago. I guess he calls himself 'Pastor Butch.' Youth pastor from a big interfaith church in Singapore. Canadian, I guess, and lots of fun. He says he can come if we throw in an extra plane ticket for his wife too."

"That's not too much. What, a couple hundred?" She shook her head, then flicked her own forearm. "I've been here two years and I still keep thinking in terms of dollars all the time. Sorry."

"Well, you're pretty much right on the button, though. Khemkaeng called his guy down at Thai Airways, and it's right at seven thousand baht. Which is . . ."

"Two hundred dollars." Rachel Marie grinned.

"Actually, the exchange rate went nasty on us. It's more like two fifteen right now. But who's keeping track?"

Rachel Marie finished off the plate of fruit. "And you've learned enough Thai that you can be this guy's translator?"

"Very amusing."

"You've done great, though." She gave her principal an admiring thumbs-up. "You've learned more words in a month than I've picked up in two years of teaching."

The rain had let up by the end of the lunch hour, and Sue didn't bother with the umbrella as she hiked back over to the main building. Stepping carefully around the sidewalk puddles, she greeted two seniors who were giggling over a picture on one of their iPhones. Just as she reached the front door, she spotted Miles, who was getting to his Honda in the parking lot. She flushed with pleasure as he waved.

He'd continued to swing over to the school at least once a week since the poolside explosion, always popping by her office to say hi, or chatting in the parking lot for a few minutes. His was an expressive face, and she was intrigued by his lively Aussie accent and the cheery euphemisms that punctuated his speech. Just once, Gino had been in the passenger seat of the car, waiting for a ride home, and the youth studiously avoided her as she and Miles discussed a possible science fair scheduled for January.

It was cute the following weekend when Tommy dragged Pranom to the front of United Christian Church for the praise music. The eighth-grader had a passable voice for the melody lines, and he proudly sang a harmony around his stepdaughter as his fingers danced over the keyboard.

"You two should take that act on the road," Sue told him, giving Pranom a hug. "I can't remember the last time I heard such good music."

The Thai girl beamed. "Thank you, Missie Baines. I like to sing with Daddy now."

"Well, I know Jesus is glad for your talents too." Sue pretended to be sad. "And I hope November and December go by really, really slow." They both laughed.

"By the way," Tommy added, holding up the church bulletin, "did you guys see this?"

"What?" Rachel Marie came up and gave her niece a one-armed hug. "That was awesome, kid."

"Bangkok Combined Choir is doing Handel's *Messiah* again," he grinned. "Course, they perform it every Christmas, is what they say."

"Really?" Sue reached out for the insert. "That's the greatest music in the world. I mean, I can barely do the easy parts, but it's my total favorite. What's this about, Tommy?"

"I took eight of my *Matthayom* kids last year. About five of the Christian churches here in Bangkok, including us, spend Wednesday nights–starting in two weeks–practicing over at Wattana Church. Biggest in town. Then the weekend before Christmas, they perform it Saturday night and Sunday night both."

"How many singers?" Rachel Marie wanted to know.

"Oh, last time was at least a hundred. It's pretty cool." He flashed his characteristic grin. "But the awesome thing is, they've got connections with the Austrian Embassy, which sends a whole orchestra over for the gala performances. So it's the full show, man. They even have that trumpet doing the little run right at the end of 'Hallelujah Chorus.'"

"We should all do it," Rachel Marie declared. "I don't read music terrifically well, but if we all sat in the alto section, I bet we could pick it up." She glanced over at Pranom. "What do you think, sweetie? Could you work hard and get all your homework done before supper?" The girl nodded, grinning.

"Well," Sue declared, "I'll tell you what. If you let me join you, I'll pay for all the taxis." She laughed. "I was sitting by Khemkaeng just now. The way he sings, I assume he's not interested."

NINE

The Asian city was ablaze in lights as the crowded taxi threaded its way through the November traffic. Sue, enjoying the extra legroom of the front passenger seat, tried a few mangled Thai words on the cabbie, and felt a tinge of pride when he responded. "He says he's married," she informed Rachel Marie. "Three kids."

"He's ahead of me by one," Tommy said. "But tell him I've got the prettiest daughters in the world."

"I could," Sue laughed, "but don't know how diplomatic that would be. He might drop us off in a rice paddy."

Wattana Church was a large, spacious sanctuary halfway down the main Sukhumvit thoroughfare running through the eastern sector of Bangkok. "This place has been going since 1874," Tommy said admiringly as the quartet entered. He pointed to a makeshift sign. "See, the four vocal parts divvy up like that. You guys'll be on the left side behind the sopranos."

Sue was pleased to see both Lee and Miles already seated in the bass section with a group of Thai vocalists, clutching *Messiah* scores. She wondered if Miles' standoffish son was there too; moments later, she spotted the sullen teen sitting alone in the back row of the sanctuary, tiny ear buds drowning out the holiday oratorio.

The practice session was about to commence when she saw a familiar sight. Coming through a side door was Marilyn, and just behind her, shuffling with a cane, was John Garvey.

"Oh, you guys!" She rushed over and hugged the older woman, then carefully embraced John. "It's so wonderful to have you out and about." She looked him over. "How are you feeling?"

The cheerful principal had dropped at least twenty pounds and his face had a grayish pallor. But he lit up as Tommy and Rachel Marie came over, murmuring their greetings. "Well, I'm not ready to take up skydiving just yet," he joked. Even his voice was reedy, and Sue felt a pang of concern. "But Marilyn wanted to sing, and I didn't feel like being home alone."

"Is there still quite a bit of pain?"

He shook his head. "Thanks to modern pharmacology, not really. Dr. Wilamart says I can be up for maybe three hours a day if I move real slow. Which we did tonight." A smile. "And of course, the diet is very plain–which is killing me. I haven't had a cookie since the Fourth of July." Everyone laughed.

He reached out and offered Pranom an avuncular embrace. "Hi, sweetie. So good to see you."

"We pray for you every day, Mr. G," she assured him. "Me and my daddy."

"I know you do, honey."

Tommy came over, wagging his head, and draped an arm around his old mentor. "Awesome to see you, boss. And we miss you big-time." A glance at Sue. "Course, the pinch-hitter Scioscia sent in did okay, you understand."

John smiled, appreciating the Angels reference. "How are the wedding plans coming along?"

"Oh, Samantha emails me about twenty times a day with bright ideas. Pranom and I looked over a whole bunch of photos of wedding dresses, and sent her our votes last night. Huh, sweetie?" The girl smiled and moved closer to him. "And we just got word that Pastor Mike will be able to fly up and perform the ceremony. So that's awesome."

"Man, I hate to miss it," he said. "But even if my ticker was up to the airplane ride, Marilyn read me the riot act last week. Said that everybody who comes out to Bangkok Christian School finds a spouse right away, and then I want to keep flying clear to Seattle for weddings at eleven hundred bucks a pop. Can't afford it." Even in his fragile condition, he shot Sue a teasing glance. "Be on your guard, Miss Baines. This city seems to be the happy hunting grounds for anybody who'd like to snag a mate."

She racked her brain for an appropriate rejoinder, but just then the director, a polished Thai woman, took her place and invited Wattana Church's senior pastor to offer an opening prayer. Sue picked out just a word here and there, but noticed when the man launched into the now-familiar "*Nai pra nahm Pra Jesu Cris Jao.*" Together with the amassed choir, she murmured: "Amen."

It was a delightful two hours of rehearsal as Charunee took the four groups through their tricky parts on "And the Glory of the Lord." "Alto ladies, we must count on you!" the director said brightly. "On this first song, you come in first, and all other parts will depend on you to do well." Sue at least knew how to count time, and had mastered the rudiments of reading treble-clef music clear back at John Muir High School. Pranom, who had three semesters of Tommy's music instruction under her belt, seemed to be holding her own, glowing at the thrill of participating with adults in such inspiring classical music.

Everyone took a ten-minute juice break at eight, and Miles wandered over to greet the ladies. "It's quite something, eh?" He shook hands gravely with Pranom. "I heard a truly heavenly voice coming from your section. It had to be you, I reckon." He slipped an affirming arm around the teen. "Soon you'll be joining your new mum is what Miss Baines tells me. Are you excited?" Pranom nodded, then skipped off when she spied one of her classmates from the soprano section.

At the close of rehearsal, Charunee motioned for everyone's attention again. "Next week we will be here at the same time. Please be punctual if you can." A big smile. "I realize that Bangkok traffic is so bad in the evening time. In Thai we always say: '*rote dhit.*' It means that the cars are all stuck together!" Everyone laughed. "But leave your homes a little bit early, and we can begin together at seven o'clock. You sounded so heavenly tonight, and I know our singing will bless Bangkok in a special way." She paused, glancing warmly at each vocal section. "Now, we have asked Pastor Munir, who serves Jesus at United Christian

Church, to say a small message and then pray for us."

Sue had already established a cheerful rapport with the colorful Pakistani minister, whose church was rapidly growing in the heart of downtown Bangkok. His notoriety came from inventive sermon illustrations and also from the vivid shirts he wore, tooling around the city on his Yamaha motorbike. Tonight's was bright pink, and there were soft chuckles from the gathered musicians as he accepted the microphone.

"Thank you, Miss Charunee," he said, beaming. "Ladies and gentlemen, I have been so wonderfully blessed tonight. The music is from heaven, the friendships are from heaven, and of course, this music came through the pen of *Kuhn* Handel but also from heaven; you can be sure of that."

His voice sobered as he shared his main point. "You know, I think about the words of this glorious second song we rehearsed. 'For Unto *Us* a Child Is Born.' Think of it. We live and work here in this beautiful, precious land which is ninety-five percent Buddhist. And such dear, wonderful people they are. But here in this song we find that the Christ Child, our beloved Savior Jesus, is born unto . . . who? He is born unto *us*! The entire world! All seven billion of this planet's citizens. Week by week at my church and also at your churches, this is the message we must share. Jesus is God's gift to all people, especially the people of Bangkok."

His voice almost choked up for a moment, and he had to regain his composure. "You know, my brothers and sisters, I pray that every song we sing in this grand oratorio will let Thailand know what an amazing gift Jesus Christ is. He didn't come to this world to tell the Buddhist people they were wrong. He didn't come to our broken planet to inform people in Bangkok of his condemnation for them. No, he came here to redeem, to offer to be their 'Wonderful Counselor, their Mighty God, their Everlasting Father and Prince of Peace.'" For a moment Pastor Munir's eyes fell on Pranom, now arm in arm with her adopted dad. "Let's all commit the fullness of our talents to sharing this wonderful news, not just in song, but in our lives, in every moment of personal connection with the people of this great land."

He invited everyone to join hands in prayer, and Sue flushed when Miles reached across the center aisle and took her hand. Munir offered a stirring invocation, and she felt a wonderful sense of kinship with all these musicians, coming together from many ethnicities and a variety of denominational persuasions–all to adore and worship the Baby in a manger.

She and the others were about to hail a cab back to the city when Miles hurried over, his reluctant son in tow. "Miss Baines," he said firmly, "please forgive us both. But my boy has something to say. Eh?"

Sue turned to face Gino, who had pulled his earphones out and had his hands thrust in his pockets. "Go ahead now," Miles prompted.

"I'm sorry for . . . how . . . I was at the pool," he muttered. "Dad says I shouldn't have."

It was an artless apology, and she could feel the intensity of Tommy's fascinated stare. Rachel Marie tugged surreptitiously on Pranom's sleeve, and the two slipped to the other side of the cab, getting into the back seat.

"Well, it's okay," she managed, trying to be low-key. "Thanks for saying so. I appreciate it."

The boy hesitated, his eyes still dark with

resentment. "That's . . . it, then," he said, wheeling around and walking away from his own father.

Miles was about to speak, but Sue gave a dismissive wave. "Good enough," she assured him, putting a hand on his forearm. "Maybe next time he'll mean it."

"You're a queen," he nodded, relieved. "I'm coming by tomorrow to hear that new preacher from Singapore. If you've truly forgiven me, then wear that black blouse I like so much. As a signal."

It was the perfect thing to say, and she grinned, feeling better. "Nice to see you guys tonight. I'll enjoy coming to rehearsal, knowing you're here."

He brightened and opened the car door for her, reaching out to help her in. The touch of his hand sent a nice quiver through her, and she hoped Rachel Marie didn't notice the scarlet creeping into her cheeks.

IT WAS ENJOYABLE, she thought, as she wandered the aisles of the grocery store, to manage independently so far away from her usual world. In two short months, she had become adept at shopping with Thai currency, bargaining with merchants and taking taxis into the city and back home. It was an adventure to hit a linguistic impasse or an unexpected thorny problem at the thriving Christian school and confidently improvise a path to success.

She paused at the freezer section, noticing a colorful new batch of fruit-flavored ice cream bars. *Pineapple with chocolate?* Chuckling to herself, she counted out twenty of the exotic treats and plopped them in her cart.

"Drive fast," she instructed Khemkaeng, who was chatting with Rachel Marie out by the car. "Otherwise these are going to melt on us." He grinned.

Mr. Somsak, a wealthy Christian entrepreneur who adopted BCS as a pet project, had invited the school group to use his estate for their baptism following the Week of Spiritual Focus. Located twenty kilometers north of the traffic-choked city was a cluster of elegant homes set into the verdant hillside, and the twinkling garden lights surrounding the home created a picturesque paradise. The nine students who had committed their lives to Jesus were already waiting there, eager to begin their new life in the Christian faith. A long table was covered with delicacies, and faculty members chattered contentedly as they waited for Pastor Munir to arrive.

A nearly full moon crept its way to an opening in the clouds, and Tommy cleared his throat. "This is a miracle night," he told everyone. "Nine of our kids in *Matthayom* Five and Six have made decisions to serve Jesus all their lives–and we're thankful that all their parents are okay with it." He glanced around at the six girls and three young men who had ridden in the school van over to the palatial estate. "And it seems like this has kind of become our signature song at Bangkok Christian School." He motioned to a young college student. "Ratana made this same decision two years ago when Pastor Mike visited us. Now she's at Chulalongkorn University, and I know she just keep witnessing there too as she get ready to be Christian doctors."

There was a sound at the gate, and everyone beamed as Marilyn pushed a wheelchair into their midst. John, holding a camera, gave the crowd a wave. "Since this is such a night of celebrating, I thought I should arrive in style." A ripple of cheerful amusement spread through the group of believers.

One of the senior boys picked up his guitar and did an acoustical intro. Sue watched, fascinated, as Ratana began to sing one of her California favorites from New Hope. *Amazing love, how can it be, that you, my King, should die for me?* Standing in the shadows, she spotted Miles next to Dr. Wilamart. He caught her eye and smiled.

"Are we ready?" A sacred hush fell over the group as the last notes hung in the dewy air . "That was perfect, Ratana," Tommy said. "Thanks so much. Your talents are just so awesome."

Pastor Munir hopped into the pool and gestured. "Shall we baptize the ladies first?" he beamed. "This is a glorious night of victory for our wonderful King, eh? And the kind of work I love to do!"

The quiet splashing of the baptisms, one by one, seemed an elegant heralding of the daily victories being won in this faraway place. Sue realized that years of arduous mission work had prepared the way for tonight's celebration, but inwardly rejoiced that the Lord had called her to at least play a small role. She went down the line, embracing the juniors and seniors. "We're very, very proud of you young people," she said, not minding the dampness of their clothes. "And BCS will always be your family; I promise you. Whatever you may need, just come and ask me."

People lingered after the event, basking in the glow of the spiritual highlight and nibbling on the pineapple ice cream popsicles Sue had brought. She relaxed in a poolside chair next to Miles, who kept shaking his head. "What beautiful kids. This is just the best, I say."

He began to describe a difficult surgery from that

morning, and she listened in fascination. Bangkok was a notorious city with more than its share of traffic pileups and street crime. Bloody messes routinely stumbled to the emergency room doors that were open to the public on *Thanon* Phitsanulok, and physicians were a fragile line of defense against the violence.

"Were you here when Rachel Marie had her . . . you know, accident?"

Miles nodded. "I wasn't on duty that night. But that was a rough bit of work. Pradchaphet did okay, though. Had her in the OR within about five minutes, and was able to get everything clamped off tight." He wagged his shiny dome, gratified. "Man, times like those are when you thank God for all that he's shown medical folks how to do. 'Cause that was one we could have lost. And she's a dear."

At that very moment, Rachel Marie walked over, hand in hand with Khemkaeng. "We're about ready if you are."

"Aaaaah." Miles pretended to be grumpy. "It's lovely here in paradise, and I'm trying to win me some points with BCS's boss lady. And now you're about to whisk her away from me."

"Sorry," Rachel Marie laughed. "But I don't think Pranom should be up till four in the morning."

"Hmmm. That's right. She's bunking with the two of you until all the proper 'I do's' have been witnessed and notarized, eh?"

"Something like that," Tommy admitted. He reached out and nuzzled the teen. "Seven more weeks, though, and we're an official family."

"Excellent." Miles thought for a moment. "How's about this? I've got my car here as well. Why don't you all run along; I'll be pleased to drive Miss Susan back to town in a bit. That is, if you think we can be counted on." He added the last with a wink.

"I don't know," Rachel Marie said slowly, mimicking a concerned mother. "We'd end up just waiting up anyway, worrying and looking through the curtains. How do we know we can trust you?"

"I promise I'll be good, Mom," Sue giggled, getting into the spirit of it.

"See there?" Miles waved them away. "I'll be on my proper best."

Sue watched the retreating taillights of Khemkaeng's car. "Where's Gino tonight?"

He ambled over to the table where there were still a few half-filled plates. Perching two pieces of banana bread on a napkin, he returned and handed one to her. "He's got a friend. Michael something or other. Five floors up from us. Attends the same school and they have most classes together. Good news, actually, 'cause this kid does all right with his classwork and all. So that's nudged Gino in a better direction."

"Huh.

"Anyhows, he wanted to spend the night. Some big basketball match, they said. Coming in from the States."

Sue chose her words carefully. "Does Gino handle himself all right with–you know–being with friends. Being unsupervised and . . . like that?"

"Well, it is what it is. Kid's sixteen now. I've had to snip a few of the apron strings, but still try to know what's happening best I can."

"Sure."

They talked a bit more, and he began to pour out his soul about the challenges of being a single parent. "It pains me, you know, because my heart swells up with love for the Lord. And my kid, he just plain doesn't get it. So I pretty much back off. Read my Bible when I'm by myself, go to church, of course. But Gino won't have any of it. And of course, you saw what a snot he can be."

"That's hard." She felt a growing closeness to this unique man with his rough-edged sweetness that was indefinably precious. "We had a lot of that at New Hope. Parents would find Christ through some event, maybe a family seminar. And they'd hear Pastor Mike preach–he's just amazing–but their kids . . . no way. I've had people just *sob* in my office. 'Why, Pastor Sue? What can I do? It's so obvious! It's so beautiful.' And their kid just turns and walks away."

"Yeh." He sat and stared at the elegant mirror of aqua water as the stars danced in the symmetrical ripples. "That would be Gino and his papa, that's for sure."

Their host, Mr. Somsak, came over, wringing his hands apologetically. "I have a drive I must make into town. Our main store on this side has alarm system that is functioning not so well. Not a serious thing, but it is late and I am the one who must go and make adjustment." He looked down at his watch. "Please, you are so welcome to remain and enjoy. Also to swim in pool if you wish. But I will return in maybe one hour."

"We were about to leave anyway," Miles said quickly, noticing that the other BCS guests had all departed.

"No, please take your time. If you leave, then just shut the gate on this side. Okay?"

"Sure."

There was one last bottle of diet Coke, and the

couple passed it back and forth, savoring the quiet comfort of being with a good friend. She felt a strange, feminine urge to delay, to sit close to Miles, to hide his car keys and spend nice hours with him, to bask in having a man be more than just the next name over on a corporate flow chart. "Miss Baines, I must tell you this in the strictest of confidence," Miles said suddenly, setting the bottle down next to his lounge chair.

"Yes, sir. What is it?"

He reached out and picked up her hand, inspecting it for a moment. "It's just that I have truly come to enjoy knowing you as a friend."

"Oh." She brightened. "And you know what? That goes double for me. This is very nice, Dr. C."

There was a comforting minute of silence, and it took her that long to notice that her hand was still in his. "Anything else?" She hoped her voice wouldn't betray the butterflies that had found their way to her stomach.

"No, that's kind of it. But maybe just this one more thing." He shifted his chair around until he was facing her. In the waltzing bits of moonlight that softly pirouetted off the surface of the pool, she could see something new and wonderfully warm in his eyes. *Lazy day, Sunday afternoon. Like to put your feet up, watch TV.* Oddly, the tune from the old Moody Blues song began to play in her brain and she flushed, feeling wildly feminine.

"Don't back up on me, Susie B," he murmured. Leaning closer, he suddenly breathed in as if wanting to hold this lovely moment as a shared memorial in time. His fingers were entwined in hers, tightening, as he kissed her.

TEN

She flopped down on top of her bed, still wearing the slightly damp clothes from the baptism party, her mind helplessly and joyously whirring. *What just happened to me?* She was a fifty-six-year-old gray-haired lady, sister to a grandmother, titular head of a major educational institution . . . and she'd just ridden into Bangkok holding hands with her new boyfriend, heart thumping in her chest like a tom-tom. With the dashboard clock in Miles' car reading way past midnight. She could still replay in digital perfection the feel of his strong hand enfolding her own as he managed a one-handed steering of the Honda. At her front door, he had pulled her close for an extra goodnight kiss. "Once more, love?"

"If Khemkaeng and Rachel Marie find out, we're both in such trouble," she had managed almost breathlessly before fleeing inside and leaning against the inside of the front door, weak in the knees and feeling pleasantly foolish.

Bar none, it was the dumbest thing she'd ever done. She knew that, and yet the memory of it all was delicious beyond anything she'd felt her whole life. The magic was akin to the adolescent miracle with Arnaud, and her face crinkled into an amused reverie. As Cubs fans were wont to say, "Anybody can go through a dry spell." It had been forty years between kisses, and at this rate the next one might not come until she was ninety-six years old. *Better get it while you can, honey.*

There was a formidable, even unscalable mountain of objections to consider, and the practical guardian who dwelt within her was knocking sharply on the door even now, demanding to be heard. But for a sweet moment, she simply swept aside the daunting issues and glowed like a schoolgirl. This moment was so glorious, it was all right to postpone being practical. *He likes me. I don't know why, but he does. And he's so cool!* She loved his passion for Christ and for dynamic teaching, the barking laugh that punctuated his Aussie slang, his finely honed surgical skill as a saver of lives. He was magnetic, exciting, even sexy in a rawboned, outback kind of way.

And, though the truth had to be dragged out of her sedate, practical soul, she melted at Miles' hulking physicality. He was big in spirit and bigger in body, and she felt special by his side, pleasantly dwarfed by his imposing 6' 4" figure. Ever since high school, she had blocked out the plain sturdiness of her own frame. But standing in the spreading presence of his shadow gave her a comparative daintiness that added, she realized now, a subconscious sparkle to their moments together. Any plant next to an oak tree may as well be a rose.

The lingering wetness of her blouse brought a sudden chill, and she reached out to pull a corner of the bedspread over herself. To think such sensuous thoughts while lying on a bed seemed raw, almost illicit, and she blushed. For these four long, barren decades, there had been no one. No one had asked her on a date. No man had paid attention. No one had taken her hand to help her into a car or across the street. She sensed with wonder that there was still a needy engine inside her, cylinders capable of arousal, of firing. The sparkplugs were unused, still wrapped in cellophane, with the factory warranty intact. But in so many years, there hadn't been anyone to even find a key and turn it in the ignition.

Since Arnaud and the frosty evening of teen angst, she had dreamily thought of these matters . . . many times. She had hoped for a man; she had leafed through bridal magazines. She had dared to be wistful. But not for a long time now. The impulses had lain dormant for so long that it was astonishing to have them rush back like uncaged lions in this short and tumultuous time in Bangkok.

Setting aside the stark mission boundaries of her current assignment, she floated away on a violin-bathed reverie of hope. She wanted to see Miles again, to feel his hand confidently taking hers. To have his arm around her as they walked along a beach. To be enfolded in his embrace. This evening's two kisses made her entire body long for more, for the untested but oft-imagined intensity and ache of what she and Karen used to laughingly call make-out sessions. She even–*God, forgive me*–allowed her mind to soar to a sacred image of Miles sharing this bed with her, taking the entirety of her into the glory of his embrace.

Okay, Baines, now let's get real. She was keenly

aware that Miles' kiss had seriously realigned her tidy world. It was one thing to be mission pals with a fascinating man, to share rides, to pray together before singing the "Hallelujah Chorus." An occasional lunch at a five-star international restaurant was a tidy, acceptable entry in her iPhone schedule. These moments of interaction were simply random *events*, one following another, positive serendipities without any cumulative impact.

But a kiss put things on a moving track. A relationship with physical touches needed to go somewhere. *A* on a first date was always followed by *B* on the second. Kisses brought a flurry of attendant questions. What are we? Where is this going? What do you wish to have happen? Are the two of us "on the same page"? A hundred pizzas at the Narai Hotel didn't create as much dangerous momentum as a single kiss. One had to now consider the destination.

And Sue Baines, for her entire adult life, had spun many relational tapestries—none which had destinations. She was good to people for Jesus' sake. She made phone calls to encourage; when she hugged a parishioner it was to give comfort or to thicken the bonds of the body of Christ. But now, in this suddenly dizzying canoe ride with her beautiful Miles, she had to know—and longed to know—where the flowing river would take them.

In a few short weeks, she was slated to hand BCS's office keys back over to a restored and robust John Garvey, then ride the green school van out to Suvarnabhumi Airport and resume her California life. Now, so suddenly, she yearned to envision, despite the towering impossibility of it all, a new path of adventure where she and Miles could walk hand in hand.

But what? Could she live in Thailand? Could he move to America? Whose career was more crucial in heaven's blueprint: Miles' medical ministry in this land of sometimes volcanic pain? Or her efficient, statistically impressive career as a ministry specialist back home in the Golden State? The two talent bundles were so disparate that it seemed petty, almost rank, to set them in a scales in order to see which way her destiny tipped.

She drifted off to a sweet land of new dreams, wondering if there was someone in whom she could confide. John and Marilyn? Natalie? Pastor Mike? Rachel Marie? It was too strange and volatile a tale to share. And really, what would any of these goodhearted friends be able to say that would help? It was a delicious and undefined mess; only God in heaven knew the possible avenues that led through the Christmas break and beyond. She was comforted to realize that, before Creation Week, God had already scoped out the poolside intersection of these two dynamic lives. Heaven would love her no matter how human choices–hers and Miles'–unfolded the miracle.

KHEMKAENG'S TAN NISSAN was pulling into the school parking lot the following Monday when the other shoe dropped. *Gino Carington. That sullen, petulant, potty-mouthed plague on the human race. How did I forget? Dear God, I really do hate that kid!*

The romantic interlude had so sweetly swept away the unassailable fact that her Miles came with a millstone: a sour, disdainful teenage son. Dazed and impatient with herself, she scanned the crowded commons, with literally hundreds of boys that same age jostling here and there, tossing basketballs back and forth, scanning their trig notes. In her mind, one could line up all of this school's 675 boys, and every single one of them would far outclass Miles Carington's objectionable son.

"Here we go again," Rachel Marie chirped brightly, blissfully unaware of the civil war so suddenly entrenched in her friend's mind. Sue watched, conflicted, as the colors were raised, the Thai flag snapping briskly in the December air. The term let out in three weeks; the *Messiah* concert was slated for the 16th and 17th. Then . . . what?

She went to her office, scanning the to-do list for the week, but the overhead clouds were joined by her own sodden depression. It seemed impossible to envision any future with Miles where Gino didn't infect and destroy it all. The boy was a pestilence; he openly disdained all authority–especially his father's new lady friend.

She had often remarked to John Garvey, during their fragile moments of consultation, what a pleasure it was to deal with Thai children. Theirs was a culture of devoted work and respectful attitudes. Behavior issues were few and far between. Parents demanded and expected compliance, and in the classrooms of Bangkok Christian School, the obedience was generally bathed in optimistic goodwill. All of which was seemingly can-celled out by her two prickly encounters with the obnoxious son of her possible paramour.

She chaired the after-school *Matthayom* staff meet-ing, distracted and ill at ease. Excusing the group with two agenda items unresolved, she went back to her office and tossed her briefcase in the corner. "Get a grip, Sue," she muttered out loud, forcing herself to concentrate on the duties at hand.

"Got a minute, Miss Baines?" She flushed at the sound of his voice. Miles, his white surgical coat framing his bulging upper body, leaned against the doorpost, a boyish grin on his face.

"Hey." A ragged army of fragmented thoughts lunged at her, but she still felt a cautious thrill of pleasure at seeing him. "Come on in."

He eased into the room and took the seat next to her desk. "How was the rest of the weekend?"

"All right."

"I've been thinking a bit about the other night," he said, giving away nothing.

"Oh really?" It didn't hurt to simply be herself. "I kind of had that bouncing around in my mind too."

The tall man peeked back at the open door, making sure they had some privacy. "I don't know what's going to happen," he admitted. "You came into my world, and *boom!*" A grin. "I didn't see it coming, and of course, I take all the blame. You were just sitting here at your desk trying to make a living and lift up the mighty name of Jesus . . . then I got it in my mind to up and kiss you." He said the last in a lowered voice, eyes dancing.

She reddened. "That's very true. What do you have to say for yourself?"

Miles suddenly sobered. "Well, look, Sue. I'm a grownup; so are you. I don't know where all this leads. And I definitely don't want to make things a mess for you. You've got a mission to accomplish, and of course, that comes first. But I like you. I mean, a whole lot. I'd like to see you again if you're willing." He held her with his gaze and she felt the surge of his emotions.

"Yeah." She picked up a pen and nervously twirled

it. "I have some blockbuster questions, but I like you too. Obviously. And I guess we both believe that God has answers for any questions that stand in the way." *Meaning your idiot son!* She knew there was time later for that, but was impatient with herself for giddily ignoring such a plain pothole in the road ahead.

He climbed to his feet. "I've got a quick trip out to a village forty-five minutes on the other side of Chao Phraya," he explained. "I volunteer once a month, just stethoscope-and-aspirin stuff mostly. On behalf of Redeemer Christian. But if you could ease away from here, it'd give us a chance to talk." He managed a crooked grin. "We're both adults. If there's just too much sagebrush in the way, let's say so and then get back to being excellent good friends. But who knows?"

His vulnerability was so disarming that she smiled in spite of herself. "Can you wait ten more minutes? I have one thing to check with Rungsit about the email newsletters, and then better touch base with Khemkaeng."

"Good enough." He was astute enough to add: "I'll just wait outside. Come find me when you're ready."

Khemkaeng couldn't hide a smile when she told him about the medical outing to the village. "It seems you have found a new chauffeur," he observed, face impassive. "I hope Dr. Carington is a careful driver."

"It is very nice of you," she responded, "to care for your friends' safety."

"Have a good time."

They visited about mundane things as he carefully navigated their way across Memorial Bridge, the tall span over the muddy river ringing the outer perimeter of *Krung Thep*. The skyscrapers and throttled avenues of the capital city soon gave way to a narrow two-lane road bordered by the verdant rice paddies, with carefully sculpted mounds of dirt marking out individual fields. Golden images of Buddha were everywhere, and he pointed out various local landscapes. "'Bout two kilometers now."

A smaller dirt road peeled off to the left, unmarked and seldom used. She was surprised to see what could only be described as a village just a few hundred meters removed from civilization. Several random thatched-roof huts were clustered together, set into the side of a hill, and children in tattered clothing wandered between the fragile dwellings. There was a larger *sala*, or open-air gazebo of sorts, where villagers could gather for important events. Already fifteen or so adults were waiting, and Sue watched, fascinated, as a designated headman approached. He addressed Miles in Thai, who managed a monosyllabic response. "A bit of flu this past month," he murmured to Sue.

There was a rickety table where he could set his bag, and Miles plopped down in a seat and motioned to the first person in line. The headman spoke a bit of English, and between pantomime and Miles' limited Thai arsenal of medical terms, he was able to decipher the person's stomach cramps. He fished in the bag for a sample bottle of tablets, gesturing as he did so toward a bottle of water. *"Samkahn,"* he repeated somberly several times. "Important." To Sue: "They don't have much access to potable water out this way, but they've simply got to scrape together the funds to get bottled water here. They can do it if they lay off cigarettes."

He measured the heartbeat of a toddler, handing her mother a small foil packet of pills. "This will take away the fever," he explained to the village leader, and the man translated. A woman with a runny discharge from her right eye offered Miles a grateful *wai* as he bathed the infection with some antiseptic salve. Sue felt a quiver of admiration as the hulking physician cradled a naked newborn, still with the umbilical stump oozing a greenish pus. Wiping the worst of it away, he had Sue hold the baby while he bandaged the infected area and gave simple instructions on changing the dressing each day.

In less than an hour, the line had dissipated, even though most of the infirm had lingered around the *sala*, eager to show their appreciation. Motioning the villagers closer, Miles explained in halting Thai that it was the love of Jesus that had brought him here to help. At one point he gestured toward Sue, who gave a start. "I told them you were my friend who came to have our prayer," he grinned. "In English; I'll try to translate a bit if I can."

"Oh." She gulped, reddening, then took a breath. "Dear Lord, we thank you for giving us medicine that makes things better." *Translation.* "Please bless all those who came today for help." *Translation.* She marveled at Miles' ability to even stammer through an intelligible thought in this exotic language. "Help them to know of your eternal love for them." Miles hesitated, and the village headman murmured helpfully, offering the needed phraseology. "In Jesus' name, Amen."

"That was amazing," she told him as Miles turned the key in the ignition.

"Aaah, just simple stuff."

"I know, but you always knew what to do. Even with, you know, not knowing all that much Thai."

He gave his staccato laugh, amused, as he related a

story from a previous visit. "I was out to another village a bit farther on. And we had a couple of people who I suspected were suffering from diarrhea. Only thing is, I didn't quite know the word for that. So I tried to clarify by talking about how many times they were hiking out behind the nearest clump of trees. A bit distasteful, eh?" Sue grinned in spite of herself. "You can be sure I got home, fished out my dictionary, and got *roke tong see-a* in my head for the next time."

"What's that mean? 'Run really fast'?"

He roared with laughter, leaning pleasantly toward her before straightening up to focus on the winding dirt road. "Good one. But actually, it means: 'my tum's busted.' *See-a* is the Thai expression for 'broken.'"

"Huh."

They reached the highway, and as naturally as drawing a breath, he reached out and cradled her hand. "I got a good one for you. In Thai, the preacher says this for the word 'repent': '*glahp jie.*' Which literally means: 'your heart returns.' Not bad, eh?"

Just before they reached Memorial Bridge, he pointed to a restaurant over on the right. "I've been here once, and they've got decent food. Mostly Thai, but mild if we want. How about it?"

"Sure," she nodded, her appetite kicking in.

They dined under the stars, feasting on endless bowls filled with rice porridge, a salad made of *noy-nah* or custard apples, and the standard offering of *pad thai*. Sue nibbled contentedly on the fried noodles, grateful for the cool evening air that danced its way through the colored lights ringing the perimeter of the dining area.

"It's pretty here."

"Yeh." He gestured toward the lights. "Course, for

about the last sixty years, the whole kingdom has always put up lights in December."

"How come?" She set down her spoon, confused. "I mean, they don't observe Christmas at all, do they?" She had spotted a couple of stray Christmas trees in major department stores and one that Khemkaeng pointed to, defiantly occupying the lobby of a large luxury hotel catering to westerners.

"Huh uh. It's a monarchy thing. King's birthday." A grin. "But if you're into Christmas, it works out for that just as well."

The waiter brought the requisite *kow neo mah-muang*, and Sue dug into the delicious sticky rice. "This is incredible."

"Yeah, not bad, I must say."

The couple finished up with their dessert, and Miles took his opportunity. "Look, Sue," he said comfortably, "let's go ahead and chat a bit. If you've got the time right now."

"Sure." She peeked at her own watch. "You don't have to get back for Gino?"

He shook his head. "He has a study group at the school and won't get out till 9:30. So we've got time." He spread out his hands, examining his close-cropped nails. "I hope you feel like I do, because I just think we make a really decent pair."

She felt a touch of scarlet creep into her cheeks. "I think so too, but I'll let you embellish your thought."

He smiled, enjoying the moment. "I like you. I find our conversations stimulating; I admire your wit and the five million things you do well. You're a consummate pro, and in the line of work I'm in, that's a winsome plus. And of course, we're both determined to make a difference for the Lord Jesus."

It was an impressive speech, and she impulsively reached out and took his hand. "That's me too," she admitted. "My times with you have been the highlight of coming to Bangkok. Which–considering the entire experience has been terrific–is high praise, doc."

He lowered his eyes, thankful for the compliment. "So where does this leave us, Susie?"

For a long moment she didn't respond. She longed to give an answer bathed with heaven's wisdom; the hard fact was that this moment, this adult conversation, was a critical fork in the road. At this blinking signal were several possible avenues, each of them disappearing into a metaphorical clump of thick trees or a damp cloak of fog.

"May I speak my mind?"

"Of course, love."

Her hand tightened in his own. "There are two hard things I have to pray my way through. First is this. I may be leaving Thailand before Christmas. Or I might be here a couple of months. It all depends on John Garvey and how he's doing."

"And?"

She eyed him. "I thought you might know that better than I do."

Miles shook his head. "Well, you know he was discharged from the hospital quite a while back. Although Wilamart mentioned the other day that he'd checked back in for a weekend due to some infection. He definitely looks weak; I'll say that."

"I know." She remembered being concerned when John had arrived at the baptism in a wheelchair, which was definitely a downgrade from going around with just a cane.

"If things were shipshape with him, what would your plans have been?" There was a touch of anxiety in his voice, and he reached out with his other hand to cradle hers.

"Well, I kind of figured that when we got to the Christmas break, I'd head home. That's what I was thinking back in August. That would mean staying through that weekend where we all do the 'Messiah.' Last day of school is the following Thursday, which is the 21st." She scanned her iPhone with her free hand, then set it back down. "I was toying with the idea of changing my ticket and heading back by way of Portland." A smile. "In order to crash Tommy's wedding."

"That would be aces. But, as things appear, I wouldn't think that Mr. G is anywhere close to coming back to work by the end of the year."

"I know. But even then, I might take that ten-day holiday and zip back to the States."

"Really?"

"Well, all my family's there in Southern California. I can get there in about a day, enjoy Christmas with everyone, say hi to the folks at New Hope, be back here in time for the January rush." She shrugged. "I guess I could even duck in the wedding in Portland, since they're getting married that first Sunday. Christmas Eve."

Miles digested the timeline, his ruddy face impassive. "I loathe myself for secretly being glad that John's still ailing," he said, forcing a crooked grin.

"I won't tell," she commiserated. "I've struggled with the same thoughts too."

He let go of her hands in order to pour himself a bit more of his 7-Up. "You?" She shook her head quickly.

"I got something I'd like to invite you to consider," he said. "Hasn't got anything to do with our long-term dilemma. But just in case it catches your fancy . . ."

"What is it?"

He fished in the back pocket of his khakis. "I did it last year and it's a powerhouse experience." Smoothing out a crumpled sheet of blue paper, he set it in front of her, pushing her dessert plate out of the way. It showed a photograph of what appeared to be a Boy Scout camp site.

"I don't get it."

He pointed to a map in the lower corner. "For many years–ever since some of the wars across the border– there have been permanent refugee camps here in Thailand. Up north, right near Burma. Sometimes a few hundred people, sometimes a few thousand. But with various military skirmishes that have happened now and again, it's something the Thai government has had to cope with."

"What's up there?"

"Just people. Homeless. Political refugees. Kids whose parents were killed in a police action or because of the drug trade." He took another swallow of his soda, eyeing her. "And so they have a rudimentary school going. As permanent as they can make it. Then some adult-ed classes for parents. Medical clinics, even a bit of fly-by-night surgery if the situation warrants. And the nice thing is that the government allows church groups to have a presence, sharing Christianity to anyone willing to sit and listen."

Sue listened, intrigued. "But what's that got to do

with you?"

"It's not much of a contribution," he admitted. "It takes a long day there and a long day back. But if you're willing to surrender your Christmas break, it can sure make a huge difference to those desperate people up there. I talked with Khemkaeng and his bride; they're thinking about coming. We'd take the overnight train to Chiang Mai, then rent a van the rest of the way."

"And you can get away from Mission Hospital for that long?"

He nodded. "I've worked an extra shift here and there, building up a cushion of time."

"Where do you stay while you're there?"

"Well, I won't sugarcoat it. It's real Spartan. Last year there were six or seven of us all packed into this pretty threadbare building. Just sleeping bags on a dirt floor, you know."

She flushed. "Sounds palatial." She tried to add a touch of levity, but something inside her quailed. A week of grit and poverty sounded arduous compared with a week at her parents' pristine villa overlooking the San Diego beaches, with twinkling Christmas trees and elegant comfort and a veritable feast three times daily. Not to mention being wrapped in a holiday blanket of affable and loving relatives. A vague memory stirred in her mind, where Pastor Mike had kindly said to her: *You don't have to volunteer for every single thing that comes along. It's all right to say no to something really distasteful.*

"Well, just an idea," he hastened. "If it doesn't suit you . . ."

She took a deep breath, dreading the rest of the conversation. "Well, we may as well just suck it up and start talking about the elephant here in the room."

The metaphor was obscure, and his forehead wrinkled up. "Now it's your turn," he retorted pleasantly. "Please define, principal lady."

"Well, the other nasty thing we both know is out there," she said evenly. "Meaning your son. I just don't see how there can really be any kind of relationship for us as long as Gino *loathes* me. Which he clearly does."

The statement pained him, but Sue refused to back down. "I mean, the way he acted at the pool was unforgivable, Miles. I know he's your son and you're doing your best. But I'm not about to subject myself to that on a regular basis."

He nodded, accepting the stark reality of what faced them. "Is it all right if I give you a couple of mitigating factors?"

"Sure."

"Well, first off, you're right. He's my son. I try hard, but he's a messed-up kid. I admit it. It brings me pain but I don't have the option of just wandering off and leaving him be. I've got to do my best with God's help."

"Of course."

"I hope you understand that Gino doesn't have anything personally against *you*. I mean, he snapped at you that night by the pool even though he'd never met you before. He was just in an angry mood and you happened to be the one sitting there. If it was someone else, he'd have treated them shabbily instead."

Sue refused to be mollified. "That doesn't really help. If he's rude to whoever's in the chair, and I start being your main friend in the chair, I'm setting myself up for some nonstop unpleasantness."

He shook his head. "I don't know if this will help," he said, shamefaced. "But I think if we plan carefully, it might be possible to stay out of his way."

"What do you mean?"

"Gino's sixteen, coming up on seventeen. He's with his friends a lot; he's got stuff at school. He's just the kind who goes his own way." Miles gestured around at the cheerful ambience of the restaurant. "Like now. I think if we simply stayed low-key, it wouldn't have to be a lot of major battles."

Sue weighed his words. Did she want to spend the next few months endlessly scheming to dodge confrontations? "Sounds kind of weird, Miles." She looked right at him.

"I suppose." His frankness was disarming, and she felt a renewed affection for what he had to be going through. "Like I'm saying, though. He'll be on his own soon enough. I don't intend to be held hostage to his whims forever. No way."

She took the final bite of her sticky rice, the sweetness of the mango nuggets an odd intrusion into this charged moment. "Why *is* he so filled with hate?"

"Well, like I was saying. He always missed his mother, blamed me for the mistakes and all."

"Anything else?"

"I don't think so." He paused. "Well, seems like the last year he's been ill a lot. So I guess when he feels messed up, maybe he lashes out then."

"Ill like how?" She gave him a teasing smile. "You're a doctor."

"I know. But nothing specific. Just drags himself to the breakfast table, says he feels like . . . well, he's got certain impolite words he uses to describe it. Then either goes off to school and toughs it out, or back to bed. There's been a few days lately where he skipped classes."

"Nothing serious?"

"If it keeps up, I may have to run him over to the hospital for some diagnostic tests and all." He gave a pained shrug. "I only bring it up so you'll know–it's not just pure wickedness."

"I suppose not."

Miles picked up the check and motioned for a passing waitress. "Deep down, I'm figuring that Gino does love me. In his own microscopic little way." They both smiled. "And if I sit him down and tell him just how much Miss Baines is starting to mean to me, maybe that will warm things up a bit."

"But you're not counting on it?"

He shook his head with a weary grin. "Not really."

Sue reached for her purse and motioned toward the door. "Come on, Dr. Miles. Drive your new girlfriend home."

He seemed pleased by her self-description. "For real? You're my girl now?"

"I'm thinking about it."

ELEVEN

D aily life at BCS was such a dizzying flurry of duties and administrivia, it was rare for Sue to run mundane errands. But Rachel Marie was a favorite of hers, she mused; it was always a delight to pop into the young teacher's vibrantly decorated Form Six classroom. From her first days in charge, Sue had guardedly asked teachers if they minded the impromptu visits. "I promise you–I'm not out on the warpath, looking to get you in any trouble," she explained. "It's just that I want to mingle, to enjoy seeing you in action, and to connect with as many of these great kids as I can. So if I come by and say hi, it's totally in a supportive way."

It was especially gratifying to observe Rachel Marie's prowess as a teacher, probably because her successful adventure here in Thailand had been Sue's own doing. She stifled a smile as she bounded up the stairs, remembering the pasta lunch in Glendale more than two years earlier, where they had prayerfully discussed the temporary teaching post. Now Rachel Marie and Khemkaeng were permanent pillars at the Bangkok school, with a widening influence throughout the city's elite young families.

"Hi, kids!" She offered an awkward *wai,* clutching a sheaf of bright blue photocopies in one hand. "Are you guys having a game?"

"We are almost winning." Sumalee, a gangly girl with rimless glasses, bounced up and down. "Against boys."

"Excellent." Sue shot the boys a daring look. "Men, are you going to allow this?"

She watched, bemused, as Rachel Marie clicked her remote mouse and a silhouette map appeared on the PowerPoint screen. "Kulap, your turn. If you can identify this county, then the ladies will finally have achieved victory. After a million years of waiting and waiting and waiting."

There were nervous peals of laughter, and the boys leaned forward, eager to steal away the prize. "And Miss Baines, you mustn't help," the teacher admonished. "Even though I'm sure you're rooting for the females."

"I'm trying to be fair."

Kulap, who had perhaps the longest braids in the school, squinted comically, trying to resurrect a lost piece of geography. "I think is maybe . . . Korea. Both north and south all in one?"

"Correct!" There were squeals of triumph on the feminine side of the room, and the girls leaped from their chairs, hugging each other. The boys, downcast, began to fish in desks for their textbooks and lunch pails.

"It looks like Miss Baines has something to give us," Rachel Marie announced. "Why don't you all get packed up, and we'll hear what our excellent leader has to share. And then closing prayer."

"Thank you, Mrs. C." Sue went to the front of the room and began distributing the handouts. "I want you to give this to your parents so they'll all come to Bangkok Christian School's holiday program this Thursday night. I think about half of you are in Mr. Daggett's choir, and your parents will enjoy all the excellent songs you've learned. Plus"–she gave a woeful shake of her head–"we must soon say goodbye to Mr. Daggett and Pranom. You know that he's going back to America to get married to Missie Kidd."

There was a cheerful hubbub at the romantic reminder. Samantha Kidd taught for just one semester in the upper *Matthayom* grades, but had been a vivacious force for change on the entire campus the previous year. And Tommy was a huge favorite among all the kids, routinely mobbed in hallways and out on the playground as he made his way from room to room.

"Okay, then." Rachel Marie glanced around the room. "Miss Baines, I hope you can stay for prayer, because our 6C young people do the nicest ones in all of Bangkok."

"That's what I've heard." Smiling, Sue settled into a corner of the room, waiting.

"Let's see. I think it should be . . . Virote. Okay?"

The slight boy hesitated, then nodded timidly.

"Okay, then. Shh, men and ladies."

"Dear Jesus, thank you for good day. And also for school and we have so many friends. Give us safe going to homes and also please bless moms and dads and family members of . . . that we have. And also we wish for God to give blessing to Thailand and family of king.

Amen."

"Very nice. Excellent." Rachel Marie nodded approvingly, and Sue gave the boy a thumbs-up. "Now, don't forget, kids. What is the great truth at BCS?"

"God is good! All the time!"

"And what is the number two truth that can never change?"

"6C rocks!" Giggling and eyeing the principal for affirmation, the boys and girls trooped out the door and down the hallway. Bits of illegal Thai chatter mingled in with the mandated English and Sue pretended to scowl. "Better chase after them with your conduct report pad."

"Nah. It's Christmas," Rachel Marie laughed. "I'm in a good mood."

"The time has really zoomed by, hasn't it?" Sue pulled up a chair and sank into it, fanning herself with a couple of leftover flyers.

"Are you keeping up with everything?"

"I think so. There's a couple of long-term things I just stuck in a drawer, figuring John can get to them whenever. But most Fridays, I really try to not go home until my desk is cleared off." She reached over and put a hand on Rachel Marie's arm. "Of course, that boy you married is a whiz. Unbelievable how much he knows. I've really appreciated working with him."

"Yeah, he's all right." Rachel Marie began organizing the papers on her desk into distinct piles.

"Do you mind if I ask you a medium-level favor?"

"Well, like I said, I'm in a Christmas mood. Better get while the gettin's good."

"Ah. Well, here's the thing. We've got the big *Messiah* concerts weekend after next."

"Uh huh." She laughed. "If you want for me to do

any tutoring on 'And He Shall Purify,' forget it. When we get to those long runs, I try to hit the first note and the last one, and essentially lip-sync the rest."

"That puts you two notes ahead of me." Sue sighed. "Maybe I can ask Pranom for some help."

"Or Tommy."

"Actually, what I need is a bit of wardrobe counseling."

"Oh. You haven't got a black dress?"

"Huh uh. I figured with this being the tropics, I brought out mostly light-colored stuff. And really not that much. Six or seven outfits, and I've kind of just rotated them around."

Rachel Marie nodded. "Well, you came to the right place, boss. When I first got here, that's how Khemkaeng made his move. Offered to take me out to a tailor shop so I could get some new duds. Then he began plying me with free food and pineapple smoothies and just melted all my willpower." They both laughed.

"You still have the name of the place?"

"Oh, sure. I had to go back twice for fittings, and then I got some more stuff later." Rachel Marie flushed, remembering the romantic date at Le Normandie that finally sealed the deal. "In fact, the dress I'm wearing for the concerts is from there."

"How can I bribe you to take me?"

She grinned. "Hmm. Let me think about that. Tommy's got Pranom for the evening; they always go out Mondays for something special. And it seems like Khem-kaeng's on some committee over at UCC. Hang on." Reaching for the phone, she punched in a four-digit code. "I'll try to ditch him."

After a couple of rings, he came on. "Hey,

handsome VP," she teased. "Are you doing all right?" There was a pause and she blushed. "Now don't say that. I've got Sue here, and what if this is on speaker phone?" Another moment. "No, but it might have been." She giggled. "Anyway, don't you have that meeting at the church? Why don't you just get some supper there at that Indian place right up the street? Yeah. 'Cause Sue and I are going to hit the tailor shop, which might take five hours or so."

She gossiped a bit more, then replaced the receiver. "We're good. Let me just wrap up all the paper flow and check my email and we can scoot out of here."

"Are you sure?"

"Absolutely. That concert's going to be a big night, and you and I'll knock the guys' socks off with our hot outfits."

Sue flushed, pleased.

Out on the main thoroughfare fronting the big Christian campus, Rachel Marie consulted the business card as she waved for a cab. Bangkok was like an upended ant hill, with taxis emanating out of every nook and cranny. Drivers without fares glumly trolled all the main roads, hoping for some pickup business. One of the city's blue-and-red Toyota specials rumbled over to the curb and she handed the address to the driver. He inspected it briefly, then nodded.

"Off we go, then." Rachel Marie followed Sue into the back seat and sighed contentedly. "Even in December, that AC feels good." It was a warmer than usual afternoon as the cab driver nosed his way into the snarl of traffic heading north into the main part of town.

"Hey, what's that?" Sue craned her neck to peer at a golden display surrounded by a troupe of Thai dancers.

"I'm trying to remember. Seems like Khemkaeng told me about it once. They call it the 'Erawan Shrine.'" Rachel Marie squinted as the late afternoon sun penetrated the car window. "'Cause that's the Erawan Hotel right there. One of the fanciest in town. Run by Hyatt."

Sue could see a palatial edifice just beyond the golden image, with well-manicured gardens and a sumptuous pool off to the left.

"Buddhist, I assume. The shrine, I mean."

"Actually, no. I forget what exactly, but he said it was more of a Hindu monument. And tourists pay those dancers to perform, figuring it'll bring them good luck or a bit of karma. But we've never stopped for a closer look."

"Huh."

The proprietor of the tailor shop bounded over enthusiastically as the ladies entered his shop. "Missie Stone," he said effusively. "Except I must remember— now you are Mrs. Chaisurivirat."

"Please. Just call me Rachel Marie," she chided.

"Of course."

"And this is Miss Baines, who is serving as our principal while *Kuhn* Garvey is recovering."

The Thai man's face sobered. "We have been so sad to hear of his illness. But he is doing better?"

Sue smiled. "Yes, much. We all pray every day for his recovery."

"Of course." He gestured around the shop. "Are you both here to look for material? And dresses?"

"Just Miss Baines," Rachel Marie said quickly. "We need a black dress for a special night."

"Yes! Excellent!" He motioned politely toward a tall rack filled with richly brocaded fabrics. "Here we have many beautiful selections." The man made a self-deprecating gesture. "And of course, as you are important friends at BCS, the lowest prices, always."

"Thank you," Sue said, wondering if the discounts were real.

"Don't fret it," Rachel Marie whispered in a low voice. "This stuff is so inexpensive it's amazing."

Wandee, the demure assistant, began jotting down measurement numbers, and Rachel Marie entertained herself by wandering through the display area, tracing along various imported fabrics. The owner noticed. "If you see cloth that is favorite selection, perhaps you can buy new as well?"

"Oh, probably not," she laughed. "But it's fun to look."

"Certainly. Please feel at home."

He helped Sue flip through a French magazine offering a number of styles. "If you like long, is only one hundred baht additional." He pointed to a floor-length banquet gown.

"Oh, I don't think so." She shook her head. "That'd be too hot for Bangkok."

"Ah, yes. You are thinking so wisely." There was a teasing bit of banter in the man's demeanor, and the ladies grinned at each other. "Perhaps with sleeves that are long, and then length down to just below knee. Eh?"

"Yes, that's better."

"And with neck high or low?

Sue blushed, imagining herself out with Miles for a night on the town. She was still acutely aware of her self-image as an ugly duckling, and felt conflicted but hopeful about this attempt to dress up her deficiencies. "High, I think."

"Very good." He nodded enthusiastically. "This dress will be so beautiful." He tried to coax Sue toward an additional stack of bolts of cloth. "If you wish, we can do second dress with same style and pattern, etc. Only eight hundred baht for second selection. It is okay?"

Sue looked to her companion for counsel. "You're the expert around here. What do you think?"

"Well, you're talking about something like twenty-five more bucks. And it'll fit you perfectly. If there's a fabric that you like, hey, you're nuts not to get a two-fer."

"I guess." She scanned the stack, noticing an ivory-colored choice that had a subdued pattern of maroon orchids woven into the background. "Now that's exquisite."

"Yes! This is special order," the proprietor beamed. "From Chiang Mai province." He pulled it out, and generously draped the cloth over the table. "And color for you is so beautiful." He chortled. "All gentlemen of Bangkok will notice and say, 'Introduce me to lovely lady, please.'"

They all laughed, and Sue surrendered cheerfully, knowing she was being played. "Young man, in America we would call that 'selling up.' I come in here for one dress, and now you have sold me two."

He affected a pained look. "No, madam. I only wish to serve you well. With excellent bargains."

"I'm teasing." She fished in her purse. "So tell me what the damages are."

She made an appointment to return late Thursday for a trial fitting, and the two women ambled down the crowded street, enjoying the pungent Thai ambience. "I could use a little coin purse," Sue said suddenly, noticing a makeshift stall with handcrafted items for sale. "Let's see how much these are." She picked up a turquoise one decorated with tiny elephants. "*Tao rai?*"

The girl perked up. "*Sahm roi baht.*"

Sue feigned disinterest. "She says she wants three hundred baht for that."

"No good?"

"Huh uh." To the clerk: "*Paeng mahk. Song roi.*"

Rachel Marie knew enough Thai to recognize the counteroffer. "No way. She'll never go for two."

"Probably not." Sue set the little purse back down and gave a casually dismissive sniff.

The salesgirl inexplicably broke into English. "You give two-fifty, okay."

"Really?"

"Yes, madam. For you only."

Rolling her eyes, Sue fished in her purse for the currency.

"Not bad, Sue." Rachel Marie felt a touch of envy. "You know more of the language than I do, and I climb into bed with a Thai guy every single night."

Sue laughed. "Well, all the time you're doing . . . that kind of thing, I'm sitting at home just studying my Berlitz language CDs."

The sun had just disappeared behind the western landscape ringing the Asian capital as the taxi wheeled into their housing development. "How about some supper?" Rachel Marie dug in the pocket of her blazer for some money.

"Hey, put that away," Sue ordered. "This whole trip was for me."

"You're the boss."

"And in terms of supper, sure, that'd be great."

"We got the place to ourselves," Rachel Marie reminded her. "What are you in the mood for?"

They dined on bowls of steaming potato soup, and Rachel Marie rummaged through the pantry for some bread from a local bakery. "Here. Put some of this on it."

It was a thick brown goo with a sugary sweetness. "That's incredible. What is it?"

"It's some kind of local honey made out of coconuts, if you can believe that. There's a little gourmet health food store over at that Christian hospital where Dr. Carington works. Back when I was . . . you know, Khemkaeng happened to sample a bit of it, and now we're hooked. Every couple months I make him go and buy us another stash."

It was the opening she'd been waiting for. "Speaking of Dr. Carington . . ."

Rachel Marie peered at her over her glass of bottled water. "Yes?"

Sue blushed. "Well, in the interest of full disclosure, I've got a bit of a crush on him."

Rachel Marie pretended to do a Hollywood spit take, comically spraying the tablecloth. "What!" Then a laugh. "Sue, are you serious? Is there something going on with you and the good doctor?"

"Well, you know what? It just kind of happened." She wasn't quite sure why she was blurting out her romantic tale, but impulsively felt that she needed an ally for the complicated journey ahead. "I mean, he's just great to talk to. He loves BCS; he's terrific with kids. We've had a couple of, you know, things at restaurants here and there, and somehow three hours go by and we just enjoy each other. And all of a sudden . .

." She felt the crimson rush to her face. "Did you and Khemkaeng know? He acted kind of funny the other day when I mentioned we were going to that village across Chao Phraya."

Rachel Marie shook her head, cheerful and bemused. "Well, I was starting to notice, maybe just a little bit. But I didn't take it seriously. I mean, look. You've spent your whole life . . ." It was a clumsy thought to finish and she fumbled for words. "After all this time being the girl scout, you trot out here to Bangkok and all of a sudden have a gentlemen friend? That cracks me up, Miss Baines." She was almost laughing, but managed to keep a lid on her mirth. "And by the way, who all knows about this? The kids at BCS are going to have a field day if they figure out that Miles Carington is your *fan*."

"That's the Thai word for 'boyfriend,' isn't it? Seems like I've heard it in the hallway a few trillion times."

"Yeah. I think *fan* is the one Thai word where we don't slap kids with the twenty-baht fine. Especially in the *Matthayom* grades. There's a lot of romantic pairing up that goes on up there. Samantha told me once she could hardly keep track of all the musical chairs. But even my girls are constantly whispering about this or that cute guy." Rachel Marie's eyes danced wickedly. "And now Susie Baines has got a fella too. Who'd have thunk it?"

"Well, look. I spilled the beans for a reason. 'Cause I kind of need somebody's advice."

"Sure." Rachel Marie took a last bite of her cake, then shook her head. "No, first tell me how this happened. I'm dying to hear the story."

Sue gave a delicately expurgated account of the growing saga, beginning with the lunch at the Sheraton. "And then, along around the night of the baptism, I think we both realized that something was happening."

"There's a question that's just trembling on my lips," Rachel Marie told her. "Speaking of lips, I mean. But I'm not going to ask."

"Well, that's very prudent," Sue countered. "'Cause I only kiss and tell the first time it happens." She grinned. "And this was the second time." Surrendering cheerfully, she launched into a glowing account.

"Very nice." Rachel Marie felt a rush of affection for her pleasantly flustered mentor. "Let me dump these dishes in the sink, and then we can start planning the wedding."

"You're hilarious, Mrs. Chaisurivirat."

They settled down in the living room and Rachel Marie went over to open the drapes. It was a beautiful evening; the elegant lights of distant skyscrapers barely penetrated the quiet neighborhood as people still getting off work motored silently past the picture window. "So tell me what your dilemma is, Sue."

There was a poignant pause as Sue weighed the variables pressing down upon her. "Well, obviously it's a massive disruption to what I thought was going to happen. As soon as John's well, I'm supposed to pack and go home. New Hope Church is waiting for my return because I'm just on loan here. I live there; Miles lives here. There's no big deal about it except for the whole Pacific Ocean separating the two worlds."

"Yeah." Rachel Marie reflected back to her own tumultuous nights where the geography of her own love life threatened to engulf her in despair. "I went through this same thing, you know. With Khemkaeng. If something comes of your . . . love, then it involves a pretty wrenching choice for either him or you."

"Well, I don't know if this all goes that far," she said quickly.

"But what's the point of putting your heart out there on the target range unless you're willing to consider the possibilities?"

"Yeah."

Rachel Marie scooted her chair closer. "I think I can say this for sure."

Sue waited pensively.

"If you really decided that you were in love, and that Miles could be the one, for sure there'd be a way for you to stay here in Thailand."

"And do what?" She felt a twinge of frustration. "I know John's recovery is a lot slower than we thought, but at some point he's going to pick up the reins again."

"So?" Rachel Marie curled her legs up underneath her and looked directly at her friend. "Look at all the stuff you've done for the school, Sue. It's been amazing. BCS has got room for both of you. There'd be all sorts of ways you could serve the Lord here."

She hadn't considered that. "Do you really think so?"

"You'd know better than I do. But I would think if you and John and Khemkaeng put your heads together, you could carve out some kind of triumvirate that would be totally awesome."

It was an intriguing idea and she warmed, considering the possibilities.

"But that has you changing your whole life. Bangkok instead of Pasadena. That's a seismic shift."

Rachel Marie sighed, remembering. "Trust me."

"It worked out for you."

"I know. But I can tell you this: I spent a lot of nights fretting until two in the morning. Just because you're stepping off the edge of the world and you don't know." She traced her toe in the carpeting, reliving her own giddy tumble into a relationship with someone special. "It's great, though, isn't it?"

"What?"

"Falling in love."

There was no sense being evasive. "Yeah, it's pretty much wonderful."

A car eased around the corner, its headlights bathing the nearby shrubs that Thai gardeners had planted around each home in the project. "I thought that was Khem-kaeng," Rachel Marie murmured. She suddenly wheeled around and faced her friend. "What a minute, though. What about that clunky kid of his? I mean, you guys had a couple of real hoo-rahs."

Sue felt a tightening around her heart. "I know," she sagged. "That's the other thing. I just don't see how I could ever make it work with that Gino in the way. He's a total snot."

"Things are still terrible?"

"I've only bumped into him the two times, actually. When we had that nightmare intro at Miles' pool. And then when Daddy put a gun to his head two months after the fact and he came over with his poison apology that wasn't worth five baht." She grimaced.

"Hey." Rachel Marie got up and switched on a nearby lamp. "If he's nearly grown, maybe you wouldn't have to actually spend that much time near each other. A couple of years from now, he'll be off to some college, and maybe you can get him shipped off to a school in . . . I don't know, the South Pole."

"That's what Miles was saying too. That we could just try to arrange our lives to have a minimum of him distracting us. But that's no way to live, hiding from your own stepson."

"No. I can see that."

There was the quiet hum of Khemkaeng's car gliding into the carport just to the right of the living room. "So what's the rule here?" Rachel Marie said suddenly. "My sweetie's home. Is Miles being your boyfriend a secret or can I tell Khemkaeng?"

"Can he keep a lid on it?"

"He's like a CIA agent. Leak-proof," she said. "He is kind of a terrible liar, though."

"Well, if he blabs, you kill him and then I kill you."

Khemkaeng grinned cheerfully as he digested the romantic news. "I thought Dr. Carington was always coming to BCS out of deep Christian concern for our students."

"Don't be mean." Rachel Marie pretended to aim a *muay thai* boxing kick in the general direction of his hindquarters. "And you can only tease Sue when we're here at the house. Never at school."

"Of course." He pulled his necktie free and flopped down on the just vacated couch, an uncharacteristic move for such a usually reserved and precise man, Sue thought to herself. "But this is very good. I'm happy for you, Sue."

"Thanks." She peeked at her watch. "I better hike home, but let me real quick ask you guys about this trip to that refugee camp. Are you for sure going?"

Khemkaeng nodded. "Yes, we just purchased the

train tickets yesterday."

"What? For the whole Christmas break?"

Rachel Marie came out from the kitchen with a tall glass of juice. "Here, sweetie." Then to Sue: "Yeah. I thought about going back to Seattle to have Christmas with my folks, since I haven't seen them since the wedding. But we decided to wait until next summer so we can take a bit more time off. Anyway, so you're right–the entire holiday we'll be in the trenches, working. It's kind of a bummer, because the very day after school lets out, we go up there. I imagine we'll be working right through Christmas Day itself."

"Wow. And just refugee stuff?"

"Uh huh. I can teach English. Khemkaeng is going to be helping people gather paperwork for visas, stuff like that. Plus just helping organize and revamp their, you know, camp schedule. Who helps with what volunteer jobs, streamlining the kitchen detail–all the government and NGO donations of food that get trucked in. We don't totally know all that stuff till we arrive, but Munir says that any time a volunteer arrives, they have meaningful things to do. For sure, Miles will be busy at the clinic." She peered at her friend. "Are you seriously thinking about coming along? I'm sure Miles would be thrilled."

"Well, and that's part of it. I'd love spending a whole week in ministry together," Sue told her. "Except for the primitive part. I'm actually kind of a stay-at-the-Hyatt kind of girl, to tell you the truth." A vision of the sumptuous high-rise hotel popped into her brain. "But I guess a week of anything wouldn't kill me."

"I definitely think you should come," Khemkaeng put in. "Instead of such a short trip back to California."

He gave her a sympathetic look. "I know you probably wish to see your family during the holiday. But suppose John is well by March. You would be able to go home then anyway–which is only three more months. I can book the train ticket for you if you wish."

The trio fell silent, weighing the choices and the possible threads of an unknown future fabric. Could she thrive in this exotic but uncertain world as the life partner of Dr. Miles Carington? Could her God help forge yet another match birthed in Bangkok?

There was just one way to find out. "Yeah, go ahead and put me down," she told him, feeling another anxious flush creep over her entire body. "If I haven't killed Gino and gone to the Thai slammer by then, it might actually be kind of fun."

"And we'll be right there to chaperone," Rachel Marie declared. "Come on, Susie. Now that you've got a boyfriend, you need your beauty sleep. I'll walk you home."

TWELVE

The chemical warmth of their hair dryers mingled with the beauty parlor's ambient flow of chilled air to create a festive cross-current of emotional anticipation. "I haven't done this in a long while," Rachel Marie confessed gaily. "Khemkaeng keeps telling me I should pamper myself, since these Bangkok prices are so low. But I just don't get around to it."

Sue was aimlessly leafing through a French magazine offering a garish photo spread of skimpy models, but set it down with a contented sigh. "Silly to go through such a fuss just to stand in the back row of a church choir."

"Aha. But also right across the aisle from a rather dashing and hunky M.D. from koala country. You take that slinky dress we just picked up, plus your avant-garde new hairdo, plus all the ten-baht makeup we're going to slather on when we get back to the house, plus your heart-melting alto voice . . ."

"Which people only hear when I come in a measure

too soon."

Rachel Marie ignored her. "Miss Baines, I predict that your lovestruck Dr. Carington will take one look, go into cardiac arrest, and thereafter be putty in your hands."

Despite the clumsy mechanical contraption aiming its flaming oxygen jets at her stubborn locks, Sue shook her head in protest. "I should never have opened my big mouth. You've done nothing but tease me ever since."

"Don't be silly. Half the fun in having a boyfriend is telling your friends about it."

"We're not in ninth grade anymore."

"Doesn't matter," Rachel Marie said airily. "Some things never change."

Sue had put a minimalist spin on the Carington report during her parents' weekly phone call. And Mike was his unflappable self: a sensitive listening post when she admitted the delicate but growing flower of romantic interest. "Place it all in the hands of Christ," he said good-naturedly. "If it can bring both of you happiness as well as further his kingdom, the Lord can smooth out any bumps." The metaphor caused her to flash back to the pure tenor solo in the upcoming *Messiah*: "Every valley shall be exalted, and every mountain and hill made low, the crooked straight and the rough places plain."

The two American teachers paid their youthful beauticians and added a gratuity, exchanging grateful *wais* as they exited. "You look terrific, Sue." The novice Thai attendant had created a softly feminine cap of gray curls that added a glow to her face, and Sue savored the compliment.

"I just hope this humidity won't melt the perm

before we get on the train next Friday."

"Just as long as Miles gets one glimpse of you. That's what the nine hundred baht is for."

Clutching her dress bag in one hand, Sue scanned the onrush of traffic, then beckoned frantically. "Hey, there's a taxi. Is he empty?"

Bangkok was settling into a glorious evening, and even this Buddhist citadel seemed to faintly acknowledge there was a trace of Bethlehem presence in the air. There were Santa posters in some windows of the pricey malls towering over the business district in their twinkling splendor. Bustling crowds paused to gape at a forty-foot-high silver Christmas tree in the courtyard of a major complex of computer stores.

"Do you want to just get dressed at our place? And then we can play around with some of this makeup?"

Sue flushed. She knew full well that Rachel Marie was diplomatically coaxing her toward a predestined goal. Partway through her own college experience, she had ruefully accepted the verdict of the dormitory mirrors and stopped wasting money on mascara and eyeliner. It didn't seem to help; guys didn't notice; what was the point? Ever after that, through graduation and beyond, she had done the expected minimum to survive corporate job interviews and meet the blandly unstated appearance rules of the marketplace.

But now, without him ever having said so, she felt this new reality fluttering within her breast: *Miles seems to find me appealing.* He had never said the words "pretty" or "beautiful." But somehow, as the affections swelled, she felt an awakening desire to be attractive in every way she could–for him–to bolster her unstated gratitude for the sweet gift.

Khemkaeng loitered in the living room, halfheartedly watching a locally produced film as the two ladies primped and dabbed on the rouge. "Ten minutes more," he called out. "Traffic could be quite bad, I think."

"Okay, babe," his wife responded, giving Sue's mascara a final touch of sisterly attention.

Pranom emerged from the upstairs bathroom, a virginal cloud of awakening adolescent beauty. "Sweetheart, you look amazing," her aunt beamed, giving the girl an affectionate hug. "Your daddy's going to be so proud of you tonight."

As if on cue, Tommy rapped on the front door. "Everyone ready?" He was freshly moussed, wearing his best black suit, and there was an aromatic air of elegance as the five of them squeezed into the Nissan.

"I wish you were singing, honey," Rachel Marie said; she reached out and rested a hand on Khemkaeng's shoulder as he drove.

He snorted cheerfully. "With one hundred good singers in Miss Charunee's choir, I think what they need most is people like me to sit and listen."

Sue sat in the back seat, aware of the chatter around her but not noticing. In just these few months she had come to love Bangkok and the immense vistas of mission opportunity here. The sidewalks were jostling masses of people going home from jobs and university lectures. There were crowded clothing stores, a sidewalk stand offering a dizzying array of colorful newspapers and magazines, both local and foreign. Five jewelry stores in succession, advertising heavy gold chains draped around black velvet mannequin heads. An Internet café vibrated with adolescent energy as teens with spare change huddled over violent video games. At an ice cream store, young Thai girls with corporate miniskirts bantered with tourists eager for a familiar treat.

The Christmas season had descended upon Wattana Church; the sanctuary was bedecked with a tasteful array of subdued lights, garlands taped to each pew, even a makeshift crèche in the foyer. Already the Austrian Embassy orchestra was in place, and the candlelight flickers seemed to move in time with the tuning notes as the string section prepared for the grand overture. The church was nearly filled with a curious, somewhat international congregation.

Sue felt a delicious thrill as Miles swept in through the back door moments before the concert began. His complexion looked even more ruddy and *alive* against the crisp white shirt of his tuxedo as he flashed a wink at her and headed toward the bass section. Hesitating, he peeled away and lumbered over to her row of alto singers. "Merry Christmas, ladies." He solemnly shook hands with both Rachel Marie and Pranom, then paused to take in the visual package Sue had prepared for her man. "Now *you* . . . are a Christmas delight." He glowed in his approval. "Miss Baines, you look absolutely breathtaking. I may not hit a single right note tonight." He nudged closer to her and, despite the crowds all around, actually kissed her cheek.

In all her life Sue had never had a man say such a thing to her, and she felt her mascara threatening to melt underneath the romantic heat of the moment. "Thank you, Miles. You look very elegant too."

Wattana's senior pastor greeted the many guests and offered a brief prayer in Thai. Sue settled into her seat, basking in the splendid spiritual festivity of the night, and let the overture and opening solos sweep over her soul.

The orchestra was exquisite, and the swelling beauty of Handel's magnificent creation seemed to pour into all of Bangkok with the glory of the Christ child. Sue stood and sang with the others, Christians of many faiths bonding together in telling the hopeful tale of Bethle-hem's redeemer.

Toward the close, as the musical odyssey marched toward the inevitable "Hallelujah Chorus," the conductor motioned for the orchestra's introduction to the slow, sweeping "Surely He Hath Borne Our Griefs." It was Sue's favorite, and as the majestic largo filled the sanctuary, she glanced over at Pranom. The eighth grader was exquisitely beautiful with jet-black hair, wide, wor-shipful eyes, and her sequined frock. Proudly clutching her own score, she came in on cue with the rest of the mass choir: *Surely He hath borne our griefs and carried our sorrows.*

Sue realized with a stab of wonder, as the lyrics carried her along in the grand Calvary swell, that she knew the barest details of the teenager's agonies. As a prepubescent seventh-grader Pranom had lost her own mother. Her dad had succumbed to the throbbing temptations of the city and been arrested for dealing narcotics. And then the *coup de grace*–an opportunistic uncle seizing her and forcing this woman/child into Thailand's pervasive sex trade at Pattaya Beach. Only by the most improbable of rescues had she been reclaimed and restored, her former horrors erased.

Now Pranom sang, the picture of pure innocence, her clear voice mingling with her adopted aunt's. In eight days she would stand as maid of honor in a

Christian church–Portland,   Oregon, her adopted home nine time zones away–and be embraced into a newly birthed family that worshiped at the altar of the slain Redeemer. *He was wounded for our transgressions; He was bruised for our iniquities.*

Unmindful of her makeup, Sue mopped at her eyes, suddenly overcome by the healing glory of this anthem and the fragile, hopeful teen trophy worshiping before her. She chanced to peer over to where Miles and Tommy were sharing a songbook. Tommy had stopped singing, and was gazing in awe at his stepdaughter, unabashed tears streaming down his cheeks.

And with His stripes we are healed.

They came to the oratorio's grand climax, and the Austrian musicians began the opening to the "Hallelujah Chorus." The gathered Thai worshipers and guests were well versed in the performance tradition, instinctively rising to their feet to savor the celestial chords. Just two blocks away from the Christian church, golden Buddhist monuments ascended into the skies, good-hearted expressions of man's eternal search for a caring Deity. Sue felt a rush of love for the citizens of Thailand as she joined her fellow believers in the gospel's generous guarantee: *The kingdom of this world has become the kingdom of our Lord, and of His Christ. And He shall reign forever and ever.*

The last triumphant note held forth in glory, and the congregation burst into applause. Misty-eyed, Sue happened to glance out into the gathered throng. Khemkaeng was still on his feet, clapping, a broad smile on his face.

What in the world? Standing next to him was Gino, wearing a dark green shirt and yellow tie pulled down a bit. The ever-present earbuds were dangling around his neck, but he was actually applauding heartily along with the others. She felt a confused cacophony of emotions as the teenager leaned over and said something to Khem-kaeng, who nodded as the four soloists came to the front of the sanctuary to accept their bouquets.

THE LAST FOUR DAYS of the fall term slipped into history and Sue went about her duties, filled with a kind of wistful longing. BCS was a cheerful island of Christmas awareness, but she keenly missed the yuletide trappings that made Decembers at New Hope Church a heartfelt pleasure. It was painful to envision Tommy and Pranom boarding a plane bound for the United States, and then her own grungy journey into the muddy camps of northern Thailand.

She had spent several restless nights second-guessing her decision to stay. Her prospects with Miles were iffy at best; he was an expatriate, ensconced in his Asian world. Gino was an incorrigible and gloomy specter hovering over her hopes. But the rational part of her mind forced a reconsideration of the equation. Miles was still a good and amiable friend and a possible grand adventure. The Christmas tinsel of Glendale would be there in future seasons; this opportunity was *now*. A tough week of sacrificial service, of grit and malarial mosquitoes, was a reasonable investment. The days would go by; she would get to see Miles in his heroic day-to-day ordinariness. And she might as well find out if she and Gino could carve out a tenuous détente.

Tommy popped his head into her office just as she was closing up the school's main Excel account. "Hey, venerated principal." He had a cheerful arm draped around his stepdaughter.

"Hey, yourself." She smiled at Pranom. "Ready to fly home to be with your new mom and sister?"

The girl beamed. "Yes. I am so excited to go."

"You know we'll miss you very much, Pranom. You've been a wonderful part of Bangkok Christian School. We will always think of you."

"Thank you, Missie Baines."

Sue picked up a folder. "Rungsit dropped this off," she told Tommy. "It's her transcripts. So she should be able to slide right over to the school in Portland."

He grinned. "Awesome! And I don't have to even look; I know they're all A's." Pranom blushed and snuggled closer to him.

"Well, that's going to be a sad ride to the airport tomorrow. For the rest of us, I mean." Sue pretended to scowl. "Here we have to get up at five in the morning. Thanks so much, Mr. Daggett."

"I know." A shake of his shaggy head. "Plus we'll be out late tonight." His cell buzzed and he glanced down before switching it off. "Are you coming with us?"

"I'm not sure." She pushed her chair away from the desk. "What time are you guys singing?"

"Siroj said between ten and ten-thirty. Four songs."

"And you got a driver arranged? For the students?"

"Uh huh."

She hesitated. "Well, let's do this. I'm kind of lined up to have dinner with a friend. But when it's done, I'll really try to come over. Okay?"

Tommy tried vainly to stifle an owlish smile. Despite Sue's best efforts at containment, news had begun to seep out among the BCS staff about her tenuous romance. Several *Matthayom* students had actually witnessed the casual kiss at the Wattana Church concert; now their eyes danced knowingly as they passed her in the hallways of the high school part of campus.

"Well, it's going to be really great. I hope you'll come."

"That's a short night for the two of you."

He shrugged. "We can sleep on the plane."

The campus slowly emptied out and she stayed at her desk in the gathering twilight, stolidly working to tie up loose ends. She toyed with the idea of calling Natalie for some sisterly commiseration, but a quick bit of math reminded her that it was just coming up on three in the morning in Los Angeles. With a nervous sigh, she shoved the last unfinished project into her catch-all procrasti-nation drawer and snapped off the light. It was nearly dark in the hallway as she went to the stairwell and out to the bare parking lot.

Miles was just pulling in as she emerged, and he swung over to the curb and leaned over to open her door. "Hiya."

"Merry Christmas." She felt another flush of feminine pleasure as she accepted a kiss on the cheek. "Thanks for picking me up."

"Thought of you all day, love." He was still wearing his white medical coat, a couple of unclipped pens bouncing around in the breast pocket. She noticed that his stethoscope was still absent-mindedly draped around his neck, and she carefully unpeeled it for him and set it in the back seat.

"Are you all packed up for the trip?"

He shook his head. "You're joking. I always wait till about an hour out, then toss a load of clothes in a duffel bag and off I go."

"Really?"

"Well, not quite that bad." He emitted his barking laugh while changing lanes. "I've actually done a bit of packing of the medical supplies we need. Hospital admin donated quite a boxful of this and that. But my own undies and clean socks–haven't got to that yet, I fear."

Traffic thickened as they approached the Chao Phraya River area of the city, and Miles drummed anxiously on the steering wheel. "I told Gino I wanted him on his best behavior tonight."

Sue tried to keep her tone even. "Think it'll work?"

The big man shrugged. "Dunno. School's out for the kid, so maybe he'll be in a pleasant mood about that."

"Is he looking forward to the trip?"

"Not likely. I mean, I've got no choice but to have him along. Can't leave him here in Bangkok for eight days unattended. But he won't lift a finger to help out once we're there. Just sit under a tree and text his friends, I reckon. That and a week of nonstop rock-and-roll with the iPod." His face tightened.

The luxury high-rise condos came into view and he carefully pointed the Honda toward the gated entrance. "Sure is good of you to come over, Sue. Hope it goes well."

There was a smallish elevator that whisked them up to the twenty-seventh floor. The hallway's windows afforded a magnificent view of the river, and she gaped at the nocturnal glory below them. "Bangkok looks a lot better at night," she grinned.

"It does that." He fished in his pocket for an apartment key. "Brace yourself, Susie."

The condo was spacious and decently decorated for

a bachelor father who spent such long hours working and doing mission projects. The living room was on two levels with an expensive teakwood table and four chairs; a large TV was mounted on the wall, and lights flickered on as the couple entered. He pointed. "If you need a bit of freshening up after all that traffic, it's right in there. Number one door on the left." He peeled off his lab coat and put it away in a hall closet. "Gino!"

There was a moment before the teen shuffled out from his bedroom, a bit bleary-eyed. "Hey."

"You remember Sue Baines."

Gino nodded absently, both hands thrust into his pockets. "Yeh."

Her heart lurching unhappily, she forced a smile. "How are things? I guess you're glad school is out."

A shrug. "Sure. We only get a week, is all." He flopped down on the couch and gazed past her.

The tension was vibrating in the room, but she managed to sit across from him and affect a pleasant look. "I'd love to hear about your school and everything. Since I do that kind of work too. What school subject do you like best?"

To her surprise he uncrossed his legs and showed the slightest evidence of perking up. "They're all okay. But I like government studies the best." He spoke with a clipped accent not quite as pronounced as his father's.

"Really? How come?"

"Just . . . it's interesting. How the Thai system works, then compared to, like, America and what Europe's got. We got this lady, Mrs. Lefevre, teaching. And she gets films off the Internet and all that. Kind of cool stuff."

Miles was in the kitchen, efficiently concocting a

menu, and she seized the opportunity before her. "I have this awful confession," she told the boy. "I've been here since August but really haven't learned a single thing about the Thai system of government beyond the fact of a monarchy and them having a female prime minister. I'd love it if you'd give me a fifteen-minute tutorial before dinner."

"For real?" He shrugged. "What do you want to know?"

"Everything. Just figure I know zero, and start from there."

Gino launched into a slang-punctuated dissertation about the kingdom's bicameral legislature and the government's relationship with the hereditary monarchy. Sue listened intently, prodding him with questions and praising his knowledge. "This is really a nice surprise. Finding out that you know all this. I really appreciate it."

The generous words were met with a shrug. "Whatever. I just like comparing, you know, one system with another."

"It's a lot like back home," she mused. "Interesting that they have a house and a senate, just like in America."

To her surprise he rattled off the long Thai names for both institutions. "Don't know why I got that in my head. Mrs. L said we didn't need it, but I wrote it down and I guess I memorized it without thinking much." He actually flashed what passed for a smile. "Weird."

"Ready to eat?" Miles came into the living room. "It's not fancy grub, but I think it'll do." They sat down, and without fanfare he offered up a quick prayer. "Thank you, Lord God, for this marvelous time of year when the birth of your Son gives us such hope and joy. Bless our trip to the camps. Keep us safe and healthy. And we offer thanks for this food. Thanks also that Sue can join us; we ask your blessing on her family and all the good work she does at BCS. In the name of Jesus, Amen."

Gino was already spooning string beans onto his plate before the benediction, and he seemed disdainful of Miles' spiritual expressions. But he participated in an amiable conversation about the hit films currently playing in Bangkok, and how prices at the local cinema were a sixth of what they might be in Brisbane.

"Tickets there are worst in the world," Gino told the two adults, sniffing disdainfully. "Mr. Metcalf said the other day that people go to the movies there, costs them like eighteen dollars. Just the ticket."

Sue swallowed the last of her rice cake. "Australian dollars?"

"Huh uh. American. Course most of the time, the two are kind of the same. Within, like, five points of each other. Not always, though. If one's economy goes into a dive."

"Huh." Impressed, she set down her fork. "Do you pay much attention to, you know, news and stuff from Brisbane? Even though you've lived so long right here?"

"Some." He reached across her for another piece of bread. "'Scuse me. I just, you know, watch CNN International and all that. There's, like, a half hour each weekend where a lot of news is from Australia/New Zealand. And sometimes I see stuff on the Internet."

"You guys want some dessert?" Miles was clearly pleased at the amiable nature of the dinner conversation. "I stopped at Beard Papa's before picking Sue up. I think you'll like these." He went into the kitchen and returned with three coconut cream puffs oozing over with Asian flavor. "Try these, eh?"

Sue took a careful bite and was dazzled by the exotic taste. "Oh dear oh dear," she murmured. "This is a wicked discovery, Dr. Carington. What have you done?"

He grinned. "What do you think, son?"

The boy was careful to never let his enthusiasm show. "They're all right." He finished the sugary treat and wiped his hands on his khaki pants. "May I be excused?"

"Sure."

"It was nice meeting you again," Sue told him, trying to mean it. "And thanks again for telling me all that about the government here. It's really great how you know so much."

The compliment seemed to land on deaf ears. "Yeh." He shuffled away.

Stifling a sigh, she pulled her chair back and went over to the balcony door. The moon was just coming up over the bridges spanning the river far below. A pair of water taxis made their lazy way north, and she peered out at the cruise ships that offered on-board dinners and cocktail parties. "Have you been on one of those?"

Miles shook his head. "A couple of the docs at Mission said it was a good show. Nice food and all." He laughed, plainly relieved at the way the evening had turned out. "I just never had anyone pretty enough to take on a boat ride. Till now." He undid the latch and slid the glass door open. "Care to take a closer look?"

The cool December air was pleasantly humid and their lofty position high above the uncollected refuse in the streets erased the sometimes pungent atmosphere of Bangkok. Hotels on both sides of the river were towers of dazzling light, and neon ads chased their merry way around digital billboards lining the highways exiting the city.

"I need to leave in a bit," she told him regretfully. "I promised Tommy I'd go to this mini-concert he and a few of the choir kids are doing."

"I heard about it," he responded. Casting a glance at the darkened bedrooms off the main hallway, he added in a lowered voice: "Care if I join you?"

"Gino doesn't mind?"

"Kid's on vacation. He's got films all piled up he wants to watch. Plus games on the computer. But I'll make sure."

"Of course, then." She felt a flush of anticipation. "That'd be great."

He slipped his muscular arm around her waist and pulled her close. "I know it doesn't mean a thing. 'Cause next time out, Jekyll could turn right back into Hyde again. But at least tonight was all right, eh?"

"Uh huh." It was an odd metaphor, and she tried to erase it from her mind. All she could do was to be bright and winsome; Gino could warm up or disdain every overture. It was essentially out of her hands now.

In the far distance, an airplane slipped into the silvery curtains ringing the city and she remembered that her family would soon be gathering around the Christmas tree, boisterously teasing each other and tearing off wrapping paper. Going out for an extended feast at the El Torito champagne buffet. Without meaning to, she eased her own arm around Miles and savored the closeness, the comfort of having a strong man in her life. "I sure appreciate you, Dr. C.," she murmured.

The couple chatted for a few minutes, drinking in

the insulated beauty of Thailand's legendary nightlife. "We'd best be off if we want to get to your show on time," he said at last, giving her a last squeeze. "But I'd enjoy just standing here with an arm around my lady love for the next decade or so."

She laughed. "Let's see if we're still friends after a week in the jungle fighting off snakes and malaria."

They went back inside and he fished in the closet for a sport coat. "Gino! We're going out for a bit for a thing Miss Baines has got to attend to. I'll be late, so get some sleep, eh?"

There was a long pause before Gino appeared at his doorway. "All right then. Cheers." His father gave him a pointed look, and the boy finally mumbled the requisite addendum in Sue's general direction. "Nice seeing you and all."

"It was." Trying to appear as platonic as possible, she subconsciously pulled away from Miles. "I'll enjoy getting more acquainted on the train tomorrow."

He wheeled back into his room, the door closing with a thud. "See?" she said brightly. "We're fast friends."

Miles laughed. "You didn't kick the kid under the table and he didn't use any of his seven dirty words. I figure the evening was a grand success."

Traffic had ebbed by the time they passed Mission Hospital and got back to Petchaburi, the main east-west thoroughfare going through the heart of downtown. Still, an entire brigade of *tuk-tuks* and trucks soon filled the boulevard, and it took nearly half an hour to ease their way south to Rama Road.

"Which hotel did Tommy say?"

He pointed to his right. "It's the Siam Square

Novotel. Pretty nice place, maybe three-and-a-half stars."

"Huh." She gazed at the towering edifice.

He parked the car down a small *soi* a block away. "World Trade Center Mall is just there." He gestured behind them. "One of these times we'll go and do a bit of shopping. A lot of nice stuff."

The sidewalk was nearly empty, and she felt a sweet tingle when he reached for her hand again. "What's the connection you folks have with this place?" he asked.

"I'm really not sure myself," she confessed. "But I imagine we'll find out."

The hotel lobby had some Christmas lights hastily strung along the eaves, and there was an artificial tree with faux presents pressed against an ignored corner. Guests from a charter flight were checking in at the front desk and bell boys jockeyed for tips, wheeling luggage carts toward a bank of elevators.

"Should be down here." Miles pointed to a large sign above a flight of stairs. A gaudy banner proclaimed Concept CM^2 to be the hottest nightclub in all of Bangkok, with the most dynamic dance music to be found.

"What are we getting into?" she fretted as they went downstairs into the cavernous basement. A thumping bass line greeted them, and the dance floor was pulsating with young Asians and a mix of European and American tourists.

Miles bent closer to her. "Better stay close, eh? This place isn't for the faint of heart."

On the stage, a rock band was belting out standard pop hits from the U.S., the speakers throbbing with energy. A lead singer in a sequined miniskirt was gyrating as she belted out the suggestive lyrics; scantily clad waitresses flitted from table to table, delivering ornate cocktails and making change for customers.

Tommy spotted them and came over, leaning close to make himself heard above the thunder of decibel overload. "Good! You found us."

Sue fixed him with a scolding look. "Mr. Daggett, what in the world are we doing here?"

He grinned. "I know. Pretty lively stuff. But they say we're on in five minutes."

The band's backup singers stepped up to their own mikes as the song began to come in for a landing. The club's percussive power seemed to assault the walls, and it was difficult to even converse, but after an extended finale the sound and the strobe lights all went off with a synchronized *pouff!* In the alcoholic haze, it took a few seconds for the nightclub's patrons to respond, but they offered up a smattering of applause.

The club's emcee was a beautiful Thai woman in her late thirties, with spiked hair and an excess of garish makeup. She accepted the mike from the lead singer. "Ladies and gentlemen, please, one more round of applause for the band. *Kop kuhn kah.* They will be back in a little while, and we plan to rock all of Bangkok until closing time, so keep on your dancing shoes." The invitation was met with drunken hoots and Sue colored.

"But in the meantime, we know that a lot of you visiting our City of Angels are perhaps missing something here on December 21. True? It is almost Christmastime, and you know that Santa Claus has Bangkok on his map this year. We don't wish for you to be homesick, and so we invited some special friends to come and make Christmas happen." She glanced down at a small piece of paper in her hand. "So here for your holiday pleasure is Mr. Tommy Daggett. He leads a choir at a place called Bangkok Christian School. Without further ado, let us get into the Christmas mood and do some caroling." She emitted a phony but cheerful laugh. "I don't know if his songs are for dancing or what, but please enjoy."

Miles spotted Khemkaeng and Rachel Marie at a table close to the back of the club, and he ushered Sue over to join them. She watched, fascinated, as Tommy and a row of BCS students went to the stage. A smaller boy, around fourteen, perched himself at the drum kit, and Tommy walked up to the keyboard. "*Sawatdee*, everyone," he said easily, his voice booming through the nightclub's house PA. "It's great to be here, and we hope you're having a good stay in Bangkok. But for many of you, it's not Christmas without a bit of 'Jingle Bells,' and that's where we come in."

"Rudolph!" A drunken pair of college students in the corner hollered out the suggestion, and the place erupted in laughter.

"We'll see what the tips are like." Tommy's rejoinder brought more raucous hilarity, and he launched into a thumping version of "Santa Claus Is Coming to Town." The ten *Matthayom* students he'd brought with him were using a laptop as their own impromptu TelePrompTer, and the infectious tune soon had the place clapping and singing along.

"He's not bad," Miles grinned, motioning for a wait-ress and dickering for a couple of sodas. He leaned closer to Rachel Marie. "How about you two? My treat?" She nodded.

Sue beamed proudly, enjoying the odd scene as revelers sipped on their martinis and clapped zestfully. Tommy added a cute joke or two following each number, introducing the students and bragging about the school. "And this prettiest girl on the front row," he beamed, "is my stepdaughter. Say hello to Pranom, everyone. Tomorrow we fly to Portland, Oregon, where I'm marry-ing her mama. If she'll still have me." The announcement was met with hoots of approval.

"Now here's something you'll like, *meine Damen und Herren,*" he grinned, gesturing toward the boy play-ing the drums. "This young man, Siroj, is one of our finest. He's in eighth form at school, and his dad is a musician right here at this lovely hotel."

Miles leaned closer, nodding in understanding. "There's your connection," he whispered.

"So we offer you a special blessing tonight," Tommy went on. "It's entitled 'Little Drummer Boy.'"

The Thai youth began a slow, rhythmic cadence on the snare, just a percussive whisper, and Tommy eased into a series of chords. "*Come, they told me, pah rumpa-pum-pum. Our newborn King to see, pah rumpa-pum-pum.*"

The Christmas carol unfolded exquisitely as the keyboard's arpeggios rolled around the escalating drum solo. The ten singers gathered around two microphones, building a sacred harmony that filled the place. Sue reached for Miles' hand, dabbing at her eyes as she did so. "*I played my drum for him. I played my best for him.*"

The song seemed an anthem of commitment, of offering Christ one's best efforts, the most diligent and winsome panoply of talents and grit a disciple could muster. Sue reflected on her decision to come to this city, to sacrifice comfort and stability in order to make a difference where the yawning gaps between goals and realities demanded so much. She felt a stab of shame at her earlier reluctance to journey on dirt roads to the camps, to sleep on a floor and mingle with the neediest of God's children. *"Then he smiled at me, pah rumpa-pum-pum. Me and my drum."*

There was a cathedral-like hush as the last drumbeats melted into the midnight of the club. Revelers seemed to sense that something noble and nice had just been offered to them, and the applause filling the dance hall was respectful. *"Sehr gut!"* a European lady near the front cried out, clinking her cocktail glass with a spoon. "More!"

The bearded musician turned to the eighth-grade boy and invited him to stand and take a bow. More applause. "And please thank our choir," he added. "Folks, I get to make a living simply teaching these young people how to honor God with their voices. What do you think?"

"They're all right!" A florid man wearing a Braves baseball hat stood up, his beer glass still in hand. "Give us another."

Tommy played a slow and familiar sequence of chords. "How about this one? And if you know the words, please sing along."

All at once the nightclub was ringed with vibrant color as the entire bank of plasma screens was filled with images of the Christ child in the manger. The piano was muted, a sweet orchestral whisper, as the BCS choir began to quietly sing. *"Silent night, holy night; All is calm, all is bright."*

The PowerPoint slides sanctified the nightclub as halfway intoxicated partygoers set down their glasses and began to sing along. Sue, proud and overcome, leaned her head against Miles' shoulder, barely able to manage the words herself. This place was a den of shallow pleasure; seductive bottles of gin, vodka, and other exotic spirits sparkled through the tall stacks of cocktail glasses. But on the platform, surrounded by mike cables and electric guitars and the accoutrements of rock-and-roll music, were the trophies of Bangkok Christian School. Young men and women who had listened to Christian chapel services, written term papers about missionaries and Martin Luther, about the theology to be found in the book of Philippians. They had listened to prayers and watched Christian instructors respond with grace and Calvary wisdom to a myriad of challenges. And now they sang as one: "*Son of God, love's pure light; Radiant beams from thy holy face, With the dawn of redeeming grace.*"

It was the most perfect and wonderful thing she had ever seen–this heavenly invasion of a fallen world's inner sanctum. The last notes died away and before any applause could truncate the moment, Tommy simply held up a hand. "Lord Jesus," he prayed, "we thank you for this wonderful time of year. Thank you for Christmas and for your gift. Bless and safeguard all these nice people who have traveled to Bangkok in search of happiness. Thank you for being our greatest and eternal happiness. Amen."

It took a holy moment before the party crowd could collect its breath. The clapping was reverent and imbued with grace. Smiling, Tommy motioned, and the BCS choir took a bow to a swelling of applause. He hopped off the stage, holding Pranom's hand, and came over to Sue's table. "What do you guys think?"

She gave him a lingering hug. "Thank you, Tommy. You're a missionary in the most beautiful sense of the word. Your witness here will last a long, long time." She stepped back and eyed him with wonder. "When in the world did you find time to do that beautiful slide show?"

He gave her a weary smile. "Last night till around midnight."

"Well, it was perfect."

Sue exchanged hugs with all her students, dabbing at her eyes as she did so. "You guys are just amazing. I'll never forget your songs. And don't forget: we'll see you after the Christmas break. Okay?"

"Thank you, Missie Baines. Merry Christmas." Their eyes followed her as she walked, hand in hand with Miles, toward the exit.

THIRTEEN

Hua Lamphong, the legendary station in downtown Bangkok, was a buzzing den of commercial activity as the small Christian entourage boarded the northbound train the following evening. Armed with a jumbo bag of M&M candy and three bottles of drinking water, Sue handed over her ticket and let Miles heave her carefully packed duffel bag into an overhead rack. "Now we'll get a real taste of mission-ary life," he smirked, huffing as he made a second trip to get his medical supplies safely stashed away. "No more HBO, Miss Baines."

"Don't worry about me," she retorted, beginning to worry more than a little bit. Even the train station was a massive but dilapidated barn of a structure, with grime and foul-smelling restrooms. Dingy food stalls ringed the upstairs area, and tourists shopped for last-minute bags of snacks and pungent indigenous fruit.

The overnight express train offered pairs of facing seats on both sides, and Gino quickly commandeered the isolated fifth seat away from the adults, burying himself in a sports magazine. The train jerked twice, then slowly crept out of the terminal, rumbling noisily through the center of the city.

"Peek over here and you'll see again where I work." There was a sharp *ding ding ding* as a red-and-white barrier pole came down, cutting off the late-afternoon traffic darting through a busy three-way intersection. Miles pointed through the window. "Right past that gray wall."

Sue hadn't been to Mission Hospital since her initial visit with John Garvey shortly after arriving, and she eyed the quiet campus with the familiar green neon cross heralding the medical center's presence. "You like working there?"

"Yeah." He grunted heavily as he sank down into the blue leatherette seat. "The folks there are aces, CEO's excellent, and most of the staff is Christian." He motioned to the seat across from him. "Take a load off, Miss Baines." He ruminated for a moment. "I especially like the chaplain. Guy named Lopes."

"He was so awesome." Rachel Marie came across the aisle and perched herself on the edge of Sue's seat. "When I was in for those four days, he came by every single evening to pray with me. I was really going through some things in my head. 'Cause, you know, these kids just up and attacked me out of the clear blue sky. For no reason. So I was pretty much filled up with resentment and hate. But when David came by, he was able to help me remember that Jesus went through that too. Trying to help people and getting attacked for it."

"Wow." Miles nodded sagely. "Yeah, he's a good guy. We have lunch together in the hospital cafeteria every now and again."

Sue had packed a whole shopping bag of peanut-butter-jelly sandwiches, and the four adults munched cheerfully, gossiping about their respective churches and BCS politics. "Gino! Want some of these?" Miles held up an extra sandwich, and shrugged when the offer was disdained. "He'll be crying about midnight, I reckon. But tough luck to him."

There was a portable snack table travelers could erect between the two seats, and Khemkaeng carefully set up a Scrabble board. "I don't know why Rachel Marie makes me play this game," he confessed. "And then doesn't permit Thai words. So I always lose." With Sue keeping score, they managed to balance tile holders on their laps, and to everyone's surprise, Khemkaeng eked out a win, victoriously landing a big triple-word score that began with a "Q."

"I don't love you anymore," Rachel Marie sniffed, pretending to stalk off. "I guess I'll go sit by Gino."

It was fascinating, as the sun slowly disappeared from view, to experience Thailand through the glass pane of a train. The verdant hills of the north were yet to come; for now, one small town flowed into the next, with the *Thai*-ness more pervasive than in the capital. Most passing cities were marked by aging infrastructure and insistent outdoor advertising. Local artisans were inventive at preparing huge displays hawking the latest deodorants or flat-screen TVs, and sumptuous light-skinned models beamed down on the tracks from a multitude of billboards. Rows of cars and motorbikes lined up and idled their engines patiently as the train slowly slid past them and into the rural darkness.

Fishing in her bag, Sue dug out the last sandwich and went over to where Gino was nodding his head in time to his own silent symphony, his eyes lidded. She paused for a moment, unwilling to interrupt, but the teen suddenly jerked up and peered at her. "Huh?"

"We do have one sandwich left," she told him. "You might get hungry later on."

The offer hung in the air; he seemed torn between an instinctive array of disdainful responses. Finally, un-adorned practicality won out. "Thanks," he muttered, nodding toward the empty space next to his magazines. "There's fine." Trying to not roll her eyes, she set the offering down and rejoined the adults.

Miles was an ebullient host as the pleasant evening clicked by, tossing out stray bits of Thai to each passing entrepreneur who plied the passengers with offers of late-night snacks and overpriced orange-flavored drinks. "I know my accent's a frightful mess," he lamented cheerfully to Khemkaeng.

"No, you do very well."

The conversation strayed into an edgy free-for-all on the comparative efficacy of strategies to reach a growing segment of the kingdom with the Christian message. "Hands down," Miles declared, slapping his meaty hand against his own knee. "What you folks are doing at BCS. Getting young people exposed to the beauty of Jesus' message. Nothing works better than that. And like Daggett did last night, taking those kids to sing Christmas carols in a nightclub. That was prime."

"It is very slow work, though," Khemkaeng conceded. "We have many of our older students who quietly tell us: 'I believe Christianity to be true. But I cannot make such a decision as long as I am with my parents. It would be too much controversy.' They think that someday, when they're independent and finished with university, perhaps even married, they will find the freedom to become Christians. Of course, often by then they have drifted away from contact with the school or any church." He shook his head ruefully.

Rachel Marie leaned against him, stifling a yawn. "We've got to find a way to simply stay in touch with these kids after they graduate. Maybe have a massive alumni mailing list and be sure to keep sending them newsletters every quarter. Or have Rungsit organize a Facebook club where everyone who attends BCS stays in the loop."

They continued to brainstorm, but the energy level was flagging and Khemkaeng motioned for the night porter. "Since we slept so little last night, we should try to get more rest."

In the flurry of a few efficient moments, four cozy beds had been prepared and the train employee gave a slight bow before heading to the next car. Miles eased over and casually pecked Sue on the cheek. "Have a good rest, dear thing."

"You too." Despite Rachel Marie's teasing presence, she reached down and gave his hand a squeeze. "It's very nice traveling with you, Miles."

Her lower berth provided a cocoon of pleasant reveries as she carefully changed into a pair of sweat pants and T-shirt, tugging on the green curtain to ensure privacy. The awareness of her boyfriend's bulky presence just a few feet above her in the upper berth gave her a nice glow and she sat on the sheeted mattress for a long half hour, gazing contentedly out the window at the late-night visions gliding past her.

Even in the inky darkness of this isolated terrain she felt a keen sense of a vast and searching kingdom of good people. Every few kilometers a distant pinprick of light served as reminder that along these twin strips of steel there were people here and there in small houses, insignificant but cohesive communities. Migrant farm workers, plucky entrepreneurs, Buddhist priests, *Prathom* teachers in makeshift village schools doing long division problems on scratchy blackboards with a piece of chalk. Rising with the crow of a rooster, scratching out their daily bread, watching a news feed from Bangkok via a tiny color TV fed by satellite dishes. Burying their dead in respectful ceremonies replete with ancient chants and the comforting presence of incense.

It sometimes felt like a daunting Everest climb,

attempting to penetrate this lovely, lost place–now rolled out under the December moonlight–with the story of Calvary. The Christian faith claimed less than one percent of all Thailand's citizens. Millions of earnest, diligent people went through the karma-like cycle of birth, bicycling to school, finding work, raising families, retiring, and dying . . . without ever truly hearing an invitation to even consider Jesus' offer of grace and eternal life. She realized this, but without any daunting sense of inevitable failure. The kingdom of heaven's galactic armies already had a faithful Commander; she was a simple and obedient foot soldier. Her role was to do good where she could, to make the better of two choices at every intersection, to smile and love and heal and instruct whoever came into her sphere of influence. "Love God and the person standing in front of you."

She flipped off the night light and lay in the murky elegance of the night, praying silently and hearing the *ta-tick . . . ta-tick . . . ta-tick* of the train sliding over the nearly seamless rails. The teak forests were barely visible now, and as the car was enveloped by a tunnel, even the sound beneath her seemed to be muted.

Patches of sleep were restless and haphazard, and Sue shifted frequently, trying to find a sustainable comfort zone. There was a slight but insistent need for a hike to the bathroom at the end of the car, but she squinted unhappily, trying to will the matter away. Could she get back to sleep as things were? She waited hopefully for slumber to erase the problem, but alas. Grumpily surrendering to the realities of female biology, she fished for her glasses and the slip-ons at the foot of her bed. There was a small overhead light in the aisle, and she stepped carefully around Miles' duffel bag.

It was amazing how speedily a grownup could accomplish a response to the call of nature under conditions as unseemly as those on a Thai train. *And you probably ain't seen nothing yet,* she grudgingly concluded as she washed her hands in the tiny metal sink and headed back toward her bunk.

She came to Gino's lower berth and noticed that his curtain was only partially closed. The sandwich she had offered him was half-eaten, a leftover piece of crust on the floor next to his mattress. Curled up in a fetal position, he stared, unblinking, out into the dull murkiness of the aisle. Without meaning to, she paused. His face was a sickening sheen, perspiration dotting his forehead, and he seemed almost to be moaning.

"Gino? Are you all right? What's the matter?"

"Nothing."

"Do you feel okay?"

"I said nothing. Get the hell away, would you?"

She flushed. All her life, she had been a helper; it was wired into her DNA to copy Jesus in acts of service: the cups of water, the prison visits, the deeds of charity even for those who were ungrateful. "Are you sure? Can I get you a drink?"

He twitched angrily on his pillow, and she spotted an odd coloration on the sheet, as if he had been dabbing at something messy. "Leave me alone, eh? Christ!" He spat out a colorful obscenity and turned away from her.

Sue's cheeks scarlet, she stumbled to her own bunk and pulled the green curtain taut to ward off the hostility emanating from the insolent teen. What had she been thinking? Détente with Gino Carington was an emotional impossibility. The boy was a jangle of psychotic dysfunction and rude impulses. Not to mention his expletive-laced diatribes whenever he felt subpar. Minutes later, it occurred to her that the stains on the boy's pillow might possibly have come from him feeling motion-sick and even throwing up.

In the morning she whispered her concerns to Miles as the quartet dined warily on over-easy eggs and small pieces of white toast. "I'll ask when he wakes up," Miles said, his face a mask. "Hope he's not coming down with some bug he picked up at school."

The morning scenery was almost surreal in its beauty, though, and she put the barbed encounter out of her mind. Northern Thailand was a stunning blanket of rolling greenery, its high hills thick with trees and gentle clouds floating in between the waves of forest cover. The endless miles of untouched nature on all sides seemed so complete the train itself was the barest whisper, a tiny thread on a grand tapestry. Every now and then a golden spire would punctuate the rural perfection, and travelers could spot a silent row of saffron-clad priests making their way toward the Buddhist *wat*.

Gino finally staggered out of bed, pushing his dark curls away from his eyes and dabbing at his nose with the corner of his shirt sleeve. "What's there to eat?"

Miles went over and put a hand on his shoulder. "Doing okay?"

"Yeh. Just hungry is all. Can I get some pineapple?"

"Sure." The older man pointed. "Lady just went that way selling some. See if you can catch her." He fished in his pants pocket for a couple of bills.

The train pulled into Chiang Mai a half hour behind schedule, and Gino sat off to the side on a wooden bench as the adults tugged at the bulky suitcases stuffed with supplies. Khemkaeng greeted his parents, and introduced everyone. "My father's name is Aroon, and this is Pakpao," he told Miles and Sue. "We can rest for a few hours at their home and then we should begin our trip. It will take three hours, at least, to get to the border camp."

Khemkaeng had already arranged for the rental van, and cheerfully pointed out various sites as they made their way through the picturesque city with its water fountains dotting the center canal. "Perhaps on our way back home we can do sightseeing," he said apologetically. "Sue, you must see Doi Suthep. Our best temple, and in a beautiful spot high in the mountains. But not today."

They spent a leisurely three hours at the Chaisuri-virats' comfortable home out in the country. Khemkaeng and Rachel Marie chatted easily with his parents; she clearly enjoyed her in-laws and had an affable rapport with the Thai family. Miles herded Gino into a spare bedroom, and Sue could hear the soft rumble of his interrogation. He emerged a few minutes later, mildly frustrated. "Says it's nothing. Just got to feeling bodgy around midnight."

She pursed her lips. "Was he sick to his stomach? Did he . . ."

Miles shook his head. "He says he didn't. But he did look rather green this morning, eh?" A careful shrug. "I'll keep an eye on things. And I got pills in case he gets any intestinal disorder." He came over and put an arm around her. "Thanks for noticing, though. And if any of the rest of us gets a case of *roke tong see-a,* I'll be ready and waiting." She smiled, remembering the Thai expression.

Lunch was a feast of corn on the cob–blackened almost to a crisp in the Thai style–and large platters with cold, crunchy circles of cucumber serrated in a festive design. "The food at this camp will be so plain," Aroon commented with a big smile. "You should eat well before going."

Khemkaeng took over the driving chores as the expedition headed northwest toward the Thailand-Myanmar border. Sue gazed, fascinated, at the colorful tapestry of Asian life clicking by their green rental van in a never-ending series of portraits. Along the side of the road, farm workers putted slowly along on cheap motorbikes; aging rice farmers bent low in the paddies, painstakingly nurturing the prized cash crop that was the boast of the kingdom. Every few kilometers there was a fruit stand or farmer's market where piles of indigenous produce could be purchased for a few baht. Dirt roads peeled off on both sides, and pairs of water buffalo stood in knee-deep brownish water, using their tail to flick at an occasional fly lighting on their back.

"Anyone need a rest stop?" Khemkaeng slowed as he noticed a western-style snack shop. The group piled out and Miles fished through a freezer for some ice cream bars. "Take your pick, son." Gino, his face still a bit waxy, numbly accepted a chocolate-covered treat and peeled away the paper wrapping without acknowledging the gift.

"How far are we from the Burmese border?" Rachel Marie caught herself and flicked her own forearm as punishment. "I mean Myanmar." A laugh. "I should know better. Don't tell my students I flubbed that."

Her husband peeked at his wristwatch before answering. "Only perhaps ten kilometers. Maybe we can drive there one afternoon and see the crossing area."

"Can we go over to the other side?" Miles wanted to know.

Khemkaeng frowned. "Yes, but I think the border police charge quite a high price. It is like eight hundred baht just to cross, get a stamp in your passport, and walk right back to the Thai side. Some visitors do so, only so that they can say, 'I have been to Myanmar.'"

"Not worth it," Rachel Marie muttered idly, pressing her face against the glass.

Khemkaeng carefully wheeled the Toyota van along a bumpy dirt trail that wound its way through a series of makeshift tin buildings. In a grassy area, a long row of crude tables had been set up, some of them lopsidedly sinking into a patch of mud. Huge pots were suspended over charcoal stoves, and the newcomers could see thick clouds of steam slowly floating over the cooking area. Already children of all ages and sizes were beginning to shove and push to get into line, each clutching a small tin plate.

"I think we check in over there." Miles pointed to a small but trim stucco building that had the Thai flag waving briskly in the December breeze.

"Yes." Khemkaeng nodded, maneuvering the van into an available parking spot.

Sue emerged carefully, not wanting to sink up to her ankles in a mud hole. "It must have rained here not too long ago."

Samud was a graying, distinguished-looking administrator who stepped out from behind his desk and greeted the newcomers with a generous *wai*. "Dr. Carington, we are grateful that you have come again! And also your son." He bowed slightly in Gino's direction. Sue colored in irritation as the boy, hands shoved in his jean pockets, stared at a painting on the far wall, ignoring the overture.

The Thai man, apparently unruffled, warmly greeted Khemkaeng, Rachel Marie, and Sue. "It is a fine honor that you come during your Christian holiday time," he smiled. "And doctor, I must personally thank you for the financial gifts you send us each month. Your checks have provided many meals." Sue's eyes widened.

Samud led them outside and pointed to the west side of the camp. "Do you see that green building on the end? You can stay there. Already three women are using it, but it has eight beds, so this is a good place. You will like them so much; they come from Italy and have been helping in the clinic." He beamed at Miles. "Tomorrow you will meet them and begin to work together."

"What can we do to help right now?" Sue was eager to get started and the Thai leader nodded gratefully.

"After supper we like to have a story time for the small children, and those who are older usually choose to play football." He bent his head down in a kind of cheerful apology. "Sorry—you always say 'soccer.'"

"Gino, maybe you could help with that," Miles put in. "I reckon they could use an extra referee.

"Yes, that is a good suggestion," Samud nodded. "And here in the office, I am endeavoring to organize classes for older people. We have six instructors at this time, but only four rooms that are good for school. If someone can help to make a new schedule, then I will have opportunity to travel to the town where we must arrange with market truck to bring next week's supply."

"I guess that would be me." Sue raised her hand.

"Can you make chart on computer and arrange all

classes for a time of one and half hours? Begin at nine o'clock and then from there?"

"I'm on it."

Rachel Marie grinned. "I guess I'll just climb trees and have fun."

"Never!" Samud seemed to have a pleasant sense of humor, and he immediately picked up on the American style of teasing. "Khemkaeng already send me email and suggest that you can teach young students in all subjects. Most of all, can you teach them small amounts of English? Most know some already, but they are eager for improvement. We have many who pray for opportunity to leave here and be received in U.S.A. as immigrants. If they can learn 'hello' and 'goodbye,' that is good, eh?" They all laughed.

Sue was surprised when Khemkaeng tossed the van's ignition key to Gino. "Why not drive over to where we are staying? The rest of us can walk and stretch our legs."

Gino gulped. "Really? Me?"

"It's only a short ways. And the van is easy to drive, with automatic transmission, not stick."

"Cool."

An uncharacteristically pleasant look flickered on the teen's face, and Khemkaeng masked a grin as he walked toward Sue. "It is probably the last thing he will help do."

"Good idea, though." She kept her voice equally low.

Supper was a tangy delight, with generous portions of spicy curry atop the fluffy white rice that was a staple at each meal. "Thailand's the world's number one exporter of this stuff," Miles commented between bites, "and I can see why. This rice is delicious."

A sudden stench wafted in their direction and Sue winced, putting the back of her hand up to her nose. "Yikes! What in the world is that? Did something die out here?"

Khemkaeng began laughing and couldn't stop. "The camp must have received a gift of durian."

"Oh, man." Sue had spent five pleasant months in Thailand without a single encounter with the pungent tropical delicacy. "I asked God to protect me from durian, and now here it is right in our faces." The smell almost made her eyes water, and she leaned against Miles, almost laughing and crying at the same time. "Yow. That is an unbelievable stink."

"No! Come on, Bainesy. When in Thailand, do as the Thai folks do," he admonished. Already a long and eager queue was forming, as four volunteers handed out small plates of the formidable delicacy. Hopping up from the table, Miles ambled over to the line. Towering as he did over most of the refugees, he was able to teasingly inveigle a plate from the cook, and he returned in triumph. "There you go, dear people. Bon appétit. The king of fruits!"

"No way." Comically pinching her nose, Rachel Marie picked up a small bit as though handling the carcass of an objectionable animal. "It smells like rotten onions. I mean, really." She took a delicate bite, wincing as if expecting her innards to explode like in an *Alien* double feature. "Actually, not bad, though." She let go of her nose and rolled the fruit around in her mouth. "Kind of a custard feel to it, I think."

"Like almonds," Sue declared, slapping Miles' hand and helping herself to a bit more. "You should have offered me some earlier, Dr. C. This is pretty good stuff."

"Ah, another convert," he grinned, nudging a slice over toward his son. "They say most visitors to Thailand who get up the courage end up writing poetry about durian."

"Now there's an English assignment I can take back to BCS," Rachel Marie snickered. "A poem about durian. 'An apple a day keeps the doctor away; a durian a day   . . .'"

". . . Would keep the whole world away." Sue swallowed the last of hers, and felt the odor lingering in her entire upper body, rolling rebelliously up and down her esophagus.

"They say the odor stays with you for three days," Khemkaeng warned. He lowered his voice discreetly. "A person finds themselves belching up the taste for a long time."

"Oh, great." Sue craned her neck. "Maybe we should try to neutralize it with some papaya then."

There were juvenile shouts of enthusiasm as youths tried to push a lopsided soccer ball between two upended fruit baskets that served as a goal at the far end of a pockmarked field. Gino, following the action with a whistle in his mouth, intervened timidly when errant shots skidded out of bounds. With almost zero knowledge of the local dialect, he was reduced to awkward gestures, but the boys cheerfully accepted his ruling whenever one of them illegally touched the ball with his hand or had a kick sail out of bounds. He trotted up and down along the sidelines, his sweaty jersey sticking to his skin as twilight stole over the ramshackle community.

Sue watched from the back of the community *sala* as Rachel Marie mesmerized the younger children with a whiz-bang ghost story imported from BCS. She and Khemkaeng were natural entertainers; he translated the tale mimicking her gestures and even the comic squeak she put in her voice. Kids chortled with laughter, and at one point Rachel Marie leaned against her husband, almost unable to go on. He feigned exasperation with her and she concluded in triumph by delivering the memorized punch line in Thai herself, much to the approval of the listening parents.

"You guys are too much," Sue told them, meaning it. "That was marvelous."

The encampment was an open field lacking fences or marked boundaries, with high mountains swooping into the richly indigo sky on the north border facing Myanmar. The rising moon was nearly full and kids continued to frolic and play the eternal game of tag, reluctant to peel away to their assigned sleeping quarters. Gino, his earplugs firmly in place, sat alone underneath a bare light bulb dangling from a nearby tree branch, a thick novel in hand. Miles ambled over to Sue, nibbling on a bonus piece of pineapple swiped from the kitchen. "It's still early," he said. "How about a walk about the camp just to get our bearings?"

"Sure." She never tired of the confident way he reached for her hand, and they did a slow, lazy loop around the outer perimeter. Along the western portion of the makeshift city, the government had set up three rows of semi-permanent canvas tents; Thai lettering stamped on the crude canvas seemed to indicate a military authorization of some kind. In between two of the tents, a single faucet provided a trickle of water for washing, and there was a snaking line of people waiting with jars and small basins.

"Can we drink that?" she asked, feeling anxious.

Miles shook his head. "Probably not safe. Samud makes a run into town every couple of days and gets a good stash of bottled water at a subsidized discount. We'd best stick with that." He slipped an arm around her. "You have enough for tonight?"

She nodded. "Speaking of water and its effects, next time we pass the ladies' room, you let me know."

"Ah." There was a moment of easy silence, and when he spoke again there was mirth in his voice. "This may not be your favorite ministry moment, dearie."

"What do you mean?"

He hesitated, then pointed to a small shed. "There she be. That's for you on one side and your boyfriend on the other."

"And . . ."

He said no more, and as they got closer, a foul odor assaulted her senses. It was clearly a makeshift bathroom, dimly lit and surrounded by a weedy patch of oozing mud. "Lovely," she grunted, trying to spot a firm bit of soil in order to step safely toward the door marked by a generic cutout of a figure in a dress.

"I'll be around the other side, eh? It's a race."

"You're on."

She went in, trying to adjust her eyesight to the nearly pitch black interior. There was nothing but a bare spigot against one corner; in the gloom she could make out a rancid puddle of water on the cracked tile of the floor. It took another moment before the unpleasant truth hit her. This camp had nothing but four "squat" toilets, low-slung porcelain beasts that were hardly more than a hole in the ground. Someone had left a damp half-roll of toilet paper lying between two of the horrid contraptions, and the tissue was matted, almost unusable. There were no stalls, no privacy . . . and the third toilet was clogged and overflowing with refuse.

A gagging feeling threatened to overwhelm her. Her innate sense of dignity, of propriety and longing for comfort and sanitary seclusion, was a powerful, desolate wave and she felt unhappy tears springing into her eyes. *Dear God . . .*

But it made sense to do her business quickly, with darkness being her friend. Peeling desperately at the soggy bits of rough paper, she finished in record time, adjusting her clothing and feeling a mingled sense of relief and resolve that by the end of this missionary trip– if she, Pastor Susan Baines had anything to say about it– refugees would be lining up to pee in a sanitized lavatory fit for the Bellagio Hotel.

"Still my friend?" Miles slipped a comforting arm around her as the pair exited the squalid little dungeon.

"You're on very thin ice," she said rather coolly. "My advice is that you walk me over to that pretty clump of trees on the other side of Camp Paradise here . . . and think of a romantic way to help me forget what just happened."

FOURTEEN

Charcoal fires the following morning added an acrid but crackling cheer to the hardscrabble ambience of the camp. Sue helped out as volunteers spooned out endless plates of rice and scrambled eggs flecked with tiny mint leaves. Ivory-colored slices of *somoh*, the local grapefruit, were a tart, juicy pleasure, and the Bangkok visitors ate with relish.

"Some who are Christian meet for short church worship," Samud explained as he offered her a portion of mango. "Since you are pastor, perhaps you could share–not sermon, but brief message from Bible. I will translate." His broad smile was infectious. "If you do not use hard English words."

Approximately fifty refugees and aid workers convened in the *sala*, where they sang a number of familiar choruses, accompanied by a Burmese woman who strummed a weather-beaten guitar. One of the European volunteers offered a lengthy prayer in Italian, and then Samud launched into an animated Thai introduction of the new arrivals. Switching into English, he added: "And Miss Sue will teach us from Word of God."

Preaching had never been her assignment at New Hope Church, but with the natural breaks provided by a translator, she was able to share a brief object lesson from the story of Joseph. "Many of you here have known the hard experience of being far from your own homes," she concluded, waiting for Samud to express the idea in the local idiom. "'How can I go on?' you wonder. 'Does God have any plan at all for my life? Does he care?' But this true story from the holy Bible gives each of us a wonderful comfort, when we know that God is always shaping the pains of our life into a new plan that will be good for us and also good for his kingdom." In the dusty background, she could see Gino leaning against a supporting post, a carefully bored expression arranging his features.

"That is excellent message, Sue." Samud was effusive in his praise. "I see in the eyes of those who come that they find hope in what you share with them."

She found a host of things to do in the office, first organizing the January schedule of adult classes, then going through Samud's monthly fundraising newsletter, still in the rough-draft stage, with a critical eye for typos and awkward grammar. A sudden flash of inspiration from BCS took her back to the first page, where she dutifully respelled *programme* and *labour* to fit the British usage common throughout the kingdom. Scanning through the list of agencies that donated foodstuffs, she compared lists and noted that no one from the camp had followed up on two substantial offers from charity organizations in Chiang Mai. She quickly typed notes to both groups, printed them out, and set them on Samud's desk for translation into Thai.

A mid-morning trip out to the same dingy restroom strengthened her resolve to spruce up the building and its primitive plumbing. She did a quick twenty minutes of surfing the Internet and discovered that decent-sized stores in the nearby town of Fang would have western toilets, stall dividers, and fresh tile for the floors. *And a Costco-sized jumbo pack of TP*, she muttered absently to herself.

Just before lunchtime she picked up a pair of water bottles and trudged through the soggy side road to the classroom where Rachel Marie was teaching. Using a BCS video projector, she had compiled a cute collection of PowerPoint slides illustrating the tricky conjugation of English verbs. A row of Thai women, one openly nursing her baby, peered in fascination at the slides, obediently parroting the phrases. "*Tomorrow I will eat at da restaurant. Today I am eating at da restaurant. Yesterday I ate at da restaurant.*"

"Dis so hard to say, ma'am!" A gray-haired woman with a crinkly smile moaned cheerfully and the group guffawed. "English language is not possible!"

"It is hard," Rachel Marie said brightly. "But you guys are doing great." She gave Sue a cheerful wave. "Let's show Miss Sue all we've learned. Okay? Here we go. *Hello, how are you?*"

"*Senk you, I am fine,*" they chorused, beaming and looking at Sue for affirmation.

In the afternoon, the Bangkok entourage enjoyed a jovial time painting the interior walls of an unused extra classroom. Even Gino got into the act, parrying and thrusting with a broom to sweep spider webs out of the corners.

"Can you reach clear up there?" Sue, determined to put the pile of unpleasant moments behind her, pointed to a thick wad of leaves that looked like an abandoned bird's nest high in a ceiling corner. He dragged a chair over and managed to poke the crusty sediment into submission. "Good job."

There was a kind of native spirituality about the camp's evenings, she noticed, as the moon rose into the heavens and the hubbub slowly faded into a gentle rhythm of communal grace. There was no television up here, no blaring boom boxes or electronic distractions– except for the Australian crime dramas on Gino's miniature iPod screen. The rest of the tent city eased into quiet conversations, children playing under a tree in the silvery elegance of nightfall, mothers nursing their young. A few with spare cash smoked cigarettes, the tiny orange bits of glow bobbing as they trudged to the restroom or sat at a dining table, isolated with their lonely thoughts.

Miles, still in his white lab coat, ambled back over to the bunk house where Sue was perched on her bed, listening idly as Rachel Marie and Khemkaeng bantered about some Thai game the children had tried to teach them. "It's nice out," Miles observed, jerking his head toward the door. "Care to come sample the moonlight?"

"Sure." She fished in her duffel bag for a light sweater. "Do I need this?"

"Not at all. It's very tropical out."

Hand in hand, he led her to the northeast quadrant of the encampment. A smallish trail led up an incline treacherous with exposed tree roots, and she huffed as they climbed. "Come on, doc." She deliberately added a childish whine to her voice. "Can you carry me?"

"Shush now, pretty lady."

Twenty minutes later, they came out on a small park area, now abandoned in the late evening shadows. He pointed to a nearby pair of benches. "See, lovey? We've got all of Club Med to ourselves, eh?"

He sank down on the bench and pulled her close. "By the way, I must say this one thing, Susie dear."

"What?"

With a smile he bent over and kissed her. "Merry Christmas. Eve, anyway."

"Oh, yeah." She had almost forgotten that the December calendar was registering a twenty-four. Back home, choirs were singing. Snow was on the ground. Elegant parties were going on, the eggnog was flowing, and eager kids were pleading with parents to release at least a sample present. Cookies and milk for Santa were perched on TV trays next to the chimney, and Christmas trees were blinking in all their glory.

And here she sat in this barren but beautiful land, next to such a prince of a man. What a rich Christmas indeed. She rested her head on his shoulder and sighed, contented and grateful. "You're a dear."

He sat next to her for a moment, then pulled free. "Don't get too cozy," he warned.

"Huh?"

He fumbled in the right-hand coat pocket. "Just for you, my precious." Wrapped in a tissue-thin napkin was a small cupcake.

"Where'd you get this?"

He grinned. "Local bakery came by today with a major stash of bread. We hadn't ordered these, of course, but the man had a spare rack of them in the truck. So I bought me a few of 'em."

"Where's yours then?"

He grinned. "I couldn't resist; it disappeared a few hours ago."

"Oh."

The confection was a sugary delight, and she held the frosting in her mouth for as long as she could. "Not bad, Dr. Carington. But you know you're corrupting the morals of an innocent maiden here."

"Well, you're so near to perfect, a bit of sugar and a few kisses under the stars won't hurt you much."

She finished the cupcake and peered up at him. "Did you say a few kisses? I can only remember getting one from you, Miles."

"Ah." He plucked the napkin out of her hand and wadded it back into his coat pocket. "I acknowledge this deficiency with grave resolve." He reached out and turned her face toward his own. "I love you, Sue Baines." He kissed her again.

The words lingered joyously between them as she responded to his kisses. It was strange–in a divinely ordained way–that the long wait now seemed like nothing. All her life she'd waited to hear a good man say *I love you*. It had happened in her dreams; she had filled up pages in diaries, wistfully imagining the soaring violins and roses that would accompany this moment. More than half a century had gone by without the fulfillment of what every girl always wanted. But now, on a Christmas Eve in Thailand, Miles Carington loved her . . . and had plainly said so.

"I love you too, sweetheart." She murmured the response, flushing with gratitude as she leaned up and kissed him again, the sweetness of the cupcake's frosting lingering and blessing the moment. She pulled free and looked him right in the eyes. "You make me very happy, you know."

"Likewise." He held her two hands in his own. "I came here from Australia, never figuring I would love again. After the messes back there." For a moment his deep eyes seemed to well up, and he smiled, unembarrassed by his own emotions. "But I walked into that faculty room one morning, and there you were."

"Amazing, huh?"

"It surely is." His strong arm around her, the couple simply rested in the goodness of the Lord and his artful designs.

EVEN ON CHRISTMAS DAY itself, it seemed only right to follow the pattern of the Christ child–to arrive in a faraway universe and cheerfully labor and create a better world. A friendly Thai man in his early twenties arrived from the plumbing store in Fang, and Sue supervised as two pristine white thrones were installed, one in each restroom. "I don't care what everyone else does around here," she muttered comically to Miles, who lent a practiced hand with putting down some new tile. "But at least I'm going to do my business in comfort and privacy."

He smirked, holding a screwdriver between his teeth as he expertly installed a toilet-roll holder on the side of the stall. "Shall we have a dedication ceremony here and serve some punch and cake?"

"Very amusing."

Huay, a refugee from a nearby Thai village, nodded enthusiastically as Sue outlined her new duties in keeping the restrooms spotless. "Each day you check to see there is paper," she explained, using pantomime to help illustrate the instructions. "And mop up the floor each morning and evening. So we don't get mud on this new tile." She held up the newly purchased mop, then pointed to two large floor mats now set outside both entrances. "With these, people should come in with clean feet. And every morning both water buckets must be filled. Okay?"

One of the main goals of the camp was to give refugees marketable skills, and the Thai government had allocated a pittance of money to be used as "salaries" for the smallish jobs that were available. The young girl beamed as Sue held up fingers to convey that she would receive thirty baht for each day of work.

Samud actually surprised the visitors with a pair of huge sheet cakes prepared by the kitchen ladies. *Happy Chrismas and love of Jesus Christ* read the bright red frosting, and all the refugees lined up, pushing and cheerfully devouring thin slices of the unexpected treat. Miles dug into his suitcase and pulled free a soccer jersey for Gino, who smiled and actually gave his dad a stiff embrace.

"And for you, Susie dear," Miles added, "is this." He pulled out a small, exquisitely wrapped package.

"No way." She blushed. "Sweetie, I didn't get anything for you."

"Doesn't matter," he said dismissively. "Just the glory of your presence is enough."

"I know, but . . ." She tore off the wrapping. Inside was a pink blouse made of exquisite sheer Thai silk. Tiny white orchids, laboriously embroidered, formed their own edenic garden throughout the luxurious fabric, and her eyes welled up. "It's the most beautiful thing I ever owned."

He grinned. "Well, don't wear it out here in all the mud, eh? But when we get back home to Bangkok, maybe you'll join me for a fancy supper out by that Sheraton pool and I'll show you off for the whole kingdom to watch."

To hear a man speak about her in terms of beauty was a rare and precious thing, and she eased over to him. "You're a prince."

The days of Christmas vacation slipped past in a seesaw of emotions: frustration and grit one moment, and breathtaking sunsets or an impish smile and a hug from an orphan child the next. A Christian organization from Maryland had funded ongoing adult classes in sewing, welding, and hair styling; Sue bounced from one to the next, looking for ways to help streamline the educational process so that refugees could obtain certificates and quickly find gainful employment in nearby cities.

"Whooh, I'm beat," she sighed Wednesday evening as the group dined on *khao dhom kai,* rice soup flavored with bits of chicken. "We've got fourteen men all trying to fix the carburetor of one car engine, and it took Paiboon two hours to let them all have at least a peek at it. Then about half of them don't know how to drive, and Khemkaeng took most of the afternoon and helped teach them out on that dirt road that goes toward the lake."

Miles shook his head, baffled. "So they can . . . what? Become taxi drivers?"

"Well, it pays a lot more than unemployment," she said. "Or chauffeurs. That's actually a decent living down in Bangkok, they tell me. If you can find a wealthy family or a diplomat to take you on. Course, then, it helps to manage a bit in English."

"Which we're doing too, eh?" He shot Rachel Marie an appreciative look.

She took a sip of her fruit punch before replying. "There's only so much you can do in a week. But bless their hearts, they're sure trying."

"That's some terrific computer stuff you put together, dearie," Miles complimented. "PowerPoint and all. And inserting the Thai underneath the English expressions–that's genius. Did Khemkaeng help with that part?"

"Uh huh. His computer has both languages, of course, and he just zips it out in about ten seconds."

"Sweet."

Samud walked over to their table carrying two supper plates, his wife following close behind. "Everyone is okay?"

"Yes, excellent. *Dee mahk.*" Miles slid over to make room. "Please join us."

The Thai director helped Boonmee get seated, then fished in his pocket. "This email has come for you," he told Miles. "Sorry."

Miles scanned the document, his brow furrowing as he read.

"Anything wrong?"

He leaned heavily on his elbows, rereading the note. "Typhus outbreak in part of Bangkok, I guess. Several thousand people down with it, and the hospitals are filling up fast." He glanced over at the group. "Wilson wants to know if I can cut the trip short and get home tomorrow. Says to fly if necessary; hospital will approve it."

"Oh, no!" Rachel Marie put a hand to her mouth.

"What if some of our students are infected? Or their families?"

Miles sat for a moment, weighing the situation. "Well, it'll probably hit mostly in the slum parts of the city. Which wouldn't be BCS kids, most likely. But where the diet's lousy and people don't have good water, that's where it lands. So we've got to get them into hospital beds and then pump them full of tetracycline."

Khemkaeng pushed his plate to the side. "If you wish, I can drive you back to Chiang Mai early in the morning so you can fly out immediately. I believe there is a daily flight at seven."

"Course, then we lose half that train ticket," Miles sighed.

"Yes. But if you took tomorrow night's train, you would lose the entire day tomorrow," the younger man pointed out. "And there is always a chance the train would come late to Bangkok. You could possibly not get to the hospital before noon on Friday."

"You're right." Miles shook his head, frustrated. "This is bad! We've planned this for months."

Sue slipped her hand into the crook of his arm. "Has the clinic here been very busy?"

"Not really," he admitted. "Couple of minor things. But most of these folks are in surprisingly good health. And Busaya has been a crackerjack of a nurse. Plus we have those three women from Italy. One of them's a physician's assistant; she knows her way around– anything except regular surgery." He glanced at his watch. "No chance for tonight, I assume. Flying out, I mean."

Khemkaeng shook his head. "By the time we could get to Chiang Mai, the last flight would have gone out.

But I could drive you there tonight, so that you didn't have to get up so early in the morning."

Miles shook his head. "No, that's okay." He reached out and gave Sue's hand a squeeze. "Let's at least enjoy this evening, eh?"

A knot of refugees from a Burmese village perched precariously on the border entertained the entire encampment with a concert of *angklung* tunes performed on finely tuned bamboo shakers. Most of the songs were a tedious mix of extremely Asian harmonies, but the concluding number was delivered in all good humor, and it took Sue half the song before she recognized it as "Surfin' U.S.A.," a 60s Beach Boys hit.

"How in the world did they figure that one out?" she grinned, enjoying the delightfully quirky juxtaposition of cultures. "Amazing!"

"Somebody way out here had a radio," Miles observed. "Cute, eh?"

Just as the concert was concluding, Miles motioned Khemkaeng and Rachel Marie to join them. "Listen, you guys. I need to make a decision about Gino."

Sue felt a spot of color appear in both cheeks. For most of the trip, the disdainful teen had simply absented himself from his duties. He would show up at mealtime, wordlessly bolt down a plate of food, then wander off to lounge underneath a tree with his music, or hike up the jagged peaks that stood to the north. Occasionally, Miles was able to bribe him with an insignificant chore, which he performed with a petulant scowl. But at least there had been no profane outbursts, she noted with relief.

"Meaning?"

"Well, on the one hand, I guess he should go home with me. Being his dad, and all. On the other hand, if this typhus explosion is as bad as it sounds–and I just checked on the Internet–I might be pulling an all-nighter or two."

Khemkaeng chose his words carefully. "You are wondering if he can remain here at the camp with us? And go home Saturday night as scheduled."

"Well, yeah." Miles had the good grace to blush. "I know he's not done a lick of work. And he runs around too much with that . . . whoever kid from Bangkok."

The last brought an awkward pause, and the adults looked at one another. One of the aid workers arriving Christmas Day from Bangkok was dragging around an accompanying Thai stepson named Leekpai. The youth spoke broken English, punctuated with current slang and a haughtily impatient air. The two rebels had quickly fallen in with each other, and spent long hours absent from the camp.

Sue, wanting to be diplomatic, was nonetheless a realist. "Look," she said evenly. "The fact is that without you, there'd be no one in charge. Who'd be responsible for him if anything went wrong?" She looked directly at Miles. "I mean, Gino barely does what you tell him. Any of the rest of us, if we crossed swords, he'd just tell us to go straight to the hot place and that'd be the end of it." Her face reddened, but she felt it was important to stand her ground.

"Yeah, but . . ." Rachel Marie's face was sober, but she fumbled with her words, trying to find an amicable solution. "Look, you guys. At least he's here where we're all serving. He heard your awesome little sermon the other day, Sue. We have a few songs at night and he picks up on them." She looked beseechingly at Khemkaeng. "Who knows? Maybe being here, he'll start comprehending the tiniest idea of what it means to serve the Lord and all."

Miles, looking miserable, said nothing. Khemkaeng weighed the situation. "I don't think he would do any harm. We would have to have him agree that if we truly needed something from him, he would do it." He gestured toward Sue and Rachel Marie. "Meaning, all three of us would share an authority. And unless he accepts this, he would have to go to Bangkok with you, Miles." He said the last without flinching.

"Does he even know you're returning to Bangkok?" Sue wanted to know.

Miles nodded. "Yeah. He didn't say anything, but probably figures he's heading out with me. And if you guys say so, I'll just leave it at that. But I thought I would at least get your opinion."

"Ask him." Khemkaeng, ever the practical one, spread out both hands, palm up in a gesture of reasonableness. "If he is willing to be a good mission partner, then we are happy to have him. If not, home is the best place for him."

The trio waited in the *sala* while Miles went out into the December gloom to track down his son. The search took more than twenty minutes, and Sue found herself doing a slow burn as she made small talk with Khemkaeng and Rachel Marie. "I don't want to be a wet blanket. But you guys can see the problem. Here it's almost ten o'clock at night and who knows where Gino is?"

Rachel Marie nodded, then forced a smile. "Come on, Sue," she said lightly. "You were sixteen once. Ten o'clock's nothing. Kids are just warming up by then."

Miles finally walked back into the dim light of the

unwalled building, his son in tow. "Sorry," he huffed, red-faced. "He was asleep and it took a bit to rouse him." He nudged Gino toward a seat. "If you're going to stay, then these folks all need to hear that it'll be all right. Eh?"

Gino, bleary-eyed, rarely spoke in anything but monosyllables, and this was no exception. "So . . . what?"

There was another pained moment of quiet, and Sue decided to speak her mind. "Well, look, Gino. We've got three more days here and a lot of pretty important things we want to get done. Your dad has to leave, but we'd be glad to have your help around here if you want to stay on."

Khemkaeng nodded his assent. "Since you are sixteen, it is important that you are willing to be with our group. And if we need something done, to know that you will help in a good way."

Oddly, the precise Thai way he expressed the situation seemed not to ruffle Gino's dignity. "I . . . well, yeah. I guess. I don't know much about stuff, but I'll try."

"That's not enough," Miles said quickly, his voice unusually firm. "Khemkaeng, here, is standing in my place. If he says you do something, you do it. No fuss, no pouting, no calling in sick, no F-words. The same for Rachel Marie here, and Sue too. Clear?"

Gino eyed the women with barely disguised hostility, then nodded. "Yeh."

Khemkaeng tried to smooth the moment over. "So this is good." He turned to Miles. "We must leave for Chiang Mai at three. I guess our bedtime has come."

FIFTEEN

The morning dawned under a thick, almost alien bank of rolling black clouds silently shouting the impending arrival of rain. Rachel Marie and Sue dined together, carefully spooning watery oatmeal into their mouths. "Tastes flat," Rachel Marie grumbled. "But at least they've got pineapple this time. Which saves almost anything."

"Did you hear anything when the guys left?"

"Huh uh. Khemkaeng probably set his watch to just vibrate or something. I got up to go to the bathroom around four, and they were already long gone." She managed a bit of a smile. "By the way, going to the potty is a whole new glorious adventure, Susie. All thanks to you." She popped a piece of the delicious tropical fruit into her mouth. "Is there a plaque somewhere? 'This john made possible by the generosity of Sue Baines'?"

"Very amusing." Sue peered around a crowd of young girls who had just trooped into the kitchen area. "Should we get Gino up?"

"Somebody better. Otherwise he'll miss breakfast and be down our throats for that."

"I'll do it." Sue grimaced as she pulled herself free. "You pray for me, you hear?"

Gino cast a baleful eye at her when she gently nudged the corner of his cot. "They're closing the cafeteria line in about ten minutes. I didn't want you to miss breakfast."

"What is it?" The words came out sharply, and she recoiled.

"Oatmeal and pineapple."

"Aaah. Don't want none."

"That's okay. But there won't be more until lunch."

He hesitated, then pushed the covers away and grunted himself into a sitting position. "What the hell. I guess I better . . ."

Sue was about to leave, then abruptly made up her mind. "Look," she told him, determined to keep her tone neutral. "You and I had a couple of run-ins. Okay. You can like me or not like me; that's your business. But I'm here to do God's work, and as far as I'm concerned, our little battles from before are over and done with. If you want to be friends, I'm ready to go."

He digested the offer, his face an impassive mask. "Well, yahoo for that."

Don't kill him. Just . . . She stood her ground, unwilling to step aside and let him pass. "You've already figured out that I think your father is a pretty awesome guy. I like him; he likes me. And I'm not about to let you drive me off. Get that through your head right now. But I'm just telling you–I can get along with you. So the ball's in your court. Your dad and I are having a great time; you're welcome to join us."

He still didn't say anything, apparently shell-shocked. After a moment's pause, she turned on her heel and headed out. "See you at breakfast," she tossed over her shoulder.

She rejoined Rachel Marie and clicked her iPhone calendar through her Thursday list. "So Khemkaeng and Samud are essentially out for the day."

"Yeah." Rachel Marie was still nursing the oatmeal, grimacing with each insipid bite. "I don't know the details, though."

"I guess there's a pretty decent-sized industrial factory just outside that town." Sue grinned, red-faced. "I thought it was *Fang*–like on a cobra–but then I heard one of the ladies yesterday afternoon. And they were saying 'fahng.' So people were probably laughing behind my back all afternoon. Especially that guy who sold us the toilets."

"Oh well." Rachel Marie snickered.

"Anyway, these people manufacture hard disk drives. Way out here in the sticks, and they've got a decent-sized contract with two major Taiwanese computer firms. Thailand's the second biggest maker in the world, right after China. Go figure. But I guess the owner says he can maybe take about eight people from here, start them working almost immediately. Only problem is, we've got, like, thirty in the camp who want to take a shot at it."

"So what happens then?"

"Well, we've got that old orange bus parked out by the front office. They'll go over there–drive takes about an hour. Tour the factory, and I guess they have some assembly line people work on. Everyone gets a try, and those that do the best are offered positions. Just like that."

"Huh."

Sue pecked out a note to herself. "Speaking of which, I need to have the kitchen put together something they can take along for lunch." She hesitated. "And I think I'll exert my authority and have Gino and his friend wash the bus. It's pretty much caked with mud top to bottom."

"Go for it."

Tucking her phone into a shirt pocket, she slipped over to where the dour teen was smearing peanut butter on two slices of bread to make a sandwich. "I've got a job you might actually enjoy."

The knife paused in mid-air. "What?"

She described the bus-scrubbing assignment. "It's really a mess and I don't want Samud having to drive it until we get it cleaned off. The windows are too gunked up to even see out of. I know it might rain, but even that wouldn't be enough for how much mud it's carrying around." She paused, looking around. "If your friend's anywhere about, you can ask him to help you. There's a faucet right next to the office building, and you'll find sponges and a big hose in the supply shed on the other side of the road there."

He grunted a response that she took to be in the affirmative, and eased away. Khemkaeng's green van was just pulling in and she hurried to greet him. "How'd the trip go?"

He nodded, stifling a yawn. "All right. We arrived at the airport by six, and they had room for Miles on the flight. I had some very quick breakfast with my father at the airport restaurant and then returned."

"Your parents are lovely people. How's your dad?"

"Thank you. Both are very good." A glance at his watch. "Only an hour until we take the group to Fang and the HDD factory. And first I must show all of them the training DVD provided by the factory."

"That's really a great deal," she enthused. "I hope our people land all eight positions."

"Yes, the manager has helped us before, is what Samud says. So we want to offer him the best people we have." He fished in his pocket and handed her a small slip of paper. "By the way, Miles asked me to give you this." His inscrutable Asian features gave way to a mischievous look. "It is probably a list of medical definitions."

She reached out with her foot and stepped down hard on his toes. "Mr. C, I warn you. Teasing an older woman is considered very bad form in your kingdom."

He laughed. "So true. I better check on Rachel Marie and her English class before we go to Fang."

She busied herself in the office, tapping out replies to several emails and juggling housing needs for three homeless families that had come across the border early that morning. A quarter before eleven, she turned off the computer and leisurely hiked across camp to stop in at the clinic. Fortunately, business was slow; Busaya was changing the dressing on a little girl's ulcerated leg, with Sophie, the physician's assistant, looking on. "You ladies are doing all right?"

"Yes, quite." The Italian woman nodded as she handed the nurse a metal clip for the Ace bandage. "And the new doctor will come to us when?"

"Not till next Tuesday," Sue said guardedly. "So we must pray that God only permits small problems to come to us! No heart surgeries."

With a cheerful wave, she was off. A few stray children scurried across the path, glancing guiltily at her, but most everyone was in a class. She headed toward the bus-loading area and noticed that already most of the hopeful refugees had climbed aboard. Samud was carrying over a large plastic tray filled with sandwiches from the kitchen.

"All set?" She hurried to assist him. "Here, let me take one side of that."

"Thank you, Miss Sue." He beamed gratefully. "This food is so heavy."

They got to the sagging orange vehicle, and she suddenly felt a sharp spike in her emotional temperature. Only the back of the bus had been washed clean, and streaks of mud, plainly visible, were still smearing up the rear windows. The sides and front of the bus remained untouched, and flecks of caked dirt made the windshield an impenetrable mess. The hose, still attached to the faucet, had been carelessly tossed to one side of the road, and the bucket of soapy water abandoned.

"Curse that child! I told Gino to wash this thing for you guys," she fumed. "And now I have no idea where he's gone off to."

Even Khemkaeng, normally unflappable, shook his head. "I hope our decision was not the wrong one," he sighed. "Here. At least we shall wash the front before going." He motioned to a pair of young men in their early thirties, jabbering in Thai. They nodded eagerly at his suggestion and seized the hose and sponge. In just a few minutes, the front of the bus was gleaming. The younger of the two refugees pointed at the right-hand side of the bus and queried Khemkaeng, who shook his head.

"We shall be back before the supper hour," he told Sue, glancing warily at the still threatening clouds. "Perhaps a bit later if there is rain. I think the road there is only dirt for part of the way, and it could be slow driving. But hopefully not."

"Okay." She climbed aboard for a moment and gave the excited group an encouraging wave. "*Kaw hai choke dee.* Good luck, you guys!"

"Senk you!" The chorus was a cheerful hubbub.

She stepped back down, bemused at the innate enthusiasm Thai citizens invariably displayed for the idea of *bhai teo*–an expedition to anywhere. There was a serene sweetness to their one-day-at-a-time ability to survive and take pleasure in small moments of hope.

She hiked back to the office, suddenly remembering the folded bit of paper in her pocket. Reddening slightly, she glanced around before opening it. "Hey, dearest. Got to CM safe and sound. Will catch a bit of a nap on the plane. I trust Gino will do as told. Feel free to kill the boy if you feel so led. It was good to have these days with you, love. You're a fine soldier in Christ's army– and right pretty as well. Love for always, Miles."

My first love letter. Her first impulse was to go find Rachel Marie and spend an hour giggling and analyzing every heart-tingling phrase. But they could gossip at lunch, she decided–and besides, English classes were still in session.

"Yikes. I miss him already, though," she murmured happily to herself. Even though he was probably already in Mission Hospital's emergency room, making triage decisions six hundred kilometers away, she felt a nice feminine closeness, a spiritual intimacy with the rawboned physician's beefy but tender touch.

It was quiet in the office with Samud away, and she indulged in a second reading of the hastily penned note. "Love for always, Miles." How much more precious were the three words when appended to that name–Miles. The promise was from her beloved Miles. Love for always from this caring and generous man. Miles. Sue and Miles. Love for . . .

"Missie Baines?"

She jerked to attention. The small portable printer was humming out a report, but a Thai boy wearing a Coors Lite T-shirt was standing before her, wringing his hands in anxious suspense.

"Oh, hi. Sorry, I remember your name starts with L is all. Gino's friend, right?"

At least for the moment, the insolence was gone. "My name Leekpai. I know Gino little bit, yes."

She wanted to snap out an accusing complaint about the abandoned bus-washing task, but bit her tongue. "What can I do for you, Leekpai?"

"Please, ma'am. Is Gino. He fall down." The boy hesitated. "I think he is hurt so much."

The words snapped her to reality. "Where is he?"

Leekpai pointed toward the eastern perimeter of the refugee camp. "We go to climb mountain. Only little ways. And then think we come back to wash bus again. But we come onto high rock and is fun to climb. Except then Gino, he fall off rock. Very far of fall. And I think so, his arm is very bad now."

Her resentful words abruptly shoved back into a corner of her mind, she seized him by the arm. "Hurry! You show me where."

"Yes, okay." He broke into a near trot and she

struggled to keep up. Classes were just beginning to dismiss for the noon hour, and the pair had to dodge twos and threes ambling lazily toward the lunch area and the billowing pots of rice.

"How far away is he?"

"Not so far, ma'am." He pointed. "This road is how we go."

They moved at a rapid clip up the same path she and Miles had hiked on just a few short days ago. Partway up, the trail split in two, and he took the higher path. "I think so close now."

The trail was cut out into a side of a fairly steep hill with jagged rocks on the right and a tangle of thick bramble bushes growing wild on the lower side. Around a sharp bend there was a towering pile of boulders looming as an almost perpendicular cliff. Gino was huddled at the base of the incline, now pulled into a sitting position. His right arm dangled uselessly from his shoulder, and there were several bleeding cuts on his cheek and forehead.

"Oh, no." She moved quickly to his side. "What happened?"

He was almost in tears, his lips cracked, as he tried to respond. "We were up top, eh? Just looking about. And then I guess I lost my balance and all. Fell all the way down. I tried to stop myself, but went over and over. Hit my arm real bad on that rock right there." He pointed to a scarred boulder jutting out about seven feet above them.

"Does it hurt pretty bad?" It seemed like an obvious thing, but she didn't know how else to ask.

"Yeh. Don't know if it's broken, but it feels really bad. Plus . . ." He gestured to his face with his good hand, then at his badly bloodied shirt. "Bleeding and all. Tried to stop some of it with my sleeve."

Sue hesitated. Miles was clear down in Bangkok. The clinic was basically unstaffed, with just a nurse and physician's assistant on duty. "If Leekpai and I help, can you walk back to camp?"

"I reckon."

They helped him to his feet, carefully supporting the crushed arm. Despite her gingerly care, the first steps were excruciating, and he moaned out loud, tears springing to his eyes. "Easy," she said. "If you can't make it, we'll send Leekpai to bring someone here for you."

"No, I think I can."

Each step an arduous trek, the trio eased down the mountain trail. Gino, his face a pasty mask, fought back tears, whispering soft obscenities to himself as he thudded unevenly toward the tents.

As they approached civilization, Sue pointed. "Leek-pai, you run and tell Busaya we're coming. We'll need something for the pain immediately, and then antiseptic for where Gino cut his face. Okay?"

"Yes." Relieved, the boy broke into a fast trot and disappeared around the bend.

"Just a bit more," Sue murmured, her former hostility buried for the moment. "I know you're hurting real bad."

"Yeh."

Busaya pointed to a gurney, inviting and cool with the shade of the overhead tarp. "Lie down on this. We have injection for pain first, then we look."

The sedative did its work, and the boy was soon breathing more easily. Busaya and the trio of assistants from Italy gathered around, and Sophie very gently traced a finger along the rapidly swelling tissue. "It is definitely a fracture," she announced, sighing. "Bad luck. You can feel bone fragments right along this line. Almost puncturing skin but not quite."

"And . . ." Sue looked from one to the other.

"Definitely he must go to hospital."

Busaya, whose command of English was limited, quickly nodded assent. "Yes, it will be best to go." She searched for the proper word. "Doctor of *orthopedic* matters must give assist."

Sue's mind whirred with the possibilities. Would the town of Fang have proper medical facilities? Her Internet search had included a brief photo gallery of a thriving main street and local commerce. Would it be possible to find a decently managed ER? On the other hand, she recalled that there was a fairly large and modern hospital on this side of Chiang Mai. The group had commented on it while motoring north to begin this trip.

"I'm thinking we should take him to Chiang Mai," she told the others, making a quick decision. "For sure he could get proper care."

"Chiang Mai has *roang payaban,* very good one," Busara assented. "But quite long to drive."

"I know, but at least it's a sure thing. And paved highway the whole way." Sue turned her attention to the prostrate teen. "Gino, how are you feeling? Did the shot kick in yet?"

"A bit better," he managed.

"You rest right here. I'm going to go find Mrs. C and make some plans. I'll be back in just a couple minutes."

"Okay."

The first drops of rain were beginning to fall as she went at a half-trot toward the open-air cafeteria. Rachel Marie was critiquing a young man's schoolwork, pointing to his sheet of paper, and Sue made an apologetic gesture. "Sorry to interrupt."

"That's okay." Rachel Marie handed the Thai student's homework back. "You did very well! *Dee mahk!*"

"We got a bad problem," Sue blurted out without preamble. "Gino had a pretty nasty fall and broke his arm, we think."

"Oh no!" Rachel Marie's hands flew to her face. "For sure?"

"Yeah. Well, he slipped and fell from about twenty feet up. It could have been worse, actually."

"So what can we do?"

"I think Chiang Mai's our best bet. We've got to get him to where there's something pretty full service, and that's all I can think of." She hesitated. "I guess we could try to get Samud on the phone and find something closer, but my inclination is to get on the road ASAP."

"Oh, sure." Rachel Marie thought for a moment. "Hang on. Good thing Khemkaeng gave me back the keys to the van; otherwise, we'd really be in the soup." She tugged on Sue's sleeve. "Come on. My bag's in the classroom right there."

"I'm trying to think of how to go."

"Well, that main highway's just right past the gas station. I think you head straight south and should be all right."

"Wasn't that big hospital we saw on the east side of the highway? With the green cross?"

"Uh huh. So from this direction, you'd see it on the left."

"That's what I figured."

Rachel Marie fished in her purse and pulled the ignition key out. "Should I come with you guys? Or do you want me to drive and you stay here?"

Sue's mind was a convoluted whirlpool of options. She was in a foreign land with a damaged and dysfunctional kid who despised her. Miles was down in Bangkok. Khemkaeng and Samud were hours away. The nearest culture and any semblance of medical structure were in Chiang Mai.

"I'd love for you to come too, but maybe you'd better stay here," Sue said slowly. "I know we're all just fellow volunteers, but until the guys get back from the computer factory, you'd kind of be it here at camp."

"Tell you what," Rachel Marie said, suddenly inspired. "You run to the cabin and grab what you need. I'll try to get Khemkaeng on the phone and see what he advises."

"Good enough."

She noted thankfully that the rain, though threatening, was being held at bay, but with the gray clouds sliding ominously toward them from the Myanmar border. Tucking the van keys into her pocket, she broke into a trot and arrived all out of breath at the bunkhouse. Even in the few days at camp, the Spartan dorm had become a kind of sweet mission haven–especially with Miles' ebullient good cheer warming the place. Now it was just a bare repository for people's belongings, and she hesitated, standing over her own suitcase. Would they definitely be back by nightfall? What if there were complications? What if Gino required surgery and an overnight stay?

She made an abrupt decision and simply scooped all her things into the duffel bag and closed it. Better to be safe and prepared, and she hastily dumped Gino's scattered clothes and a soggy towel into his backpack. Perching both bags on the front doorstep, she went to the bare dirt lot where Khemkaeng had parked the rental van earlier that morning. "Lord, I'm going to need a triple blessing and battalion of angels," she murmured aloud as she climbed into the right-hand driver's seat. She had no valid license; this was a wrong-side steering wheel designed for a wrong-side highway system in a scarily foreign world.

At least it's not a stick shift. She started the engine and breathed one more prayer as she adjusted the mirrors. The van gave an initial lurch as if to sternly inquire about the authority of the alien driver, but she bumped cautiously back to the hostelry. Grunting as she hoisted the two bags into the rear luggage compartment, she bounced around the perimeter of the encampment and pulled up close to the clinic's dusty entrance.

"How's he doing?"

Busara was sponging Gino's forehead. "Most cuts are not so bad. This one is maybe good to have two stitches put in. But butterfly bandage is okay until Chiang Mai."

"Excellent." Sue gave the Thai nurse an affirming hug. "You did so well. I thank God for your good work and all the help you give here at the camp."

"Yes, okay."

Sophie helped as they got Gino to his feet. "Here is more medication," the physician's assistant offered, handing Sue a packet of pills and a small bottle of drinking water. "If the injection wears off."

Rachel Marie was breathless as she came in. "Are you ready?"

"Yeah." Sue's pulse skipped at the intimidating situation facing her. "Did you get Khemkaeng?"

"Yeah. He says to go right now. Chiang Mai. They weren't sure what Fang had, and the road had a half-hour detour anyway. So they're running substantially late. Just get the van up to one-ten and keep the pedal on the metal, he says."

Despite the gruesome situation, Sue managed a tight smile. "And he said it exactly like that?"

"Well, I might have paraphrased just the tiniest bit." Rachel Marie assisted as they helped Gino into the passenger side of the van and tucked a pair of pillows in between the two front seats. "That should help hold things in place."

"You guys are the best." Sue exchanged quick hugs with everyone, then hopped into the driver's seat. "Say a prayer."

"Promise."

There was a moment of panic when she got to the main highway. Temporarily disoriented, she had to peer back at the camp and remember that north was off to the right, facing the border hills of Myanmar. *So Chiang Mai is here to the left.* Just as she sorted out the navigational threads, she spotted a green sign boldly pointing left and announcing "Chiang Mai" in both Thai and English. "Brilliant, Baines," she muttered.

Remembering to nose the van over to the left side of the highway, it gave her a slightly disoriented feeling to be steering the vehicle from the "wrong" side. Thankfully, the two-lane concrete was fairly empty, and soon the van was hurtling southward with the odometer needle edging its way toward 110 kilometers per hour.

"Are you doing all right?" Despite her stiff dislike for Gino, his fragility at this moment–combined with her impulses of Christian compassion–brought out her solicitous side. "If you need anything at all, just tell me. Okay?"

"Yeh." His eyes were half closed, and he shifted in his seat, grimacing sharply with the tiniest move.

There was a slow-moving *songthaew* taxi puttering contentedly along in front of her; peering anxiously around the vehicle, she measured the distance from an oncoming truck and managed a successful pass. There was a spattering of light rain that lasted just a few minutes, ebbing into a mottled bit of sunlight that pierced the clouds and brightened up the watery brown patches of rice paddies. Gino dozed fitfully, an occasional bump jarring him to semi-consciousness.

Every few kilometers, modern-appearing petrol stations appeared on either side of the highway, with an extended bank of pumps and convenience stores. But they were clicking along at a high rate of speed, and she was loath to stop. She glanced down at the gas gauge, and was relieved to see that there was still more than half a tank. "Khemkaeng must have filled up in Chiang Mai," she muttered to herself, grateful for his efficient thoughtful-ness.

There was a sudden high-pitched cry; startled, she almost ran the van onto the metallic dots separating the two lanes. "What?"

Gino leaned forward in his seat, his slight frame tugging at the seat belt. "Stop the car, eh?"

"What is it?"

"I got to puke! That's what!"

She slammed on the brakes, the van bucking and coming to a shuddering halt. "What can . . ."

"Just leave me be!" Clumsily fumbling with his seatbelt, his right arm dangling uselessly, he bellowed an obscenity. The door finally sprang open, and he tugged himself free, the two pillows tumbling into the dirt next to the roadway. Barely leaning over, he heaved his guts out in an astonishing stream of vomit.

Stunned, Sue switched off the motor and scurried around the back of the van. Still heaving, Gino leaned over, pausing, then retching as another dose of breakfast came out. *$#*! $#*!* Half-sobbing and punctuating the air with his oaths, he held his stomach with his left arm, tears and additional remnants of his last meal dribbling into the scrawny bits of grass lining the road.

"Better?" She eased closer and impulsively put an arm around his shoulder. "I'm so sorry."

"Oh my God." His face streaming with perspiration, he tried to straighten up. "I feel so messed up . . ." The same harsh word popped loose again and he leaned his head against the side of the van. "Sorry."

"It's all right." As if comforting a small child, she rubbed small circles in his back. "Just one of those days, isn't it?"

"Yeh." Something seemed to collapse in the boy, and he burst into tears, burying his face in the crook of his good elbow. "Everything's such a *$#*!* mess!"

Sue remained by his side for several minutes, simply holding him, murmuring what comfort she could think of. "I know you feel awful. And you miss your dad. But let me get you to the hospital and things'll be better."

At last he nodded. "Okay."

She picked up the pillows and carefully brushed away the dirt. "Here. Let me help you back in." Traffic was whizzing past on both sides, but she tried to block out everything except the needs of this fragile, broken lamb.

"Better?" She began to hand him the small packet of pills, then stopped. "No, let me open it for you." She took his left hand and gently tapped on the envelope until two tablets popped free. "Here you go, sweetie." The maternal endearment popped out without either of them noticing. She dug in her purse for the bottle of water and undid the lid. "Let me hold it for you." He took a swallow and the pills eased their way into his bloodstream.

"All right then." She started the engine and waited for an opening in the traffic. "Keep your eyes open for that hospital, okay? It should be on your side."

A tense thirty minutes later, the welcome green neon cross came into view. "Thank you, Lord," she whispered aloud, slowing down and flipping on the van's turn signal. Then to Gino: "I just want you to know: whatever they need to do to help you, I'll be right here."

He peered at her, his eyes bloodshot from the tears, and with the horrid ache of the day's events still imprinted on his face. "Thanks," he whispered, his voice clotted in near surrender.

"There we are." A bilingual sign pointed to a small road curving around to the right. "Emergency Room."

"Stay right here." She parked the van and got out. "I'll get a wheelchair."

"I can walk," he protested.

"Are you sure?"

"I think so."

He climbed free, carefully protecting the injured limb. He was about to straighten up, then suddenly paused. "I got to tell you something," he said all at once, his voice hoarse.

"What?"

"I . . ." His look was one of juvenile confusion, that of a child whose playing board was askew, with kings and bishops and rooks scattered on all sides, white and black players switching loyalties. Sue felt her own scattered, tumbling emotions bumping into one another, as this prickly adversary now cowered helplessly before her, so needy and supplicating. "I fell off that hill . . . 'cause me and Leekpai . . ."

She waited, curious and sympathetic.

"I mean, he brought a big stash of weed up from Bangkok. So we were both kind of high. And . . . I guess that's why I fell."

SIXTEEN

The visitors' area was bright and decently comfortable with a row of blue plastic chairs and newspapers from both Bangkok and Chiang Mai. Sue picked aimlessly through a German-language magazine, trying to glean bits of recent international news from the photos and occasionally recognizable names. High on the wall, a TV monitor broadcast a slow stream of Thai sitcoms; intermittent bursts of subdued laughter punctuated the interminable afternoon of waiting.

She tried to thumb in a few halfhearted solutions on her growing file of unaccomplished camp priorities, but her mind was on the dilemma before her. Gino was a tragic train wreck of a boy; his fractured right arm was one more assault on an obviously ravaged physical frame. His violent vomiting by the side of the road seemed to indicate internal despair of a lasting nature, and her mind bounced from one possible cause to the next. Had he maybe gotten a whiff of the typhus bug before boarding the train in Bangkok?

Ever since the sullen tempest by the pool in August she had harbored an unkind disdain for Gino. And his continuing insolence still raised her hackles–but now at least mingled with a discordant pity. The scars in him ran deep and lasting, his deviant behavior patterns perhaps bathed by a steady stream of physical pain. Here in this Chiang Mai medical building, she felt honest doubts about whether someone like him could possibly be reclaimed and made whole.

She walked over to the far side of the waiting area, peering out into the approaching twilight and the nondescript cars and vans in the parking lot, wondering idly about the wrenching stories and decisions represented by each mud-spattered vehicle. Loved ones who stood on the sidelines at a hospital often faced life-changing choices, and she felt a stab of anxiety about her relationship with Miles. She loved him–of that she was now sure. But was he facing his own marathon of all-nighters just dealing with Gino? Perhaps the repairing of his own broken-down family was so all-consuming a task she ought to step aside. The thought tore at her and she felt a sad tightening in her throat.

A short woman appeared at the door with a clipboard. "Susan *Bay-ness*?"

It took Sue a moment to realize the page was for her. "Er, I think that's me."

"Please come."

She followed the Thai clerk to a small examining room in the back of the emergency room. Gino's face had more color, and his right arm was snugly trussed up in a cast that ran from his wrist almost up to his shoulder. "How're you feeling?"

"Okay."

The doctor was finishing the last scribblings in his chart. "You are Gino's relative?"

"Uh, no. I'm a friend of his father's. Dr. Carington. He was with us at the refugee camp but had to fly down to Bangkok this morning to help with the typhus outbreak."

"Oh, yes." The physician offered a handshake. "I am Dr. Weerasethakul." A nice smile. "You have come to know many Thai people with long last names, I am sure."

She nodded, instinctively liking him. "Oh, yes. At the Christian school where I work, I spend half my day typing students' long names into our computers. And my best friend just married a man whose last name is Chairusivirat."

He gave what passed for an apologetic shrug. "Well, we have done x-rays and the arm is broken in two places. He will be in this cast for one month, possibly six weeks."

"But other than that, he'll be okay?" She glanced over at Gino, who was looking down at his feet, downcast.

"Yes, okay. And of course, in Bangkok his father can oversee the process of healing, etc."

Sue eased closer to Gino and put an awkward arm around his shoulders. "I know the pain was pretty bad coming down. How will that be for the next few days?"

"Probably quite severe for forty-eight hours." Then to the teen: "But I can prescribe pills that will make you comfortable, Gino."

"What's your advice about travel?" she asked.

"What are your plans?"

"Well, we were going to be at the camp for two more days, then go back to Bangkok on the Saturday night train."

"It is your choice," he said slowly. "The train journey is quite difficult, I think. Not so comfortable. But this is your decision, surely."

"Well, we'll see how things go." She flashed him a grateful smile and remembered to offer a *wai*. He set down his clipboard and reciprocated, patting Gino on the shoulder. "I wish you a safe journey home and a good conclusion to your Christmas time also."

"Thank you."

It took several minutes to navigate their way to the accounting office and Sue struggled to complete the necessary paperwork, vainly coping with the Thai/English forms and Gino's monosyllabic responses about the family history. The clerk accepted her credit card and she glumly considered the upcoming insurance intricacies. "Come on, let's go find the pharmacy," she said, trying to be upbeat. "For the next couple days, these pills are going to be your best friend." She hesitated. "Did the doctor say anything about your getting sick in the van?"

"Huh uh."

Nighttime had stolen over Chiang Mai by the time they got out to the parking lot. She helped him into the passenger side, and then paused before fastening her own safety belt. "Look. You've been through a nasty day and I'm really sorry. But if you're up to it, we should talk about what to do. I imagine your dad's up to his ears in patients, but we can try and call him. Or . . . let's just talk it out. Do you want to simply go home?"

He stared straight ahead through the dust-streaked

windshield at the shrubs and trees ringing the hospital. "Yeh," he muttered. "I reckon."

"Okay, then." She glanced at her watch. "I wasn't figuring we'd want to drive back to the camp in the dark anyway. So what are our choices?" She thought hard. "The train's probably not an option, because it's too late for tonight's anyway. Plus I think that would be a really uncomfortable trip. Do you think if I got you to the airport that you could fly back to Bangkok by yourself? If your dad picked you up? It's just an hour flight."

He weighed the challenge, then nodded. "I guess."

"Right now? Or in the morning?"

A shrug. "Dunno."

"Let me think." Getting out her iPhone, she got online and typed in a couple of search questions. "Come on . . . come on . . ." She peered into the screen, trying to decipher the options. "There's one more flight tonight," she concluded. "But I don't think we could make it. By the time we found the airport and all."

Gino was in a near-catatonic state. "Then what?"

"Just a minute." She keyed in "December 30" and peered at the web site. "Tomorrow at seven a.m.–I guess that's the same flight your dad took. Or nine-thirty. How's that sound?"

"I . . . uh, sure."

She tried to *will* a feeling of positive support. "So all we have to do is to find Chiang Mai, then a place to stay, then something to eat, and then the airport . . . and that's it." A quick laugh. "How about if I drive and you handle the navigation?"

Her attempt at humor was lost on him. "I stink at stuff like that."

"I was just kidding." She turned the key and

carefully backed out toward the highway. "We'll find something."

Traffic was thicker now as they came to the sprawling suburbs of the northern city. It was an appealing place, with neatly ordered streets and a thriving night market. Sue drove carefully, still apprehensive about the reversed polarity of all her motoring instincts. A high-rise building loomed on the left and she peered through the darkness to read the sign. "That looks okay," she murmured. "Let's go see."

A young Thai girl wearing the requisite business suit of a hotel clerk accepted her credit card and typed names into a data bank, her elegant nails making a rhythmic clicking pattern on the keyboard. Sue pulled Gino to the side. "Do you want to have your own room? I know kids want their privacy, but you might have a hard time managing with your bad arm. Whatever you want is okay." She tried not to picture Miles' face when all the day's invoices landed in his IN box.

"Is it expensive?"

Sue shook her head. "Don't worry about that. Your dad's good for it."

His eyes dull, he gave his characteristic shrug. "Don't care." A moment later he shook his head. "I still feel pretty messed up."

"Okay." She went back to the clerk. "We need one room, but big. So I can take care of him."

"Yes, ma'am." The young girl picked up the phone and murmured a question in Thai, then nodded to Sue. "We have very fine room on Floor Nine. Two big beds and view is so nice of Ping River."

Sue accepted the room key and fished in her purse for cash to tip the bellboy. "Let's go, Mr. Carington.

We'll find a way you can enjoy a hot shower without getting that pretty cast all wet."

The room was spacious, with two queen beds and a large picture window overlooking the main part of Chiang Mai. "I think you should just soak in the shower for a while," she offered. "That would feel really good, I bet. And maybe we can order some room service."

She fished in the small cupboard and found a plastic laundry bag. "Here," she suggested. "I'll help you peel off your shirt and then we'll fasten this around your arm. Will that work?"

With the hot water running in the next room, she sank into one of the two easy chairs facing the nighttime beauty far below them and wearily dialed Miles' number. His voice mail came on, and she left a detailed account of the day. "We'll aim for the nine-thirty flight, so if you can sneak out to the airport to pick him up, that'd be great. I'll call in the morning just to confirm." She hesitated, then added: "I love you, doc. We'll get through all this fun stuff."

Khemkaeng gave a good report of the job-seeking expedition to the computer factory, then cheerfully affirmed her decision to send Gino on his way in the morning. "Sure, that will be best. The train is too long of a trip, and he needs to be home now."

"I'm kind of worried about how sick he seems to be," she told him. "I mean, the way he was heaving up his guts this morning was a world record."

"Did the injection Busara gave him possibly cause a bad reaction?"

"I guess." She remembered Miles' observation about his son's spasmodic health. "Hopefully that was all."

"Good luck," Khemkaeng offered. "Gino is probably your last choice for a roommate, but at least you will have a clean bed and a very nice shower."

"Speaking of which, I think it's about my turn in there." She heard the dwindling water flow from the bathroom. "I'll be back sometime around noon tomorrow."

"Drive carefully."

Two plates containing sandwiches and French fries arrived, and Gino, his wet hair slicked back, ate gingerly, holding the food in his left hand.

"Getting enough?"

"Yeh."

The meal concluded, she piled up the empty plates and set them out in the hallway. Returning, she sat back down and faced him. "Do you mind if I ask you something?" A forced smile. "Since we're roommates and all that?"

His look was expressionless. Picking up a leftover napkin, he dabbed at his nose.

"First of all, how are you feeling? How's the pain?"

He examined his bruised arm as if to read the answer off a meter. "Right now it's not so bad. I mean, when I move it kind of hurts."

"We'll fish out a couple more of those pills before you go to sleep."

"Okay." He was silent for a moment, then added: "Thanks for helping today. I know I messed up and all that. Not washing the bus. Sorry."

She waved dismissively. "That's past. But I do want to ask you something else if you'll let me."

He waited.

Sue leaned forward in her chair, both hands on her

knees, and then blurted it out. "Gino, why are you so unhappy? I mean, why live this way–angry all the time?"

Gino seemed nonplussed by the question. "Who says I'm angry all the time?"

"Oh, come on." She shook her head. "I met you that night by the pool. I didn't know you; you didn't know me. And you just about tore my head off." She held up a hand as if to ward off his objections. "I mean, that's way over and done with. You asked me to forgive you and I said sure. But I still want to know: *why?* I hate to see anybody unhappy, and you're the son of the man I'm starting to love."

His dark eyes were brooding and he appeared to be constructing an emotional fortress to keep out her questions. But she bore in, without speaking, and at last he gave a little nod. "I just . . . it's all 'cause of how things were when I was a kid. My dad and mum had a lot of fights. I figured he could fix it, and he never did. For a long time, I really missed my mum a lot. I'd cry in bed and couldn't sleep. But Dad said, 'No, it's over; she won't have us back and all.' Said he was sorry, but what the hell good did that do?"

"Do you love your dad?" She asked it softly, but the query still jolted the boy.

"I dunno. Sure, I guess. He's my dad and all."

"And wasn't this years ago? When you were, like, eight?"

"Yeh."

She pulled her chair a bit closer and peered into his face. "And your dad's a Christian, but not you. How come?"

"'Cause it seems like it's all bull. You know?" It took an effort for him to trim the offensive language from his explanation, and she noticed, giving him a grateful smile.

"Do you think the things your dad believes are true? About God and Jesus and heaven and all that?"

"I don't know." He carefully moved his encased arm, a wince crossing his face. "How would I know that? I mean, you don't know for sure either. It's all a bunch of theories is all."

"Okay." She nodded, accepting that. "But do you mind if I tell you something?"

He snorted. "You're going to anyway, so I may as well let you dish it out."

"No, I won't. If you say 'shut up,' I'll shut up. I'll go soak in the shower and you can watch TV and that'll be the end of it."

He jutted out his chin, chewing on his lower lip, then suddenly shook his head. "No, let me hear it. I guess I owe you one good listen after all your driving me down here and everything."

Sue smiled, feeling a flickering pulse of affection for this lost boy. "Let me try two ideas on for you. First is this. Your dad's an amazing Christian, and he's happy. Everything you went through, he went through too. But having Jesus in his life makes him happy. You don't have Jesus in your life . . . and you're not happy. So there's that. I know there are Christians in this world who aren't happy, and maybe there are atheists who walk around town ecstatic all day every day. But for the most part, having Jesus does seem to bring joy and peace and a feeling of hopefulness. Which you don't have–and it'd be great if you did."

The observation hung in the air between them. Finally he gave a noncommittal shrug as if to accede to the scored point. "Maybe."

Sue breathed an inward prayer before continuing. In her mind's eye, she pictured a lost child, an eight-year-old waif watching by the window as the car of his mother's new lover disappeared down the street, its glowing taillights spelling the end of a cupcake adventure and the grim heartache of many lost tomorrows. The tears on the pillow, the birthdays with nothing for him but an empty mailbox. An eighth grade graduation announcement coming back from the post office, defiantly untouched. The high tower of accumulated sorrows had defeated this child who didn't know how to find or operate a bulldozer in order to dig his way clear.

"I was talking to a preacher one day," she told him. "He worked at a church where there were so many people like you. Parents who split up. They'd lost their jobs. Had painful pasts. Some had gone through years of alcoholism; stuff like that. I mean, this guy told me two hours' worth of really sad stories."

"And did they all just come to Jesus and live happily ever after?" he asked scornfully.

"Huh uh," she admitted. "Well, I'm sure some did. But here's what he said to them. Always the same thing. He would tell them, 'It's my number one job as a Christian pastor to help you give up . . . I mean, *give up* . . . on the idea that you can somehow have a better *past*.'"

He rested his chin on his knees, brooding. "I don't get it. What's that mean?"

She reached out and took his good hand in her own. "It means that nobody can go back and change what happened eight years ago. Your dad's not a time traveler.

He can't spin things back eight years and somehow make his marriage to your mom spring to life again. All that stuff happened. It was sad and it was wrong and your dad and mom messed up. You've messed up, I've messed up, and your own father's not such a superman that he didn't mess up too. He loves you with all his heart; if he could take you by the hand and go through a time tunnel and start that marriage all over again, I'm sure he'd do it. And I'd be the first to give him a goodbye hug and say, 'Miles, go. I'll stay here and pray for you.'" She drew a breath and could feel moisture in her eyes. "But life doesn't work that way. We don't get do-overs of the past. All we get is the amazing reality that Jesus comes in and gives us a new future instead. He forgives our past, and then says: 'Let me heal you. Let me bring new joy into your life. Let me comfort you for the things that scarred you from before and then stand by your side as your new life starts up right now.'"

It was a jumbled, nakedly honest speech and she simply let the ideas pour out, bubbling and confused and earnestly optimistic. "I've spent years going through one lonely experience after another," she told him. "But Jesus was always there, making up for my tears and giving me joy as a counterweight to the hard times. Always. And then I came here to Bangkok and found this incredible guy. Whose son could be just as incredible–and happy–if he ever decided to start things all over again."

Gino was quiet, his stare at the pattern in the hotel room carpeting giving away nothing. At last she pulled herself away from the fragile détente. "Well, that's Pastor Sue's sermon for the night," she said lightly. "I'm going to go in there and take the longest shower I've had in the last five years. Why don't you watch a little TV and, if you feel like it, call up room service again and order us up two of those ice creamy things on the menu?"

THEIR LAST DAY IN CAMP, Samud surprised the American visitors with a splashy outing to a waterfall twenty kilometers to the west, tucked right up next to the Myanmar border. Tumbling its way down two levels of rolling rock formations, the clear water created a delightful mist, and refugee children splashed delightedly in the small pool down at the base. Her pant legs rolled above her knees, Sue hiked carefully up to the halfway point and perched herself on a mossy log overlooking the idyllic scene.

Rachel Marie, slightly sunburned from the afternoon activities all week long, handed her a plastic bag filled with pistachios, and the two women traded samples as they gossiped. "So you survived your night in enemy-occupied territory," she teased.

"I guess." Sue was still feeling conflicted about Gino and being drafted as his adult comforter. "What else could I do?"

Three little girls raced past them, shrieking in joy as one tried to douse her peers with a small tin cup spilling over with water. The innocent scene provided a stark contrast with the jagged childhood moments she imagined had been Gino's early lot in life, and she flushed with a new resolve to be charitable.

"This is the hard thing," she blurted out, setting down the homegrown delicacy and facing her friend. "If I really try, I actually have Christian impulses toward that kid. He's a lost soul; he needs salvation. He's trying to navigate life without Jesus, and just making a royal mess of it all."

"Yeah."

"But it feels to me right now like all those lofty resolutions are a figment of my imagination. That kid needs a home in heaven–but that doesn't feel real. Christ paid his penalty on the cross, and right now that idea feels kind of vapory as well."

"How come?"

"I don't know. I'm torn between spiritual duty and my own carnal resentment. Because in contrast to all my 'God duties,' when I look in my own heart, I really and truly do despise that kid. I mean, really bad. He's just plain a jerk." Sue sighed heavily and chomped down angrily on another nut. "He was just the tiniest bit not terrible the night of the accident. I'd helped him out all day, he was full of meds, and I guess that melted his nasty heart a bit. So I went to sleep thinking, 'This isn't so awful.' But by the next morning he was as snotty as ever. Complained all through breakfast how all of life was so stinking unfair. 'Poor, poor me.' Dropped a couple of F bombs on me as I took him to the airport. I got him a plane ticket, put it all on my credit card–and sure, I'm going to get a refund from his dad. But still, I went seriously out of my way to kind of fluff up his pillows and make nice to him. And when it was time to board the plane, he just marched off, dragging his backpack in his good arm, and didn't even look back."

Rachel Marie reached out and gave her a sympathetic hug. "Yikes. So the garbage of planet earth is more tangible than the golden streets and river of life?"

"At least at the moment, it sure is." Sue felt a flush

of concern creep into her cheeks. "And I don't like that about myself. My kingdom impulses should be the strongest ones. In my heart, I know that Calvary's real and that I've got to love this redeemable enemy. But I look in the mirror and have to admit I've got a visceral hatred for that clunky kid."

"Do you think you and Miles can still make a go of it?" Rachel Marie laughed uneasily. "'Cause it sure looked like the fires of love were burning bright all week long."

"I don't know. Honestly, I don't." Choosing her words carefully, she described her state of mind while waiting at the Chiang Mai hospital. "With all the parenting issues Miles has got on his plate, maybe I need to step back and recuse myself. You know? Just let him focus on saving his son."

"Huh." Rachel Marie struggled to climb off the log and waded carefully until she was up to her ankles. "That's some serious baggage, Missie Baines."

"Tell me about it."

IT WAS A QUIET train ride back to the capital city later that night. Khemkaeng and his bride were gracious and thoughtful traveling companions, and although she missed Miles with an ache that frightened her, the quiet tapestry of conversation was a satisfying conclusion to the mission adventure.

"I feel sure that John will want you to stay for the rest of our school term," Khemkaeng told her as they finished off a late supper of mango and fried rice. "He feels better, he says, but even on the phone he sounds very weak still. It will be a long time before he can work as he did before."

"I'm afraid you're right."

He handed her an open tin with some sugar-coated fruit drops. "From my parents' factory. You will like them."

"Fair warning," Rachel Marie laughed. "Once you start with these, you're not going to want to stop any time soon."

Sue grinned. "That was kind of a meager menu up at camp. I probably lost five pounds, and this candy will get half of it back right now."

She lay awake for a good hour, enfolded within the security of her private lower berth as the darkened landscape of a slumbering kingdom glided by in the sacred silence. Mission work was a dizzying, sometimes roller coaster ride of highs and lurching lows, opulent comfort interrupted by the stench of a squat toilet and unflushed miseries. Her rented house in Bangkok was clean and well-ordered; students at BCS arrived each morning smelling of talcum powder and exotic deodorants. But just blocks away from the leafy, spacious campus were squalid tenements and even a kind of shantytown, where ten adults would sleep in a single room and share an outdoor bush as a latrine. Moments with Miles were a giddy pleasure, an invigorating and mentally stimulating funfest followed by tender kisses and his rawboned, masculine endearments. Then his son would puncture the mood, snarling and deadening a room with his blank, uneducated hostility.

Sigh.

SEVENTEEN

It was a windy January morning, the first Friday back at school, and Sue needed an excuse to get out of the principal's office. The new semester had hit like a New Year's Eve fireworks show, with an explosion of meetings and paperwork. Occasionally, when she wanted to just clear her head, she liked slipping down to Bangkok Christian School's well-stocked library. It was a quiet haven, mostly populated by students in the *Matthayom* level, and she went from table to table, greeting knots of high school juniors and seniors.

"Did you enjoy your break from BCS?" she asked Wismita and Ngam, two of her favorites. The girls were due to graduate in June, both new Christian converts and very popular. The older one nodded, setting aside her notebook filled with precisely penned physics notes.

"Yes, my family took me to Penang for the week."

"Excellent! I bet you had a good time." It was one of Malaysia's most popular resort destinations, and many of BCS's wealthy families made annual pilgrimages.

"Yes, it is so nice. We went to museums and also swimming each day." The girl giggled. "And my mom and I spent so much money shopping."

Sue was about to move on when one of the girls whispered something to the other. They both tittered, and Ngam blushed.

"Something you ladies want to ask me?"

"No." They giggled again and Sue pulled up a chair.

"Come on. I won't bite you."

After another pause, Wismita blurted it out. "Students all say that Miss Baines now has *fan*. That you and Dr. Carington are in love together."

Despite both girls' fluency in English, the clumsy phraseology was a delightful bit of mirth and the girls almost squealed. Sue put a warning finger to her lips. "Shhh."

"But it is true?"

She weighed the question and decided to be honest. "He is a very special man and, yes, I like him a lot. But I'm an old lady, already fifty-six. I don't know yet what plans God has for me." She looked from one to the other. "I pray each morning that Jesus will guide in my life and show me what I should do. When Mr. Garvey comes back to us, maybe it is heaven's plan for me to go back to America. Or . . . maybe stay here for a longer time." She smiled at them. "Of course, Dr. Carington has something to say about it too, you know. Just because we ladies find a *fan* that we like doesn't mean that anything will happen."

"But, Missie Baines, you are so nice! Of course he will love you very much," they chorused. All at once Ngam covered her mouth to stifle a near-shout. Pointing to the library entrance, she leaned against her friend, laughing helplessly.

"What?" Sue turned to look. Framed in the doorway, his surgical coat slightly rumpled, was Miles. "Ah. There he is. Should I go and say hi to him?"

"Of course, Missie Baines. Ask him to be your *fan.* And when you marry him, we will come to the wedding and do a beautiful Thai dance. Okay?"

"I think we're getting ahead of ourselves." Embarrassed but pleased, she got up and sidled over to him. "Hey, doc."

He managed a smile, but seemed strangely distracted. "How's your first week back?"

"Hectic. Everything's going two hundred kilometers an hour around here. I had three committees last night; Khemkaeng and I didn't get out of here till a quarter to ten."

"That's tough."

"How about you? Are things at the hospital calming down?"

He nodded. "It seems like Wednesday was the peak. We had a good thirty-five come in that day, but there's been a lot of discharges this morning, I know. Almost back to normal, I'd say."

"How's Gino's bad arm?"

"Sore. But healing all right. The physician in Chiang Mai sent along a copy of his X rays, and it's a fairly simple break."

"That's good."

The big man hesitated, and she eased closer to him, feeling the eyes of her students cheerfully following every move. "We're being watched, I figure."

"Yeh." He shoved both hands in his pockets and looked directly at her. "It's Gino I wanted to talk about."

"Oh. Okay." She felt a disquieting flutter in her stomach and hoped her expression didn't give anything away. "My office?"

He motioned with his head toward the door and they slipped into the hallway. "I hate to ask you this," he implored, "but could you slip away? Like, right now?" He swallowed hard, and she saw pain written on his face. "Let's get away from here, eh?"

"Is something wrong?" Without speaking further, she followed him out to the parking lot and let him drive her away from the Christian campus. He went about a kilometer, his eyes fixed on the slowly oozing traffic in front of him. She was about to speak, but the tension in the car was terrific and she bit her tongue, aching for her man. A small, unkempt park on the left had several vacant parking stalls next to the trees, and the car lurched toward them. He switched off the engine and stared dully at the vacant greenery on the other side of the sidewalk.

"Miles . . . sweetie." Alarmed now, she reached over and took his hand in her own. "I can see that you're hurt. Whatever it is, just tell me." For a fleeting moment, she wondered if the same dreaded thought had occurred to him–that Gino's urgent needs trumped their romantic interest in each other.

He stared dully at the dashboard, then turned to face her. When he spoke, his voice was trembling. "I took Gino over to Saint Catherine's to get some lab tests done. Just in case his being sick lately was more than just . . . you know . . ."

A feeling of raw, female dread swept over her, an intuition of wrenching certainty. "Oh, sweetheart," she whispered. "Oh, no. What is it?"

He was about to speak, then suddenly dissolved into huge, silent sobs, burying his face in the crook of his right arm. His shoulders heaved against the steering wheel as he wept, his audible cries punctuating the dread stillness there in the car. Desperate now, she clutched his hand to her heart and squeezed tightly, breathing a wordless prayer. "Please, dearest," she managed. "Please tell me."

For a moment he didn't answer. Finally, sucking in a rasping breath, a death rattle of grief, he blurted out the awful news. "My boy has lymphoma. Gino . . . he's dying."

The news ripped a hole in her soul and she stared at him in disbelief. "What?"

"Lymphoma. Cancer of the lymph system. The blood work came in, they double-checked it, and . . ."

She felt tears running down her own face as all the equations of this mad, wonderful relationship inverted themselves and splattered against the windshield. This kid she despised and hated, who by all accounts had chosen her as an enemy–now was facing a far more menacing foe. The often-rehearsed rationale for her resentments had just been sledge-hammered, and her shame added to the horror of the moment.

"Dear God, sweetie," she whispered, leaning her head against his shoulder. "I'm so sorry."

He strained against the seatbelt to pull a handkerchief from the side pocket of his laboratory smock. He gently dabbed at her face and then wiped his own tears away as well. "What a pair we are," he groaned, trying through the gloom to force a tiny smile.

She clutched his muscular bicep and peered into his face. "Well, please tell me everything. But first, honey . . ." She felt a flooding desire to simply escape with Miles to a distant haven, to hold him and love him and care for him. To soar arm in arm beyond the conflict of this moment and the dread duties that lay before them both. "I just want you to know something. Whatever you need, that's what we'll do. I love you with all my heart. If you need me with you, then I'm with you. If you need me to step back so that you can just pour yourself into all you need to do for Gino, then that's okay too. But first, tell me what happened."

He nodded. "Well, he got home all right that Friday morning. We spent a couple hours together before I had to rush back to the ward, and he said he was okay, that the pills were working. But all weekend long, then, he was feeling lousy. More than just the arm. So first thing Monday I took off work, drove him over to Saint Catherine and said, 'Please do a full workup, stat. Everything.' They're the best in Bangkok for that sort of thing. Our place doesn't handle much beyond just the routine; in fact, we ship all our hard cases over there anyway."

"So how long before you heard back?"

He didn't reply at first, and she could see Miles fighting his emotions again. "Sorry," she whispered.

"No, it's okay." He drew a deep breath, his eyes closed. "Their main hematopathologist called me yesterday, mid-afternoon. Said maybe I should come in. He had some numbers that concerned him. Which is a diplomatic way of saying trouble."

"So . . ."

"Well, I drove over, and he went right to the issue. Gino's got lymphoma, full-scale. Needs to get into treatment immediately."

"Which is what?"

His face sagged. "First off, they try aggressive chemotherapy. Which is a God-awful thing for a kid. I mean, if he feels sick now, just wait. Hair falls out, retching half the day and night."

Sue felt a bilious sense of sympathy rising up inside her. "Poor baby." She reached out and plucked the handkerchief out of his hand, mopping at her eyes again. "I feel just awful for the fact that, you know, he and I had some battles. Course, all that seems so petty and . . . *nothing* now."

"Yeh." Miles' right hand was making aimless little *pops* on the steering wheel, his head bobbing sadly in time to the cadence of the mournful tune playing in his heart. "Anyway, if we don't get results from that, then his best hope is to go into the lottery pool and take a shot at a bone marrow transplant."

"Yikes. I heard about that once," she murmured. "Pretty tough ordeal too, isn't it?"

"Yeah. For Gino and the lucky whoever. So let's hope it doesn't come to that."

She pressed his hand to her lips and simply held it there for a healing minute. "I love you so much. How can I help?" She caught herself. "I guess, first things first. Did you tell Gino already?"

He nodded abjectly. "Yeh. Wouldn't be fair not to tell him right off. So I went straight home and we sat down together."

Sue's mind raced, picturing the precarious anguish

of the moment. "How . . . how was he?"

"Well . . . scared in a blanked-out kind of way. On the one hand, kids sometimes feel invulnerable. Like nothing can beat them. But not him so much, 'cause he's been puking up his guts the past couple months already. And on the other hand, the medical complications of something like this overwhelm them to the point where all they can do is go blank and maybe cry a little. Which he did for sure."

She weighed the imagined scene, then turned his face toward her own and carefully kissed him, trying to pour the fullness of her reserve of charity and Christian hope into this man she loved with desperate fervor. "What all did you say to him about it?"

"I . . . well, just . . . I laid it out. Said it was a tough disease. That he'd have a fight on his hands. But that I loved him, that we'd go at this enemy together, him and me. That we'd grab every advantage, try to push up our odds. And that I figured with God's blessing, he'd come out all right."

"How'd he do with the God part?" She recalled her own witnessing moment in the Chiang Mai hotel room and Gino's reluctant nibble of interest.

"Well, when you're drowning, you don't particularly care what color the life preserver is. But I have no idea what's in his head about that."

"I guess not." She rested her head against his shoulder again, grateful for the comfort that came from two people pooling their fragile pockets of strength. "Where is he right now?"

"Home. I told him I was going to come over to BCS and tell you."

"What'd he say?"

"Nothing." Miles managed the barest trace of a smile. "In a funny way, I think maybe he was glad. None of his friends know yet, and your little adventure together at the camp made him feel like you were at least a spiritual ally. He'd never say that out loud, of course."

Sue pulled herself free and faced him with determined confidence. "I think we should go home. Let's just spend some time together, the three of us." Carefully attendant to each word, she added: "I don't know if we'll ever be a family. But to the extent that we already are, we may as well let that be one of God's advantages." She peered into Miles' beautiful, broken face. "Let me just take care of you guys . . . and cook supper for the two men in my life."

She dug into her purse for her phone as Miles started up the car and headed back in the other direction. "Need to stop by the school for anything?" She shook her head.

Mallika, the main administrative secretary, answered the call. "This is Miss Baines. Sorry–I had to leave campus for an emergency. Is *Kuhn* Khemkaeng in right now?"

"Yes, Missie Baines. He came to pick up medicine folders for *Prathom* One and Two."

"Oh, yes. See if he can talk to me for a minute."

"Yes, okay."

A moment later, he came on the line. "Hello, Sue. Is everything all right?"

Save it for later. This news was too significant to relate over a telephone line, especially with Miles sitting right there. "Yeah. I just had a bit of an emergency pop up. Personal, not BCS. Anyway, I don't think I'll be back by five, so your little carpool is down to just two.

Tell Rachel Marie too, okay?"

"All right." Sue could hear the typical office bustle and nearby student chatter associated with the school's dismissal hour. "We'll see you later then."

"Sure."

She held Miles' hand as they drove toward the river, sending up wordless prayers of entreaty to her merciful Father in heaven. "Is the typhus outbreak pretty much under control?"

He nodded. "Yeh. Worst of it's contained."

"That's good."

A pleasant sunset blessed with cloud streaks in the western sky bathed the condominium towers and the lazily flowing river far below. Sue eased herself next to Miles' comforting bulk as they rode up in the elevator. "It'll be all right," she said, trying to believe it herself.

Miles inserted the key in the lock and pushed the door open. In the shadows of an unlit living room, Gino stood before her, fragile and wounded with his encased arm and the creeping virus none of them could see or measure. For a moment the two of them simply stared at each other. She motioned instinctively, and the boy fled to her embrace.

"I'm really sorry," she soothed, hugging him in the gentle gloom. "I know it's a big and scary mess. Not very good, huh? But your dad loves you a lot, and I'm here to help. And our mighty God is already working on it."

The boy was taller than her by a couple of inches, and it was a clumsy physical moment. He pulled himself free, awkward and embarrassed. "Dad told you every-thing?"

"Yeah. Well, just . . . what I needed to know." She

took him by the hand and led him to a nearby couch as Miles flipped on some lights. "How are you feeling?" She hesitated. "Arm . . . and then this other?"

Gino twisted around on the couch so that he could face her, his broken arm resting carefully on the edge of the furniture. "Arm's better," he admitted. "No more pain pills as of yesterday." He paused, glancing at his father. "And then this other thing, I don't know what to say. I mean, I don't feel any different. I haven't, you know, thrown up since that time in the van. But from what Dad says, once I start the treatment, I'll be barfing every time I breathe."

"I know." Her face softened. "I'm so sorry. I mean, really. But you're a good kid and you're going to find the toughness to fight through it. I totally believe that." It was halfway true, she realized. There was good in this boy; there was something worth healing. Christ considered him of supreme value, and all at once, her own shepherding impulses came flooding back, restored by the unassailable beauty of the gospel. "How soon will you begin your treatments?"

"This next Monday," he whispered, suddenly vulnerable again. "Two times every week for four months."

"Can you still go to school?"

Miles eased his considerable bulk down next to his son and draped an arm around him. "Don't think so. There's a decent chance he'll go through without much nausea; that's what we'll pray for. Perhaps we'll get lucky. But it's still a good-sized challenge for a kid, and we need to harness every bit of strength we've got. Gino and me both, eh?"

"Yeh."

Impulsively, Sue got to her feet and walked over to the lad. "Well, let's make it official," she said, leaning over and kissing the top of his head. "I'm Miles' Carington's lady friend, and that makes me Gino Carington's biggest fan . . . and supporter . . . and prayer warrior." She looked right into his eyes, then kissed him lightly on the cheek. "I promise you, sweetie. I will pray for you morning, noon, and night. Every single day until you're well. And anything I can do in all this world, you just raise your hand and ask. I'm a lady who knows how to get things done."

EIGHTEEN

What followed was four months of what Sue later remembered as a kind of desperate purgatory. Chemotherapy was a relentless, clawing, coldhearted adversary, and the twice-weekly medicines tore into Gino Carington without mercy. Saint Catherine Hospital scheduled the sessions for Wednesday and Saturday evenings, and she often sat with him at his bedside as the IV did its tormenting work. The aftermath of each chemical baptism was hours of unending nausea and profane pleading for the ordeal to end.

She plodded through her administrative routine at BCS with a kind of stolid perseverance, remarking to Khemkaeng that the curse of disease was the only reason she was still in Thailand. "First John, now this," she sighed as the trio ate lunch together in the crowded food court. "I always figured I'd be home for Christmas."

"How are you hanging in there?" Rachel Marie handed Sue one of her two cookies. "Here. You could probably use a pill or two yourself."

Sue shook her head wearily. "Well, Miles and I hoped for an easy time of it, and we sure didn't get that. I mean, in between chemo appointments he does okay. Once in a while he even manages to do a bit of school work."

"Yeah, I saw him here this morning."

It had been Sue's suggestion that, rather than drop out completely and lose an academic year, Gino could endeavor to catch a few BCS *Matthayom* lectures here and there and possibly salvage the semester. He would edge into the back of a classroom and sit in isolation by the door, an obvious visitor in his civilian clothes and American baseball hat to cover his thinning locks.

"How is that going?" Khemkaeng wanted to know.

Sue shrugged. "It's just too hit and miss to really do any good. There were two tests in Algebra II last month; he was too sick to come in for either one of them."

The trio fell into a glum silence. The stark truth, Sue realized, was that the situation felt–to her–bleak, almost hopeless. Okay, the kid could audit a few classes, but why bother? The chemo seemed a futile token, his body obviously beyond repair. This brave project was failing before her eyes.

"You were saying about last night?" Rachel Marie glanced around to make sure they still had some privacy.

"Yeah. Pretty bad."

"What happened?"

"Well, he gets home, he gets in bed, and he knows what's coming. Like waiting for a hurricane to hit. Ten minutes later he vomits up just unbelievable amounts. It tears you up to watch. Sometimes he makes it to the bathroom; sometimes he doesn't. So I try to clean things up, change the sheets, and get him comfortable. Twenty minutes later, he's at it again. It kills me; it really does. Miles has this little washing machine unit, so we've got that going–I mean, all the time. The other night he was stuck in surgery until three in the morning. I did Gino's sheets four times. After a massive sedative, he sometimes finally gets to sleep."

"Oh, dear God." Rachel Marie shook her head, overwhelmed. "Sue, I'm so sorry."

"Well, this is bad too. I mean, I know Gino's coping with stuff beyond my imagining. But when he's all twisted up like that, the language is just *blue* in the room. He's crying; he's screaming, and every other word is that certain one. For the first couple times, he was just shouting at me: 'Get the *hell* out! Just get out of here! Leave me be!' But now it's that other word nonstop. He's at death's door and it's not good."

The barren despair of it all shook her even as they sat there, and she dabbed at her eyes. "Yikes. Don't let the students see this."

"It's all right." Khemkaeng shifted in his chair in order to shield her from view. "I'm very sorry, Sue."

"You guys pray for me, okay?"

"Of course." Rachel Marie draped a compassionate arm around her friend. "You're an incredible blessing; you know that."

She digested the well-intentioned compliment. "Well, I have to tell you both this–and just between us, okay?"

"Sure."

It was painful to express the vivid handwriting she saw on the wall of this deteriorating story. "I actually love Gino now, but he's just completely lost. In every way."

The young couple waited, their faces soft but questioning.

"In my heart, I don't see a way for him to get well. There was one batch of numbers where things ticked up just a bit. But the next week all the markers were down, worse than ever. And he's got just three weeks to go in the cycle." She had to swallow hard to keep down the lump in her throat. "But the worse thing is that he's just a lost soul. Somehow all his messes from before–the divorce, all his anger, his screaming hatred–he's so poisoned that it's honestly what's keeping him from having any chance, I think."

Rachel Marie stared at her. "What do you mean?"

"Just that. To beat a thing like lymphoma, you've got to have every advantage. You need optimism. You need hope and prayer. You need to feel like your team, your family, is there with you, pulling for you. For sure, it helps if you cast your cares on Jesus and, you know, get some spiritual rest. But this kid has none of that. Miles loves him just . . . *desperately*. He's learned some lessons and now he's an amazing dad. But Gino's built up such a barrier of piled-up resentment that everything we do for him basically bounces off." Tears flooded her eyes and she almost had to put her head down on the table. "When I first came to New Hope as a pastor, I wasn't for sure convinced that Satan was a real being. I thought, well, maybe that's just a personification for all the evil messes in this world. But no more; I'm telling you that. 'Cause Satan wants this boy bad. I'm watching this slow-moving collision that's happening, and neither of us can stop it or even slow it down."

DESPITE THE FIERCE HEAT that attacked the capital city without fail every April, most evenings provided a pleasant respite. Tropical breezes blew through Bangkok, and the array of lights as the city prepared for evening *sanuk*–entertainment and fun–made her life seem almost human again, if only for right now. Despite the grueling twice-weekly battles in Miles' high-rise apartment, she was pleased when an email popped onto her screen right as school was letting out. *Hey, love. Two surgeries got canceled for tonite. Gino's feeling alright and has plans to see some film with his fr Michael. How about a night under the stars? Despite hosp bills, I've enough baht left to treat my queen to that long-promised boat ride on the river. Please say yes. You deserve it and millions more. Love for always, M.*

There was a sweetness to the artificial normalcy of the note: Gino's got plans with friends; we've got reservations for two on the "River Queen"; love is in the air, etc. She grinned, grateful to God for small but precious blessings.

"This is the best idea anybody's had in about a hundred years." She climbed into his Honda and, glancing about the parking lot, kissed him enthusiastically on the lips. "Take that, doc."

"Well." Despite the careworn lines, his face creased into a smile. "Offer a boat ride, get a kiss. Tell your calculus teacher here I intend to memorize that math equation and put it to good use."

She laughed. "There may come a day when favors are paid off even more generously than that."

"Ah." He peered in the rear view mirror to make sure there was an opening in the relentless traffic. "All good things come to those who wait, eh?"

"Something like that."

It was a beastly drive creeping along Ratchadamnoen Road, but traffic finally loosened up and they made the boarding time with fifteen minutes to spare. Miles shoveled out a large stack of Thai baht, and the couple accepted ornate flower leis as they stepped aboard the floating restaurant. Already the spicy aromas of sweet-and-sour fish, rice soup, and pans of Italian pasta were mingling with the faint scent of imported wine being served at the bar.

Miles led Sue to an upper-deck table where they could see the glowing patterns of neon that spelled out commercial seductions on both sides of the Chao Phraya River. With a pair of enthusiastic toots, the boat eased away from the wharf and the stately elegance of nearby hotels.

A jazz combo from the Philippines lent a soft sophistication to the evening, as waiters scurried between tables, bringing extra dishes and an array of Thai confections for dessert. Sue sipped on a pineapple malt and felt a bit of emotional rejuvenation. "This is absolutely perfect, sweetheart," she said, squeezing his hand. "I'm so glad Gino felt a bit better so you could get away. You deserve it."

"You too." His visage, scarred by the recent battles, showed a trace of peace, one evening's badly needed respite. "You've sure carried us along, eh?"

"My pleasure," she told him, meaning it. At the outset of the crisis, they had spent a long, desperate evening praying together about putting the romance on hold or even just breaking up. But the swiftness of Lucifer's attack had forcibly thrown them together as two doves caught in a thunderstorm. Clinging to their friendship had quickly become a matter of mere survival.

Another tour boat, this one churning past in the opposite direction, tooted on the foghorn, and partygoers sitting near Miles and Sue hollered inebriated greetings. She finished her dessert and scooted her chair around to be closer to him. "Thank you, sweetheart. This is all very nice."

"Yeh." He slipped an arm around her and managed to inveigle a kiss before the band began playing again. "Hey, I love this song."

A young female began the slow, sultry anthem made famous by blues singer Etta James. *At last my love has come along. My lonely days are over, and life is like a song.*

Sue felt a tear slowly slip down her cheek. She had grown up in a conservative Christian home; dancing had never been a part of her life. But all at once she found herself in Miles' arms and they stood on the deck, being touched by the music and Bangkok's comforting beauties that outlasted a multitude of bad dreams. *I found a dream that I could speak to—a dream that I can call my own. I found a thrill to press my cheek to, a thrill that I have never known.*

For all of her quiet, efficient life, she, Sue Baines, had waited and hoped . . . until toil and time had chased the dreams away. And then came Miles Carington, this flawed but earnest and noble gentleman who held her cheek against his own, humming quietly in his rough bass voice as he and she slowly swayed in each other's arms, thanking God for being present in their lives and simply loving them.

"I love you so much," she whispered, overcome and once again at peace. "Thank you, Miles, for finding me and loving me." *Then the spell was cast. And here we are in Heaven. For you are mine at last.*

AND THEN, IN ONE merciless onslaught of sweat and screaming that left the family nearly broken . . . it was over. With two weeks left to go, the quest was abandoned. Gino's spasms threw him to the floor where he huddled in a fetal position, sobbing out his anguished surrender. "No more! I'd rather be dead already than do another two minutes of this!"

Together Miles and Sue bathed and nursed him until the sun rose in the east, but the boy was adamant. He was through with chemo, and if that meant the end for him, well, he would face his fate with stoic resignation. All their cajoling and appeals to logic were drowned out by the tidal wave of pain.

"Can't say that I blame him," Sue whispered the following morning as, groggy and despairing, she rode with Khemkaeng and Rachel Marie to the school. "Poor little lamb–he's hanging by a thread and knows it."

She realized full well that, without saying anything, Khemkaeng was doing yeoman work, staying extra hours at BCS and multitasking at home, trying to alleviate her own emotional overload. John, still fragile, shuffled in for a few hours here and there and buoyed her up as best he could with his hugs and stray contributions.

It was that pleasant time of afternoon the next Thursday; the campus was nearly empty, with a few stray students lazily loitering for rides and teachers polishing off the day's paperwork. Sue was perusing the minutes of the March board meeting and typing explanatory notes to append to the document before emailing it to the members.

"Miss Baines? Telephone is for you."

She jerked to attention, realizing that she'd actually dozed for a few minutes over her keyboard. "Thank you, Mallika. Who's calling? Did they say?"

"Sorry, no. I think it is a doctor, but not Dr. C."

She stifled a smile. Miles was such a frequent visitor to her office that all the staff helpers traded gossip about the growing romantic entanglement. "Okay." She picked up the phone. "Miss Baines here."

The caller on the other end was clearly American, a man's voice revealing an East Coast accent. "Yes, hello. Miss Baines, this is Dr. Powell from over at Saint Catherine Hospital. Have you got a moment?"

Hearing from another doctor put her guard up, and she responded carefully. "Yes, if you wish."

"I'd like to be able to talk with you privately about Mr. Carington. Gino, that is." His voice softened. "I know your friend Miles quite well; we've conversed at citywide medical conventions a couple times, so I know what he and his boy are going through."

She relaxed. "I know. It's been a tough situation, and not getting any better."

"Yes. And I know Gino suspended his treatments– which I can certainly understand. His chemo reactions were more brutal than most, unfortunately." There was a pause before he added: "Excuse me just a moment." Sue could hear him say something in clumsy Thai before coming back on the line. "In any case, I wonder if you might be willing to come out our way. Something I'd like to discuss."

"You mean, like, right now?"

He hesitated. "If possible. It's rather important, actually."

"Of course. If you think I should. But I really don't know how to get there."

"You don't drive?"

"Huh uh. I'm only assigned here in Bangkok for a few months."

"I see. Well, you basically say to any cab driver, *'Roang payaban.'* Which means 'hospital.'"

"Oh, sure."

"And then just tack on 'Catherine.' Most any cabbie will know that's us."

"Huh. And how do I find you?"

"Fifth floor. Just ask for Dr. Powell at the nurses' station. They'll be able to page me."

"All right then." She thought for a moment about her schedule, but decided nothing should keep her from what sounded like a significant matter. "I'll go extricate myself from my carpool and get right on the road."

There was an odd moment of silence before the doctor responded. "May I ask you a big favor?"

"I think so."

"For now at least, this really ought to be confidential. You'll understand when we visit."

"Oh. Okay."

The cabdriver was the tiniest little guy she'd ever seen operate a car; propped up on a purple seat cushion, he peered over the steering wheel, vainly trying to spot openings. Sue gazed at the passing scenery, imagining that in a city of teeming millions, there were countless life entrances and exits. Babies were being born; people were dying. This was the inexorable flow of a slowly expiring planet, and all a kind friend could do was to facilitate the first and postpone the last. Residents in Bangkok joked cynically about someone "sleeping under newspapers," referring to the cultural habit of covering bloody corpses with a handy newspaper following a fatal traffic accident. But throughout this hyperkinetic city, if one traveled down any small *soi*, you would encounter moments of dying. Some expired in isolated squalor; others breathed their last in perfumed comfort, with the finest of medical care and attention. But still they died . . .

There was an ornate water fountain gracing the front entrance to the hospital, and after paying the fare, Sue paused for a moment to simply drink in the pastoral serenity of the Catholic medical center. On the way over, she had tried not to think about what this Dr. Powell might be wanting from her. She and Miles were already stretched thin, to the point of breaking, but hey, she could do all things through Christ. Or so the teaching went.

The lobby was still busy with early-evening visitors coming and going; it took several minutes to squeeze into an elevator and ride to the fifth floor. Two Thai nurses were making notations in charts, and one looked up. "May I help you?"

"I'm here to see Dr. Powell."

"Yes. He is in 508. Down hall and then to left side."

"Thank you."

A bit of sunset poked through the western windows as she went down the long hallway. In the past four months, the disinfecting odors of medical care had become all too familiar, and she noted with appreciation a large spray of orchids someone had brought in. She tapped on the door of 508, still feeling some trepidation.

"Come in."

Dr. Powell was a dapper man with a Bostonian look

and accent about him. Short-cropped black hair with a touch of gray on the sideburns. Rimless glasses, a friendly face guarded by his professional demeanor. "Sue?"

"Yes. Hi."

"Thanks for coming over." He had just finished dictating into a small handheld device, which he shoved into a drawer. "So the taxi driver knew about us."

"Yes, you were right."

They chatted socially for a couple of minutes; he described his four years of medical experience in Bangkok. "My wife and I always hankered to try out a foreign experience, so when we spotted this opening at Saint Catherine's, we said to ourselves: 'Maybe this is it.' We'd just emptied out our nest, and no grandkids as of yet, so it seemed like an opportune time." He paused, eyeing her. "I take it you're unattached. No children back home?"

Sue shook her head. "Huh uh. Just Dr. Carington. Which, of course, takes second place to all of this."

"Sure." The physician's face softened. "Well, anyway, let me simply open up to you. And I have to say right here: our meeting is a bit irregular. You'll see why in a moment."

"Let's hear it."

Dr. Powell seemed to slip into a kind of thoughtful reverie before he spoke. "The thing is this. Again, Gino finally just had enough. The chemo wasn't working; we all knew it. The numbers were piling up against us. And at some point, especially with a young person, sometimes they just hit the wall and they can't take it any longer." His eyes revealed an understanding of the pain of these trials. "So Miles and I both agreed that it just wasn't worth pursuing, especially for only two more weeks. I didn't see much likelihood of–all of a sudden– things turning around."

"So now what?"

"Okay. Well, that takes Gino to Option Two. Which, frankly, is his last hope. If this doesn't work out, it's basically a matter of making him comfortable and everybody getting ready for the last vigil."

Sue felt moisture spring into her eyes. She still felt a sharp sense of confliction about Gino, but he was the son of the man she loved. Dr. Powell noticed and his face softened. "I'm truly sorry. I know this has taken a toll on all three of you."

She gestured for him to continue.

"So it's down to hoping that a bone marrow transplant might work out for him. Even at the beginning of the chemo protocols, of course, we had already sent in his tissue samples, so that the global registry could begin to search for some possible matches."

"How did that go?"

Dr. Powell reached into a drawer and fished through it for a folder. "Well, the first hope is always that a family member will match. Once in a while that does happen. But the laboratory ran Miles' samples through, and they didn't work at all. Bad luck, because that would have been ideal. So the next option was that perhaps Gino's birth mother might possibly line up. And of course, as you know, that family has been separated for quite a few years. Miles didn't even have contact information for his ex-wife. Living in New Zealand now, divorced a second time, into a third husband, etc. Elena Bedeau's what it is, now. And, unfortunately, she really did not wish to reestablish any connection with her former life, so didn't even respond."

Sue digested this. "I didn't realize it had come to this. Miles didn't say anything about it."

"Well, and I can understand why. He and I both hoped that the chemotherapy would work. So this was always a secondary possibility–and a distant one at that."

"Huh." She felt a surge of maternal sympathy for Gino and his quickly diminishing hopes. "So now . . . what? I guess it's simply a case of hoping the computers find a generic match?"

"That's right. We needed to get lucky, is about the gist of it." He flipped the folder open and pulled out a single sheet of paper. It had a logo on the top, and he slid the document toward her. "No one has seen this but me, but I thought this was a startling thing. I mean, truly a one-in-a-million moment."

She picked up the piece of paper. Halfway down were printed four names. Her hands shook slightly as she read in silence: "Waterford, Douglas M.; Legard, Francois P.; Okonkow, Jumoke W. B.; Baines, Susan C."

Nineteen

It was at once a terrible and surreal moment, white noise roaring in her ears. Fifty alibis and rebuttals pounded in her mind like an alien army's battering ram, but the stark fact was that she absolutely did not want to hear this plea or consider the possibility. She, Sue Baines, be a bone marrow donor? To endure pain and anesthesia and complications and the terror of a mask over her face, the darkness closing in, the needles and the ooze of her life forces ebbing away? *And all for Gino Carington,* easily the most unpleasant child she'd ever met?

She pushed away the scarlet collection of petty impulses and set the paper back down. "Wow," she confessed. "I can see why that made you jump. It looks like a lottery miracle, sure. But there's no way that's me."

"Beg your pardon?" He took the sheet and murmured the last name. "'Baines, Susan C.' I guess, sure, there's more than one person named that in the whole world. But you're sitting right here. I knew Miles and you were close friends; as soon as I read this list, I figured this was something you folks planned and we just got incredibly lucky."

"Oh, my, no." She spoke rapidly, almost stammering, feeling the blood course to her cheeks. "It's never once come up. And I'm assuming that I'd be no more likely to match than any of the other seven billion people walking around. There's no genetic connection whatsoever."

"True." Dr. Powell seemed to sag. "But how are you so positive this isn't you? Even then?"

"Well, first of all, that's not even my full name," she explained. "It's Susan *Louise* Baines. This sheet has someone with a 'C' for a middle initial." She felt like she was grasping at a technicality, like a lawyer who finds a seldom invoked loophole and brandishes the ruling in the jury's face.

"Could be a mistake," the physician said hopefully.

"Oh, sure. I guess." Sue could sense the defensive intensity of her denials and tried to force her galloping pulse to settle down. "But the other thing is that I'm not in any kind of registry. At least as far as I know. How would someone have ever gotten my name? Don't you have to volunteer for things like that?"

"Oh, certainly. They work off a worldwide data bank. Something like ten million registrants." He peered at her over the top of his glasses. "And you're not in it? Absolutely?"

"No. Never have been. I'm positive."

He thought hard. "Back in the States, were you a regular, like, plasma donor? Have you given a lot of blood through the years?"

The question brought a rare moment of levity. "That's very amusing. 'Cause it's been a family joke since I was a kid. Scared of needles, screaming tantrums every time I had a shot. I've spent my entire life hiding in the closet anytime somebody ever asked me to give a pint of blood. 'I'll send fifty dollars in' has always been my stock answer. 'Go poke somebody else.'" For a moment, she recalled the fainting spell at New Hope Church, and it filled her with a sturdy resolve to evade this missionary moment.

Dr. Powell nodded glumly. "Well, that's a shame." He drummed his fingers on the desk, thinking hard. "See, here's the thing. And it's why I asked you to make it a quiet cab ride over here."

She waited, picturing in her mind's eye a huge mainframe computer in New York City with blinking panels and humming hard drives, scouring all seven continents for a donor whose numbers magically lined up with a lost and unlovable teen boy in Bangkok.

"See, unless the donor is a family member, this entire process is generally kept confidential. We don't tell patients who a donor is, and we don't tell the donor who their possible recipient is. Sometimes we do tell them the cancer patient's age and gender, but that's it."

"How come?"

"Because it's such a high-pressure demand," he explained reluctantly. "This is a rough procedure. It's grueling, it hurts, it's got some tough aftereffects."

Sue felt a slow wave of revulsion beginning to well up within her. Despite her hope that Gino could find a cure, it was a frank relief to know that the four names on this list were faceless strangers, living in far-flung and anonymous corners of the world.

"So we never want for a donor to feel pressured to make this commitment. At any time, a donor needs to be able to say, 'You know, I just can't do it. It's too much.' And we respect that. People are allowed to walk away." He looked directly into her eyes. "That's why Miles and Gino have no idea that I have this list, or that your name's on it." He caught himself. "I should say–that this person's name is on it, rather similar to yours. Because we absolutely do not want for you, or anybody else, to feel inordinate pressure to do something you're not ready to do."

An odd memory came into her mind, of how Pastor Mike had given her a hug after the fainting debacle at New Hope. *You don't have to do every single ministry thing that comes along,* he soothed her. *There are many ways to serve the people of God. Find ones you enjoy and just do them well.*

"Well, since I spent two hundred seventy baht riding over here," she said with a taut smile, "you may as well tell me what the procedure entails. If you don't mind."

He was clearly downcast, but finally nodded. "Sure. And of course, I hope you'll get right on your knees every day and start saying prayers that one of these four names might pan out. One's clear out in Nigeria, so lining up that one's going to be an adventure."

"Oh, of course," she assured him, grateful to be back to such an innocuous assignment.

"Here's what happens. These four names are simply possible matches. When they registered, it took account of various 'markers' in their blood. Human leukocyte antigens, we call them. HLA. If we can get hold of any of these people, and they're willing, then they provide us with some additional samples and we look for an improved set of matches. There are six lottery numbers, or proteins, that really count; if a person matches on all six, that's just about heavenly. Five is pretty good too. And we have a decent chance that one of these four names is going to work out. Then, if there's still a green light, they undergo a physical exam to make sure they're in acceptable health."

She listened, fascinated and relieved that the conversation had moved safely beyond her own situation.

"Then we come right down to it. Gino's case, unfortunately, is one that really does require bone marrow rather than stem cells, which is a much easier process. Less invasive and all that. But what happens is that the donor comes into surgery. They go under general anesthetic, and you'll understand why when I tell you." He gestured with his hands. "They use a pretty long needle, like this, and have to insert it into the pelvic bones. Quite a few jabs, but of course, the patient is completely knocked out. They extract a sufficient amount of bone marrow, the patient goes to post-op, they generally stay in the hospital overnight, and they have a few fairly uncomfortable days afterward."

"What then?"

"Nothing. In a few weeks, most of them are a hundred percent recovered. Sometimes there's residual pain in the lower back. Occasionally there are issues with anesthesia, of course, but that's true with anything in the OR. But then the new marrow is surgically administered into the recipient and we begin hoping and praying in earnest that it'll take hold."

She was grateful for this Christian man's references

to prayer and God's intervening power, and felt a warming sense of kinship with him in the medical victories he helped to mastermind. "I've got to admit that I'm relieved this isn't me," she told him, "but I honestly hope you can find at least one of these people."

"Of course." He put the sheet of paper back in his folder. "Speaking of which, we have a good laboratory right here at Saint Catherine's, and it wouldn't take more than three days for them to run a typology on your blood. It's still a million-to-one long shot, but miracles sometimes do happen. Or for future reference, perhaps." He hesitated. "Any interest?"

She could feel her face flushing again. "Let me think about it. Truthfully, it just really freaks me out even thinking about a little needle stick. Let alone that eight-inch spike you were just describing."

He smiled. "Sure. Well, listen, it's really so nice to meet you. Miles is a good man, and he had mentioned 'Missie Baines' a few times. I hope, first of all, that Gino finds his way back to good health, and then who knows what the Lord might have in store for you and the good doctor."

"Thanks. It was good to meet you too."

The elevator was slow in coming and she decided to work off some of her built-up tension by hiking down the five flights of stairs. She plodded from one floor to the next, reliving the stab of trepidation when she first saw that name on her list. *Thank God for that wrong middle initial,* she mused idly, and was immediately ashamed of her self-centered fears.

On the ground level, she realized that she was an entire hospital wing removed from the front entrance where she might catch a taxi back home. Grumbling to herself, she traipsed the entire length of the first floor, gazing at the now-quiet hum of activity as the medical center sought to heal and restore.

The laboratory was right next to the main lobby, and she experienced an incongruous impulse to go in and offer a sample of blood, to at least say yes to Dr. Powell's request that she be typed for the marrow registry. *You're right here. It wouldn't take more than five minutes.* She already felt a twinge of shame for being so cheerfully relieved at being excused from duty, and wondered if giving a sample right now would balance the moral scales. But just as she passed the open doorway, a technician bent over a Thai woman's arm, carefully tapping in order to stimulate a vein. The thin metal spike poised, he swabbed the spot and jabbed the needle home. A thin red spider of fluid crawled along the clear tubing and Sue felt a tight fist of nausea grabbing her stomach and squeezing it. She scurried past, looking the other way and shuddering, beads of sweat leaping onto her forehead.

The taxi driver nodded affably as she gave him her home address and she sank into the back seat, enjoying a departing glimpse of the ornate water fountain. *Yikes! Needles! Blood! What were you thinking, Baines?*

The green-and-yellow car wheeled around the corner and onto Rama IV. The images of the Saint Catherine lab were still in her mind, forcing her to relive the horrible bit of comedy at New Hope Church the previous summer. The mocking teenagers in her Girl Power Ministries group, coaxing and badgering her into donating a pint. Measuring her pulse and temperature. The rubbing alcohol, the blood pressure cuff tightening around her arm. The needle stick in her finger to check her iron levels. That idiot blond nurse who couldn't tell a vein from the Holland Tunnel. All the probing lifestyle questions about recent trips to the U.K. and had she ever given anybody money or drugs for sex. Was she willing for a sample of her blood to be sent off to some data bank . . .

Oh my God.

She felt a shuddering in her brain as the scene replayed itself. In the unhappy blur of that ministry moment she had said a listless yes. *Sure. Whatever. Go for it. Just get me out of here, you dumb chick.* She could picture herself now, heart fluttering awful anticipation, penciling her name in those tiny squares. B–A–I–N–E–S. First name: S–U–S–A–N. Middle initial: she had hastily put in an 'L,' but okay, she was in a hurry. Her L's tended to lean a bit on top; somebody could have read it as a C.

No! Please, Lord. Don't make me . . .

In a moment of galactic certainty, there in the smoke-saturated back seat of a Bangkok taxicab, she knew that she was on the hook. She, Susan Louise Baines, was the match for Gino Carington that the computer had pin-pointed and unmasked. All her life, she had won the lottery. Her numbers always lined up, three cherries to beat the house. And now God was exacting his due for all the giveaway Kindles, the door prizes, the real estate bulls-eyes. An invoice had been kept and heaven now expected her to pay up in full.

Her mind was pounding with the dilemma of this crossroad. She was on her way home. She was already in the clear. Dr. Powell would spend this next week trying to find Doug Waterford or some Parisian named Monsieur Legard. A medical emissary would ride a jeep out to some village or small town on the edge of nowhere in Africa and carefully explain to a farmer's wife named Jumoke that a surly half-Australian, quarter-Caribbean, quarter-Italian teenager now dying in Thailand was desperate for her bone marrow.

Or the computer from hell might actually reveal that Susan Baines' donor sheet listed her original address as being Pasadena, California, with mail now forwarded to Bangkok. The thought made her turn scarlet with horror and embarrassed fear and she shrank into the coffee-stained plastic upholstery. How could she ever have a future with Miles, knowing that she had hidden this life-altering secret? It was an impossible prison box in every way.

There were back-alley avenues to freedom, but the call of God trumped them all. Most of all, she simply could not lie. She could not allow this taxi to continue fleeing the scene.

Her heart in her throat, she tapped the cabbie on the shoulder. He looked at her, startled.

"*Kaw todt.*" Please excuse me. There was a hard, excruciating lump in her throat, and she felt tears coursing down her cheeks. The Thai man was at a loss; baffled, he jerked his gaze back and forth between the traffic-choked thoroughfare and the weeping victim in the back seat of his cab.

"Please take me back. Sorry. *Roang payaban.* Saint Catherine."

SHE SAT IN THE Chaisurivirats' living room, Rachel Marie gazing pensively at her as the clock on the wall ticked toward eleven p.m. "I guess I don't need this." Sue peeled away the small strip of adhesive and examined the minuscule reddish dot marking the injection. Her innards lurching yet again, she plodded over to the kitchen, looking for a trash container.

"Under the sink."

"Thanks."

Her mind was still clammy with dread at the unbelievable tilting of her universe. Dr. Powell had seemed sympathetic but relieved upon her return to Saint Catherine's. "It really did seem too perfect to be a coincidence," he told her, offering a careful hug. "Thanks so much for coming back. Let me go with you and we'll get a full sample logged in even tonight."

Now hours later, she felt the walls closing in on her. Together she and Rachel Marie had gotten on the Internet and scoured the web for details about the postoperative effects of being a marrow donor. One lurid site warned that she might well have large purple bruises from her waist clear down to her knees. "Ouch," Rachel Marie murmured, putting an arm around her friend. "Missie Baines going around Bangkok with a black-and-blue butt."

Sworn to absolute secrecy, the two women sat in the inky darkness, grappling with the decision. "That's just it," Sue confessed, ashamed and yet desperate to know that someone understood. "How do I even have a choice? I've got to do it. I hate the thought; I'm scared out of my mind. But how could I ever say no to Miles?"

Rachel Marie digested this. "If it weren't for him, what would you do?"

"I don't know." In all honesty, as she peered into her own soul, she suspected that the decision would be to renege on her original offer. Her fear of needles and hospitals and pain was pathological and even a bit pathetic, but it was also real. Reading about an eight-inch needle being jammed endlessly into her hip bones, sucking out marrow, bruising nearly half her body, invading her very core with searing pain . . . it was just plain and simple too much. She didn't want to do this; everything in her quailed at the thought.

"There are other people, you know," she reminded Rachel Marie. "There's ten million people on that list. Only one person in 540 ever even gets a call, and a lot of them either say no or wash out."

"Which could happen to you. They could run these extra tests and you'll not be a match."

"I know, but . . ." How could she possibly root against a successful pairing, especially with a human life at stake? Gino was a petulant mess, a blot on the family tree. But he was still a child created in the image of God. If she didn't step forward, why should anybody else? If not her, who? Why should she request an exemption from this moment of herculean challenge?

It was impossible, she realized, to say no to Gino—and then still have a relationship with Miles. How could she attend his son's funeral, then put on a white wedding dress and marry the father, while knowing she had shirked this golden chance? It would be a lapse that would haunt her forever.

But maybe it was better to simply say no, flee to California, resume her pleasant duties at New Hope Church, and put the entire saga in the past. Miles was a good man; she loved him desperately. But he was tethered to this strange and faraway land; Bangkok was his assignment; he was going to live out his days in that high-rise condo, puttering around Thailand in his Honda in between saving lives and snacking on durian. Next to the tumultuous ups-and-downs of this battle-scarred corner of God's universe, old-maid ministry in Pasadena had its own comforting and familiar allure.

"What are you thinking?"

"I wish I could just hide from the whole thing." She swallowed hard. "There's a chance you might have to help me keep this secret for a really long time."

"I know." Rachel Marie put an arm around her mentor and leaned her head against Sue's shoulder. "And really, you should do what you feel in your heart."

Sue sighed. "Don't say that," she almost snapped. "'Obviously, the 'heart' thing is to do my duty here. Such as it is."

"Sorry." Rachel Marie comforted her for another long moment, then climbed to her feet. "Let's go out for a bit."

"How come?" Sue peeked at her watch and felt a rush of guilt. "Sweetie, it's coming up on midnight."

"I know. But this is important." Rachel Marie fished in the small basket by the refrigerator and dug out the house key.

"Will Khemkaeng wake up?"

"I don't think so."

The moon was high overhead as the pair walked out to the front of the housing tract. Most lights in the neighborhood were dim by now, and traffic was sparse on the lonely road heading toward the 7-Eleven. "We could get mango slurpees," Rachel Marie observed, trying to keep her tone light. "'Cept we haven't got any baht on us."

It seemed like a journey to nowhere, with only one possible conclusion to the matter. *I have to do this,* Sue glumly thought to herself, angry and embittered at being placed in a moral straitjacket this way. How could a Christian principal face this lifesaving opportunity and then turn away simply because a surgical needle was eight inches long? Or because of some post-operative pain? People willingly died on battlefields for their homeland; even small children bore incredible burdens on behalf of those they loved. Could she do less?

Three blocks up the street, a smallish Buddhist *wat* came into view, its courtyard dimly illuminated by a ring of lights. The golden image of the Buddha, placid face and serene lotus position, gazed unblinkingly out into the gloom of Bangkok; a lone monk was padding his way toward the back entrance as the American women came to the gate. Sue spotted a nearby bench and pointed. "Let's just rest ourselves for a bit, and then I've got to make a decision and get on with it."

"Okay."

They discussed in low voices for a little longer, and Sue felt the saga thickening in her mind. Maybe things weren't as settled as she had thought. The odds were against a match anyway. Gino was deteriorating at a frightful pace now; he might succumb even before a lab report could make its way back across the Pacific.

"Will you be mad if I put one more issue on the table?" Rachel Marie reached out and simply held Sue's arm for a nice moment.

"No. Of course not." She gazed at the ornate Buddhist architecture and reflected on how in every land people sought to do the right thing, to make a helpful difference. Whether it was to improve one's own karma or to leave the family of mankind slightly improved–or at least comforted–Christianity and Buddhism were part of a good and common effort.

"I sometimes get little ideas," Rachel Marie said, "from 'Mere Christianity.' You know, C. S. Lewis?"

"Oh, sure. I read it a long time ago."

"Okay. Anyway, he's got this line about where we have two impulses. There's this moment that comes along–maybe a really hard one. And the stronger impulse says: 'Okay, I could go here and it'd be easy. Or I can do this other thing, which is a lot tougher.'"

Sue forced a wan smile. "Well, that would be Missie Baines for sure. Easy thing: sneak home to California and never say a peep. Hard thing: let Dr. Powell stab me two hundred forty times with his great big needle, end up with a purple rear end, limp around town for a while, and who knows if it even works?" The spiel came out sounding sarcastic and small, and she sighed, feeling nearly undone.

"Well, sure. And that's right. Anyway–and you won't like this, probably–Lewis goes on to say: 'General-ly, the hard thing is the right one. And we need to try to *side* with the right one, with the weaker impulse, even though we don't want to.'"

The challenge sat there in the humid midnight air as the Buddhist culture surrounding them respectfully retreated and waited for a decision. "I know I'm going to do it," Sue said at last. "Because I honestly don't have any choice."

There was a sudden jangling, a rude intrusion into the nocturnal solemnity of the monastic haven. Rachel Marie groaned. "Oh, no. Khemkaeng must have awakened." She fished in the pocket of her shorts and pulled the phone free. "Hi, babe." She listened for a moment. "No, I'm out with Sue. We're kind of working our way through something big. But we're okay. Really." There was another brief silence, and then she handed the phone over. "Here, Miss Baines. Your vice president might try to take over the Oval Office if you don't tell him what's up."

Sue felt a rush of affection for this generous couple. "You guys." Into the phone: "Hi, Khemkaeng. I'm so sorry; I stole your bride for the night."

His voice was typically gentle. "Sue, I'm very worried. Are you all right?"

A hundred retorts pressed against her soul, and she waited before answering. "I'm going to be okay," she heard herself say. "Rachel Marie is, like, the best friend I've ever had. And I'm sorry we startled you. We'll be back in a few minutes."

"No, no," he remonstrated. "It's Friday morning. Our easy day at school. So don't worry about that. But where are you? Can I come and help?"

A passing taxi slid over to the curb adjoining the small worship grove and the cabbie made a questioning gesture. Rachel Marie waved to indicate that, no, they didn't need a ride.

"Sue? Everything's all right?"

"We'll be home in ten minutes."

She handed the phone back and sighed, desperate to recover some sense of peace. "We're out past your curfew, I'm told."

"Come on." They hiked slowly back toward their own neighborhood. Sue still felt roiled by the momentous challenge, but there was at least a nudge of relief over the finality of having made a decision. One month from now, she would have done it. The sacrifice would be accom-plished. If the medical hurdles were terrible, at least she would be seeing them in the rear view mirror, scattered and bloodstained behind her. She might faint, but nurses could revive her. Tissue might swell or ache; someone would have an ice pack and medication for the hurt. If there was residual pain, even long-term agony, she would find a way to cope. But it would be done.

"It helps to have made the decision," she told Rachel Marie as they got to the street where the Chaisurivirats lived. "It'll probably be a messy awful thing, but at least I don't have to keep going through the back-and-forth turmoil of thinking about it. I'm all in, and if it's bad, it's bad. But the Lord will see me through."

"You're so awesome. I'm hugely proud of you."

Rachel Marie was about to turn the key in the lock when it swung open. Khemkaeng, wearing a flimsy robe with Chinese artwork on it, flipped on the outdoor light and motioned the pair inside.

"It's so late. I need to leave you two alone," Sue protested.

"Please." He put an arm around her. "Sue, I hope you can tell me what the issue is. You are my good friend; it is in my heart to help you."

There was a nice tenderness to his precise Thai way of putting things, and Sue leaned against him, grateful and exhausted. "If you can spare five minutes . . ."

"Certainly." He motioned her to the couch and eased some soft light into the tastefully decorated living room.

Summarizing briefly, she outlined the miraculous train of events. "I don't know if it's going to happen," she told him. "And I'm terrified beyond words. But I've got to say yes."

He digested the improbable tale, face filled with wonder. "Amazing. So amazing." He reached out and took her hand. "Sue, despite the fear you have, you can see the hand of God. These hospitals search the entire world for a single person who can help, and then it turns out to be you. And already here in Bangkok."

"I know." Despite the overwhelming odds, though, she felt another icy wind of dread blow right through her heart, freezing her emotions. "But I dread it, and I hate the fact that I don't want to, that I'm a reluctant volunteer."

Rachel Marie turned to face her friend, her youthful face warm and lined with a goodly bit of experience. "I think you should look at it . . . cosmically."

"What do you mean?"

"Just that. Do this thing for Jesus. Okay, Gino's kind of a jerk. Why? Because he's lost. Satan got hold of him and put some scars on that boy. But he needs rescuing. You said yourself that if he dies now, he goes to the grave lost." She teared up, remembering. "Last year, Khem-kaeng and I and the others were down at Pattaya Beach when Pranom was being held captive in that prostitution nightclub. And we were scared down to our socks." She leaned her head against her husband's shoulder, remem-bering. "Khemkaeng was forced to nose around, asking questions, bumping against some pretty unsavory people. Tommy had to go right into the club, posing as a customer with a whole wallet full of bootleg Thai money. It was an awful scene. But he did it because one of God's children needed saving." Her voice trailed away. "Now, I know that Pranom's gorgeous and cute and perky and . . . redeemable. Which Gino doesn't seem to be. But really, it's the same story all over again. And it's got to be you."

The last line was stark and inescapable. The blood markers told a story and the numbers didn't lie. The computers had pinned this whole thing on her. Her resolve began to melt again, and she dabbed at her eyes.

Khemkaeng drew both women close. "Here," he offered. "This is a hard night. We should pray."

Weary but relieved at the offer, Sue felt his kind hand taking her own. There was a warm strand of love, of Christian bonding, a microcosm of the sturdy fabric–all of God's people–surrounding the globe. People praying for the lost and hurting; Christians making sacrifices. Some of them small, others substantial. And here in this quiet living room, one that loomed like the legendary cross overlooking Rio.

"Dear God," Khemkaeng began, "thank you that Sue has this opportunity. It is a hard day for her; the thing these doctors ask her to do is painful and frightening. Please give her all of your strength and your love. Help her to feel how much we love her and will lift her up and care for her through any moments that are bad. And we pray, Jesus–with all our hearts we pray–that this miracle will be one that works. Please heal Gino through the gift that Sue offers to him. We ask this great blessing, Jesus, in your own name. Amen."

Sue was overcome and burst into tears, her shoulders shaking as Khemkaeng whispered encouragement. "Everything will be fine," he soothed.

Rachel Marie took her friend's hands and pressed them to her own lips. "While Khemkaeng was praying, I had another thing come to me," she said slowly. "I think it's important."

"Okay."

"Well, it's hard to say. But before this world began, God set things up for you to be Gino's rescuer. *He made you for this.*"

Sue held the new thought in her mind, with the possible glory of this moment of ministry weighing hard on her soul. She had never believed in the idea that a cosmic engineer in the skies elaborately planned each person's moment of birth and death and then randomly dished out doses of pain.

"I don't know about that," she said slowly. "Not to argue with you. But I just have never seen God as sitting up in heaven and making each and every choice, marking up a calendar: you're born on this day and die on that one. That all the tragedies in the world are part of some overarching plan he's got. A bullet for this kid, a broken leg for you. Or that he looked down and said, 'All right, Gino. You keep messing up; so try on this lymphoma for size; see how you like that.'"

"No, of course not." Rachel Marie, confused, shook her head. "I've never thought that either." She looked from one to the other. "I mean, God is love, but this is just a sinful world. The sperm meets the egg and a baby is born. Once in a while, that baby grows up to get killed in battle. Or gets cancer. And other times, not."

Khemkaeng, his face suddenly alive with interest, leaned forward. "Before you came here," he said to his wife, "you know that a tsunami hit Thailand. Indonesia as well."

"Oh, sure."

The Thai man tried to assemble his thoughts into a coherent strand of Christian theology. "It came on the day after Christmas. 2004. More than two hundred thousand people died. All sinners, sure, but so many good people drowned. Why? Because this is simply what happens in a broken world. The flood waters come and people die. Even the grandson of the king lost his life while on a jet ski. Did you know that? God did not choose death for him. The boy had autism. God did not chose that for him either. These things come because of evil. But the healing, the volunteers who came to Thailand to help after the tsunami, the doctors who heal, people like all of us who went to that refugee camp . . . *that* is because of God's call in our lives. God is never in the breaking, but always in the healing."

"That's what I wanted to say," Rachel Marie added, her voice still and hushed in the early morning beauty that surrounded the three. "Before the creating of our world, God foresaw that Gino would have lymphoma. He didn't ordain it; he simply saw it. It unfolded before him. But when you came into being fifty-six years ago, he made sure you were equipped to be his donor. To save his life." Her eyes now filled with tears, she took Sue's hand and kissed it. "He made you for this exact moment, and if it was the only good thing you ever did– saving Gino–that would be a life well lived."

Moved and entirely undone, Sue stared at her friend. "I don't know what to say. But you're right. I never thought of it."

Rachel Marie stood up, not bothering to wipe the tears away from her face. She went over to the window, peering out into the elegant darkness of the slumbering Asian city, its minefield of hurts and wounds quieted for the moment. "Do you know what's going to happen?"

"Tell me."

The younger woman came back and put a hand on Sue's shoulder. "You're going to be a match for Gino.

The lab report's going to come back and you'll be the perfect candidate. You'll line up with him six for six. I absolutely believe it. And then . . ." Her voice quivered but she managed to go on. "You're going to give him your marrow . . . and it's going to work. Susie Baines, you're going to save his life." She dissolved into sobs and barely managed to finish. "And for the rest of your life, you'll look back and know that this was the most incredible gift God ever gave *you*."

TWENTY

S ue stood in the shower for a long while the next morning, marveling at yet another of her Lord's many mysteries. There were times when she climbed into bed at 9:30, fell asleep instantly, and yet was groggy and irritated in the morning, a sodden mess. Last night it had been nearly two before she finally said a reluctant good night to Rachel Marie and Khemkaeng. She then spent at least another hour lying in her own bed, her mind overloaded and suddenly glorying in the quest before her. And now, with less than three hours of frag-mented sleep, she felt vibrantly alive, eager, passionately ready to embrace this God-ordained quest.

She scrubbed and rinsed the nondescript mass that had always been *her*. Susan Louise Baines was 157 pounds of vanilla tissue: bones, muscles, organs. And a covering of plain, decidedly un-noteworthy skin. A surface that bulged in the wrong places, with fleshy pockets slowly surrendering to gravity. Miles Carington, perhaps leafing through a thesaurus before romantic adventures, sometimes said generous things about this female lump of humanity now lingering in the warming stream of the shower. But as she examined her frame, it thrilled her to sense that deep within, there was this divinely scripted code, this razor-perfect aligning of deoxyribonucleic acid, genome strings and hemoglobin markers that could repair Gino's ravaged frame. And which bore the divine imprint of God's personal design and involvement.

Sue longed to rush to Miles, to shout, to herald what she had been privileged to discover, to sit breathlessly next to him in some magical inner sanctum and dramatically unfold the treasure map. "Look, my darling. There is a key to unlock this chest of gold . . ."

She sighed happily, switching off the water and reaching for a towel. It was all to the glory and master plan of her Redeemer that this was about to happen. Still, she tingled with the pure joy of the telling.

"How are you, sweetie?" Rachel Marie gave her a sisterly hug as they climbed into the car. "Get some sleep?"

"Yeah. I'm good." She returned the embrace. "You guys were unbelievable last night. I just feel so blessed now."

"Wow." They drove toward BCS and Sue drank in the beauty of this day, knowing within her heart that she had been chosen. It was a challenge to still function on this Friday, to stay earthbound and fulfill her principal duties, to stand where assigned and to rise, kneel, eat, dismiss according to the April schedule. The campus emptied out quickly, with staff and families eager to begin their weekends, and she packed up her things with an almost adolescent quiver of anticipation.

There was a flower shop just a block from Mission Hospital, and she asked the cabbie to let her out. Scanning the floral offerings, she selected a mix of white roses and lisianthus lavenders. "You like these, madam?"

"Yes, please."

"These so pretty. You make good selection."

It was a short walk to the lobby of the medical center, and she paused for a moment before going to the information desk. Even the air conditioning seemed friendly today. "Is Dr. Carington here?"

The middle-aged man in a white shirt and tie examined the monochrome monitor. "Yes. He finish rounds soon on third floor. Do you wish I should call him?"

"Yes, please. Tell him Sue is here."

"Okay."

A few minutes later her heart skipped a beat as she saw him come off the elevator. Even during the wearying weeks of staying up with Gino, the sleepless nights and prayer vigils, his face still held a noble spark of dedicated service, of unswerving commitment to the cause of Christian medical service. His face wreathed in smiles, he trotted through the lobby and embraced her. "Hello, love." He held her face to his own for a precious moment, oblivious to the stares of patients and nurses. "What a marvelous surprise!"

"Are you on duty much longer?"

"Actually, I had one patient yet to see, but they got delayed and the referring doc says that all is well for tonight." He reached out and fingered the floral arrangement. "Did some other lad give you these? Because Dr. C is prepared to fight tooth and claws for thee."

She laughed, savoring the moment. "Well, I'm here to offer you an exchange. You drive your friend Missie Baines down to that very nice Sheraton Hotel dinner buffet. And in return, I have some news that I think will bring cheer to your heart."

IT WAS WONDERFUL to sit in church with Miles' strong arm around her, listening together with Rachel Marie and Khemkaeng as Pastor Munir unfolded the Christian message to a growing community of believers. It was still just the four of them who shared the secret, and Sue found herself whispering yet another inward prayer that the lab results would confirm her best friend's confident prediction.

"How's about a quick trip over to Saint Catherine's?" Miles fished in his pocket for the keys. "I've got to visit Gino for a bit, and I know he'd like it if you all came along, eh?"

"It'll be so hard not telling him." Rachel Marie, hand in hand with her husband, gathered up her purse and waved to a pair of BCS students just leaving the sanc-tuary.

"Yeh." Miles had shared in whispered tones that his son had taken a turn for the worse the previous night and had had to check into the large Catholic medical center. "Don't think he'll be home again until . . ."

There was a nice bit of banter in the Honda as Miles took Sue's hand, then dropped it in order to signal a left turn, picked it up, dropped it for a sudden whiz around one of Bangkok's ubiquitous "roundabout" intersections, seized it again . . .

"Can't decide?" Khemkaeng, amused, gave a poke at his friend's seat. "I think driving in Bangkok requires two hands on the steering wheel. All the time."

"Ah." Sue peered behind her. "And did the two of you always obey that rule back during the kissie-kissie days?"

"Oh, sure." Rachel Marie's breezy response dissolved in a fit of female giggles. "Are you kidding? Khemkaeng always said to me, 'Oh, Thai people don't hold hands in public.' But in private, never a moment's rest."

Sue felt a wrenching pang of sympathy as the foursome eased into Gino's hospital room. In just the last week, the dissolving of his will to live was a startling surrender. Pale against the hospital pillow, his head was wrapped with a blue bandanna to cover the massive hair loss. His eyebrows were patchy lines, eaten away by the chemical onslaught, and his eyes were sunken and despairing. An IV tube snaked out from his left wrist, held in place by thick bandages.

"We just got out of church," Miles boomed, trying to revive his son's spirits. "And look who tagged along. All my BCS chums."

"Hey, you guys." Gino tried to force a smile. "Thanks for coming and all."

"How are you feeling, sweetie?" Sue eased herself into the chair next to the bed and traced a motherly hand across the boy's forehead.

"Well, I was pukey this morning, but the doctor put something in the IV and so it's not as bad now."

"That's good." She eyed the television set perched on the far wall. "Able to watch some TV or is everything in Thai?"

He shook his head disinterestedly. "Flipped through once an hour ago. Nothing."

It was a discordant rendezvous, being in the purgatorial presence of certain death and unable to draw back the curtain and let in the cheering sunlight of hopeful news. But Dr. Powell had warned Sue and Miles that to raise false hopes at this preliminary stage might be devastating. The potential salvation trembled on their lips, unheralded good tidings that caused a sweet ache in her heart. *Any day now, sweetheart. Susie B's going to march in here and fix this horror.*

There was a tap on the door and the quartet glanced up. Dr. Powell, minus his usual medical smock, offered a cautious smile. "Greetings, everyone. It looks like a full house."

"Yeh. We just got in from church."

"Excellent." He made a deprecating gesture toward his polo shirt. "Sorry. I'm not on call but wanted to check in on Gino and a couple other folks."

Miles provided introductions and the Saint Catherine's physician shook hands with Rachel Marie and Khemkaeng. "So good to meet all of you." He smiled. "We have a number of nurses here who graduated from your school. Top candidates, all of them. You do a good job, I must say."

"Thank you." Khemkaeng, ever the diplomat, beamed. "Nursing is a very good field for our young people. And in a few years, I think some doctors here at Saint Catherine Hospital will be from Bangkok Christian School." To Miles he added: "At your place too, of course."

The Bostonian chatted for a moment, then paused to query Gino about how he was feeling. "Your immune system is so fragile," he warned, "and that's why there's a lot of hand-washing and bathing by the nurses and all.

So please do be patient." He initialed something on the chart, then added: "We're praying for some good news soon, of course."

He said goodbye, then added to Miles: "I have an appointment with the Minister of Health, but hoped you and I could have a quick word. Down in my office." He touched Sue lightly on the arm. "You too, if you're able."

Trying to keep her face expressionless, Sue nodded. Forcing a smile, she bent over Gino. "Don't squirm and pull all your tubes out," she teased. Bending over, she kissed him right on the border of the head scarf. "Hang in there, Mr. Carington."

"We should say a quick prayer before you guys run off," Rachel Marie suggested.

Dr. Powell eased an arm around her. "Good idea," he nodded. "Gino, is that okay with you?"

"Yeh."

The group paused and Rachel Marie cleared her throat. "Jesus, we know that you're here with us. And that you love Gino and care about his life. Please bless Dr. Powell and all the people who work here. Please work things out for this bone marrow transplant to take place. And we'll for sure give you all the glory and the praise. We love you and thank you for letting us be your sons and your daughters. Amen."

Miles went to the side of the bed and patted Gino on the left shoulder. "We'll be back in a few minutes. You and Khemkaeng and Rachel Marie can chat a bit, eh? But if you're tired, just say so."

"All right."

Her heart in her throat, Sue walked hand in hand with Miles toward the elevators. "How's he doing?" she asked the Saint Catherine's physician as they waited for the elevator.

"Well, it's dire," the younger man admitted. "I won't try to cover that up. But let's wait till we get downstairs."

The office was dimly lit for the weekend, and he flipped on a couple lights. "Have a seat, folks." He pointed to a spare couple of chairs.

"Do we have any news yet?" Miles wasted no time getting to the question that burned in his and Sue's hearts.

Dr. Powell paused as if interrupting a great condor's flight in the skies above. "Let me just say this . . ." A twinkle came into his eyes and he reached into his pocket. "Yes! This came at nine o'clock this morning!" He unfolded the sheet and thrust it into Miles' hands. "Everything we hoped for. Absolutely the jackpot."

"Praise God." Miles traced his finger across the laboratory numbers. "A perfect six."

"I never would have believed it. Miss Baines, there's no explanation for this except that God had it in his heart to work a miracle. But of these four names, you match Gino on every single marker. We couldn't have hoped for better."

"Doesn't mean it'll work." Miles, forced by the codes of his profession to be realistic, bobbed his head in a warning.

"True enough. But in a case like this, all we can hope and pray for is a chance. It's like a baseball game where you're down by four in the ninth, but do get the bases loaded and your best hitter up." His voice sobered. "Folks, we now get this one at-bat, one home run shot. One good chance to save Gino's life."

Sue felt a thrill go through her, an icy but gratifying stab of hopeful trepidation. God had revealed his will; she had been chosen. It was difficult to conceive that such a clear miracle could still fall short, but the ways of the almighty Father were beyond a mere human's understanding. She tingled with nervous, hopeful energy, wary but eager to advance the mission. "What do I need to do?"

"There's something I need to explain to you," Dr. Powell said, choosing his words with precise care. His tone put a caution into the meeting and the visitors drew themselves closer to his desk. "Gino's situation is dire. Without this"–he gestured toward the paper still in Miles' hand–"I truly believe your boy wouldn't make it until June." The jarring assessment thudded into Sue's heart and she stared at the doctor.

"So I guess we have to move quickly."

"Yes. And here's what this means." He laced and unlaced his fingers, eyeing the woman whose unassuming frame held all their hopes and prayers. "Sue, I already told you how this works. It's a purely volunteer decision. No one can make you do this. No one can demand it of you."

Miles, his voice husky, took Sue's hand in his and dabbed at his eyes with the other. "That's right, sweetheart. Gino doesn't know anything about this. I haven't said a word. And if you decided you couldn't do it, I would understand. I would never, ever . . . hold it against you. Wouldn't be fair."

"I know," she said, looking from one man to the other. "But I'm here. I'm ready and I'm doing it."

"Thank you." Dr. Powell reached across the desk and offered a handshake. "From the bottom of my heart,

Sue, thank you. It is a wonderful, magnificent, unselfish gesture. Truly in the spirit of Christ, and I know that the Lord is proud of how you minister so generously as his ambassador."

He pushed back his chair and went over to a file cabinet. "I have two things for you," he said, returning to the desk. "First of all is a printout of how this goes. You'll be in the hospital overnight, so there are a few things to pack. Miles can bring you and then take you home; I trust that will work." He smiled as the couple nodded.

"But then there's this." He pulled free a single sheet of paper that had just a few lines of print on it. "Sue, this is a very sober moment and I already know what you will say." For a moment he almost could not speak. "Again, there can be no commitment. Nothing legal. This entire matter stems from the kindness of your heart. You could never be bound to any promises you make here in this office." He handed the paper to her. "But we do want to ask you to sign this document simply as an expression of your decision. It has no legal bearing; it is absolutely unenforceable; in fact, it's worded carefully for that exact purpose. You'll see that as you read. But we just want to have your name on this, saying: 'Yes, on the given day, I'll be here.'"

"I promise." It was a vow as sacred as a wedding's, and her voice was thin and wet with emotion. She reached into her purse for a pen, but Dr. Powell stayed the motion.

"There's more."

"Oh. Sorry."

He shook his head. "Today's the twenty-second. And we really have a ticking clock here. We need to move quickly." He glanced at a large white calendar thumb-tacked to the wall. Flipping it up, he peered into the month of May. "I know it's in the middle of the week, but would you be able to come in on Wednesday the second? First thing in the morning?"

"Of course." She thought of Khemkaeng, nobly forcing amiable bits of conversation with Gino one floor up. And of course, John was available to drop in and help. This was the most poignant emergency she would ever experience in her life. "I'll be here."

"Wonderful." The man took a deep breath and seemed almost to meditate, praying for a silent moment. "And now let me tell you why I even ask you, Sue, a Christian woman who clearly keeps her word, to sign this pledge."

She listened, anxious and wondering now. Clearly the doctor had a core message yet to relate and her heart lurched, missing several beats.

"Based on your assurance," he said, addressing the pair, "we'll bring Gino into the radiology department a week before that date. So that would be this coming Wednesday." He addressed the last to Miles, who nodded. "And here's what happens. To prepare your boy for the marrow transplant, we essentially burn his existing defensive system out of existence. The fragile bits of immunity he still has, obviously failing, are then totally destroyed. To make way for the incoming healthy marrow."

Sue, white with shock, seized her beloved's arm, her nails digging into his flesh. "Oh, dear God."

"I know. It's a frightening reality. And of course, during that week we keep him in conditions of absolute sterilization. Don't worry about that part; Saint

Catherine's has perfected that matter. He'll be kept in safe seclusion." He turned to Sue and chose his words carefully. "But here's what you must understand. Even after that moment, even after Gino puts himself in our hands and surrenders his entire immune system, we could not hold you to this commitment. Even then, you could simply change your mind and say: 'I can't.'" His eyes softened and he touched the sheet of paper almost wistfully. "I know you would never do that. But you could." He bowed his head and then delivered the *coup de grace*. "And you must understand that if you were to change your mind—and depart from this equation—Gino would have played his last card. Of a certainty, he would then die. Because his last hope will have been lost."

The announcement was said in a low-key, professional way, but the words struck right to her heart. She stared at the doctor, unblinking and not truly able to fathom the spiritual mystery of what she had heard. It felt like her own heart had stopped beating in her chest, frozen by the terrifying, raw significance of his pronouncement. "You mean . . ."

Dr. Powell nodded. "This is it," he said simply. "This is everything." He pointed to the second sheet, the list of four names. "There wouldn't even be time to find and process another name. And we'd never find another perfect six in any case; I'm convinced of that." He paused, then delivered his verdict. "After this Wednesday, Sue, it's on you. Gino will have absolutely passed the point of no return."

"Oh my God." Sue felt her insides collapsing. "Oh my God. Miles." She began to sob, a lost, frightened child, unable to find her emotional bearings. Dizzy and swaying, she fell into his arms. "I never heard anything like this before. How can it be like this?" She tried to find words for what this meant, for the awesome, holy, Calvary reality of the calling. There was a boy, a human being–son of Adam–whose entire life would be in her hands. For one week, one hundred sixty-eight hours, he would have given away everything but the power of her promise. The two of them would stand alone on the battlefield.

"You'll be fine, my love." Miles caressed her cheek, his own face wet with the reality of what he had just heard.

TWENTY-ONE

The city was still slumbering as Miles navigated the nearly empty streets of Bangkok. Sue tried to doze but her mind was on full alert, alive, humming with intense concentration as she anticipated the mission. The Honda's seatbelt, pulled more taut than usual, pinned her to the passenger seat like in a Six Flags thrill ride, and she smiled, remembering. It chilled the two of them, hearing Dr. Powell's unvarnished warning about Gino's utter dependence on her. For the following week, she had warned Khemkaeng and Miles: "When I'm in the car, it's like an ambulance. Gino's life is in my pocket—we can't even dent a fender." Aware of her innate sweet tooth, she had scrupulously foregone sugary treats for the week, unwilling to risk even a slight cold. The healthy marrow buried deep within her bones was a unique and precious Fort Knox commodity, not to be jeopardized by inept carelessness.

"You've done good, baby. Don't hit any trees now," she murmured, reaching out and patting his thigh for a brief moment.

"Yes, boss." He flashed the grin that always gave her a womanly tingle. "Eyes on the road and not on the pretty lady."

"After today I'll be the purple lady." There was still a ripple of nervous trepidation; the aftermath of today's battle would involve bruises and bandages. That was a certainty. But as the car stole into the parking lot of Saint Catherine Hospital, she felt briefly like a Christian warrior who arose before dawn to stand at the edge of a field where the conflict was about to commence. The theater of operations was still shrouded in white fog, the unstained grasses shimmering with virginal dew. As the morning sun burst over the landscape, cannons would fire and the ground would heave; men would fall. Generals would issue commands and heroes would obediently do their duty. But if the cause was righteous, if the leader of the liberating force was noble and worthy of his command, then all would be well when the smoke cleared.

Miles parked the car and hesitated. Leaning across the bucket seats, he kissed his lady friend. "I love you, Susie Baines. Thank you, my precious, for doing this wonderful, sacred thing."

"It's my pleasure," she responded, meaning it. "Just promise me you'll hold my hand while that IV needle goes in."

"Done."

They checked in with a minimum of fuss and Dr. Powell came over to greet her. "Are you ready to help make a miracle?"

"I'll do my part. You do yours–God does his. We should be okay."

"Attagirl." He caught himself. "Sorry. That wasn't exactly in the professional spirit of Saint Catherine's."

Despite her jitters, Sue managed a dismissive wave. "Call me 'girl' anytime, doc. I'd like my marrow to feel as youthful and invigorated as possible just now." He laughed.

A nursing attendant pointed to a small private room. "Please put on gown. You can leave clothes there. We will take later to post-op for you. Okay?"

"Sure." She went in and closed the door, sensing immediately the isolation and a warning trickle of nervous perspiration beading its way down the small of her back. *Please, Jesus . . .*

The blinds were nearly drawn, but the first hints of a breaking dawn were beginning to tiptoe across the still slumbering city. Sue carefully removed her clothing, her underthings falling to the floor. There in the darkness, she felt naked and vulnerable. For fifty-six years her Lord had guarded this life-preserving fluid deep within her bones. Oh, she had experienced bruises and scrapes, falls and fractures. Once while driving across the U.S., a pickup truck had plowed into the family car, giving her a concussion and a one-night stay in a Kansas hospital. But she had been kept for this very moment. Now she stood alone in the room, bare and unprotected, the tile cold beneath her feet, her skin uncovered and apprehensive. She picked up the gown, unfolded it, and groped for the arm holes. It was open in the back–that made sense, she mused. But she still felt exposed and fragile as she struggled to manage the flimsy ties that left a considerable expanse of pasty American flesh open to public view.

She resolved not to blush as Miles and a Saint

Catherine's nurse led her down a long corridor and into the outer part of an operating suite. "You can lie on the bed, please," the hospital employee told her, and she climbed aboard, thankful to be able to recline on her back and reclaim a bit of her modesty.

Miles chatted with her for a few minutes, their voices muted, trying to cling to easy trivialities. "Khemkaeng can cover all of BCS for the rest of the week?"

"Oh, sure. Hopefully I can crawl back in by Monday if my sore hindquarters will permit me." He grinned.

A gangly woman with very dark skin came over, wheeling a medical cart. "Miss Baines?"

"That's me, I'm afraid."

The Indian physician's face crinkled into a smile. "Are you nervous?"

"Oh, on a scale of one to ten, I'm at a six . . . and the elevator's heading up, not down."

"Ah. Well, we're about to begin. And I understand you are not so much in love with needles."

Sue shot Miles an accusing look. "Did you blab on me?"

He feigned ignorance. "Probably Dr. Powell."

The anesthesiologist put a hand on her shoulder. "That's why I'm here. Usually we'd have an assistant put in the line, but I'm going to do it myself."

"Thank you."

Dr. Pradesh explained carefully that the anesthesia would be administered through a needle inserted into the back of her wrist. "Any preference which side?"

A shrug. "Huh uh."

"Are you right-handed?"

"Yes."

"All right. Since we're already here on the left side, we'll take that one." She quickly prepared her materials. "Since you're somewhat sensitive, I'm going to apply some topical anesthetic first. It will numb your skin."

Miles went around to the far side of the gurney and pulled a chair close. "Here's the plan, Bainesey. At the big moment, I'll distract you with a kiss. You won't feel a thing."

She chuckled despite her qualms. "From the needle or from you?"

"You're a mean one."

The Saint Catherine's doctor felt for the vein. "All right, then. Just a quick little stick, eh?"

Miles bent close and carefully turned her face toward his own. "I love you truly, truly, truly." The kiss was a good one, robustly moist and startling in its enthusiasm, and Sue felt color splashing into her cheeks. There was an insignificant *bzzz* down around her left wrist, and suddenly it was done. "Dr. C, you have an excellent bedside manner, but I hope that didn't violate some Hippocratic oath." She carefully averted her eyes, unwilling to look at the invading spike of cold steel.

Dr. Pradesh nodded, pleased. "Not too bad?"

"No, it was fine."

"Good." She paused. "In a few minutes, you may begin to feel a slight chill. Not only from our hospital air conditioning, but because of the meds coming into your system." She went to a closet and brought out a thin blanket. "Here." Carefully she draped it over the patient and, with a smile, slipped away.

The starched white pillow was wonderfully soft and Sue soon felt enveloped by an electric warmth that reached into her bones, relaxing her. Miles was still by her side and that was so nice, his presence a masculine fence to keep away her fears. The surgical anteroom was tastefully decorated, with wall paintings from the rolling mountains of Chiang Mai. The scenes reminded her of the refugee camp and her evening hikes with Miles up to the high vantage point overlooking the border. A whimsical smile crept over her face as she remembered the sugary pastry he had pulled out of his pocket, a bit crumpled it was, to be sure, but not bad for only five baht, and how he wiped a tiny smudge of the frosting away from where it trembled on the corner of her lower lip, and popped it, grinning, into his own mouth, and then eased a protective arm around her waist as they managed the treacherous path back down to the tents, the jagged potholes looming and shifting in the shadows, and then the dinner by the Sheraton pool, as they dined and smelled the lisianthus flowers of her bouquet, and talked with guarded hope about how Gino would react when he found that his own father's lady friend held the possible key to his survival, the mysterious, never seen spongy healing tissue; would he like her more after all this was done, considering the sacrifice, and really, she was glad to do it because there was something good, something worth saving in just about anybody; all those kids in the camp were infinitely valuable to Jesus, and it was so cute the way they dashed from one place to the next, always zooming along the dirt paths with startling speed despite wearing donated rubber flip-flops instead of shoes, pausing almost in mid-flight to offer her a shy smile, and even though the camp was so quiet at night, the twilight pouring out of the Asian sky into the little valley where the orderly rows of tents and classrooms spelled rescue and redemption and hope and a new, safer beginning, but the nicest thing was all the flowers that children loved to pick in the nearby forest and then bring up to her, usually not saying a word at all because they didn't speak English but just handing her their tattered but sincere little bouquets as if to say, Missie Baines, thank you for helping us, and we want to show you our gratitude if we can, and the flowers filled up her heart and made a lovely garden of memories, with the soft violets and the roses, and Thailand really had the prettiest orchids, if you thought about it, but it was lovely how there were so many flowers.

She stirred in the bed, wondering if perhaps she had dozed off for a moment. Which made sense considering the anesthetic flow through that tube going into her left wrist. Miles was still there, her beautiful and God-sent friend, perhaps lover, and he smiled. "Hey, Susie dear. Are you awake?"

"I think I slipped into dreamland for a moment," she murmured. "But it's very cozy here. How long before they wheel me into OR?"

Miles leaned against her cheek and gave it a sweet row of his affections: *kiss kiss kiss kiss kiss*. "You're a love," he said, slipping around and managing a discreet kiss right on her lips. "It's all done, my precious."

She was too sedated to actually be startled, but tried to weigh the odd possibility that she had time-traveled right through to the other side of the war. "Huh?"

"All done," he assured her. "Sweetheart, it's one in the afternoon."

She gaped. "What happened?"

Miles laughed, a melody low and wonderfully cheering, masculine in his comforting way. "You were mumbling something about flowers, and just like that you were out like a light. They wheeled you into the operating room, they did their thing, and now we're up on the sixth floor."

She peered around, the wallpaper vibrating woozily as she scanned her surroundings. Oddly, the Thai-themed frescoes on the wall had disappeared. She was in a private room with a nondescript ocean landscape against the far wall. A television set next to the window was on but the sound was muted; a news anchor was speaking underneath an international CNN logo that said "London."

"How long have I been here?"

"A couple hours."

It boggled her imagination to have half a day simply evaporate into her dreams, with the worst of the ordeal miraculously behind her. It was as if an entire reel of an R-rated horror film–the eight-inch spike, the digging, the probing for tissue, the seeping of blood into a test tube, the hurt and the wincing and the dread–had been deliberately incinerated by a concerned friend. Like it never happened.

"Well, that was quick," she told him, her voice weak but grateful. "Wow. I feel like I dozed off for maybe two minutes, and here we are."

"Thank God for modern medicine."

"I know."

She squinted, trying to recall the tapestry of dreams, the kaleidoscope of slowly sliding images as they had poured one into the next. So many flowers . . . and as she looked at the dresser, Sue suddenly realized that dreams and reality often intersected in weird but wonderful ways when a patient was anesthetized. Because the hospital room was awash in bouquets and floral arrangements.

"It looks like somebody died," she murmured. "Did I pass on and head into the afterlife? And if so, what are you doing here too?"

He grinned. "All the flowers?"

"Yeah."

He pointed. "Those are from Khemkaeng and all the kids at BCS."

Tears sprang into her eyes as she pictured her *Matthayom* students reacting to the announcement at assembly. "That's so sweet."

"That one's from the church. UCC. Munir brought it while you were in surgery. Sends his love. The little one next to it is from the surgical team here at Saint Catherine's. I don't reckon they donate flowers all the time, but this is a special case, eh?"

"How about those?"

His chair on rollers, he slid over and fetched the tiny card for her. The writing was in a precise feminine script, obviously dictated to a florist downstairs. "From Pastor Mike and Christian friends at New Hope Church."

She dabbed at her eyes again, feeling bathed and healed by the love of such a noble and global family. "This is all too much." Then a smile. "The flower shop in the lobby must be loving me; that's for sure."

"Well, I had to make sure of it," Miles said, bemused. He went over to the little closet next to the door leading to the lavatory. "So how about one more?" He came to her with a small ceramic pot overflowing with pure, white orchids mingled with baby's breath. "This one's from the Carington boys. Gino and me."

Overcome, Sue reached out with her good right

hand and hugged him tight around the neck. "They're my favorites then. They're beautiful, and I surely do love the guy who bought them." He lifted them up to her and she buried her face in the sweet aromatic splendor of the offering. "Lovely." She kissed him, then added: "And you know, I love Gino as well. Be sure to thank him for me."

"Yeh."

There was a tap at the door and they both turned. Dr. Powell, his stethoscope draped around his neck, peered in. "May I come in?"

Strangely, Miles reacted with a frown. "How about in ten minutes?" He added: "I don't want you to see her this way."

Still a bit awash in painkillers, Sue shook her head, not comprehending. Dr. Powell nodded, his expression giving away nothing, and pulled the door closed.

"Wh . . . what?" She looked at Miles, not understanding at all.

He set the bouquet of orchids on the nightstand and carefully held her untethered right hand. "Susie, my love, I've got a bit of something to ask you." His eyes took in the battered female form in the bed next to him, the bandages and the wrinkled hospital gown, the rumpled sheets slightly soiled by bits of her blood oozing out from behind the gauze.

"Okay."

His fingers tightened around her own. "There are things we don't know," he said, carefully searching for and weighing each word. "What you did for us may work; it may not work. Gino understands this. And it's all right. The Lord gave us a good shot, and we're both grateful. But what both of us realize as well is that we want to be a family again. Whether it's for a few weeks or the next forty years. We both want to know that we did this thing together, united, holding each other up." He was taken with a wave of emotion, and she smiled, waiting.

"Anyway, you know how things were for us. For all the bad years in Australia, then here too. Broken and not doing too good. But then you came along."

A strange, sweet feeling, almost a divinely prepared extra *sense*, began to seep into her heart, like hearing the first tuning notes of the violin section before the opening theme of a long-awaited concert. Miles lifted her hand to his lips, then set it back down. "You brought a wonderful sense of completeness into my life, Sue. I loved ministry, and I did my jagged, haphazard bits of it this way and that. But so many things were missing, and you filled them all up. Every one. I think of you a million times a day, knowing that you serve as I do, that you're praying for me when we're apart, that you want what I want and love what I love. Most of all, you found it in your heart to forgive and then love my boy Gino. Despite all he did to send you packing, your love pushed through all that and helped save us."

Not meaning to, he brushed at his eyes and then leaned close, his rugged physician's heart right up next to her own, scars and all. "Sue, I love you with everything that's in me. And I know we're going to be praying together and hoping together, you and me, for some good news in the next few weeks. But I want us to do our waiting, not just as friends, but as lovers promised to each other. I want with all my heart, before God Almighty, to be your husband, and for you to be my wife."

There was a moment of holy awe and glory that passed between them. Sue thought of the kiss at the airport so long ago where a beautiful French boy had flown away into the fog. And then of the endless lonely years that followed: high school, college, work, ministry. Always alone. Always a bridesmaid, never a bride. Driving home alone after work. Celebrating birthdays and Christmas holidays with friends who gave her funny cards and gag gifts . . . but never a present from a man, a lover, a life partner. No one had ever said "I love you" until this man did. No man had ever wanted to spend a lifetime by her side until this man said he did. No man had ever shown the slightest inclination to ask for her hand in marriage   . . . and now this amazing, exciting, precious, generous, devoted friend had done just exactly that.

Until the dreams had surrendered to time and reality, there had been imagined scenes, girlish fantasies where the handsome prince would bend on one knee, surrounded on all sides by sand dunes and rolling waves, or the exotic recipes of an Italian restaurant where the violinist would bathe their intimate candlelit table with romantic arias, or on a bluff overlooking vast pastures and a white farm house, with rippling fields of flowers and horses lazily dotting the verdant landscape. Instead, she was limp in a hospital bed, her backside bruised and battered, her hair unkempt, her bed linens tangled and tinged with perspiration. But it was the most glorious moment of her fifty-six years, and she felt a tear of joy trickle down her cheek.

"Are you . . . going to put that in the form of a question?"

Miles brought back the bouquet of orchids and

placed them on the bed next to her. Buried underneath the fronds and the delicate greenery in the potting soil was a small silver box. He pulled it free and carefully undid the latch. "Sue, my dearest friend and love of my life, will you marry me? Please?"

The ring was a beautiful, simple band of polished gold; the diamond twinkled in the muted light of Saint Catherine's healing aura. Sue bowed her head and whispered a prayer aloud. "Thank you, Lord Jesus. Thank you, thank you, thank you. Thank you for Miles, this wonderful man. I accept him as your gift to me. For all of our lives, we will both serve you." She bypassed the ring and slipped her good hand around his neck. "Yes, Miles. I will marry you and love you for as long as we live."

He kissed her, then took the ring out of the box and brought it around to the other side. "I'm sorry this is the bandaged hand," he said cheerfully. "But I'm a doctor. We'll get this done." With the tender precision that she so loved about him, he eased it onto her finger and stepped back to inspect. The royal elegance of the jewel seemed to subdue the harsh and continuing presence of the long needle encased in heavy surgical tape, and he nodded, pleased. "A beautiful ring for my beautiful lady. And now Dr. Powell can come in and take a look-see at this beautiful hand."

"Well, first, dearie," Sue responded, "since I am now a promised woman, there are certain privileges that go with engagement to a famous doctor. Am I right?"

"Absolutely," he assured her. "My vast estate is yours, my lady. What can I do?"

She grimaced. "I've been meaning to say something. 'Cause I need for a very devoted and loving friend to help me pee."

SHE HADN'T NOTICED BEFORE, but the moon was full outside as if to indicate heaven's undivided interest in the spiritual saga unfolding at Saint Catherine Hospital. The nocturnal splendor tumbled through the louvered windows and into the hallways and surgical wards, anointing the place with reborn hope. It was nearly midnight now; Miles wheeled her to the fifth floor where Gino was being prepared for the next day's delicate operation.

A thin protective plastic cube shielded the teen's bed from contamination, and Miles pushed her as close as he dared. There was a rhythmic hiss as a bedside tank delivered small doses of oxygen; there was a maze of tubes and needles running everywhere.

They had both agreed to hold off on telling Gino who his donor was, and Sue fretted now about whether her arrival in a wheelchair would create confusion in his mind. But the teen was only semi-conscious; he nodded feebly and managed a listless acknowledgment with his left hand as she waved to him.

In the past ten days her mind had been flooded with rescue impulses, and with the poignant reality that she had been chosen as Gino's last hope. In her ministry at New Hope Church, she and Pastor Mike had often prayed together about the gospel commission: taking the Calvary message to a dying world. So many busy Californians–sometime cheerful, always frantic and anxious–lived and worked nearby. Their lives were focused on pleasure and survival. They drifted into the sphere of the church, then away again. But countless times, she wrestled with the hard fact that people were mildly interested in Jesus as just one of many ways they might be rescued. Yes, there was Jesus, but there was also the panacea, the hoped-for college credits due to their good citizenship, their orderly lifestyle, their generous impulses, even their manicured front lawns. People fed their pets; they filled out 1040 forms without coloring outside the lines. Was this enough? Did they need a spiritual marrow transplant that only the Man from Galilee could give? Was there just the single option, or could they hold out, delaying, pro-crastinating until a more convenient season, assuming there were many other freeways whereby one might get home?

Here in Thailand, where Buddhism was a pervasive and positive force, it took heavenly diplomacy to suggest that Jesus offered something unique and urgent, something beyond the normal scope of the national faith. She had listened once in a Bangkok McDonald's as Rachel Marie and Khemkaeng described his own conversion path two years earlier. "I am a Thai man, a Buddhist man. But I need a King to die for me."

Sue held hands with Miles, and she said a short prayer for the boy, but he had lapsed into a troubled sleep. Miles wheeled her back to the elevator, nodding a greeting to the two nurses who joined them for the ride upstairs. "Big day tomorrow," he said quietly, resting a hand on her shoulder.

"Yeah."

There was some residual pain as the night wore on, but Miles summoned a ward nurse, who efficiently increased the flow of meds. She was a bit groggy now, but they discussed the waiting game that lay before them.

"Probably two weeks before we know," he said. "If

it gets to be a month and there's no jump in his white cell count, that'll be bad news. So we have some serious praying to do, sweetheart."

She looked at him. "What about . . . you know . . . a decision? By him?"

Miles sighed heavily. "No. Nothing yet." He hesitated. "It's hard, love. I mean, I know it's urgent. Life and death. But I don't want him to be thinking: 'Well, Sue did this for me, and now I owe her.' Like spiritual blackmail. So I don't know how hard to push."

She digested the idea. It was tempting to weigh this campaign at Saint Catherine's in mathematical terms, and to present Gino with a claim stub. She had sacrificed her bone marrow for the lad; she had suffered and bled in a tiny microcosm of Calvary itself; now a decision for Jesus Christ was her due! Here's the invoice, buster; pay up.

"It can't be like that." She nodded her agreement. "I read once that in the U. S. Army Rangers, their motto is something like *sua sponte*."

"Which means?"

She gestured feebly at the medical trappings of the hospital room: the tubes, the IV bottles, the flickering digital readouts that flashed blue and green warnings for the nurses to take note of. "Meaning: I'm a private in God's army. I do this because I love people. I do it because it's my duty as a person who serves Jesus. Nobody owes me anything. I don't have any claim on Gino for his love . . . or for . . . anything. He can choose the things that matter to you and me, or he can get well and go his own way." She swallowed hard, feeling her emotions rise to just below the surface. "It's always going to be his choice."

"Yeah." Miles sat with her in the tender blanket of slowly cascading moonlight, the beams reflecting off the tiny gold circle on her ring finger.

TWENTY-TWO

She crept back to work at Bangkok Christian School Monday morning and eased herself into her chair with a gingerly dose of caution. Flowing up and down the hallways was an energetic river of neatly pleated maroon skirts and ironed shirts; Thai students tended to be an immaculate lot, with perfectly groomed hair and crisp ribbons for the girls. She, on the other hand, was wearing a loose-fitting pair of sweat pants, and she blushed whenever anyone came in.

"How're you feeling, Professor Plum?" Rachel Marie's teasing smirk preceded her entrance. "Referring to the new vivid coloration of certain parts of your anatomy."

"That's just very amusing." Sue made a big show out of clicking onto the school web page. "Let's see. Salary scale for Mrs. Chaisurivirat: now cut down by . . . *fifty percent.* Let's find out how you survive on two hundred baht a month."

"I'll be good. But really, you're okay?"

"Yeah."

"How purple are you? And are there any photos posted online?"

Sue forced a smile. "They weren't kidding about being black and blue down to my knees. Actually, the rainbow is essentially decorating just where I sit down."

"Yikes." Rachel Marie set down her case and came over. "I'll hug you really carefully, Sue. But sweetie, we're hugely proud of you. It's amazing what you did."

"Thanks."

"Gorgeous ring, by the way. Congratulations."

The next two weeks of waiting slipped slowly into the past like very thick syrup stubbornly oozing onto a pancake, or a TV serial drama where the bomb squad has five minutes to defuse an IED and it seems to take an hour. After ten days, the medical team at Saint Catherine's began daily blood tests, hoping for a noticeable spike in Gino's white cell numbers.

Sue's bruises faded with stubborn slowness and Rachel Marie graciously surrendered the front seat of Khemkaeng's little Nissan, so that she could enjoy a bit of padded comfort. Often the trio would pray aloud together during the short commute back home, giving all their hopes and anxieties over to their caring Father.

Friday morning, Day Fifteen, dawned with a harsh tent of rain clouds blocking out the sun. *Matthayom* chapel had just let out–a youth ministry DVD Lee had brought back from the States–and Sue was walking gingerly across the concrete athletic court back to her office. Ngam and Wismita were gossiping about some stray bit of inside humor regarding Benjie Cey, and she pulled out her iPhone in order to mask the fact of her eavesdropping. Sliding over to her incoming messages, her heart suddenly did a skip and a jump. *Something new from Miles . . .*

Her impulse was to stop and pray first, but the curiosity was too strong. She clicked on it and stared at a single word. "YES!!!!!!!!!!!!!"

The campus was split by a piercing female scream, a high-pitched, ecstatic cry of exultation. "Yes! Yes! Yes! Thank you, Jesus! Yes!" Shrieking like a junior high cheerleader watching a winning three-point buzzer-beater at a basketball game, Sue held the phone aloft, jumping up and down. The two Thai girls rushed over. "Missie Baines! Is it Gino? He is well?"

"Yes!" She thrust the phone into their faces, then resumed her dance with wild abandon, her own stiffness forgotten. "He's going to be well!"

Students crowded around, hugging her and high-fiving one another with pleasure. Amid the pandemonium, Sue happened to glance clear across the campus. In a second-story window, a veiled form turned to face the giddy mob scene below. She could see Rachel Marie, just a tiny figure, raising both hands in a querying gesture. Sue held her arms up, thumbs pointing skyward, signaling the victory. The distant form, barely seen through the heavy glass, began to bounce up and down in her own frenetic dance of celebration.

AT LONG LAST, it was Graduation Night for the *Matthayom* Six students. Sue felt a tangle of bittersweet emotions as she fluffed up her hair and dabbed on makeup. It was wonderfully gratifying to don a robe signifying her own academic successes and also her contributions to the growth and maturation of ninety-four beautiful young people, Thailand's finest. She knew most of the graduating seniors by name, and felt a wistful bond of affection with the young men and women who would march up the aisle tonight.

The doorbell rang and she eased her way downstairs with the robe half-zipped, still protecting her slightly fragile frame. "Hey, Mrs. C. What's up?"

"Sorry," Rachel Marie wheezed, her hair in slight disarray. "I was getting dressed and all at once the light bulb in our bathroom blew out. The upstairs one, I mean, where there's a good mirror. Do you mind if I borrow yours for, like, eight minutes?"

"Be my guest. I'm all done up there." She grinned. "I'll just peek at my little speech while we wait for Khemkaeng." She hesitated. "You're marching tonight?"

"I wouldn't normally. 'Cause our kids graduated yesterday. But I know a lot of the older students by now and it's fun to take part. I own my own robe so it doesn't cost anything."

"Go for it."

Rachel Marie bounded upstairs, a grocery bag of mascara goodies bouncing against her right leg. "Don't steal any of my imported French perfume," Sue hollered up the stairs.

The graduating class had voted to hold their commencement exercises at the elegant Siam Garden Palace Hotel, and Sue gasped as she entered the ornate ballroom. Seniors had spent most of the day decorating, and the hall was splendid with a fluttering maze of streamers and flower sprays. Student photographers had recorded digital highlights of the academic year, and large blow-up posters had been placed on easels lining the two side walls.

"These kids are too much," Sue murmured to

Khemkaeng and Rachel Marie, taking in the elegant décor. "But their parents wanted to spring for this place, and who am I to say no?" She went over to the table at the entrance of the hall and picked up an ornate brochure, fragrant from the printers, that had *Graduation Pro-gramme–Bangkok Christian School* emblazoned on the front.

John, nearly his old self now, came over and offered Sue a careful hug. "Marilyn and I just can't get over how the Lord worked this out. And as soon as all this finery settles down, we'll sit down and sort out our future together."

Marilyn bustled up and offered her own embrace. "We were over at Mission Hospital yesterday," she laughed, "and you should have seen Dr. C. All he could talk about was his beautiful fiancée and weddings and honeymoon cruises. The poor man could hardly take somebody's temperature." They all laughed.

The banquet hall was nearly filled now with parents and guests, and Sue felt a swelling burst of Christian pride as the grand theme music from "Pomp and Circumstance" began. Heading the procession, she led her fellow *Matthayom* teachers up the aisle to the platform, and they turned to face the long row of maroon-clad graduates.

It was a poignant and pleasant evening, drawn out as students fanned out into the crowd to give flowers and gifts to their parents. Sue delivered a short address, thanking families for their patience during John Garvey's illness, and promising that Bangkok Christian School would be there to serve their families and younger siblings for many years to come. "You young people are the future of this beautiful kingdom," she told them. "I think of your aim: 'To Serve Family and King.' What a wonderful goal–and I know you will do this so well. Remember to also serve your heavenly King who has given you many special blessings." She paused, catching Miles' eye in the back of the auditorium, and it took a moment before she could continue. "I will always be very proud of this outstanding class. Thank you for letting me serve each of you. It was a wonderful pleasure and great personal honor."

She gravely shook hands with each graduate as the names were read, posing together with John as a hired photographer snapped shot after shot. At the end, she graciously deferred and allowed John to step up to the microphone and declare: "As of this moment, you are now graduates! Ready for university and also to be generous alumni of Bangkok Christian School!" A great whoop went up from the adolescent crowd.

Wismata, the class president, then stepped forward. "We have a special gift for Missie Baines. All *Matthayom* students realize that our principal made a great sacrifice this year. Our friend Dr. Carington–his son Gino was so sick with lymphoma. But with the blessing of God, it was found that Missie Baines was the very person who could save him. She gave of her life, her bone marrow–it is hard to understand all the things, but this is what I know–and now Gino will live a long life!"

The crowd burst into spontaneous applause, with all of the seniors rising to their feet as one. Geerasak, one of the boys, bounced up to the platform with a bouquet and a wrapped package. Sue tore it open and held aloft a large box of expensive candies. "Thank you," she beamed. "During the time of getting ready for being in the hospital, I was careful to not eat sweet things. Now I can make up for it!" The crowd laughed and clapped again, pleased.

"Now we have additional surprise." Wismita peered toward the back. "This is not in the program, but I know that students will all enjoy one more thing. Miss Baines, this will make you so happy."

A significant silence filled the banquet room. Slowly making his way up the center aisle with the help of a cane, Gino Carington came to the platform. Still a slight and fragile figure, he was wearing a brand new navy blue suit and there was a nice thatch of jet-black hair already beginning to grow again. He came over and gave Sue an awkward hug, then accepted the microphone from the Thai girl. "Hey, everybody," he said hesitantly. "It was pretty cool being able to come and do a few classes here with you guys while I was going through, you know, the chemo thing. Sorry I didn't ever finish."

The audience, most of whom spoke passable English, waited pensively. "Anyway," Gino went on, "like Wismita said, I was pretty much down to having one shot left at living. And then God brought my dad's girlfriend into the picture. Kind of weird, eh? I mean, you go looking all around the world for someone who's got the same blood tissues and all, and it turns out she's already here in Bangkok and my dad's fallen in love with her."

The atmosphere in the hall was electric, with a supercharged stillness, the crowd in complete silence. Sue felt a strange, almost heavenly glow at the mention of God. Her pulse was pounding, eager, intensely curious, as though she was waiting, not with bated breath, but with bated *everything.*

Gino looked around at the seniors, now clutching bouquets and diplomas. "I guess some of you guys are Christians now. Which is awesome. The rest of you–I hope you're thinking about it. Because when I finally realized that I wasn't going to die, and that God had spared my life, I figured out that I had to make a choice. I'd put it off for such a long time because I was mad about a whole bunch of things that didn't really matter. But when God showed me how much he loved me, man. I finally got it."

No one spoke. The room was as silent as a cathedral on a winter Tuesday. Next to her, John and Khemkaeng leaned forward, their eyes fixed on the drama. The boy with the microphone glanced around. "So I guess some of you guys are going to help me sing. Right?"

Baffled and surprised beyond words, Sue watched as six of the graduates doffed their mortarboards and came up to surround Gino on the stage. A moment later a contemporary track began to roll through the Christian school's PA system and the visitor sang.

His voice was a bit unsure, but a decently pleasant baritone. The familiar old hymn seemed a clean, unbroken testimony unfiltered by faculty intervention or editing, the lyrics penned for this exact story and miracle from Bangkok, Thailand. *I hear the Savior say, "Thy strength indeed is small. Child of weakness, watch and pray. Find in me thine all in all."*

Sue felt a tear slip down her cheek and she reached out without realizing it and clutched John Garvey's hand. "Child of weakness." For so many months, Gino had been exactly that, a broken and imprisoned waif, lost in his own rage and despair and obscene wanderings.

Now the surrounding Thai students joined him as they sang the chorus together: *Jesus paid it all; all to him I owe. Sin had left a crimson stain; he washed it white as snow.*

It was the Calvary message Sue had longed to share with the son of her beloved Miles. Jesus the Redeemer had bled out his life for a lost and dying world. She owed him; Miles owed him; all of them owed him. And now, before her eyes, Gino and these beautiful Asian graduates, some of them still occupying a Buddhist landscape, sang it together. *Jesus paid it all; all to him I owe.*

There was a flurry of percussion as the praise song abruptly segued into its powerful climax. *O praise the one who paid my debt; And raised this life up from the dead.* The refrain repeated itself three times, growing in spiritual intensity, and she could see power pouring into Gino as he sang, lifting his free hand and pointing to the sky. The last notes died away and the girls in the impromptu singing ensemble each embraced the rescued boy as applause washed over the crowd.

Wismita, one of those who had helped sing, accepted the microphone once again. "Now we need for Missie Baines to do one more thing," she said with a teasing smile. "We have so many good things to eat and drink in the party area by the pool. So we want all parents and friends to stay for this and to have a very good time. But it is also true that in America, Missie Baines had the name of 'Pastor Sue.' She worked for God at a church. So we believe she is able to do a baptism right now! Gino Carington has this plan to serve God now, with Jesus in his heart, and it is our surprise to have Pastor Sue Baines do a baptism in the pool here.

And then our party can begin!"

The principal gaped at her. What? Perform a baptism? Her mind was joyously pounding with a million issues and debate questions and theological ponderings, but all of them were shouted into submission by the fact that Gino Carington had once been lost and now was found. Sick and miraculously made well. Dying and now vibrantly alive. Making the sure journey from hell to heaven–and now, today, was the moment of victory. Like an Ethiopian prince from long ago, her beloved Gino was a visitor in a strange land who had miraculously come to know Jesus . . . and who was now standing close to a convenient body of water.

"What do I do?" she hissed at John.

His infectious grin threatened to melt the chandeliers. "Are you kidding? Go! This is the most awesome thing to ever happen to BCS."

The PA abruptly burst forth with a flurry of trumpets, the regal chords of the recessional fanfare, and students bounded out of the banquet center, giddy and buzzing in illegal Thai, all orderly marching forgotten in the thrill of the moment. They congregated out by the pool in knots of three and four, gesturing to each other and muscling close to the water for coveted positions. Sue, still flabbergasted and overwhelmed at the thrilling turn of events, hesitated on the platform, her mind in a celebration overload. "Come on, boss lady!" The faculty members dragged her forward, smiles wreathing their faces.

It was not quite dark out by the swimming pool, a majestic liquid paradise, in appearance a vast aqua teardrop of joy that rippled in the moonlight, garden lights ringing the area like a row of angels. The hotel was a silent pillar of extravagant glory serving as a backdrop, with lights twinkling down from the luxury suites on the upper floors. There were shrubs trimmed to resemble exotic Thai gods, but the local deities seemed to shrink back respectfully as Sue approached the water's edge. Waiters in their short white coats, sensing the unfolding drama, held back, some setting their silver trays on nearby trolley carts.

Gino stood alone by the steps leading into the shallow end of the pool. He had doffed his dress shoes and Sue could see Ngam proudly holding his new suit jacket. Sue came to him and, without planning it, they found themselves in a long embrace. "You sure you want to do this?"

He nodded eagerly, his eyes moist. "Yeh. Absolutely."

The *Matthayom* graduates began to applaud, a rhythmic, respectful, united show of support for this shared experience of conversion and rescue. Sue hesitated for just a moment, wrestling with a petty concern about her clothes. The duties of the kingdom trumped everything, of course, but she didn't relish the thought of standing around in wet clothes for the rest of the evening. Then, throwing caution to the wind, she kicked off her shoes, flung an arm around Gino's shoulders, and the pair waded into the water, laughing and excited.

The pool's underwater lights were glowing, the ripples almost alive as they came to embraced the couple. For a comic moment Sue's professorial robe billowed up to her waist and she enjoyed the high school giggles as she smoothed everything down. "Oops." Then a moment later: "Okay, I think we're deep enough."

Despite being surrounded by more than three hundred students, family friends, and her own BCS team, there was a sweet interlude where it was just the two of them: Sue and Gino. Both of them bruised yet recovering. Both eager now for a new life and the embrace of a restored family. It struck her that, as much as God had created her for the bone marrow miracle, he had also ordained from all eternity that she serve this child here in the water, and then for the rest of Gino's life. An old hit from the 70s flashed through her mind–"Mother and Child Reunion"–and she felt damp with emotional joy. "Someday, sonny boy," she told him, "you're going to have to tell me how all this happened."

"I will." He flashed her a grin, innocent and eager, the birthmarks and scars of his past erased in the beauty of this fine Calvary moment. "And by the way, thank you for saving my life."

"Well, that was Jesus, not me," she countered. "He made my blood; I didn't. He planned the whole thing quite a while back. But to the extent that I got to be here, it was my pleasure." Then she added: "I love you very much, you know."

"Yeah. Me too."

"Okay. You ready?" He nodded.

It took a moment to remember just how the watery liturgy went, but Sue nudged her young charge into position and then put a hand on his shoulder. For an anxious moment she wondered about the local sensitivities and the visiting parents observing this quintessential Christian moment. But as she looked around, the pool area was thronged by an unbroken army of supportive faces. Even parents whose Buddhist ways were vital to their Asian identity seemed accepting of this unique and sacred rite of passage.

Despite the distant rumble of Bangkok street traffic and the normal boisterous hubbub of a poolside party, a respectful hush swept over the scene as Sue spoke. "It's not often that a person faces death . . . and then receives the gift of life," she began. "I want all of you to know that it was not me who saved my son Gino. It was God in heaven who brought this beautiful miracle to Bangkok. I was simply here to be used, just like all of our BCS teachers. But I hope all of you who were so kind to come here tonight will have your hearts filled with this wonderful good news. God wishes for all of us to be rescued from the hospital and from the surgery room and from the cemetery. The gift that God gave to Gino–it is in his heart to give the same gift to each of you. It is wonderful beyond words that Gino Carington will not just live to be a man; he will live forever in God's eternal kingdom. And just as it was in God's plan to rescue Gino and make him anew, he wants to do the same for each young person who graduated here tonight. And all of your families."

Sensing that she had said enough, Sue pointed her left hand up toward heaven in the ancient gesture familiar around the globe, marking a new life in Jesus. "So Gino, now your family is here with you as I baptize you in the name of the Father, Son, and Holy Spirit."

She dipped him beneath the healing currents and then hugged him hard. Both of them were crying, and most in the adolescent crowd as well. There was a sudden splashing sound, and Miles, not mindful of his dress clothes, strode into the water to embrace his family. "My boy–and my sweetheart." He enfolded them both in his strong arms as the BCS crowd buzzed with another sustained round of applause. Someone by the banquet hall entrance flipped a switch and the classic party song pounded from the outdoor pool speakers and into the beautiful night. *Celebrate good times–come on!*

Gino and his father, arm in arm, climbed the steps and stood grinning like twins on the edge of the pool. Sue, her heart wondrously full, followed behind them, her graduation robe heavy and wet, dragging her down as she pulled herself free. One of the senior boys brought her a towel and she dabbed at her face.

Rachel Marie came over and gave her a lingering hug. "That was amazing," she said. "Best thing I've ever seen."

"I know." Sue was still glowing, but did feel a twinge of concern. Thai parties tended to run on and on; already students were milling around, eager to introduce her to their parents. The next two hours standing around in wet clothes loomed as a damp and uncomfortable challenge, especially in her weakened state. Out of the corner of her eye, she could already see Gino fishing in an athletic tote for a dry pair of slacks.

"By the way," Rachel Marie added, hoisting up a duffel bag she had in her left hand. "I've got a change of clothes for you too. That dress you had made with the maroon orchids? Got it right here."

Sue stared at her, flushed and confused. "How in the world did you get that?"

Rachel Marie started laughing and couldn't stop. "Sue, you're so cute. These houses we're in are almost brand new still. Bathroom light bulbs aren't already burning out. Come on! We've been planning this for two weeks."

It took Sue a moment to comprehend the elaborate subterfuge. Lifting up the corner of her soggy graduation robe, she tried to wring it out and aim the drops of chlorinated water on her friend's party shoes. "This time you're really fired, you fiend. No kidding."

REWARDS

Natalie cocked her head to one side, admiring her cosmetic handiwork. "Still a tad crooked," she murmured, a mascara stick between her teeth. She nudged Sue's veil slightly to the right. "Okay, I think that'll do it. Now just don't move your head the rest of the day."

"Thank you, maid of honor. Matron, I mean."

"I've been waiting to do your wedding day makeup for thirty-five years. So it's my pleasure. And by the way, Padres beat the Dodgers four to two this afternoon. So you owe me a quarter."

"Get it from my rich doctor husband," Sue sniffed. "All my debts are on him now."

Dr. Baines tapped reluctantly on the door. "Come on, girlies," he prodded. "We're ten minutes late as it is. Church is packed and restless for some wedding cake. Are we ready?"

"Uh huh."

It was a glorious California evening, with a billowing, scarlet sunset blowing past the Hollywood sign and surrounding New Hope Church like an affectionate halo. Sue took her dad's arm as they headed for the sanctuary. "Ready to walk your baby down the aisle?" she teased, even though her heart was pounding with the drama of it all.

"I never had any doubt that this day would come." He glanced down at her. "You just had to wait a bit longer for Mr. Right to show."

There was a satisfying sweetness to the short walk, a divine reminder that fathers do provide well for good girls who obey. Sue leaned against Dr. Baines' shoulder as they passed the water fountain, remembering the poignant moments in her hospital room at Saint Catherine's, looking out onto a similar display. It had been a hard adventure–this trip to Thailand. The hospital battles had tested her mettle almost to the point of breaking. The thing with Gino had been a close call, a wrenching choice and saga. But now the war had come to a good end.

She thought of battle-weary soldiers who survived a hellish conflict, and finally were able to board the troop transport headed for New York Harbor and the welcoming light of Lady Liberty. There might yet be ocean swells and petty annoyances. But they had the Medal of Honor safely stored in a footlocker and the secure knowledge that their hard-earned victory gladdened the heart of their Commander in Chief. Everything would be different now.

"Happy, baby?" They stood together, daughter and dad, in the back of the sanctuary, and she gazed up to the front where the wedding party smiled down at her. Miles was resplendent and oh so beautiful in his tuxedo, beaming out as he gazed at the lady of his dreams. Sue felt overcome by the joy of this moment, the waves of sheer happiness that washed over her, healing and cleansing her entire life.

There had been a dark Friday night back in Bangkok where Gino's medical horrors and desperate profanities had simply overwhelmed the couple. His sweat-drenched tirade had finally spent itself and he lapsed into a drugged stupor. She and Miles left the condo and walked, hand in hand, for nearly an hour, staggering down to the Chao Phraya and wandering aimlessly along the muddy currents, alone and frightened without a route or a plan.

It was a small crisis, looking back on it later, but they had abruptly stopped in their tracks, realizing that they were a long ways from the comforts of home. Even at 1:30 a.m., it was a viciously humid night down close to the fetid river, with endless rows of locked-up shops lining the uneven sidewalks . . . and they were suddenly aware of a desperate thirst. There were no restaurants open, no taxis prowling the lonely streets. They passed a 7-Eleven, its long rows of refrigerated bottles beckoning with cool sadism, but neither of them had any Thai currency.

There had been nothing to do except to retrace their steps and stagger back, assaulted by the sticky heat, the parched dryness in their throats multiplying exponentially with each step. Every block, every intersection, every endless traffic light seemed to mock their desperation. But finally they were home: the tall tower, the parking stalls, the welcoming sign, the elevator ride to the twenty-seventh floor, fumbling with the key in the lock. And then that beautiful refrigerator, the bottled water so cold and icy-sweet that words couldn't tell the story of how it felt to have a drink and know that one had survived a hard night.

Now she stood with her father in the back of a church. She looked up the long, splendid aisle, with ivory ribbons gaily decorating the bouquets pinned to each pew. The long white runner, so smooth and straight, belied the tortuous route God had asked her to navigate–but now the sweet moment was at hand and she had no complaints. The organ music filled the sanctuary with Mendelssohn's great march and she stepped into her new adventure.

There was a moment of comic relief as they reached the sanctuary platform. Always a master of dramatic pauses, Pastor Mike eyed the father and daughter before calling out: "Who gives this young woman to be married to this man?"

Sue's dad hesitated, then replied: "We had to save for thirty years till we could afford this, but her mother and I do!" The church erupted in laughter, and Sue gave her dad a fake glare before kissing him on the cheek and taking Miles' arm. Just to his left, Gino stood tall and perfectly groomed, now the glowing picture of health.

Mike launched into his homily, warm and homespun, but Sue's mind traveled back to a casual lunch three years ago. Over a plate of ravioli, she had urged a confused young schoolteacher not to settle for a marriage of elegant spiritual emptiness. To leave her familiar comforts and reach for the Bangkok stars. Rachel Marie had arrived in Thailand with two suitcases and a newly fractured heart, but an all-caring heavenly Father had rebuilt her life. Now the dream had come full circle. She glanced to her left and caught her bridesmaid's eye. *Are you thinking about that too?*

"Do you, Susan, take Miles to be your husband to live together in the holy state of matrimony? Will you love and comfort him, honor him, cherish him, for better or for worse, in sickness and in health, in prosperity and in poverty, in gloom and in glory, in this land and in every land where God calls you to serve him? Do you so promise?"

The high calling, the sacred pledge, lingered in the candle-kissed air surrounding the couple. Sue thought of her signature on a piece of paper, now filed in a doctor's office on the fifth floor of a Catholic hospital in Bangkok. By the power of her Savior, she had kept her promise–as she would now defend and keep this one. "I do." She glanced up at her beloved Miles and squeezed his hand.

Pastor Mike paused, acknowledging and honoring the vow. He motioned slightly and Gino stepped closer. "Sue," he said softly, "while hanging on the cross, Jesus said seven words which echo through the centuries and into this holy moment. He cared about a hurting and broken family–a bond about to be torn apart by his own sacrifice. And right here, I want to set his words before you as an everlasting relationship."

Sue could tell what was to come, and her eyes filled with tears. Even Pastor Mike had to swallow before continuing. "Woman," he said gently, then nodding toward Gino: "behold thy son." Next to her, Miles blinked furiously, trying to keep his emotions in check. "And Gino . . . behold thy mother."

As Sue knelt on the white cushion for the prayer, her hand clutched the crook of Miles' strong arm. *All things work together for good to them that love God, to them who are the called according to his purpose.* What had happened in Bangkok with Miles and Gino defied all the odds; the staff at Saint Catherine's had marveled at the miracle numbers lining up just so. Even Tong Inn, BCS's new calculus teacher, had come to her with a broad grin. "To have this happen truly proves the power of God," he admitted. "How could it be otherwise?"

There were those, of course, who would carelessly discount the improbable statistics. Lucky things happen. Some people get well. Underdogs do occasionally win the Super Bowl and million-to-one medical anomalies baffle the Vegas odds-makers. Saving Gino, and now finding this handsome Mr. Right in a high school lobby nine time zones away could simply be one more roll in the Sue Baines lucky streak. Christians were sometimes accused of looking so hard for miracles that every stray blip in the readout of life captured their attention.

She thought of the young man who was touched by a Galilean stranger he had never met. Was his healing a miracle? Was there a God in the story? Or was it just the luck of the tumbling dice, the roulette wheel finally finding your number? *One thing I do know,* the man had declared later. *I was blind but now I see!* The flute solo faded into a beautiful stillness and Miles helped his bride to her feet. *All I know is that Gino's well. I have a new life and Miles is my beloved.*

After the reception, she gave the youth a motherly embrace. "So you're good for tonight at Pastor Mike's? Your dad and I'll be back tomorrow 'cause the three of us need to get to the Carnival boat dock by four."

"It'll be fun." He pulled his black velvet tie free and stuffed it in his pocket. "I think we're taking Rachel Marie back to the airport first."

"Good deal."

In a flurry of rice and irreverent catcalls from Sue's former Girl Power pals, Miles opened the car door for his bride, then waved to the crowd. "Thanks, all," he called out. "Pray for me now. I haven't driven a car from this side for a good long bit, eh?"

She was still in her bridal gown, savoring the sweetness of being beautiful and treasured by such a good man. "You can get us to the honeymoon suite at Newport Beach?"

"I reckon I can manage with the help of my little friend here." He flashed a grin, pointing a stubby finger at the in-dash navigator before taking her hand as they headed toward the freeway.

"Don't forget to stop at a store somewhere along the way."

"Ah, yes. That had slipped away from me." It was nearly dark now, and he slowed, scanning the boulevard on both sides. "Looks like one right here. Mrs. Carington, your run of good luck never ceases to amaze." He eyed her worshipfully. "Are you really going to walk into the store looking like that to buy . . . well, you know?"

Sue snickered. "Absolutely. And with a straight face too."

"Can I come with you?"

"Not a chance." She sniffed dismissively. "I'll go quick. Just keep the engine running."

He gave his barking laugh, squeezing her hand affectionately before setting the parking brake. "Hurry along, then. 'Cause this rental car's not the only thing with a humming motor."

She climbed out, careful to keep her flowing skirts

clear of the dusty parking lot. She clutched her Thai coin purse and headed for the supermarket entrance. A bevy of teenage girls was loitering around the soda fountain and they snickered as she pushed past them and headed for the pharmacy area. "Good luck, lady," one of them called out, and she colored.

The clerk accepted her $10 bill and handed back two dollars and a few loose coins. She hesitated, then shoved a single bill back across the counter. "You know what? Just for fun, give me one of those." She had never purchased a lottery scratcher, but, hey, it was her honeymoon. It would be fun to test the Baines magic one final time before getting on the Love Boat tomorrow.

The pudgy employee shoved the extra dollar in the drawer and tore off the garish little stub with its coated secrets. *Dumb*, she thought to herself. *But Miles will get a kick out of it.*

Just outside the supermarket door, a woman with broken teeth and a small child in tow edged toward her. "Please? You can help with dollar for baby?"

She was about to hasten past when something caught her attention. It was nothing about the woman or her clothes; she looked like the typical panhandler. Dirty jeans, torn bandanna, a lean and desperate look, the homemade cardboard sign, now drooping in her free hand. *Homeless. Please help. God bless you.* But something in this lost woman's eyes reminded Sue that those who had all the blessings should share. All her life she had gotten the winning numbers, the good marrow, now the bridal dress and reservations to the honeymoon suite. An incredible repeat gig in Bangkok for the coming school year. And just across the parking lot, the generous and perfect Miles Carington.

"Here, sweetheart." She fished in the white bag and handed the woman the leftover dollar. "God bless you." After a bare moment of consideration, she gave her the lotto stub as well. *Who knows?*

She climbed into the car and took a moment to adjust the flowing material and get a seatbelt around all her lacy finery. As the door closed, she heard a joyous scream coming from the elegant darkness behind her.

THIS WORD FROM THE AUTHOR:

All the Winning Numbers is an intensely personal saga for me! Here's why.

Around twenty years ago, I was stunned to hear that a little Korean boy was dying of leukemia . . . and I was his one and only perfect DNA match. Six for six! No other possible bone-marrow donor came even close.

To be honest with you, I was flabbergasted and resentful. Why me? I didn't even remember agreeing to have my name put on any master list. But the blood markers were there in stark black-and-white. City of Hope did want to test me once more to make sure, and I'm ashamed to confess I was essentially rooting against myself. As the sample flowed into the vial, I was almost chanting at my own blood: "No match no match no match." Which is a shameful way to respond when an innocent boy's life is at stake.

Thankfully, the Lord worked a miracle on this stubborn heart of mine. When I realized that a family in Seoul was in anguish, waiting by the computer for a reluctant yes from this aging white guy in California, it hit like a thunderbolt: *God chose ME for this miracle!*

Still, here's the kicker to the story–as you just read in these pages. City of Hope asked me to sign this non-binding "letter of intent." By this point, I was humbly glad to do so.

Based on my signature on a piece of paper, the doctors brought that busted-up kid in a week ahead of me. They burned his own immune system right out of him. Whatever busted-up, fragile white-cell armies were still staggering around inside him, the medical team took him clear down to zero.

What they said next chilled me right down to my socks. "Even in that last week," the doctor said, "David, you could still back out. If you felt overwhelmed, you could simply go home. And that'd be it. But for sure this little boy would die. *Because he and his family would have already played their last card."*

Nothing I've heard before or since has ever gotten to me like those words. What a picture of Calvary! Thank God we have Jesus! He is our last card! We have nothing else! All other options have fallen to the side. No other salvation strategy offers any hope whatever.

But we have Jesus.

You can understand why "All the Winning Numbers" is one of my favorite stories to tell! Every now and then I'm invited to share it with a church group, and the ending still gives me goose bumps every time.

By the way, our transplant was a success and that sweet little boy got a new life from heaven. And for me, hey, I was right there with a front-row seat when our amazing Jesus performed a miracle.

To request this heartwarming story for your church group or retreat feature, please email me at davidb-smith2@yahoo.com. I'd love to come share this miracle with your friends!

Book Four

Bump, Set, Love

Chloe Gainsborough is England's fearsome weapon on a volleyball court. But Dad accepting an assignment as deputy ambassador to Bangkok severely disrupts both her collegiate and competitive dreams. Is she up for finishing her grueling degree in Pharmacy when all the lectures and textbooks are in Thai?

Her new life in Asia is a funky blend of classes, part-time volleyball coaching at Bangkok Christian School, and fending off the romantic overtures of BCS's colorful agnostic and misfit, Benjamin Cey. She also makes the team at Chulalongkorn University and has a shot at representing Thailand in next year's prestigious Asian Games–except for the fact that Team Chula's lead scorer bitterly resents this light-skinned newcomer.

What follows is a stirring thrill ride through the mean streets of Bangkok and then off to the Games, where a brutal surprise will test Chloe's ability to love and forgive her enemies.

Grace-Filled Christian Reading for You and Your Friends

All of us who write appreciate beyond words the affirmation of our readers! If this special story was a blessing to you, I hope you'll take a few moments and post a quick review on Amazon. I also have readers who then cut-and-paste their kind impressions for www.goodreads.com and www.bookbub.com. Many readers glean suggestions from these interactive web pages, so your suggestions go a long way.

www.davidbsmithbooks.com

 David B. Smith Books

Discussion Questions

All the Winning Numbers

1.   If we believe God directs in our lives and relationships, why does a devout Christian servant like Sue Baines spend years in lonely isolation? To what extent does heaven "help" us meet that perfect partner?

2.   Is it selfish to say no to a discipleship task that is menial, boring, or even scary? Some church jobs are drudgery for anybody. Do we have a right to turn down unpleasant ministry requests?

3.   How do you responsibly deal with a huge ministry call, e.g. an overseas stint to an unfamiliar part of the world? What questions/issues ought to be considered?

4.   Sue is asked to whisk herself to Bangkok and immediately accept the top position at the school. Is this wise? Khemkaeng assures her he's okay with it, but should she have turned it down anyway? Is it acceptable to go along with existing stereotyping of ministry roles?

5.   Sue has acutely painful memories of a teen romance. Is it healthy to treasure and replay long-ago moments despite the angst such a reverie creates? Once a person marries, should they resolutely block sweet earlier trysts from their mental hard drive?

6.   She's almost immediately drawn to Miles Carington because of his evident Christian faith. If a potential love

interest doesn't quickly ooze piety, should a person hasten to their next dating opportunity?

7.   Any potential relationship quickly involves the relatives. Sue and Gino Carington are immediate and instinctive adversaries. "I really do hate that kid!" Does Sue make the right decision in continuing to accept Dr. Carington's overtures? How would you handle a case where a love interest's child or, say, parent was a true stumbling block?

8.   Miles is in Bangkok as a: 1) foreigner, 2) divorced man, 3) father stuck in a dysfunctional parent/child relationship. A lot of baggage! Despite the flowing chem-istry between them, is Sue being naïve in getting herself involved, especially when her own stay in Thailand is abbreviated?

9.   This Thailand series of books takes an admittedly optimistic picture of interfaith cooperation. Are we com-fortable working with other denominations for a common cause: Handel's "Messiah," interfaith concerts or social issues? Is this ever a dangerous form of compromise?

10. After the swimming-pool kiss, Sue is giddy and infatuated. A fun feeling! Why don't those feelings last longer? Why do things have to quickly "get practical"? Is it realistic for the poolside tingles to last indefinitely?

11. If you were to face Sue's Christmas choice: a luxury trip back to the U.S., or a grimy week in a refugee camp with the guy you love, what would YOU

choose? How can we overcome our distaste for Spartan service? Does it imply we are less than dedicated to Christ if we turn down tough mission assignments?

12. Sue and others are stirred as the Christian choir performs selections from "Messiah." What musical moments or traditions hold deep meaning for you? Are your friends sometimes emotionally moved by something that doesn't touch your own heart or vice versa?

13. Tommy Daggett invades a raucous nightclub with his choir in order to perform Christmas carols. There's booze all around, loud rock music, even likely some hookers or other suspect characters. In the end, tourists are inspired by his witness. Is it safe to invade the devil's playground if the goal is worthy? How does one measure the risk and either move ahead or cancel?

14. What's the toughest "God assignment" you've ever accepted? How did it turn out? Would you sign up for a repeat? Think of ways you could have improved your own mental attitude about the negative factors in the job.

15. During the missionary week, Sue has many opportu-nities to nudge refugees toward lasting success: new jobs, improved skills, an awakening Christian faith. Is it hard for God's workers in hard territories to keep their eyes on the long-term payoff? How can we better encourage one another with these realities?

16. Time after time, Gino exasperates Sue by letting the mission team down? Think of practical ways to cope

with an immature person who doesn't hold up their end of a bargain. Is endless forgiveness and forbearance always expected of a believer?

17. So Gino has leukemia. Does this excuse his years of rude behavior? How do you adjust your attitudes when you come to realize someone's frailties? Does Sue handle the relationship better once this reality becomes known?

18. In your view, does God absolutely know the future? Does he foresee someone's illness, and ordain another person as their rescuer or bone-marrow donor? If God knows all our tomorrows, does that mean fatal illness are preordained by him?

19. Was Sue obliged, from a Christian perspective, to donate her marrow (despite her wrenching dread of the procedure)? Could any factor have justified her declining the task?

20. Even though God's people pray earnestly, good Christians often succumb to leukemia or other diseases. Why are these prayers not answered? Why would God say no to requests that would be easy yeses for him?

Made in the USA
Columbia, SC
18 August 2024

40685793R00196